THE MEMORY ROOM

CHRISTOPHER KOCH

JONATHAN CAPE
LONDON

Published by Jonathan Cape 2007

2 4 6 8 10 9 7 5 3 1

Copyright © Christopher Koch 2007

Christopher Koch has asserted his right under the Copyright,
Designs and Patents Act 1988 to be identified as the author of this work

First published in Great Britain in 2007 by
Jonathan Cape
Random House, 20 Vauxhall Bridge Road,
London SW1V 2SA

www.rbooks.co.uk

Addresses for companies within The Random House Group Limited can be found at:
www.randomhouse.co.uk/offices.htm

The Random House Group Limited Reg. No. 954009

A CIP catalogue record for this book is available from the British Library

ISBN 9780224084932

Printed and bound by Griffin Press, South Australia

For Robin and Gareth

CONTENTS

Two friends who met here and embraced are gone,
Each to his own mistake; one flashes on
To fame and ruin in a rowdy lie,
A village torpor holds the other one,
Some local wrong where it takes time to die:
This empty junction glitters in the sun.

So at all quays and crossroads: who can tell
These places of decision and farewell
To what dishonour all adventure leads,
What parting gift could give that friend protection,
So orientated his vocation needs
The Bad Lands and the sinister direction?

W. H. AUDEN, 'The Crossroads'

There's something addicting about a secret.

J. EDGAR HOOVER

PART ONE

Children of the Suburbs

ONE

1

AN AFTERNOON IN March, the air cooling, the sun coming and going at the whim of slow-sailing clouds. The colouring of the day is changing from moment to moment, as it so often does in the island: colour giving way to monochrome; monochrome flooded by colour again. Birds like frowns on the glassy autumn air. Intensities of a cold climate.

Carrying his overnight bag, Bradley walks down Bay Road in the direction of the river. The road is empty, except for a bent old man in a three-piece suit wearing a grey felt hat from the 1950s, who passes by on the other side like a ghost from Bradley's childhood. There's a smell of burning leaves, and birds twitter restlessly in the well-kept gardens. Out in the east, twin-humped Mount Direction has appeared, rising above the steep, orange-tiled roof of Connie Ross's house on the corner of Swanston Street. Bradley stops at the front gate, drops his bag on the footpath, and surveys the house for some minutes.

The yellow picket fence needs a coat of paint, but the place is otherwise unchanged since his visits here in student days: a two-storeyed, red-brick Edwardian house with the steep gabled roof and white stuccoed chimneys of the period, eternally enclosed by that capsule of perfect security which preceded World War One. A glassed-in verandah converted to a sunroom runs along half the upper floor in front, with little wooden pillars at intervals, carved in the Tuscan manner and painted a mustard colour. Head tilted back, Bradley studies this sunroom with a wry, regretful attention.

This was the room that Vincent used as his study, and whose contents are the reason for Bradley's visit.

Holding her little sherry glass suspended, Connie smiles with closed lips, looking across at Bradley from the other side of the fire. 'You'll stay for a few days, won't you?' she says.

'If it's no trouble,' Bradley says. 'I've got leave, and I'm not in any hurry to get back to Canberra.'

'Stay as long as you want,' Connie says. 'It's good to see you, Derek, after all this time. Even though it's under these circumstances. Pretty funny circumstances, aren't they?'

'I'm afraid so. Things took a very tough turn, for Vincent. But you'll know about all that.'

'I know a bit,' Connie says. 'But not much. His letter didn't really explain very much at all.' Her mouth twists, and her thin, lined face takes on a pinched expression, as though she's tasted something sour. Her tone is both puzzled and disapproving, and Bradley shifts uneasily, stretching his legs across the hearth.

'He wrote me a letter as well,' he says. 'But I doubt that it explains much more than yours does, Connie.'

'Hm,' Connie says. 'Pretty strange behaviour.'

She falls silent, staring into the fire. It's now after eight o'clock. They've finished dinner, and are drinking their sherry in the dining room, sitting in the small, brocade-upholstered armchairs on either side of the hearth that have been a fixture ever since Bradley can remember. He always recalls Connie sitting in the one she's in now, with the little antique wine table at her elbow. A bowl of after-dinner mints – one of her few indulgences – sits on the table beside the decanter of sherry, her current library book and her knitting. This high-ceilinged room, with its big Victorian dining table and sideboard, is Connie's headquarters (she seldom uses the sitting room), and its still, close air has the faintly musty odour that Bradley remembers. The log fire is burning brightly in the fireplace, under its arch of glazed red bricks: Connie nearly always has a fire, even in Hobart's brief, uncertain summers, and

Bradley makes a mental note to split a good supply of kindling for her. A photo of Vincent at eighteen, smiling and formal in his inevitable collar and tie, his hair glossy with Brylcreem, stands on the mantelpiece next to the chiming mantel clock.

Connie pops a mint into her mouth and takes a small, abstemious sip of sherry. Then she looks at Bradley again, the flames of the fire reflected in her glasses. She is frowning slightly, and her dark-blue eyes, enlarged a little by the glasses, are openly watching him, apparently waiting for some statement from him that will explain things. There is nothing furtive or evasive about Connie; she is always boldly observant and outspoken, and her most constant style is one of shrewd, amused irony. Unlike a lot of aged people, she is focussed outwards, not inwards; other people interest her. Bradley has always liked her for this, and is touched as well by her lone self-sufficiency. She is now perhaps in her early seventies (he's never been sure of her exact age), but seems to look no older than when he last saw her, over three years ago. She's a little thinner, and more lined; but she has always been thin and lined. Her grey, softly waving hair is worn fairly short, done without fuss, and she has on the sort of long-sleeved cotton dress she's always worn, buttoned up to the throat and fastened there with a brooch. The rouge on her cheeks, with their round, prominent cheekbones, has been applied a little too heavily, and he realises, with a stab of pity, that this is probably because her sight is worse. Finally, when Bradley remains silent, she speaks again, in her slightly drawling voice: a country voice, with the masculine depth of old age.

'What Vin's done seems mad. His letter *sounds* a bit mad. I'd appreciate your telling me, Derek – has he had some sort of mental breakdown?'

'No,' Bradley says quickly. 'No, Connie. Nothing like that. But I think he was suffering from nervous exhaustion. So he decided to take a new direction – for all the reasons you'll know about. That's why he went overseas. I'm sure he'll have told you that, in his letter.'

Connie's eyes narrow, and she puts her head on one side. 'Yes, he told me that,' she says. '"A new life" – that's what he talked about. But what does that *mean*?'

'He didn't go into details,' Bradley says. 'But I'm sure he'll write to you again, Connie.'

'Maybe,' she says. 'But I wouldn't even be sure of that.' She leans forward, picks up the poker, and stirs one of the logs so that the flames leap higher. Then she sits back and gives Bradley a quick, shrewd look. 'Of course, being in the line of work he was in wouldn't have helped his nerves. Did *that* have anything to do with it? Was he in some sort of trouble? Some funny business?'

'I don't think so, Connie – except that he'd probably grown tired of it.'

'I'm not surprised,' she says, in her driest tone. 'Bloody outlandish occupation. And all those years he never told me. Not until the last time I saw him – when he came down here a year ago. He'd changed, then. He was very nervy and jumpy. Some-times I think his life would have been happier if he'd taken on the farm. But Vin never wanted to go farming. He wasn't the type.'

'He didn't tell *me* what he did either,' Bradley said. 'Not for a very long time.'

She stares, with pursed lips. 'Good Lord. I'd have thought you'd have known from the start, Derek.'

'No. I only found out a couple of years ago – when he and I were in China.'

Connie slowly shakes her head, continuing to stare. 'I see,' she says. 'Well, well. But Vin was always secretive, ever since he was a little boy.' She finishes her sherry, sets the glass down, and smiles across at Bradley with an expression that comes close to fondness. '*You* were never like that, Derek. You were always an open sort of chap. And I suppose you've led the normal life that Vincent pretended to lead. Isn't that right?'

'That about sums it up, Connie.' Bradley smiles back with an answering fondness. Now that his parents have moved away, he feels more at home here at Connie's than he does anywhere else, on his rare visits to Tasmania. She might well be his own aunt as well as Vincent's; he'll miss her, when he goes back to Canberra.

'And what about Erika?' Connie says suddenly. 'What happened to her must have affected him.'

'It did,' Bradley says. 'Probably more than anything else.'

'I never understood why they didn't marry,' Connie says. 'They were so wrapped up in each other. But she was a strange little thing. Poor Vin: he never found anyone else to marry.' She is looking into the fire again. 'Sometimes we love the wrong person, and there's nothing to be done about it. People tell us to give it up, but we can't, and we'd rather see our life go on the rocks than lose it. That's how it was with Vin, I suppose. Can you understand that, Derek?'

'Yes,' Bradley says. 'I can understand that.'

He leans forward, picking up the poker, and takes a turn at stirring the fire. When he looks up, flushed from the flames, he finds Connie studying him again, as though trying to read his thoughts. Then she says: 'What did *you* make of her, Derek? Did you like her?'

'Erika?'

'Yes, Erika.'

'I liked her,' Bradley says. 'But she was dangerous to like.'

'And you haven't married either.'

'I'm getting married in a few months,' Bradley says. 'I've met a girl who makes me happy. A girl who's easy to be with.'

Connie smiles. 'You're easy yourself, Derek. Well now, that's good news: I'm pleased for you. Bring her down here to meet me, won't you?'

'I'd like that, Connie.'

Her mouth tightens, and she sighs. 'I always thought I'd be saying that to Vin, some day. But there it is: Vin was never easy, the way you are. Interesting, but not easy.' She straightens herself in her chair, and her tone changes: it's practical, now, and her expression is careful. 'You'll be wanting to look in that locked room of his.'

'Yes – that's what he's asked me to do. I've got a few things to do in town tomorrow morning. I'll check his storeroom tomorrow afternoon.'

She nods. 'I'll give you the key. Why he always made me keep the place locked, I don't know. He says you're to take a lot of his papers to Professor Bobrowski.'

'That's right. But he's asked me to look through them first. It may take me a few days. Is that okay?'

'Of course it is: I've told you, Derek, stay as long as you like, if you can manage to put up with my terrible cooking. It'll be nice having you here. I've been rattling around in an empty house ever since Vin went.'

'I'll chop you some wood tomorrow, Connie.'

'That'll be handy. The fellow who brings it never cuts it small enough.'

She smiles, and picks up her knitting.

The upstairs verandah-sunroom at the front of the house that Vincent turned into a study in his undergraduate years has changed very little. All Vincent's furniture is still here, just as it was: the antique oak desk and office chair inherited from his father, the blackwood table for standing his books and papers on; his bookshelves, and even the two wicker armchairs that Bradley and he so often sat in as students, talking far into the night. But the air now is stale with absence.

Bradley stands at the desk, which is placed against the long, sliding windows that look north across Bay Road. The curtains are open, and he hasn't yet switched on the light. Like the past, like regret, the early autumn dusk is closing in: there is just enough daylight left for the dark-green cypress by Connie's front gate to keep a little of its colour, and for the roofs and hedges on the opposite side of the road to do the same. It's the moment that kindles both pleasure and foreboding: the transition that a more fanciful age saw as the dangerous time, when the human spirit lay open to enchantment, and so might be stolen. Out there, down in the valley behind the steep gabled roofs of Bay Road, with their snug dormer windows and tall, smoking chimneys from an Edwardian children's picture book, the distant lights of Risdon Road stretch across the twilight. Far beyond, the lights of Lutana Rise have come on too, trembling and winking: those lights that Vincent would no doubt have watched with a particular interest, sitting at his desk here.

Bradley turns away and walks to the door at the western end of the sunroom: the one that Vincent always kept locked, and which he said was the door to a storeroom. Bradley has never been in there. He takes out the key that Connie has given him, unlocks the door and goes in, experiencing a little surge of curiosity. He finds himself in a large, dim room like an attic: an effect created by the slope of the ceiling at the western end of the house. There is one small window on the northern side, looking out on to the street as those in the study do; otherwise, the walls are blank. Faded floral curtains are half-drawn across the window, so that the room is almost dark. Bradley switches on the light.

The floor is of dark-stained boards, with a single scatter-rug lying in the centre. A sofa bed stands against one wall, covered with a dim green spread on which faded cushions are strewn. The rest of the furniture consists of an ancient armchair of Genoa velvet, two kitchen chairs, a large and ugly kitchen table with a laminated plastic top, and an old wardrobe with a full-length mirror in its door: articles that must have been banished from the house below, or else found in a junk shop. In a corner at the back of the room, a curious structure has been built: two unpainted panels of particle board, some seven feet high, fitted into the angle of the two walls to create a sort of oblong, roofless compartment. There is a plywood door in the centre of the panel facing the room, held by a hook, and Bradley walks across and opens it.

Inside is an old-fashioned photographic darkroom. It has a sink fitted with two taps, and a bench on which stand an enlarger, a developing tank, two print trays, and some dusty bottles of hypo. A line is strung across it, no doubt for drying negatives. And there on a stool, dim with the dust of many years, is Vincent's old camera: a vintage Speed Graphic from the 1950s. Bradley knew of the camera, but has not known until now that Vincent developed his own pictures.

He turns from the darkroom and walks across to the wall adjoining the sunroom. It's fitted with four rows of broad pine shelves, rather like the shelves of a storeroom. The two top ones are empty, but the bottom two are crammed with a large number of ring-binders, some small cardboard boxes, and with what appear to be folios containing big sheets of art paper. This, clearly, is the material that Vincent has asked him to deal with. Bending, Bradley opens one of the ring-binders. It contains many hand-written pages punctuated by dates, and he quickly realises that this is one of Vincent's personal diaries – all of which Vincent has instructed him to read, before passing them on to Teodor Bobrowski.

Making a number of trips, Bradley carries the material out into the study and deposits it on the blackwood table next to Vincent's desk. He sits down at the desk, begins to examine the diaries, and releases a long breath through pursed lips. To read all this, he decides, will take at least three days.

The following evening finds Bradley seated at Vincent's desk again.

It's dark outside now, and the lights of New Town glimmer in the blackness. Vincent's archives are spread out on the table beside him: diaries, artwork, and boxes of photographs which are the products of a secret life. And the secret life was shared.

Shared. Tasting the word, Bradley looks up at the darkened windows in astonishment: an astonishment he's still digesting. The history that lies stacked on the blackwood table is not only Vincent Austin's, he finds, but Erika Lange's as well; yet it's the history of a single, shared obsession. The obsession appears to have begun as an adolescent game; but it grew into something else. It invaded the world of adulthood; it consumed the lives of its hosts. Bradley has yet to explore this in any detail: instead, he compels himself to sort through the material methodically, before he begins to examine it in any depth.

He now begins to look at the artefacts that are nearest, beginning with some of Vincent's early personal diaries, which date back to late adolescence. All are handwritten, on lined paper, and kept in the ring-binders, with the year shown at the front. They are kept, Bradley knows, all the way up to the present: that is, to the end of last year. There are also a small number of other diaries of a different kind. These are in typescript, and labelled *Contact Notes* – and Bradley knows these to be official documents. Contact notes maintain a running record of all the meetings between an intelligence operative and his subjects, to be passed on to his desk officer. Vincent clearly kept his contact notes meticulously – but why he stored some of them down here in Tasmania in his boyhood home is a mystery, and was probably against regulations.

Bradley empties out a cardboard shoebox of photographs. Vincent kept his photographs loose, in a series of such boxes, and each print is labelled and dated on the back. The batch in front of Bradley now is dated 1964, and all of the pictures are in black and white. They were taken by Vincent with one of the cheap little cameras of the time; he was only thirteen years old then, and his big Speed Graphic was yet to come. They are good, well-composed snapshots, nevertheless.

Here is Erika Lange. Bradley narrows his eyes, sitting very still with the black-and-white print in his fingers.

On the back of it, Vincent has written: *Erika, twelve years old, Lutana, 1964.* She's standing by the front gate of her home on Lutana Rise: a house which dates from the 1920s, when a set of such dwellings were built there by the Zinc Works. Double-storeyed, finished with white stucco, and with two tall white chimneys, it's dominated by a high, barn-like, steeply pitched roof which makes it look German or Swiss. Perhaps this is why her father Dietrich Lange bought it. The window of an attic room peeps out from the gable that's visible in the picture, and the secretive, multi-paned windows in front have wooden shutters. Behind the house, across the wide valley of New Town, the dim western ranges can be seen. At the corner of the street, the dry-grassed Rise stands against the sky, with receding, lonely telephone poles.

Erika, in this picture, is not the Erika that Bradley knew. He first encountered her as a young woman; here, she's a child. She wears a child's light-coloured, casual cotton dress with a spread collar and V-neck, buttoned down the front, belted at the waist, and reaching to her knees. Her sandals, worn over ankle socks, look dusty and scuffed. Clearly an outfit for being active in. It's a bright, sunny day; she squints slightly, smiling at the camera, which she faces directly, almost with a look of defiance, head tilted back, hands behind her back, feet well apart. The pose is somewhat military; she makes the dress look like a uniform. Or perhaps it's just boyishness: a boyish demeanour that combines oddly with her unequivocal prettiness: the sort of prettiness, even at twelve, that promises the beauty to come: that special kind of beauty suggestive of many possibilities.

Some people change a good deal on reaching adulthood, Bradley thinks; but Erika didn't. The straight, thick blonde hair, coming just below her ears, is worn here very much as she'd continue to wear it throughout most of her life: parted on the right, with a lock falling close to her left eyebrow. By keeping so constantly to this style, did she consciously or unconsciously wish to cling to her childish self? Be that as it may, the shield-shaped face is already showing promise of the woman's. Her eyes are wide-set and very light, in the photograph, the top lids slanting downwards to the outer corners. Her lips are closed, as she smiles; and whether this is a happy smile is difficult to discern, in such a primitive print. The lower lip has a fullness that will become more pronounced in maturity, projecting in a way that will sometimes appear truculent, sometimes humorous. Are the pale eyes happy here? It's impossible to say; she's too far away from Vincent's cheap camera. They seem perhaps to be cautious; watchful.

He puts the photograph back, and begins to consider how all this material might be organized. To get it into some sort of order ought not to be hard, since Vincent was obsessed with order – a born archivist, in fact – and the collection of pictorial and other material piled on the table is carefully labelled and dated, with cross-references to the personal diaries. In addition to this written and photographic material, however, there's another set of items which seems both incongruous and extraordinary, but which Bradley will soon discover has a direct relationship to the diaries and photographs – even though at first it doesn't seem so.

This is an original comic strip – or, to use the terminology Vincent used to prefer, an 'adventure strip'. It's executed on a hundred or more sheets of high-quality drawing paper – stiff white card about three feet by two in size – preserved in a stack of cardboard folios tied with ribbon. It's in black and white, with four panels to a sheet. On the first of the sheets is the title: *Ella of the Secret Service.* The credit underneath reads: *Artwork by E. Lange, story by V. Austin.*

This joint creation, Bradley reflects, is probably what Vincent and Erika spent much of their late adolescence engaged in – perhaps here in the study. He shuffles through the sheets. The strip owes much to the espionage thrillers of the 1960s – in particular the James Bond novels and films – and is sometimes naïve in its detail; but it's a remarkably professional production, nevertheless, and Erika's artwork is impressive. Even at that age, she was an amateur black-and-white artist of real competence: the drawing is meticulous and exquisitely detailed, so that the strip might well have been acceptable to a newspaper, or to a comic book publisher – though Vincent's dialogue might have been viewed with some dubiousness, Bradley thinks, since it's far more literary than is the norm in a comic strip, and is at times somewhat eccentric. But after all, he reflects, it was executed by a very precocious youth who was reading not only Ian Fleming and Len Deighton at that stage, but Dostoevsky, Conrad, and Graham Greene.

The central character, Ella, works for both MI6 in Britain and the Australian Secret Service. She is blonde, conventionally pretty, and her looks are clearly modelled on Erika's. No doubt she's the self that Erika wished to become: her fantasy self; her *doppelgänger*. Her creators have adhered to espionage convention by dressing Ella most of the time in a raincoat and jaunty felt hat; but in some episodes Ella is shown in alluring underwear. This follows the practice in those vintage American adventure strips from the 1930s that Vincent loved and hoarded, and which he once displayed to Bradley, in their student days – strips such as *Flash Gordon* and *Terry and the Pirates*. Erika and Vincent anticipated a modern trend in having a female as their central character: one who initiated much of the action, instead of merely following the hero into danger, as the heroines of the comic strip's golden age had done. An exception to this, Bradley recalls (and no doubt an influence on the creators of *Ella*), was the blonde, independent adventuress called Burma, in *Terry and the Pirates*.

Looking through the sheets, Bradley glimpses clues to preoccupations and attitudes that he doubts were put there intentionally by the strip's young creators. Despite her toughness, there's at times a child-like vulnerability about Ella, and an aura of pathos. Does he imagine an orphan-like quality? Perhaps he's influenced by his knowledge of Erika; but the quality is certainly there in a particular frame that he comes upon. Ella, in hat and raincoat, is trudging alone down an empty city street, in the rain. A lock of blonde hair hangs across one eye, as Erika's used to do. Tall, sterile buildings loom over her: this is New York, and she's utterly bereft. Her face expresses a profound sadness; yet a stoic endurance underlies the sadness, expressed by her out-thrust lower lip. She has two natures, this alter ego of Erika's: resourceful woman of action, and lost waif from another era.

For a moment, Bradley closes his eyes; then he gets up from Vincent's desk. It's time to go down and join Connie for dinner.

2

THERE ARE CERTAIN people who are insulated against the sharpest blows of life through an innate quality of grace, and who seem immune to common disappointments and despair. Derek Bradley was one of this kind.

As Connie Ross had said, he was an 'easy' man. Now thirty-three, he looked younger, and would probably appear youthful well into middle age. His looks were pleasing, but had never been striking enough to arouse envy or irritation. Of medium height, he was athletically built, and remained as lean as he'd been in his twenties. He had thick, light-brown hair and grey, heavy-lidded eyes that caused him to have a sleepy look. His high-arched brows, when he raised them higher, were of the kind that gave him a quizzical appearance: an effect that was emphasised by his sleepy gaze.

At school, he'd excelled at most sports, and his physical grace had been that of the natural athlete, fluid and unthinking. At university – where he and Vincent Austin first met – he had dealt with his studies with the same ease, so that he seldom had to tax himself; and if Bradley had a fault, this was where it lay. Ease was what he most valued; not idleness, but ease. Ease of spirit; ease at grasping things; the ability to float through life. What he thought of as 'floating' was fundamental to his nature, and had made him love swimming from the island's beaches; buoyed up by the sea like a bird in air, no longer held back by the thick impedimenta of reality, he was free to be himself to the ultimate degree.

Granted ease as a gift, he saw no reason to question its value. An inward grace, meanwhile, had shaped his personality, so that each time he appeared, his friends would smile with pleasure, and the tone in which they greeted him was always one of welcome. 'Here's Brad,' they would say. 'Here he is!' He was naturally inclined to like people, and to wish them well; if he sensed that they were unhappy, he was sorry for them but a little baffled, since life seemed to him so full of pleasures and fulfilments. Granted a body that served him flawlessly, with fast reflexes and a good digestion, and having had a home life without conflict or anxiety, he found unhappiness hard to understand.

Something in his soul, since early childhood, had made him cherish peace. In an unhappy child, this would have been a form of escapism; in Bradley's case, it was an inborn preoccupation, a pleasure that was almost mystical in its intensity of focus. It had always been there, and he spoke of it to no-one. Looking at illustrations in his childhood books, he had often singled out images of peace, and dwelt on them. In one of these pictures, a gabled house with dormer windows, set on an empty hill (a house that was merely portrayed as a background to the story unfolding in the foreground, and not intended to be significant), took on a special meaning and attractiveness for him: he returned to it many times, wanting to enter the picture, and to find perfect happiness there, on the quiet hillside. Some day, he would tell himself, he would own a house like that. He was not a loner; he was happy in company; happy in energetic action. But he needed at times to withdraw to quiet places; he needed the house in the picture. He didn't meditate at such times; he simply floated, enjoying his natural peace like a narcotic.

This ease with life on Bradley's part had no doubt been one of the factors that had attracted Vincent's interest at university.

When first seen, in those days, Vincent Austin had tended to give the impression of being some kind of Protestant cleric, or perhaps a member of a puritanical sect.

This was partly because his dress, in 1970, was hardly typical of a student of nineteen. Where other undergraduates such as Bradley grew their hair almost to their shoulders, and wore jeans and denim jackets and items of military surplus, Vincent's mane of thick dark hair was worn long on the top and short at the sides in the style of the 1950s and kept in place with old-fashioned hair cream, while his dress also recalled that era: drab-coloured sports jackets, white shirts, and well-pressed slacks. These outfits were unvarying, except that he sometimes wore a tie. The tie was the final touch: for a student to wear one was decidedly eccentric, making him appear prematurely middle-aged. Tall and lanky, Austin had a long, ascetic-looking face with a high, knobby white forehead and lantern jaw; he wore glasses, and his deep-set hazel eyes peered through them with a penetrating intensity. This intensity was less disturbing than it might have been, however, since he invariably wore a cheerful smile. He was clean-shaven, but his long jaw was blue with a permanent shadow of beard – since his skin, despite his dark hair, was very pale.

He introduced himself to Bradley late one afternoon in Liverpool Street. Lectures were over, and Bradley was walking up to Elizabeth Street to catch a tram home to New Town, moving beside the shop windows through late, smoky sunlight and long shadows. He first became aware of Vincent Austin's shadow, rather than his real self – or rather, of his reflection in the plate glass window of an electrical store. The mirrored, lanky figure, pacing behind him in the inevitable grey-blue sports jacket and grey slacks, loomed suddenly close to Bradley's own reflection, and Bradley turned to seek out the original. He found Austin just behind his shoulder, grinning into his face – a grin that suggested the ingratiating approach of an ideological enthusiast of some kind, seeking recruits.

'Hello, Bradley,' Austin said. 'On your way home? I live in New Town, just around the corner from you. I thought we might catch the tram together.' As Bradley stared at him, his sleepy grey eyes somewhat bemused, Austin thrust out a bony hand. 'I'm Vincent Austin,' he said.

Bradley shook hands. Austin was a second year student who was quite well known to him by sight, since he was prominent on the campus: head of the debating society, where he apparently shone as a speaker, and captain of the tennis team. Bradley was in his first year, and had only recently arrived at university, and he wondered how Vincent knew who he was, and where he lived. He felt himself to be under observation; but his sanguine nature caused him to be intrigued by this, rather than suspicious.

They sat side by side in one of the twin seats on the tram, which whined up Elizabeth Street and over Lord's Hill, carrying them north out of the city and down into New Town's wide suburban valley. The journey seemed to go more quickly than usual, as they talked. Vincent spoke with an eager rapidity he gave to all his actions, and listened to Bradley's replies with an air of deep interest. At close quarters, he gave off a high charge of energy which Bradley found stimulating. He would bend forward a little in the seat to peer sideways into Bradley's face as he spoke, which might have been irritating but was not, largely because of Vincent's good humour. His accent, like his dress, was somewhat archaic, being close to upper-middle-class English: a legacy of Knopwood Grammar, the private Anglican school he'd gone to. Bradley, who'd gone to the State High School, had an accent that was more definitely Australian.

They found that they were doing the same three subjects: Modern History, French and Political Science. When they spoke of their History professor, Vincent became dogmatic, displaying surprisingly conservative views for an undergraduate.

'Professor Robertson I find unsound,' he said, and pursed his lips in a way that made him look pedantic.

Surprised, Bradley asked him in what way this was so.

'Wait until you come to the French Revolution,' Vincent said. 'Most disappointing. The usual defence of those appalling butchers, the Jacobins. The usual crass dismissal of the slaughter of the French aristocracy. I expected better. As an antidote, young Bradley, I recommend Edmund Burke. Have you read him? No? You must.'

Briskly changing the subject, he asked Bradley what novelists he liked. Vincent proved to be unusually well-read, and Derek found that they had many twentieth-century favourites in common: Evelyn Waugh; Grahame Greene; Scott Fitzgerald. Among the nineteenth-century novelists, Vincent especially loved Dickens, in a way that went beyond a simple literary enthusiasm; and Bradley suspected that Dickens's sentimentality appealed to something deep in Vincent's nature. He and Vincent were still inhabitants of that ambiguous zone between boyhood and manhood, so that as they discovered a mutual liking for particular books, they swung backwards into immaturity's unaffected exclamations of enthusiasm and sharp barks of laughter: the euphoria on which friendship is built at that age.

Continuing to talk about books, they walked up Pirie Street together, pausing on the corner of Bay Road. They were about to go their separate ways: Vincent to his aunt's place in Bay Road, Bradley to his parental home further down Pirie Street. Before leaving, Vincent shot a question at him. 'And what about P.G. Wodehouse?'

'Wodehouse? Yes, I used to be fond of him,' Bradley said.

'But you don't read him now? You put him away with childish things?'

Something in his challenging stare made Bradley see that he was on delicate ground. 'Not exactly,' he said. 'He's always worth reading again.'

'Do it, and you'll find new levels of pleasure,' Vincent said. 'Wodehouse is wonderful. I never grow tired of him.' Head tilted back, eyes half-closed, he was looking at Bradley now with an expression that suggested religious ecstasy. 'I have almost every one of the Jeeves books, and most of the Blandings series. Sheer genius. No matter how low I feel, when I read them I'm happy again. Don't you find that?'

Bradley had last read Wodehouse at fifteen, but agreed that he did have that effect. 'I liked old Jeeves,' he said. 'I sometimes think it'd be nice to have a Jeeves.'

Vincent laughed. He had a very loud, neighing laugh, and this, combined with his mane of wavy, glossy dark hair and abrupt, jerky movements, made him seem suddenly rather horse-like. 'I've often thought that myself,' he said, and his fast, staccato voice grew excited. 'We do seem to have a lot in common, Derek. Do you remember *Carry on, Jeeves*? One of the best, I think.'

'That's where Bertie first hires him, isn't it? After Jeeves mixes him his special hangover cure.'

'Yes! Yes! That's the one. I can see that you're a true Wodehouse man.'

Beaming, he nodded with a triumphant finality which discouraged any denial, and which seemed to imply that some sort of esoteric relationship had been established between them. 'I'll lend you some you may not have read,' he said, 'if you promise to look after them.'

Bradley said that he would. In that moment, instead of seeming older than his age, Vincent seemed younger, like a boy of ten offering to share his treasures. They parted, and he called out after Bradley: 'Toodle-oo!' It was a Wodehouseism, and Bradley turned and laughed, going off down Pirie Street, to show he'd understood.

As he walked downhill towards his parents' house, he found himself turning Vincent over in his mind with considerable interest. Despite his old-fashioned dress and speech, Vincent was not the fuddy-duddy or the religious crank Bradley had half-expected. But something teased at his memory: a single image that he couldn't quite pinpoint. He had seen Vincent before he got to university; but he couldn't think where.

Then he remembered. At seventeen, in his final year at high school, he'd been walking through New Town late at night, going down Swanston Street in the direction of Risdon Road. He could no longer recall why he was there: possibly he was on his way home after taking a girlfriend to a movie. It was a dark, overcast night in winter, with a cold wind blowing, and the streetlights only just lit the way. Swanston Street, in this memory, was at first entirely empty; but just below the corner of Bay Road another pedestrian appeared, toiling up the hill towards him. As they came abreast, he saw that it was a youth a year or so older than himself, in a heavy tweed overcoat, with a large leather camera case slung over his shoulder. Bradley knew little about photography, but had guessed that a camera of this size must be of a kind used by professionals. They passed each other under a street lamp, and the young man was vividly illuminated in the yellow sodium-vapour flare. He had dark hair, tousled by the wind, a long, dead-white face, and wore spectacles. As they passed, his eyes met Bradley's, and they seemed to do so with an alarmed expression – even some kind of guilt. The impression had been very vivid, which was why the image had stayed in Bradley's mind. They had passed each other without speaking, and then the night-walking photographer was gone.

This had been Vincent Austin, Bradley now felt sure, though he'd naturally looked less mature than he did now; and he wondered why Vincent had been out with a camera at night. Perhaps he'd been visiting a friend who was also an amateur photographer; but the look of guilty alarm remained puzzling.

Vincent's speech was studded with dated slang: expressions from the Public School England of the 1920s ('*What-ho!*' '*By George!*' '*Ripping!*'). Its source was mainly the Wodehouse books; and the way in which he persisted in using it was like a private joke he had with himself. Much of his humour was like this; he made himself either deliberately absurd, or too sophisticated for his audience, and watched for a reaction. Those who were baffled or disapproving had failed his test, and were dismissed as unculti-vated boors. ('He stared at me owlishly,' he would say, relating such an encounter. 'Hadn't the faintest idea what I was talking about. An absolute *philistine.*' He was fond of this term.)

One of Bradley's earliest judgements concerning Vincent was that his humour was that of a young man who'd been forced to spend a good deal of his time alone since early boyhood. Myopic and studious (though wiry and athletic enough to excel at tennis), he'd probably been something of an outsider at school, Derek decided; and his weapon in the face of this had very likely been his humour. The weapon had never been put away. He would relish its effect on people who didn't understand it, and would take a perverse enjoyment in seeing them dismiss him as weird. His exterior was confident, cheerful and brash; he was outgoing, since he loved to talk to people, and loved to laugh; and Bradley tended to characterise his behaviour as extroverted, at first. Yet Vincent seemed to move in and out of some private world, Bradley thought – not really knowing what he meant by this.

Anyone less like a country boy would have been hard to imagine. Yet Vincent came from the country: from a modest sheep property just outside the village of Richmond, in the Coal River Valley, some fourteen miles east of Hobart. Bit by bit, Bradley learned the basic facts about his background. The property, 'Wattle Grove', had been in the Austin family for four generations, and Vincent's late father, Charles Austin, had been relatively prosperous, in times when the price of wool was good. But the family was marked by death, it seemed.

Vincent was born a twin, and his mother had died giving birth to him and his brother Douglas. Charles Austin had been a good deal older than his wife – fifty, when the boys were born – and then needed help with their upbringing. Constance Ross, who was the mother's unmarried elder sister, had offered to take on the role of surrogate mother, and had come to live on the farm. Just entering middle age, Connie was a registered nurse, and had been working as a matron in a hospital in Hobart. Whether she eventually had an intimate relationship with Charles Austin, Vincent didn't say, and Bradley didn't like to ask; but she stayed with him until he died, and Vincent said that the two of them were close. She had remained unmarried; but as Bradley would come to know, there was nothing spinsterish about her. Charles Austin had been an Anglican, but Connie and Vincent's mother Jean were of Scottish Presbyterian stock – also country people, farming in nearby Campania.

When Douglas was eight years old, he had died suddenly of whooping cough. Bradley learned this some time after his visits to Vincent's home in Bay Road began, when he and Vincent were sitting late one evening in the sunroom. Vincent and Douglas had not been identical twins, it seemed; but they'd been very close.

'It was like losing half of myself,' Vincent said, 'when Douglas died.' His face became blank and rigid, and he looked away out the window. 'He comes to me sometimes in dreams,' he said, 'and I know then that he's still with me.'

Charles Austin had died relatively young, at sixty-two. This was in 1963, when Vincent was twelve. There had been no other children, and Vincent now found himself alone in the world. In his will, Vincent's father had stipulated that the farm and stock were to be sold, and the entire proceeds left to Vincent and Constance Ross: a quarter to Connie, and the balance to Vincent. This was on the condition that Connie would act as Vincent's guardian until he came of age, with an allowance being paid to her for his upkeep. This had been agreed on between Connie and Charles Austin before he died. Vincent's money was to be held in trust until he was twenty-one, a small allowance being paid to him during his school years, and a larger amount between the ages of eighteen and twenty-one. All this was administered by a Hobart solicitor, Martin Chambers, who paid him his allowance every month. Vincent found Martin amusing, and made him into a Dickensian character for Bradley's amusement.

'Martin has no sense of humour. An owl. Once I asked him for an advance on my allowance, and he was speechless. Martin *Chambers*: don't you love that name for a lawyer? He has glasses as thick as bottles, and sits there muttering and blinking.'

Bradley asked Vincent why the farm had been sold. Wouldn't he have preferred to inherit it?

'Oh dear *no*, old chap. I'm not the type to go farming,' Vincent said. 'My father knew that, by the time I was twelve. No, no, no, farming wasn't for me – I made that very clear as a boy. My father was sad about it, since the family had owned "Wattle Grove" for so long; but he realised I was going to be the academic type, and he and Connie agreed I should go to university. He had a weak heart, and I think he knew he wouldn't live long, so they worked it all out between them. Dad was a reserved sort of chap – I never felt I knew him very well. Having dear old Connie as my guardian was the best thing that could have happened to me.'

Vincent was genuinely fond of Connie. Neither of them was demonstrative by nature, but their affection was obvious, despite its stiffness. Its expression – or at least, the only expression that Bradley ever witnessed – was an occasional swift peck on Connie's cheek from Vincent as he prepared to go out somewhere, followed by an amused chuckle from Connie (invariably seated in her chair by the dining room fire), and a swift, appreciative, upward glance. If it was winter, she would urge him to take an overcoat. The situation worked well for them both, as far as Derek could see.

After the farm was sold, when Vincent was thirteen, Connie had taken him to live in Hobart. She had bought the house in Bay Road, and went back to hospital nursing until she retired. Vincent's father had stipulated that Vincent should continue at Knopwood Grammar, where he'd boarded during term-time since he was eight years old, and Connie had complied. When he went on to university, his fees there were also being paid from the trust. So his life had been well plotted out and provided for, Bradley thought. Financial security until he finished university (his inheritance was not lavish), an indulgent aunt to look after him, and freedom to live almost how he pleased: it all recalled his beloved Bertie Wooster.

But then Bradley thought again. Vincent had never known his mother, he'd lost his twin, and his father had died when he was twelve, leaving him to live in total isolation with an ageing single woman. Perhaps he'd spun a fabric of fancy around himself for comfort. Perhaps the Victorian dream-world of Dickens, and P.G. Wodehouse's yellowing, paper-frail, far-off fantasies of the 1920s were preferred alternatives to reality. And perhaps Vincent's relentless cheerfulness was a form of discipline: a discipline he'd cultivated to make life bearable. Bradley began to admire him.

Their friendship grew, during that first term at university: the sort of close friendship that young men have at that age, where most of their thoughts and hopes are shared. Bradley had no girlfriend when he and Vincent first met, having recently recovered from an infatuation with a girl he'd known at high school, and this meant that he and Vincent had plenty of spare time to spend together, since Vincent appeared to have no girlfriend either.

They played tennis together once a week, and shared many of the same interests and enthusiasms – history and literature in particular. But Vincent's somewhat manic intellectual intensity was alien to Derek, since the life of the mind – though he lived it for short periods – hadn't the degree of importance for him that it did for Vincent. Sometimes, when Vincent grew frenzied over an idea or a train of thought (waving his long fingers, tugging at his hair), Bradley's heavy-lidded gaze would rest on him dubiously, and he would wonder whether his friend was suffering from some nervous disorder. Little, in Bradley's view, justified the loss of tranquillity and control; and his unfailing calm acted as a brake on Vincent's tensions.

Vincent was a creature of almost ritualistic routine, which he persuaded the easygoing Bradley to follow. They would see a film in town every Saturday night, at Vincent's suggestion, afterwards going back to the house in Bay Road, where Connie would make them a supper of coffee and sandwiches which they would carry up to Vincent's study in the sunroom. There they would talk for hours into the night, warmed by a two-bar electric radiator, seated in the basket chairs, while the lights of eastern New Town glimmered out the sliding windows. They would read aloud to one another, and Vincent introduced Bradley to the pleasures of classical Chinese poetry – mainly in the translations by Arthur Waley and Helen Waddell. He had memorised some of his favourites, and was fond of reciting the opening lines of one in particular, by the fourth-century poet T'ao Ch'ien:

> I built my hut in a zone of human habitation,
> Yet near me there sounds no noise of horse or coach.
> Would you know how that is possible?
> A heart that is distant creates a wilderness around it.

Their more general talk had mostly to do with the subjects they were studying, or with gossip about fellow students, or their dreams for the future. Vincent didn't go in for confessions. Despite his constant friendliness, sentimental enthusiasms and warmth, he was always essentially reticent, Bradley found, and had a way of making it clear that he gave out only essential facts about his background and his personal life. His reticence somehow went together with his physical stiffness: he had a carapace around himself which was almost visible. He also lived in compartments – an essential attribute for a spy, as Bradley would one day learn.

'I intend to join Foreign Affairs when I graduate,' Vincent said. 'I believe I'll get a good degree in Political Science, and I've begun to study Russian in my spare time. You should go for the diplomatic corps too, Derek – you'd be eminently suitable. You're doing the right sort of subjects.'

Bradley laughed. It was Vincent's habit to adopt a tone of humorous authority with him, and to treat him like a younger brother; now, it seemed, he was issuing him with orders for his future. Bradley began to say that he'd thought of an academic career, teaching Modern History; but Vincent held up his hand.

'No, no, old man! Dear old soul, *no*! You're too good-looking to be an academic, Derek. You were born for the foreign service, as I was. We'll have brilliant careers there, trust my word.'

Vincent proved to be a conservative, while Bradley was going through a radical phase, opposing the Vietnam War. But they never became heated. This was because Vincent always spoke indulgently, adopting his elder brother tone, assuming the role of a guide who would eventually alert Bradley to the truth. Although only a year Derek's senior, he looked a good deal older, which enabled him to make this performance convincing. He now addressed Derek as 'Brad', and would sometimes reach out and ruffle his hair in order to defuse his arguments, chuckling fondly: a habit Bradley found embarrassing.

It was autumn now. If it was fine, they'd meet on a Wednesday (always a Wednesday, also at Vincent's insistence), and walk out through Moonah and Glenorchy: the suburbs to the north of New Town which straggled towards the country. They'd stop in a hotel on the Main Road for a drink, and then go on: talking, always talking, wandering through the flatland riverside districts of cheap little bungalows and car yards and small factories. They sheltered from rain-showers and then went on, in their overcoats and gloves, breathing the severe, pure air of the outskirts and the river, where the rattling goods train went through to the north, and the island's tall hills loomed in the west, and distances opened up that were like the final distances of the world. Only wood-smoke from the swarms of suburban bungalows veiled the thin air, and on cloudless nights the stars were brilliant, filling the two friends with that huge exultancy of youth whose intensity is never repeated.

Vincent was curiously attached to these suburbs, despite the fact that they were scarcely Hobart's most favoured districts. 'I *like* Moonah and Glenorchy,' he said. 'Things open up, out here. One feels *possibilities*. I think it's because when I was young I used to listen to the train at night, going off through Moonah. I loved that sound. And when I was about fourteen or so, I used to catch the tram to the terminus out here – just to go as far as I could.' Then he gave a snort of laughter. 'Besides,' he said, 'the race track's here. This is the country of jockeys and trainers.'

To Bradley's surprise, Vincent was a passionate punter, going every Saturday afternoon to the track before they met in town at a cinema. Immaculate in his old-fashioned sports jacket, collar and tie and knife-edged slacks, he would have the racing section of the paper still shoved under his arm. 'I did well today, old bean,' he would say. 'Backed one straight out at ten to one in the fourth: a real outsider. I had a tip from a jockey I know: a delight-ful *gnome*, Brad. And the nag actually came in.'

He never suggested that Bradley go to the track with him: this was in another of his compartments, where he mixed with a crowd of racing cronies Bradley would never meet.

As time went on, one thing became clear to Bradley: that in spite of appearances, Vincent was actually lonely. Not for the want of friends – he seemed to have plenty of those, or at least, plenty of acquaintances. No, what he was lonely for was a conventional family; and Bradley came to realise that this was what their friendship had provided, for Vincent. Sunday night was the summit of the week for him: the night when he would come to Bradley's parents' home for dinner.

Their house in Pirie Street, some five minutes away from Aunt Connie's, was smaller and less handsome than hers. Pirie Street sloped downhill when it passed Bay Road, ending at a junction with Risdon Road, in a shallow valley to the north where the New Town Rivulet ran towards the Derwent. The street was lined with a mixture of Victorian cottages, stone Georgian houses and small modern bungalows. The Bradleys' home was a modest Californ-ian bungalow, crouched below the street on the eastern side, its flat-roofed front porch supported by pebbled pylons, its red iron roof spread like a tent. Very suburban, Bradley told Vincent: an architectural cliché from the 1930s. But he'd grown up there from infancy, and despite the way he spoke of the place, he was fond of it. From the back, which looked east, it surveyed an open, pleasant landscape that was opposite in spirit to the sombre, looming ranges of the west, on the other side of Pirie Street. By contrast, the landscape to the east had always seemed to Bradley to hold a nameless promise. Out there, half-hidden by the trees in back gardens, New Town's little streets and clusters of houses straggled downhill towards the river. Beyond – visible from one of his bedroom windows – were the distant eastern hills. Peaceful and inviting, they formed a musing borderland, beyond which lay the world. It was much the same view as Vincent had from his study, though a little less elevated.

Sunday night was when Bradley's mother always cooked a roast. As well, she would bake a chocolate cake, to be eaten later in the evening with coffee, and this cake seemed to give Vincent a special and extraordinary pleasure; in fact, he enthused over it to a degree that amused the whole family. It clearly lay at the heart of the Sunday night ritual for him. It somehow stood for family, and comfort, and shared pleasure: all the things he seemed to have found until now only in daydreams – or else in the novels of Dickens. Holding forth to Bradley about his favourites among Dickens's works, he would dwell with extraordinary fervour on the welcoming, simple-minded cosiness of Mr Peggotty's boat-house in *David Copperfield*, or Bob Cratchit's loving, threadbare family in *A Christmas Carol*. 'Utterly delightful,' he would say. 'Such simple goodness and affection! One feels one would have *loved* these people – don't you find that, Brad?' Faintly embarrassed, Derek would agree, suspecting that to do otherwise might give Vincent personal hurt.

It was always the same, on those cold winter evenings when he came to the Bradley home. Derek would let him in the front door and show him towards the dining room where a log fire was burning, hanging Vincent's overcoat and scarf in the hall on the way. Then Vincent would make his entrance, smiling and rubbing his hands together, his resonant, somewhat nasal voice that of a comical middle-aged clergyman – an effect Derek knew he exaggerated for his own private amusement.

'What ho! Here we are again! Mr Bradley, Mrs Bradley, how delightful to see you both! So kind of you to have me. Ah, what a wonderful smell of *lamb*!' Grinning, he seemed almost to smack his lips. 'And my dear Mrs Bradley, I've dreamed all the week of your delicious *chocolate* cake! I do hope you've made it?'

Bradley's mother would laugh, her far-sighted eyes dwelling on Vincent with bemusement and appreciation. 'Don't worry, Vincent, I wouldn't disappoint you. Now come and get close to the fire.' She belonged to that last generation of women who had accepted home-making as a full-time occupation, dividing her time between the work of the household, golf, and weekly bridge games with her friends. She had plenty of time to bake cakes, and must have made the picture of the traditional family complete, in Vincent's eyes. 'Poor boy,' she said to Derek, in a discussion of Vincent's enthusiasm for her cooking, 'he's never had a real home, that's obvious.'

Derek's father, as Vincent shook his hand, would be a little more guarded. He had made it plain to Derek that he found Vincent peculiar; but he had come to like him in spite of this. Both Bradley's parents came to the conclusion that Vincent's behaviour was explained by the fact that he was what they termed 'old-fashioned'. This seemed to satisfy them; they had categorised him, and it enabled them to tolerate his eccentricities, and to enjoy his unfailing ebullience and friendliness. Derek's young brother Peter, who was still at high school, found him amusing, and was always polite to him; he took a simpler view of him, however, classifying Vincent as 'weird'.

They sat around the dining room table, which was laid with a white cloth and the best china and silverware: Derek's father at one end, his mother at the other, and Vincent, Peter and Derek at the sides. This was the Sunday ritual that most families still observed at that time, and was what Vincent had apparently never known, until he met Derek. On the farm, Derek gathered, he'd eaten alone with Connie – just as he did now, at Bay Road. And Connie's cooking (as he often delicately indicated) was somewhat spartan.

'He's a queer sort of bloke,' Derek's father said to him. 'Moves a bit like a puppet, doesn't he? Jerky. But he's a brilliant chap, of course – I can see that.'

Jim Bradley was manager of the Glenorchy branch of the Hobart Savings Bank. He was a methodical, quiet man who was generally kindly, and only occasionally tense – when large bills came in, or when things went wrong at work. His faded brown hair, which Derek had inherited, was turning grey at that time, and his eyes, behind their glasses, were faded too. He seemed to expect little of a world which Derek suspected he found agreeable enough, but faintly disappointing. He too played golf, and his home was his centre and his refuge: he was quintessentially suburban. But Derek didn't condemn him for this. Unlike many of his peers at university, he didn't despise the suburbs. 'You really are a comfortable suburbanite, old Brad,' Vincent would say to him; and Bradley would smile, and not deny it. It amused him to be defined as a middle-class suburbanite, since he knew, with easy certainty, that it was not in his destiny to live a suburban life. Joining Foreign Affairs seemed a good idea: it would lift him beyond the limits of New Town and the island, and take him to the larger world; there was no need to chafe until that happened.

Like Vincent, he saw the suburbs as a frontier: dozing territories of a vast expectancy. But then, Vincent and he were children of a special sort of suburb, in a mostly rural island at the far end of the world, where town and country mingled, and where the mingling created vistas that had an odd sort of beauty: electric pylons receding across the hills; a street ending in slopes of wild grass; lights in a few last houses at night, on the edge of the land's huge dimness.

Seated at Vincent's desk in the sunroom, Bradley tries to recall now whether his friend showed a direct interest in espionage, in those days. As far as he can remember, Vincent only did so in regard to popular spy novels. But this had been at the height of the Cold War, and nearly everyone they both knew had been entertained by those novels at the time, as well as by the films that were made from them, so that Vincent had seemed to have no more interest in spying than anyone else. What comes back more vividly is Vincent's somewhat bizarre interest in vintage comic strips.

This enthusiasm, in a highly intellectual young man of nineteen, had at first seemed an aberration to Bradley: almost puerile. But he came to see it eventually as just another of Vincent's foibles, like his passionate devotion to Dickens. Vincent had a large collection of coloured American comic books from the 1930s and '40s, in perfect condition, which he kept in strict order on shelves in his study, as though they were first editions. He'd been given these by an uncle as a child, and had read and re-read them ever since, prizing them as a stamp collector prizes his philatelic rarities. They were quite valuable, he told Bradley, and he made Derek handle them gently; comic book collectors, he said, would have paid large sums for them. Vincent's knowledge of these 'adventure strips', as he called them, was considerable. He knew which artists and writers had created every one of the major strips in what is now known to aficionados as 'the golden age of the comic strip': the pre-television age which had ended at a time just before Vincent was born, at the close of the 1940s: works such as *The Phantom, Terry and the Pirates, Dick Tracy, Buck Rogers, Tarzan, Little Orphan Annie, Superman* and *Flash Gordon*.

Standing up now, going over to the blackwood table, Bradley examines the stacked-up collection of aged paperback comic books, in their lurid colours. He is remembering how Vincent first showed him the collection. His face, as he'd done so, had taken on an expression that Derek had found mildly disturbing: an expression he had described to himself as 'fanatical'. He'd known this word to be inexact; all he knew was that Vincent had shown him a quite different face from the one he normally presented. It was hard to say in what way it was different; but for a few fleeting moments, as Vincent had reverently handled a *Flash Gordon* booklet, he had seemed to be living in a private world that might not be merely immature, but in some way abnormal. Then the impression had passed.

It would manifest itself again, however. This would happen when Bradley first encountered Vincent with Erika Lange.

She had been kept until then in one of those separate compartments of Vincent's life. For a long time, Bradley had known nothing of her existence – and probably never would have known, had it not been for a single chance meeting.

This had taken place on a wet winter evening in the middle of the city, in front of the GPO. It had been at around six o'clock, he recalled: the end of the working day, with crowds going home to dinner. Bradley had been standing on the Post Office steps, his bag full of books from the Public Library. Shoals of electric trams were humming at the terminus opposite the steps, or lurching into life when their turn came to go. Lemon light from their windows was reflected in the road's wet blackness, together with the headlights of cars. Glancing towards the corner where Elizabeth Street met Macquarie, Bradley suddenly caught sight of Vincent, advancing towards him through the crowd with a blonde young woman in a beret and dark-blue raincoat.

When they drew level, and Vincent saw Bradley, his response was peculiar. His face did not break into its usual smile; instead it wore a pained, reluctant expression. But he stopped and performed introductions.

'Derek, let me introduce Erika Lange,' he said. He pronounced it 'Langer', and his voice was mechanical and almost harsh. 'Erika is a cadet journalist on the *Mail*. Erika, my friend Derek Bradley.'

'Hello Derek,' Erika said.

Her voice was low and pleasing, but without warmth; and she didn't smile. Instead, her wide-set, light-blue eyes had a look of enquiry: an enquiry entirely without friendliness, whose purpose Bradley couldn't read. She was about his own age: slim, not very tall, and quite pretty: but there had seemed to him an abstract quality about her prettiness. Her thick, straight blonde hair fell from under the beret to just below her ears.

She said no more; neither did Vincent, and an awkward pause followed. Bradley stood, searching for words, his bulging satchel of books suddenly an absurd encumbrance. Vincent glanced at it, and looked back at Bradley significantly. 'Ah,' he said. 'Working on your History essay, no doubt. You'll be busy, old chap.'

His tone was that of a man humouring an inconvenient acquaintance, and Bradley's normally calm grey eyes narrowed. He wasn't easily disconcerted, but he experienced an unaccustomed stab of annoyance at Vincent. While the girl continued to study him, he said that he had a tram to catch, and turned to make off across the road.

As he did so, Erika suddenly smiled at him; and the smile was startling. It transformed her completely, offering an intimacy as unaccountable as her aloofness had been. Under the circumstances, its true purpose had seemed to Bradley to be a kind of mockery. He stepped on to his tram, as baffled by this smile as he'd been by Vincent's coldness.

When he and Vincent next met, Bradley's annoyance had subsided; he could never be annoyed for long. It had been replaced by simple curiosity, and he asked Vincent now whether he and Erika were going out together. Derek had long ago decided that his friend was awkward with women, and doubted that Vincent was actually having an affair with Erika Lange; but he was curious to know what the basis of the relationship was, and why Vincent had kept it hidden.

Vincent, however, was not to be drawn.

'I wouldn't say I take her *out*, old chap. I run into her from time to time. We're merely acquaintances.'

Then he closed up, and Bradley shrugged inwardly. It would be useless to press him.

He leans back now in Vincent's chair, his hands behind his head. He's remembering something else about the encounter which made it disturbing. It had been an impression, merely, impossible to analyse at the time. Now, he's able to do so.

Standing in front of the Post Office, Vincent and Erika had seemed to look at him from inside a bubble: a bubble it was impossible to penetrate, and which Bradley had felt they wished no-one to penetrate. Seen with Erika, Vincent had become a different person. It was as though he and she were creatures in a dimension of their own, their eyes resting on a world which they both viewed with indifference, and perhaps even with hostility – and which they both saw in the same way.

What the exact nature of their relationship was, Bradley hadn't been able to guess, at the time; but now he sees that a clue to its peculiarity had lain in the fact that there appeared to be nothing sexual in it. He'd never known Vincent to have a girlfriend, and it had seemed unlikely that Vincent was involved with Erika, in the usual sense. The two had not stood close to each other; there had been no physical contact between them, and they'd given no impression that they were lovers – or even that they were linked by a budding romantic interest. Yet the sense of a potent yet enigmatic link had been very strong.

Late afternoon the next day, and thin autumn sun is streaming through the sliding windows, congealing in a pool on the varnish of the desk. Bradley, back at his post, opens the first of Vincent's diaries, in its blue ring-binder.

It's dated 1969. The ruled sheets of exercise paper are beginning to yellow with age, but Vincent's upright handwriting, in black fountain-pen ink, is unfaded. Bradley has glanced through a number of these diaries in the last two days, allowing passages to leap out at him – discovering, with a mixture of pleasure and sadness, that the few references to himself are fond and approving. In some of these entries, in fact, Vincent seems to regard him with a sort of wistfulness, as though Bradley represents a condition which is forever denied to him: stability, perhaps. So far, Bradley hasn't read anything thoroughly. Now he intends to do so, starting at the beginning, sitting at this desk where the early entries were written.

The diary's opening entry is dated the 7th of March, when Vincent was eighteen, and in his first year at university. Before this entry, however, a quite lengthy memoir has been inserted which acts as a preface to the diary: an autobiographical narrative dealing with Vincent's childhood and youth. The decision to write it has clearly been triggered by an unexpected meeting with Erika Lange described in the March 7th entry – and Bradley guesses that it was written a few weeks after that encounter. The old-fashioned formality of its style owes something to Vincent's infatuation with Dickens, and its fervent tone brings back the youthful Vincent in a way that makes Bradley smile.

The pages that do most to hold Bradley's attention are those which deal with Vincent's childhood friendship with Erika, and the way in which it began. In these passages, Vincent recalls his first steps into that secret zone where he and Erika would spend so much time together, possessed by a single set of dreams and obsessions which meant more to them than reality, and which they both comprehended so perfectly that they seemed to share one spirit.

This was where it began, Bradley thinks. *It all began here.*

3

Vincent Austin's Memoir

NOW THAT ERIKA Lange has come back into my life, after so long
a time, I feel compelled to record some facts about my past – as
well as the history of our childish friendship. I do so as an introduction to this diary.

My recent meeting with Erika has thrown me into joyous
turmoil. It has also caused me to mull over certain things that
have a particular, private importance for me. Principal among
these is my interest in espionage – which I find, to my surprise
and delight, Erika shares. Ah, but I shouldn't be surprised! We
always shared everything as children; why not still?

What is a spy? Are they born, or are they made? This is a
question that's of considerable interest for me, since I've decided
that my vocation will very likely lie in secret intelligence.

A number of spies are made, I imagine. They probably learn
the craft as they'd learn any other, drawn to it purely by ambition;
perhaps even by duty. But I believe that another kind of spy is
born rather than made – and this is the category to which I
belong. This kind of spy is devoted to secrecy: to secrecy in its
purest form; *to secrecy for its own sake.*

How does it begin, this addiction, and what is its nature?

In my case, it began very early. It began on the farm.

'Wattle Grove'! A strange place to have been born, for someone
like me; and I'll carry a certain guilt about it all my life. Because

I'm my father's only heir, and because I flatly refused to consider taking up my inheritance, 'Wattle Grove' has passed out of the hands of the Austin family for ever. I still see my father's quiet, thin-lipped face as he looks at me in sad resignation. But I could never have stayed; could never have been a farmer. I was meant for the world of events.

Perhaps it was the farm itself that bred my love of secrets, without my being aware of it. It was, after all, a territory of secrets, as such old properties are, in Tasmania: secrets, in the case of 'Wattle Grove', going back to the 1840s, when George Austin, my great-great-grandfather, purchased it. That was when Tasmania was still Van Diemen's Land, and the farm was worked by convict servants. The sandstone outer walls of the house, my father once told me, were cut by convicts; and there was still an old stone water trough by the house's front garden that had been hewn by convict hands. Sometimes at night, when Douglas and I were small, we'd imagine strange noises out by the stables: banging and jingling and voices. We'd tell each other there were ghosts there, but it was probably just the horses: the old Clydesdales, restless in their stalls.

The property was on the Middle Tea Tree Road, just outside the village of Richmond, whose Georgian villas, miniature brick cottages and aged stone bridge are a tourist attraction today. But when I was a child, the Coal River Valley was a quiet, half-forgotten region, its dry inland summers and dust storms making it somewhat discouraging to visitors, and the village had a forlorn, furtive air, seeming much more remote from Hobart than a mere fourteen miles. Our front drive ran for half a mile to the road, and I would sometimes walk to the gate and look west, where I could just make out the distant blue outline of Mount Wellington, rising above the invisible city of Hobart. I would contemplate the strangeness of being in an island at 42 degrees south, on the edge of the Southern Ocean; and I would dream of escape – to Hobart and beyond.

This was in the holidays, when Douglas and I were home from

school. In idle hours (when Douglas was not about, for some reason), I would roam about the property, looked down on by the dry-grassed dome of Bald Hill, which rose behind our farm in the north. The sense of unseen companions was always with me at these times, making me melancholy. Possessed by a formless apprehension, I would wander into the big, empty shearing shed with its wool table and press (alive during autumn with bleating sheep, and the shearers shouting, '*Sheep-o!*'); into the old, dim forge, with its mouldering timber walls and furnace and bellows and ancient iron tools, belonging to that stern last century of the convicts; into the stables; into the dairy. There's a particular lone-liness that some country boys have, I believe, which is not like any other. It's fed by those aged presences that are always to be found on farms that were born in the last century, with their dry whispers of a past that will not quite be buried. In other moods, of course, I was fond of the farm, and viewed tea-brown Bald Hill as my friend, and was deeply attached to my favourite dog, and to the big, comforting, butter-and-smoke-smelling kitchen with its black iron stove, where we ate all our meals. Sometimes now I see 'Wattle Grove' in my dreams, and wish I was back there, and fight back tears of regret, knowing it was lost because of me, and because Douglas died.

I should not have been idle, of course. My father, who hated idleness, gave Douglas and me many tasks – most of which I disliked. I preferred to read, unlike dear Douglas, who was always cheerful and willing. When the shearing was on, we must get under the slatted floor of what was called 'the gratings', where the sheep were held overnight, and clean out the dung that had fallen through, using long-handled rakes. We must pick up rocks in the paddocks. Or else (and this was much more pleasant) we must go up Bald Hill with our dogs and gather bark and sticks for the fire.

Sometimes, I would escape these duties by hiding in the hay shed. At times, Douglas would agree to join me; at others, I went alone. And this was where secrecy was born.

O sweet-smelling hay shed: place of solace and dreams! The bales of hay were stacked almost to the roof, and a disused tractor and an ancient Ford truck were parked there for eternity. I would hide up near the roof (usually carrying a book) in a cavity the size of a room. Here I was entirely concealed; nobody knew where I was; I could never be discovered by my quiet, patient, sober-faced father, with his long, finely cut nose and neatly parted, greying black hair and blank green eyes which seemed adjusted to staring over distances, rather than looking at people. Here, hay-sweet secrecy enclosed me. Secrecy was accompanied by the muted sounds of the farm outside: the bleating of sheep, a dog barking, and human voices too far off to understand, like voices from another country. And long after Douglas died, I would still hear his eight-year-old voice, very far off: farther than the voices outside. *'Let's go into the hay!'* Only little Douglas, with his tangled sandy hair and carefree smile, had shared with me the happiness of hiding in the hay. Now I was alone.

The next five years were not particularly happy ones – or at least, not when I was at home on the farm. I was contented enough during term-time at Knopwood College, since I did well in class, and my work distracted me from my sadness over Douglas. But 'Wattle Grove' without my brother was a desolate and empty place.

I mourned for him, and Connie and I would often take flowers to his grave in the Church of England cemetery in Richmond. I saw his lively ghost everywhere, moving about the yard. We had been so attuned to each other's thoughts that we could finish each other's sentences, and could often predict what the other would say next; we were truly variants of the one person, and I couldn't quite believe that he was gone: that he would not reappear in the attic bedroom we shared upstairs, or in the hay shed. My father and Connie mourned for him too, I'm sure, but neither of them were people who showed their emotions – at least, not to me.

My father was always a silent man, and the only sign of the way in which Douglas's death affected him was that he became more silent. I imagine he was fond of me, but he didn't find it easy to show this, and I think he was disappointed that I had short sight, and had to wear glasses. He hadn't kissed me since I was an infant of four years old or so, and a memory comes back to me now that I can never put out of my mind, although I would like to. In the week after Douglas died, I was going off to start school again. Connie was waiting in her car in the drive, ready to take me in to Hobart, and I said goodbye to my father in the kitchen. Standing over me, wearing his stained felt hat, he looked down on me with a sad and kindly expression: he was a tall man, and towered over me, when I was eight years old. I waited, thinking that today, with Douglas gone, he might actually kiss me goodbye. His blank green gaze met mine and then flickered; he coughed, and patted me on the shoulder. 'Goodbye, son. Do your best at school,' he said, and turned and went out into the yard.

The following year, when I was nine, a new figure appeared in my life. This was Uncle Kenneth: Connie's and my mother's brother. Kenneth Ross was a Presbyterian minister, and had been away from Tasmania for some years – first at a seminary in Melbourne, and then serving as minister in a country town in Victoria. Now he was back, and was minister at a Presbyterian church in central Hobart, living in the adjoining manse. He was much younger than Connie – about thirty-five – and was unmarried. He was possibly somewhat lonely, since he took to driving out to Richmond to visit us quite frequently, staying on the farm overnight.

'Kenneth's quite taken to you,' Connie told me. 'He thinks you're a very bright young fellow. Watch out, or he'll try to turn you into a Presbyterian.' She chuckled; but I think she knew there was a grain of truth in this.

Since my father had made me an Anglican – occasionally taking me to the service at St Luke's church in Richmond – I found this an odd idea, and slightly alarming. But Kenneth was certainly friendly to me, whatever his motives might have been; I was glad of any friendship shown to me at that time, and would watch for the arrival of his sedate, dark-blue Hillman, coming up the drive. He often brought me presents – usually books, since he'd discovered I loved reading. Some of them were dull, but others delighted me. He presented me with most of the English classics for children which still sit on my shelves – *Treasure Island*, *The Wind in the Willows*, *Alice in Wonderland*, *The Water Babies* and quite a few others. All were inscribed: *To Vincent, from Uncle Kenneth*, in his small, neat handwriting.

He was tall and thin, with thick, straight, dark-red hair with a tendency to spikiness: it was parted on the side and kept neat through the use of hair cream. His long face was rather pale, and his eyes, under low-set brows, were brown and penetrating and rather close-set. Connie sometimes said that I 'took after' Kenneth, in appearance, and resembled him in other ways – but I could never see it. He always arrived at the farm in a well-pressed suit – either navy or dark-brown – and a collar and tie. He liked to go for walks about the property with me, or along the road to the village, and for these expeditions he would change into a sweater, casual slacks, and thick boots. On these walks, he would question me about my work at school, and the books I'd read, and would nod (he had a habit of nodding) and glance at me with what usually seemed to be approval – although sometimes his glance seemed to have a questioning quality, as though he was trying to work something out about me. His face was usually immobile and almost expressionless, except for a very faint smile. I could never quite read this smile; it seemed partly amused and partly complacent, giving the impression that he'd discovered the answer to something. I thought of it as a religious smile, and it often appeared when he glanced at me.

In memory, Kenneth seems always to be glancing – perhaps because we were usually out walking together, and he was compelled to look at me sideways. He never held my gaze for long; his glances were quick, and would then shoot away again.

No-one else had taken such an interest in me before; I felt that he liked me, and was flattered, and decided I liked him. But although I enjoyed our walks, and although I was pleased by his interest, I was never entirely easy with him, I could not have said why. Perhaps it had to do with a sort of furtiveness about him. He was a strange man, and one I've never forgotten; I think now that much of his furtiveness was due to loneliness, and an odd shyness. What else it sprang from I'll never know. Like me, I believe, he was addicted to what was hidden; but this is only a guess.

His visits went on over the next two years, until I was eleven years old. Then he disappeared – transferred to a church in Launceston, in the north. Not long before he left, he took me on a walk to the top of Bald Hill, and on this occasion he spoke to me in a way that was very strange, and has never left my memory.

It was a fine, clear spring afternoon, and when we reached the summit of the hill, stopping in the long dry grass under a drooping she-oak, we were gazing over a view to the north that extended for miles: first, my father's pastures, beautifully green with new spring grass, then the distant paddocks of the Paterson property, and finally, very far off, the low hills and ranges, yellow-gold and then smoke-blue. Kenneth had picked up a stick to walk with; now he used it to point to this panorama.

'All the kingdoms of the world,' he said. 'You know your New Testament, Vincent?' And he glanced at me sideways, smiling his little smile, waiting for my answer.

I stared at him, baffled; I didn't know what he was referring to.

'"The devil taketh him up into an exceeding high mountain, and showeth him all the kingdoms of the world",' Kenneth said. 'That was when Satan tempted Christ, Vincent. And he said to Jesus: "All these things I will give thee, if thou wilt fall down and worship me." Do you remember now?'

I said I thought I did, although I didn't, and Kenneth looked at me seriously. 'You'd know your Bible better if you became a Presbyterian,' he said. 'We must talk to Connie about that.' Then, while I continued to stare out at the view, he did an odd thing:

he laid his hand on the top of my head, and kept it there. He was looking at me sideways again, but I refused to look at him; he had never touched me before, and I was very uncomfortable. So we stood, side by side, looking out to the hills, and he went on speaking, his hand on my head, in a low, persuasive voice.

'You're a good boy, Vincent, I know that. But one day you'll find that it's harder to be good as we go into adult life. Satan will lay many temptations for you, then. For now, just remember this: the most important thing is to keep yourself clean. You'll start to meet girls when you get older – and this is where the worst temptations lie. If you go with unclean women, you'll become unclean yourself. You must keep yourself clean for the girl you'll marry – that's if you wish to marry. Do you understand?'

I made some sort of noise in assent. I wanted him to take his hand off my head, but at the same time, I felt that he was deeply concerned for me – concerned in a way that my father had never been, and I was grateful. Finally he took his hand away, and I turned to find him smiling at me with an expression of great fondness. I was filled with a glow of gratitude, and smiled back.

'Do you remember *The Water Babies*? Remember what the Irishwoman said to Grimes,' he told me. '"Those that wish to be clean, clean they will be; and those that wish to be foul, foul they will be."' Then he ceased to smile, and spoke with sudden abruptness. 'We'd better go down for tea,' he said, and we started off down the hill.

I don't recall that he spoke again before we reached the farm, and I was not to see him very much more before he went away. I've never seen him again.

After I came to live here in New Town with Aunt Connie, secrecy changed its face.

Secrecy now was my many lone walks about New Town, this old, sprawling suburb in its wide valley which the early colonists saw as the most charming part of Hobart: a region where the Van Diemen's Land gentry built their houses, each with its own small farm. These days the villas crouch among twentieth-century bungalows, their estates swallowed up.

I was now a day boy at Knopwood Grammar, and my time was my own, after school. Secrecy was riding a tram by myself to its terminus: a journey made without apparent purpose (this was the magic of it), to a place where I had no business; a place, like the hay shed, where nobody knew where I was. I've always been fond of trams; I used to keep lists of their numbers and destinations. The whining, clanging cars on their snaking silver lines were vehicles of mystery to me, running as they did to the town's outer limits. When I rode one to its terminus, I liked the way it would sit humming on the frontier of the land, waiting to start back to town. I liked the old dry grass that grew around the tracks there, and the waiting, peaceful silence. It was possible to pretend there that I'd been brought to the border of some other country: the trams took me out of reality, and into a dimension I preferred. Out there, in those suburbs where the tramlines ended, I would walk past final houses and fields of dry grass, pretending to be someone else, observing strange lives in the windows and gardens of the last little homes. At thirteen, I was beginning to flirt with the notion of *crossing frontiers*; of taking on false identities.

And secrecy now had another dimension. It was being alone in a room which couldn't be penetrated: in what I now call my Secret Room, up here next to the sunroom, which Connie allowed me to make into my own domain entirely, and which remains so to this day. This has been a foretaste of what I feel sure is the ultimate pleasure, for a spy: the licence to be utterly alone in the still and soundless air of a private compartment, where dry sheets of paper of clandestine significance excite him as much as scented flesh might do. Safe with my secrets, I've been able to examine whatever artefacts I choose, in the Secret Room, never having to fear interruption, thanks to dear old Connie.

I've been doing this today, knowing that when a knock on the door sounds, it can only be one person in the world.

'It's me, Erika.'

She will sidle in, with her light, compelling eyes, high-arched brows and quizzical, seductive smile; and then there'll be two of us at secrecy's core, like twin kernels in a shell.

We met when I was thirteen, and she was twelve. That was in 1964, just after Connie and I came here to live.

It was my habit in that year to wander through the eastern side of New Town after school, only going back to Bay Road when dusk fell, and it was time for tea. I was still accustoming myself to being an orphan, and spent much of my spare time alone. The western limit of my wanderings was the New Town Road: the old main road that runs through New Town on its way to the north of the island, dividing the suburb's east from its west. On this border, there's a junction where four roads meet – one of them being Pirie Street, whose hill I'd climb to get home. Another was Risdon Road, whose level, sunken channel runs east from New Town Road towards the river.

On a certain showery evening in April, this became a fateful thoroughfare for me.

On that evening, instead of turning up Pirie Street, I wandered along Risdon Road towards the hillside district of Lutana. I have no idea why I did so. An impulse, dictated by fate. I was wearing a raincoat and cap, and was indifferent to the rain-showers; cars whizzed by on the wet bitumen. Risdon Road is sunk in the nineteenth century: I passed gates and driveways guarded by aged cedars, and stone Georgian houses crouching behind overgrown gardens. Below the footpath, between stone walls, the New Town Rivulet rushed along beside me, in a channel no wider than a drain; further on, where Risdon Road ended, it would emerge into the Derwent, at New Town Bay. Before this point is reached, the road passes under a high, overhead railway bridge, at the corner of Swanston Street; and here, as the rain suddenly came on heavily, I decided to take shelter.

Under the bridge, I stood against one of the tall concrete walls of the cutting, taking off my cap and shaking it, and removing my glasses to dry them with my handkerchief. A car rushed through, setting up echoes. I watched gusts of wind sweep the rain in sheets across the gleaming bitumen outside; and once a train thundered high overhead. It was now about five-thirty. Up on a green embankment beyond the bridge, giant electric pylons strode into misty remoteness: elegant, cryptic and forbidding.

For a time, I saw no-one on the footpath outside; then a figure appeared in the distance, coming from the direction of the river. At first, the driving rain made it difficult to make out anything other than the fact that it was a woman or a girl, in a wide-brimmed felt hat and overcoat. She was approaching slowly, trudging along as though unaware of the rain, hands in her pockets, head bent. When she drew closer, I saw that it was a schoolgirl around my own age: twelve, perhaps, or thirteen. The dark-blue felt hat, with its band and badge, was one that I recognised: the uniform of Riverlands College, a private school for girls here in New Town. She drew nearer, and came in under the bridge. Here she stopped, standing against the wall as I was doing, just a few yards away. But she seemed unaware of me; she kept her head bent, staring fixedly at the ground in front of her, hands remaining in the pockets of her coat, as though trying to solve a problem. Her hat was black with rain, and the brim dripped. The fair hair that hung from under it was wet, darkened and twisted. I was concerned to see that she was wet through: her grey gaberdine overcoat was saturated, and her stockings and shoes were splattered with mud.

She must have been walking for a long time, I thought, and I wondered why she carried no schoolbag, and where she'd come from. I decided to talk to her, and said that the rain should stop soon.

She looked up quickly, blankness like alarm in her face, which was wet with raindrops. Her eyes were swimming, so that she blinked. At first I thought that this was because the rain had got into them; but then I began to wonder if she'd been crying. She took some moments to answer; then she said: 'I hope so.'

She'd spoken softly. Her voice was rather deep, like a boy's, and her accent sounded English rather than Australian.

'I'll be going home, when there's a break,' I said. 'What about you?'

She looked at me now with a strange expression – almost as though I'd said something offensive. Then she said quickly: 'I'm not going home. I don't want to.' She took off her hat and shook some of the rain out of it; then pushed her hair back from her forehead and sniffed.

'You'll catch a cold, if you don't get inside soon,' I said.

I smiled to make a joke of it; but her eyes showed hostility: or was it sadness? They were eyes of a very light blue, making me uneasy.

I moved down the wall to stand next to her. 'You really ought to go home, in this weather,' I said. 'Why don't you want to?'

For a few moments she said nothing; then she looked at me with a severe expression. 'Because there's no-one there,' she said.

At this, I was reduced to silence for a moment. Then I asked her whether her mother and father were away.

'My mother's dead,' she said, 'and my father's away. He wasn't there last night either, and I don't know where he is.'

Now I understood, and was filled with pity. The girl was an orphan, like me: orphaned through the death of her mother and her father's neglect. I decided that there was only one thing to do: I must try to take her home to Aunt Connie. I didn't feel very confident that she'd accept this idea; but when I proposed it she agreed immediately, almost as though she'd been expecting it. So I led her up the hill to Bay Road.

My aunt made the girl welcome, as I'd hoped, only briefly raising her eyebrows. Connie likes to help people, and nothing much surprises her, being a nurse. She took the girl's wet overcoat and shoes and stockings, and put them to dry on the fireguard in front of the dining room fire. She led her to the bathroom for a wash, gave her a towel to dry her hair with, and then brought her back to the fire in a pair of her own slippers. The girl said her name was Erika Lange.

'Erika,' Connie said. 'That's a nice name.' She made us both sit down at the dining room table, and brought us a meal of bacon and eggs, toast and cocoa.

I'd told Connie that Erika's father was missing, and Connie had asked her no more questions; nor had she made any comment on the matter, as most other adults would have done. Erika seemed stiff and nervous at first, but Connie's friendliness seemed to make her grow easier. She ate politely but ravenously, sitting very straight in her dark-blue tunic and white, long-sleeved blouse. Meanwhile, Connie stood with her back to the fire, one arm resting on the mantelpiece. My aunt has a way of looking through her glasses that makes you feel that she's thought of something amusing which she might soon tell you about: a joke, perhaps. It was like that now; but she merely asked Erika if she liked the bacon. Erika said she did.

'You seem pretty hungry,' Connie said. 'There's more, if you want it.'

Only when the meal was over, and we'd helped her clear away, did Connie begin to ask questions. Erika and I sat in armchairs by the fire, and Connie stood by the mantelpiece again, looking down at us. She began by asking where Erika lived, and the girl told her she lived at Lutana.

Connie nodded. 'Away out there,' she said, as though Lutana was on the moon. 'And where do you think your father is? Does he work at night?'

Erika looked up. When she did this, a wing of her thick fair hair would swing back from her cheek and then fall forward again, half-hiding her face. He sometimes worked at night, she told Connie. He had an important job at the Zinc Works. But last night he'd gone out, probably to have drinks with some friends of his – and he still wasn't back. He did this sometimes, she said, staying away all night. There was usually enough food in the house for her to get herself meals, but this time there hadn't been.

Connie looked at her for some time. Her eyes had grown narrow, in the way that they sometimes do when she listens to news on the radio: news that annoys her. But when she spoke, she didn't sound annoyed; she simply asked Erika if her father ever treated her badly.

No, Erika said, he never did. She looked up at Connie almost fiercely, now. 'He's very good to me,' she said. 'I only came out tonight because I got hungry and lonely – that's all. I was going to buy a hamburger.'

Again Connie studied her without speaking. Then she said: 'Well, we can't have you being lonely. I'll tell you what: give me your phone number and we'll see if your father's there now. If he's not, you can stay here tonight. Then we'll try him again in the morning.'

Erika's father wasn't there that night, but when Connie rang in the morning, Mr Lange answered. He'd been searching for Erika and had called the police, he told Connie; now he'd have to tell them that she was back. Connie told him dryly he should do that. Her phone was in the hall; sitting in the dining room, Erika and I listened to her slow drawl. When she came back to the dining room, she told Erika that her father had said that he hadn't been well. She'd asked him if he'd like Erika to stay for another night, and he'd agreed to this.

'He reckoned you needed a bit of mothering,' Connie said.

Erika came and stayed quite frequently after that, often for days at a time, and Connie seemed happy to have her. 'She's a well-bred girl,' she told me. 'A bit quiet, but that's not surprising. It's a shame, that her father neglects her. He may send her to the best school, and buy her good clothes, but that doesn't make up for losing her mother, and being left on her own like that. We must do what we can to look after her.'

Perhaps Connie had wanted a daughter. I'd certainly wanted an orphan: one who would be like a sister or a brother. And although Erika had only lost one parent, an orphan was what she was, in my eyes: not just any orphan, either, but *my* orphan. That was how I saw her, from the very beginning.

An only child, she lived alone with her father, out on Lutana Rise. Dietrich Lange, I learned, had been a German immigrant who'd arrived in Tasmania just after World War Two. Erika's mother had been Australian, and Erika had been born here in Tasmania. Although he'd studied chemistry before the War, and had been a pilot in the Luftwaffe, Dietrich Lange had had to work as a labourer when he arrived, like most other migrants. But he'd studied at night and had qualified as a metallurgist, and now had a good position at the Electrolytic Zinc Works which squatted on the river below Lutana. When she spoke of him to me, Erika would adopt a solemn expression, saying her father was a scientist, and one of the most important people at the Works.

So Erika was half-German, at a time when memories of the War still lingered. She didn't look very different from other girls, except for her eyes. Her eyes looked somehow German to me; and she spelled her name with a 'k'. She was twelve – a year younger than me – and I found her strange and fascinating.

Because Erika lived there, Lutana became a magic hill. I'd never actually visited the small cluster of houses on that low, empty rise near the river; now, because I knew that one of these houses was Erika's home, the hill took on a mysterious quality – related, I suppose, to Erika's strangeness.

Lutana, I've discovered, was originally created to house the employees of the Zinc Works, many of whom had been brought to Tasmania from Europe in the decade after World War One. The company had built houses for them that were designed to look as European as possible, to prevent them from growing homesick: two-storeyed, steep-gabled stuccoed villas, one of which was now the home of Dietrich Lange and his daughter. The district was originally to have been named Zincville; instead, 'Lutana' was chosen: an Aboriginal word meaning 'moon'. I'd once been past the Zinc Works – driven there by Connie, in her little Morris Minor. Uncanny blue lights glowed in the windows of immensely long buildings; chimneys discharged sinister white smoke; cargo ships lay at anchor on the river, and elevated tracks, their purposes inscrutable, crossed the air between the buildings and the ships. The air reeked of sulphur. Vast and weird, the Works resembled a citadel on the planet Mongo, in my *Flash Gordon* comics: the kingdom of Ming the Merciless. And this was the world of Mr Lange, the German scientist! Was he a Nazi? I thought of Erika's father now with a chill of apprehension.

From my sunroom-study in Bay Road, I could see the Rise in the eastern distance; the Works lay hidden behind it, indicated only by shifting white banners of smoke, raised in the pure air. Only a few houses and streets clustered on Lutana's lower slopes, and two final houses could be seen on its curving, bowl-shaped top, which was treeless and empty and clothed with yellow grass. Staring across the distance, in the days before Erika took me there, I would wonder which one of these houses was hers, and imagine her walking on the Rise with the important German scientist who was her father: a master of the hidden, smoking citadel. In the late afternoons, the grass of the Rise would glow gold, and become a place of Faery: dark eyes of gorse watched from its slopes, and a line of minute telephone poles glowed in the sunset, signifying the outskirts of a land of fable, never to be reached. At night, the Rise's few, far lights became those of an alien city: a metropolis in one of those adventure strips which Erika and I would soon explore together, in the Secret Room.

Which one of us first gave this name to the storeroom off my study in the sunroom I no longer recall. So many things seemed to come from both our minds in the same instant.

At the time when we first met, the storeroom had already become my personal domain. Aunt Connie had no use for it, so she allowed me to make it my own, and to fill it with my books, my LP record-player, and my precious vintage comics. From the time when she first came to stay, Erika and I would be in there for hours at a time, and Connie wouldn't disturb us. She did look in now and then – mainly to call us to meals – but she never lingered, and was never inquisitive. I've always appreciated this in Connie.

At first, before our secret games began, Erika and I merely talked, exchanging those verbal talismans which enable the young to recognise each other: things that would seem meaningless to most adults. It's the feeling that accompanies such exchanges that causes elation at that age: an age in the borderland between childhood and adolescence. How can this elation be captured? It can't be, since it's conveyed in glances; in a lift in the voice. Initially we listened to my Beatles and Elvis Presley LPs, and discussed our favourite books and television shows. There were certain childhood books that we shared a love for, since they contained mysteries of importance to us – *Alice in Wonderland* in particular. We discovered that we'd both been fascinated by Alice's discovery of the little door behind the curtain: the one that opened with a golden key, and led to the beautiful garden. We had both wanted fervently to go through this door. Somewhere, we both knew, there was still such a doorway to be found: not one in a fairy tale, but one that led to the world's ultimate secrets.

We both read adult books as well. We found that we each had a precocious enthusiasm for Ian Fleming's James Bond thrillers – mine lent to me by Connie, while Erika's were borrowed from an older girl at school – and had both been spellbound by the film versions of *Dr No* and *From Russia with Love*. Then we discovered a mutual interest in something rather less usual: American comic strips of a past era, such as *The Phantom*, *Tarzan*, *Buck Rogers* and *Flash Gordon*. When Erika first mentioned this, I was incredulous. Comic strips were usually a boy's enthusiasm – and a rather old-fashioned one, in this age of television. But discussion soon showed that she was genuine, and I felt confident enough to reveal to her the extent of my secret devotion to the classics of the genre, and to show her the collection inherited from Uncle John. John was my father's younger brother: he had left the farm when he was in his twenties, and now ran an electrical business; and he had passed on to me his boyhood collection of comic books. To my delight, Erika was deeply impressed. More: she understood the mystical *specialness* of these strips. I found that she collected comic books too – though she was not of course in possession of the early strips that I held – and my favourites turned out to be her favourites, even though she'd met them only in their current, decadent form, carried on by contemporary writers and artists. An affinity had been confirmed: one which was deeply important. We had passed into a special country, and Erika behaved as though we'd also confessed to something: to a mutual addiction that was in some way illicit.

Illicit! I thrilled to this; and I half-understood why I did so. Some of the great adventure strips, with their violence and half-naked women, were clearly aimed at adults rather than children; and although such strips still remained within very strict limits of sexual display, and nothing more than kissing was portrayed, some older people used to find them dubious. It was plain from Erika's sly smile that she was aware of this disreputable quality. She began to hint at it; and also at something more. She began to convey the idea that she and I were special spirits, and that our recognition of the power of particular adventure strips was proof of it. As though to test this, she began to question me; and the questions usually related to one strip with which she was apparently infatuated: the one that dealt with the space adventurer, Flash Gordon.

In response, I was of course able to demonstrate a knowledge of this classic that was far more detailed then hers, causing her to look at me with solemn admiration. I showed her my precious hoard of *Flash Gordon* originals, drawn by Alex Raymond, the originator of the series: historic survivals from a time long before we were born, in the 1930s. I'd lend them to her, I said recklessly. It was an offer I'd have made to no-one else, and I was gratified to see the delight in her face. It was as though I'd offered her jewels – as indeed I had, in my own eyes. Then she resumed her interrogation.

'Isn't Flash Gordon handsome? And Dale Arden – she's beautiful, isn't she?'

Yes, I said. Flash was handsome, and Dale was beautiful.

'Yes: I can see you love Dale!'

There was something strange about these questions – or rather
about the way in which they were asked. Erika's smile challenged
me, and her wide-set eyes grew roguish and suggestive. I looked
away in confusion, while Erika began to laugh: an indulgent laugh
that was curiously mature for a twelve-year-old girl. I fought down
a certain confusion; but I was also touched by bliss. I felt myself
being drawn into a secret life that Erika led, out on Lutana Rise: a
life connected with yellow-haired Flash Gordon and his beautiful
girlfriend, Dale Arden. At the same time, a closeness was being
established between us: closeness of a kind more common between
boys, at that age, than between boys and girls. And there *was*
something boy-like about Erika: it was in her air of tough decisive-
ness; in her straight back as she walked; in her direct, narrow gaze.
All this despite her delicate prettiness and slight figure.

Ever since Douglas died, I had longed for a perfect friend, who
would be close to me as he had been. I had pictured this friend as
a beautiful girl-child, resembling one of the fairies in Arthur
Rackham's illustrations, with whom I would move through the
world in a state of perfect happiness. Now, I said, I had found her.

Sometimes, coming home from Knopwood College in the city, I
would get off the tram at the Risdon Road junction, and Erika
and I would meet there. Riverlands College was quite nearby, just
up the Main Road, and Erika always went home on foot. I would
walk part of the way with her, along Risdon Road: walks which
always ended, at Erika's request, where Risdon Road ended,
opposite the wide expanse of the river.

Here, on the corner of a little street that led up on to the hill
of Lutana, she would part from me; and before she went, she
would give me a rapid wink. The wink had a shrewdness that was
almost masculine, and was impressively mature. Then she would

be gone, marching away in her navy-blue uniform and felt hat, a bag slung over one shoulder, her back very straight, bound for Lutana Rise. *There goes my orphan*, I would say.

On these walks, she began to tell me her history. Her mother had died in hospital last year, from a wasting disease of which Erika appeared to be ignorant, but which I now believe was cancer. Erika described visiting her in the hospital with her father, and seeing her grow thinner and thinner, and her skin turning yellow. Erika remained quite calm, when she told me this; her face had no expression. Sitting beside the hospital bed, her father would hold her mother's hand and say nothing, simply looking at her. But as they went out of the hospital, Erika would see that his eyes were red, and filled with tears, and it made her frightened. She grew more frightened still when her mother told her that if she didn't get better, Erika must look after her father.

Then her mother died. After the funeral, her father did not go to work for over a week, but sat in an armchair in his work-room with a bottle of brandy next to him, drinking. Erika would come to him and try to talk; sometimes he would hug and kiss her, but at others he would shout at her to go away. Erika would sometimes come home and he would not have made dinner. He would be asleep in his bedroom or in his chair, and she couldn't wake him. But this wasn't often, she said, and looked at me warningly. She made it plain that she admired her father greatly.

'My father's very handsome,' she told me. 'He was in the Air Force in the War. No, my father wasn't a Nazi! He gets angry if people think that. He was just a pilot. I love my father; but some-times, when he drinks a lot, he's different.'

A sense of conspiracy grew, on our walks down Risdon Road. At first it wasn't even voiced; it could only be expressed by saying that we *recognised* each other. And what we recognised was that we were both in love with secrecy. Many adolescents are, of course; but with us it was different. With us it was a passion, central to our being. Nothing so eloquent was voiced by either of us at the time; but it was expressed, nevertheless, in simple ways.

'Papa doesn't mind me visiting your aunt's house,' Erika said. 'But he's beginning to ask if you think I'm your girlfriend.'

'Would you like to be?'

'I might. I like you, Vincent. You're different from other boys. You understand things. You understand about *Flash Gordon*.'

'And I like you,' I said. 'I think you're pretty, Erika.'

'Am I? My father says I am. But he says I'm too young for boyfriends – even though I'm nearly thirteen. So if I'm going to be your girlfriend, it has to be a secret, doesn't it? I like secrets. I like to spy on people. Have you ever done that?'

'No,' I said. 'Who do you spy on?'

'I'll tell you some time. Would you like to be a spy?'

'A real spy? Maybe,' I said.

'You and I are good at secrets, aren't we? We'd be good spies,' she said.

During this exchange, we had stopped walking, and stood beside a low iron fence above the rushing Rivulet, which the late light was tinting with bronze and gold. Erika was smiling at me in a very odd way now, her narrowed eyes searching mine: the sort of teasing, insistent smile that adults sometimes wore. She and I knew very little about spies then: our knowledge was mostly gained from the James Bond books, and from stories about espionage in World War Two. But these were the seeds from which everything grew.

In the Secret Room, our underground life now began.

It began with a game: a game which at first seemed suited to younger children than we were, but which quickly evolved into something far beyond childishness. We called it 'playing *Flash Gordon*'. It felt innocent enough, at first; but it was, in fact, the entry-point to certain regions *where each of us had expected to meet the other.*

Extraordinary though this seems, we discovered by comparing notes that it was actually true. Both of us, before we had ever met, had known the nature of those particular territories, and had described them as 'special' to ourselves. Special! Ah, this word now meant so much more than it had commonly done; so much more than it did to other people! We gazed at each other in glee, in triumph, our faces alight with recognition. Neither of us had believed until now that any other human being could understand the nature of this 'specialness', or knew that the 'special' world existed. Now each of us had discovered that there was another who did; and this was electrifying. Everything was confirmed for us; and when we said that *Flash Gordon* was 'special' we knew exactly what we meant, though it could never be described to anyone else. We had found each other.

It was this that drew us back constantly to the Secret Room. 'Special'! The word summed up the particular, private feeling that each of us had about *Flash Gordon* – and other adventure strips in the classic pantheon as well. Small things were associated with this specialness; even the smell of the paper on which my vintage comic books were printed. We laughed, believing that no-one else in the world knew what the smell of such paper meant. It confirmed the sacred 'specialness' of which only we were aware. The period comic books were printed in strong, almost violent colours, and these and the foreign smell of their pages intensified the thrill of studying these strange American images from the past: Flash Gordon's rocket ship roaring through space; Flash and the bearded scientist Doctor Zarkov peering through the big observation window; lovely Dale Arden (clad usually in a metallic bra-top, flowing red cloak and long skirt), running hand in hand with Flash to escape the Lizard Men, Hawkmen, Wolvrons and other grotesques of the planet Mongo.

Erika proved to have a remarkable talent for drawing – a talent which I came to greatly admire – and would copy many of these images into a drawing-book, using a set of coloured pencils. And now I discovered the origin of her interest in comic strips. Her father was fond of them, she told me, having enjoyed such strips as a boy in Germany; when she was younger, he'd encouraged her

to copy some of the artwork in the comic books he gave her –
Flash Gordon among them – and to try drawing strips of her own.

To my surprise, she brought out a pair of half-moon reading
glasses when she did her drawing: her pale and beautiful eyes
were flawed, it seemed. Another link between us! She would
go through my *Flash Gordon* books almost reverently, copying
frames from their high points with great care. In these artefacts
from the 1930s, it was noticeable that yellow-haired Flash was
seldom in his space uniform, but usually appeared naked except
for a loincloth, displaying his god-like physique as he entered into
gladiatorial combat with an endless array of alien opponents. It
was these sequences that she copied most.

Flash looked like her father, Erika said; and I wondered
whether this could be true.

We acted out whole episodes from *Flash Gordon*. We did so
mostly at Erika's direction, reciting the dialogue from the
balloons in the coloured pictures, or making up stories of our
own. And Erika insisted that we dress up. One day she brought
costumes to the room, in a shoulder bag. She drew out the leather
flying helmet and goggles her father had flown in during the War,
which I examined with awe. Her father would never know, she
said; and she asked me to put them on, in order to become Flash
Gordon. Then she crossed the room and opened the door of the
old wardrobe, disappearing behind it to dress up as Dale Arden.

I waited. After a time, the mirrored door of the wardrobe flew
back, and I stared in amazement, my heart thumping. The girl
who stood in front of me was no longer Erika Lange. She frightened me, at first. Her eyes were concealed by sinister sunglasses:
her 'space goggles'. She had exchanged her school clothes for a
navy-blue Speedo swimsuit, and early breasts I'd not suspected
stood out in it like tiny cones. Over her shoulders she wore a big
red cloak made of curtain material; she spun around, making the
cape and her yellow hair fly.

'Well? Am I Dale?'

'Yes. You're Dale.'

I meant it. In that moment, she seemed to me to have magical powers: the ability to be someone else.

The games varied. Sometimes they were directed by me, and sometimes by Erika – according to which of us had memorised one of the episodes best, or felt able to invent a new one. I was Flash Gordon, but also doubled as Doctor Zarkov; I also had to take on the roles of the various weird creatures on Mongo. Some of these creatures, such as the Lizard Men, caused Erika to scream hysterically; on these occasions she would throw herself in a corner, drawing her cloak about her, hiding her face, and crying out: *'No! No! Don't touch me!'* I found this troubling, even alarming, and feared that her screams would be heard by Aunt Connie. It was as though the fear that Erika mimed had turned into something real, and was caused by something else: something that did not belong to our game at all, but to another part of her life.

When Erika was in charge of the game, she'd occasionally allow me to kiss her: quickly, with pursed lips. This was when Flash had rescued Dale Arden, and the kiss was a reward. On these occasions, dialogue from the books themselves had to be recited faithfully. One speech seemed especially to please her, and had to be repeated often, while her face grew serious and dreamy, and her eyes looked somewhere else.

Flash: *We're on our way, darling – it's a new life, fraught with dangers – but with you by my side, I could do anything!*

Sometimes, though, Erika was not Dale Arden: she was the cruel Princess Aura, who held Flash prisoner in the torture chambers of the Hawkmen, trying to force him to marry her. On these occasions, she wore the swimsuit combined with a floor-length, transparent muslin skirt, also made from a curtain, and secured by a metal belt. Tied to a kitchen chair as her prisoner, I would see that her face had become cold and merciless, and feel almost afraid of her. And she would say something then that was not in the text:

'You can look at the Princess – but you can't touch her.'

Some six weeks after our friendship began, on a Friday afternoon in May, Erika asked me to walk all the way home with her, to meet her father. She did so with a casual air, but I knew from her sideways glance that this was important. For my part, I both wished for it and feared it.

We walked up Lennox Avenue, the long, winding street that led onto Lutana Rise, and my heart beat fast. It was just an ordinary street, I saw, with ordinary little weatherboard houses; but it had brought me onto that golden hill which had existed until now in the magical zone of distance, whose nature was a mystery.

The mystery of distance! It lay in the fact that the Lutana I saw across the miles was a different place from the one that was discovered up close. Yet I was not disillusioned. The far hill remained in another dimension, and would always remain there, inviolate.

Erika and I didn't speak much, as we walked; she seemed lost in thought, and soon we were close to the very top of the Rise, walking along Michael Street. This was where Erika lived, and I found myself in a foreign country. From up here, we looked west across the whole valley of New Town, with its miles of scattered houses, to the high rim of dark-blue ranges, and to sombre Mount Wellington, hunched above the city in the south. The low winter clouds that filled half the sky were tinted with a mixture of pink and orange: early warnings of sunset. On the eastern side of the street, habitation ended: here the tan-gold grass of the actual Rise began, with its few low bushes and gorse, running in a curve to the sky. And there on the skyline was the line of distant telephone poles that I'd so often studied. Now they were close, and strange as objects in a dream: a dream into which I had walked with Erika.

She stopped at the gate of her father's big, German-looking house, with its steep, green-tiled roof and secretive, multi-paned windows; and I was deeply impressed. I had only seen houses like this in photographs of places in Europe.

Erika led me in, and took me along a hall into a room at the back which was her father's study.

It looked west over the valley, and was lined with books. Rolled documents were piled on a table. Mr Lange was seated at a desk, in an office chair; a thin cigar smoked in an ashtray next to him. When we came in, he swivelled his chair around and stared at us without smiling, and without speaking; and something about this stare made my mouth grow dry. He was a big man in his mid-forties, with very long legs which were extended in front of him. You could see that he was German: it had something to do with his long head, his thick, powerful-looking neck, and his thinning blond hair, greying at the sides, swept back from a high forehead. But most of all it had to do with his eyes, which were Erika's eyes, but weary and much harder-looking, with bags underneath. Mr Lange's lower lip thrust out as Erika's did, but in a different way: a way that looked belligerent. Yet Erika smiled at her father as though his face was perfectly friendly, and introduced me.

Mr Lange studied me for what seemed a good half-minute, and I could hear him breathing deliberately through his nose. There was a faint medicinal smell about him which I guessed to be liquor, though no liquor was to be seen. Then he turned to Erika, and spoke to her. He had a very deep, throaty voice, and he spoke in German. To my amazement, Erika answered him in the same language. I'd never imagined that she spoke German; perhaps because she had no foreign accent, and had been born here. The dream of Lutana was complete, enclosing me like a bubble: I was truly in a foreign land.

As Erika spoke, her father slowly nodded; then he reached out and touched her cheek with his big hand. At this, she smiled with quick, radiant happiness, like a girl much younger: like a baby girl, I thought.

Mr Lange looked at me again; and now he spoke in English.

'So you are the boy Erika sees so much of. Your aunt has been very kind to her. Erika says you are clever. Are you clever?'

I've forgotten my reply; probably something foolish. My eyes wandered off about the study, and I found myself looking at a framed, black-and-white photograph on the far wall. It showed Mr Lange in flying gear, standing with two other men beside a twin-engined bomber which I recognised as a Junkers 88, the leather helmet I'd worn in the Secret Room dangling from one hand. He was young, in the picture, his hair much thicker and fairer.

He had followed my gaze, and spoke to me softly. 'You know what type of plane this is?'

'A Junkers 88,' I said.

He stared at me, picking up his cigar. He drew on it, squinting; then he exhaled the smoke. 'I see you are a clever boy,' he said. 'Yes, a Junkers. But that was a long time ago. And all a waste.' He turned away from me, looking out the window over the valley. He fell silent, his face sad, and Erika and I stood waiting. Finally he turned back again.

'So. You are clever,' he said. 'But I hope you are a good boy, Vincent. If you are not, I will not want Erika to see you. You understand?'

I said that I did, and Mr Lange nodded once. Then he swung around to his desk again, dismissing us both.

Not long after this, Erika introduced me to the practice of spying. She referred to it as 'trespassing'.

'I sometimes go trespassing. Do you want to come?'

At first, I thought she meant another piece of make-believe. 'Trespassing', however, turned out to be exactly that. Erika was in the habit of roving about New Town, climbing into people's gardens, and spying on them. Usually she did this in broad daylight; but occasionally it was done under cover of darkness. Trespassing was a summer activity, and she drew me into it in the January of 1965, in the school holidays, when warm days and evenings were back.

I protested, initially. If we were caught, the police might be sent for; we'd be breaking the law. But Erika smiled with a contempt that withered me. We wouldn't be stealing; just trespassing. And why should we be caught, if we were stealthy and clever? She had never been caught; at times she had walked right inside people's houses, and not been seen. Most people were stupid, she said; they took no notice of what was going on around them.

I was persuaded, finally. We made expeditions at night, which carried an added taste of danger. I would slip out late after Connie was asleep, and Erika would meet me in deserted Risdon Road, clad in a dark sweater and jeans. Then we'd begin to prowl, looking through lighted windows. What we saw were scenes of innocent domesticity: people sitting in their living rooms in armchairs; a woman ironing; a man sitting at a table reading a paper. Bedroom blinds were nearly always drawn; but occasionally we would glimpse people undressing, and glance at each other and laugh under our breath.

I felt no guilt over these expeditions. All the lit scenes that Erika and I watched were like the pictures in the frames of our adventure strips, existing on a level beyond mundane reality. The people we spied on were no longer New Town householders at all, but had become transfigured: figures from a story that only we were privileged to watch. Breathing and laughing in the New Town dark, we were startled at times by the piping of plover, or the hoot of the train that rattled out through Moonah. Spying gave us power: power that had the quality of a drug. This was our first taste of the craft we hoped to perfect as adults.

Without warning, our friendship ended. It ended when I was fifteen: just before Christmas in 1965, on the brink of the long summer holidays. I'd been looking forward to Erika and I spending much of our time together, as we always did in the holidays.

We met by chance on a Saturday morning, outside some shops in the New Town Road. I'd come out on an errand for Connie, and was about to go into a little supermarket there. The road was bathed in the cheerful sun of Saturday, with busy traffic passing. Turning, I saw Erika approaching, arm in arm with another girl of her own age, whom I hadn't seen before: an auburn-haired girl with a pretty, haughty face, who stared at me blankly. The two were dressed alike, in holiday jeans and T-shirts, and looked somehow older than fourteen. They talked with me, but were stiff and awkward, and barely friendly. And when I suggested to Erika that we meet soon, her eyes became empty.

'I can't,' she said. 'I'll be busy, these holidays. I'm going to stay with Barbara, up the country. Her parents have a property at Ross. She's my best friend.'

She smiled quickly at Barbara, who smiled back. Then Erika said something that pierced me. 'Don't you have other friends, Vincent?'

She was no longer the Erika I knew. She was a stranger, and cruel: no longer my twin. Everything around me became pitiless and distinct, and I can still see a newspaper banner standing by the door of the shop, reading: US War Planes Bomb Haiphong.

I went blindly into the supermarket, and after that made no attempt to contact Erika again. Nor did she contact me. Nor did I run into her in the street, over the three and a half years that followed. This was not so remarkable; after all, the route that she took to Riverlands College, on the northern edge of New Town, was quite removed from the zone that I moved in, catching a tram south to Knopwood Grammar. So a chance meeting wasn't all that likely.

I did see her once from a distance, however: from a tram window, late one afternoon in the city, about six months after our break. She was walking along Elizabeth Street with her friend Barbara, the two of them dressed identically in their dark-blue Riverlands uniforms and hats. They were laughing together, bending forward as they did so, and I saw that they were very close: members of an exclusive female society from which I was forever excluded.

I would wait until this year to see her again: my orphan, my lost twin.

4

Vincent Austin's Diary

March 7th, 1969

TO KEEP FIT, I often walk part of the way home after my lectures at university, going up Elizabeth Street to the summit of Lord's Hill, where I catch the tram home. I did this today, and stood waiting at the tram stop on the junction of New Town Road and Augusta Road.

Even before Erika appeared, I had a premonition.

I was standing in front of a paling fence that was painted dark-green, the late summer sun heating its boards. I could smell their oily fragrance, which was the smell of dying summer. A tram came over the brow of the hill: not the one I was waiting for, but the 128, bound west towards Lenah Valley. The green and yellow car, with its advertisement on the front for Kiwi boot polish, rattled and swayed across the points, going around the bend into Augusta Road and obstructing my view of New Town Road. As it receded, I had the unaccountable feeling that everything had changed: the houses in Augusta Road and the cypresses in their gardens had become like a stage backdrop, unnaturally distinct, waiting for the commencement of some unimaginable drama. I dismissed the feeling as irrational; but then I looked across to the other side of New Town Road, and saw a girl in a Riverlands College uniform standing in front of a tea room called the Granby, and seeming to look back at me.

She waved to me and smiled, and then I recognised her: Erika Lange, after more than three years.

We sat in the Granby drinking coffee, at a table next to the window. A lace curtain filtered the sun, its glowing reflection lying across the table between us: a pattern of pinpricks, touching the dark-blue sleeve of Erika's blazer. She sipped her coffee, and continued to smile at me. Her eyes examined me from under the brim of her straw hat: eyes that I remembered, but which had also changed; eyes which were no longer those of a child, but of a girl of seventeen, in her final year at school: almost a woman.

The Granby doubled as a pastry shop, and Erika told me she'd come here to buy cakes. I'd never come in here to drink coffee before: this had been her suggestion. The place was so small that there was only room for four tables, and all the others were empty: Erika and I were the only customers. A middle-aged woman with permed grey hair stood frowning at some papers by the cash register.

'You've got quite tall,' Erika said. 'You're grown up, aren't you?'

She looked amused, as though this were some clever feat I'd performed. I didn't feel grown up when she looked at me; I was trembling inwardly. To steady myself, I lit a cigarette, examining Erika without seeming to do so. She was beautiful: much more beautiful than she'd been at fourteen. Very clean and well-groomed, her blazer and tunic stainless and well-pressed, her white blouse gleaming. I'd half-forgotten her face. The way her lower lip pushed out. The way her mouth moved as she talked. The way she squinted in amusement. Her small, narrow hands now a woman's; her gestures a woman's. I knew her and yet didn't. She took the straw hat off, and shook out her thick, straight hair. It was cut in exactly the same way as always, parted on the side, with a sheaf hanging half across her forehead. Now she was Erika again: child and young woman all at once. Oh, my dear orphan!

She asked me about university, and whether I liked it.

I said I did: it was what I'd been waiting for. The lecturers were mostly good, and I was getting good marks for my essays.

She told me that she hated Riverlands now, and couldn't wait to leave. The teachers were prissy fools, she said, and the girls were stupid snobs. She leaned forward, and frowned. Her eyes, when she was serious, grew cold in the way that I remembered. They seemed to test me: to seek a response that would confirm something for her.

'I don't have any real friends there,' she said. 'I don't have a friend like *you*, Vin.'

My heart jumped again. I hadn't anticipated a conversation like this. I wondered if the woman at the counter was watching us, but didn't turn aside to see. 'What about Barbara?' I asked.

'So you remember her,' Erika said. She smiled slyly. 'Yes, we were friends, when we were younger. She kept saying she loved me. She got quite soppy.' She pushed her hair back from her forehead, glanced aside, and then looked back at me. 'But she didn't really *understand* anything,' she said. 'Do you see?'

She leaned closer, and put her hand over mine. When she spoke again, it was in a low, intense voice, as though conveying a secret. Her voice seemed deeper than it used to be: low and smooth and gliding. A woman's voice.

'She didn't understand *Flash Gordon*,' she said.

'Nobody else could,' I said. 'Nobody but us.'

'No,' Erica said. 'Nobody but us.'

We were both smiling. We had spoken in code: one which told us that everything would be as it was, between us. And yet it will all be different, I thought, now that we're not children any more. The thought made me dizzy. A current ran between us like the current in the overhead wires outside, as another electric tram clanged by. Erika's hand remained resting on mine, and we continued to look at each other. The screen door of the Granby banged, and a woman came in with a basket, going up to the counter to buy cakes; but the sound came to us muffled. Then Erica took her hand away, and leaned back.

'Of course,' she said, 'my reading has advanced a bit, since then. We're doing *The Mayor of Casterbridge*, this year. Do you like Thomas Hardy?'

I said I did, but had become much more keen on Dostoevsky. Spoke to her about *Crime and Punishment*, and she listened seriously, watching me.

'You were always clever,' she said. 'My father said that.'

I asked how her father was, and she looked away, her face going blank. 'He's well,' she said. 'He still gets on the grog, of course.'

Then she turned back to me. 'I don't want to go to university,' she said. 'I've decided to be a journalist: I'm going to try for a cadetship on the *Mail*. One of the girls at school will help me – her father's a sub-editor on the paper. I'm not a big intellect like you, Vin. I still like to read spy thrillers, in my spare time.'

'But so do I,' I said.

I reached into my briefcase and pulled out *The Ipcress File*, which I'd been reading on my way to lectures. She hadn't read it, and I told her Len Deighton was the best espionage writer I'd so far discovered. She could borrow it, I said, and she looked at me now with her old, knowing, teasing expression.

'That means I'll have to see you again, to return it,' she said. '*Will* I see you again?'

'I hope so,' I said.

'Yes. It has to happen,' she said. 'It was always going to happen.' She had spoken in an undertone, and her eyes held mine. 'We have to go back to the Secret Room,' she said.

She was asking to return to our haven of secrecy; asking to be my friend again. I was flooded with joy, knowing how fortunate I was. Unable to find words, I simply nodded.

March 27th, 1969

We're so *alike*, Erika and I! No – we're more than alike: we're one spirit, in two different people. We're truly twins, I tell her, since both of us were born under the sign of Gemini: both of us in June, a year apart.

We like exactly the same pop songs. We had chosen our greatest favourites before we came together again, in the Granby – yet the list matches almost exactly. Some are modern, but others date from before we born – from the 1930s, like the classic adventure strips.

Here is the final list:

Heartbreak Hotel
Ticket to Ride
It's All Over Now, Baby Blue
Love For Sale
Parlez-moi d'amour
Out of Nowhere

All these songs are special, we've decided. All of them have come from that other world that she and I know about, and others don't.

The most special of all is 'Out of Nowhere'. I first heard it sung by Bing Crosby (recorded in 1931), but Erika has an LP of it made much later, by Lena Horne. She plays it often, on my record-player in the Secret Room. 'Out of Nowhere' is Erika's song, since Erika herself comes from out of nowhere. Because she does, I will never really know her – even though we're so alike.

Part of her is always locked up: hidden. Sometimes she goes into silence when I want to talk, and stares into space. I hate these silences; they make me more lonely than I've ever been. Yes: Erika can make me lonely when I'm with her. The centre of her goes cold at these times. Then she's somewhere else. Why is this? Impossible to know.

March 30th, 1969
Erika and I are studying all the techniques of espionage: dead drops, secret writing, the use of hidden cameras. She says that

I should learn to take pictures at night, going out with my camera and taking pictures of people through their windows. This is a little like our games as children, and I fear being caught; but I do it to please her. She's excited when we develop the pictures.

April 10th, 1969

Erika and I have never done anything but kiss. But last night I photographed her naked.

The idea was hers. She often poses as Ella, for the adventure strip we're working on: once the photos are developed in my darkroom, she uses them for her drawings. A few weeks ago she posed in her bra and panties for a sequence where Ella is held captive in a cellar, and the pictures came out well, making her look very seductive. She was pleased with them, I could see: proud of her figure. Then, suddenly, looking at me boldly, with a small, peculiar smile, she said: 'I want you to take me in the nude, Vin.'

I stared at her, my mouth suddenly dry, a sinking feeling in my stomach. I was shocked and alarmed, and she saw it. 'In the nude?' I said. 'For *Ella*? But we can't have nudity in a comic strip. We'd never sell it.'

'Not for *Ella*,' she said. 'Just for me. I want to pose in the nude to see how I'll look. And nobody but us will ever see the pictures.' She was still looking at me directly, her smile both audacious and teasing. Perhaps she was amused at my nervousness and confusion, and the fact that I'd become flushed in the face. 'I think I've got a good enough figure to pose nude,' she said. 'Don't you think so?'

I said I did, hardly able to look at her, and she asked me again if I'd do it. I said I would, and she went into the darkroom to undress. I busied myself checking the Speed Graphic; then I set up a standard lamp near the wardrobe, trying to keep my mind empty.

When she came out, quite naked, smiling at me, not attempting to hide any part of herself, my head swam; and I knew that something had changed. She had a perfect figure, I could see that, of a kind that men would lust after. But my fairy girl, my innocent best friend? She was gone: I was looking at a young adult woman. I had wanted Erika to be a girl for ever; now she would never be that girl again.

'Where should I stand?' she asked.

Trembling, filled with an unfathomable sadness, I asked her to pose in front of the wardrobe mirror, looking at her own reflection. Then I began to take shots.

They have come out well: but what they show has been another revelation. Surveying herself in the mirror (hands behind her head; at her sides; on her hips), Erika wears an expression of open adoration, as though this perfect beauty in the mirror is the one whom she truly loves, more than anyone else in the world.

When I'd taken my last picture, I put the camera down and walked over to her. Hands crossed over her *mons pubis*, from which I kept my eyes, she stood looking at me now with a questioning expression, as though she thought I might touch her. But I knew that I wouldn't. I halted, and as I did so, she put up one hand like a traffic policeman, her arm at full length.

'Look but don't touch,' she said. 'That's the rule, remember?'

I nodded, filled with relief.

May 7th, 1969

Last night Erika talked about her father. She doesn't often do that. She admires him totally, of course, and will never criticise him – even though he drinks too much.

When he's been drinking, she told me, he sits in his study and plays old recordings over and over on the record-player. Mostly German pop music: songs that he and his comrades sang during the War. She knows then to leave him alone.

His wife's death seems to have made Mr Lange how he is, and started him drinking. He loved her mother very much, Erika said. In the year her mother died, when Erika was eleven, and she and her father were left alone, she would come into his bed at night and he would hold her, she told me. And sometimes, after she went to bed, he would come quietly into her room, and lie down beside her on her bed.

I wonder how long this went on happening. Don't dare ask.

'Sometimes,' Erika said, 'my father goes out and sits on the back porch in the dark, on the top step, staring out at the lights in the valley. I like to go and sit next to him, but he never speaks. I understand that. I'm like him: sometimes I want to be quiet too.'

May 20th, 1969
Sitting side by side on the sofa bed in the Secret Room last night, Erika and I kissed each other, and held hands.

'I do love you, Vincent,' she said. 'You're my best friend.'

It was true that we were still best friends, I thought; and yet it was different, now that she'd become a woman.

She began to talk about boys she'd met – mainly at school dances.

'Lots of boys have been in love with me,' she said. Her voice was light. Then she said: 'So have a few girls.'

This gave me a cold feeling in my stomach: a sort of dread. I knew that girls in boarding school got crushes on one another, but I hadn't thought of this happening to Erika.

'You mean Barbara,' I said.

'Yes,' she said. 'Are you jealous? Papa made me board at River-lands House last year. Barbara's a boarder, and she had quite a thing about me. I was quite fond of her too. She's a beautiful girl, don't you think?'

'Not my type,' I said.

'In the dormitory,' Erika said, 'she'd come into my bed after lights out, when the other two girls we shared with were asleep, and we'd talk and cuddle each other. But then she went a bit far.'

Her eyes were shining and excited. She seemed to like telling me this, and watched me.

'One night we had the room to ourselves,' she said, 'when the other two were away. And Barbara took off her nightie, and wanted me to take off mine.'

'And did you?' I asked.

Erika smiled at me: one of her taunting smiles, which I knew meant yes. But she said no more.

'And afterwards you stopped being friends,' I said.

'Yes. She got too serious,' Erika said. 'She wouldn't leave me alone; she was always putting her arm around me and mooning in front of the other girls, and some of them were beginning to laugh at us. So I told her it had to stop.'

I was glad to hear this. But then Erika said: 'I still talk to her, though. She'd be my friend again in a second, if I'd let her.'

'But you won't,' I said.

'I might. I might not,' she said. 'I do what I want, Vin. And I don't forget anyone who loves me.'

I feel now that I don't really know Erika as I thought I did. There are things about her I'll never understand; but I have to put this from my mind.

June 18th, 1969

Last night Erika stayed over, sleeping as always in the spare bedroom, where she won't let me visit her. She says if I did, Connie wouldn't trust us any more, and everything would be spoiled.

When she'd told me she wanted to stay, she'd looked drawn; almost ill. We were sitting on the sofa in the Secret Room again.

'I don't want to be with my father tonight,' she said.

She had spoken quickly, almost in a mutter, staring at something in her head. I took her hand, and asked had her father treated her badly in some way.

She shook her head, dumb, still not looking at me, her eyes full of sadness, as though somebody had died. At last she spoke, in a very soft voice.

'He hasn't done anything. I just don't want to be with him tonight.'

'He shouldn't drink so much,' I said. 'It's not fair to you.'

She turned to me with a fierce, warning look, snatching her hand away and breathing quickly. Then she began to shout, so loud that it frightened me.

'Don't you *dare* criticise my father! Not ever! He's a good, kind man, better than you can possibly understand!'

I told her I didn't want to criticise him, and she calmed down and went quiet. We sat without speaking for a while; then she took my hand again, and spoke in a small voice.

'Vincent. I'm sorry.'

'That's all right,' I said. 'Are you okay?'

'Yes,' she said. 'I'm fine now. I just don't want to talk about it. Are *we* all right?'

'You know we are,' I said.

'We have to be,' she said. 'You're my second self.'

5

MEMORY CIRCLES BACK constantly to this reassuring Edwardian sunroom that Vincent called his study. Bradley sees himself and Vincent sitting here always in the two wicker armchairs, legs extended, talking, smoking cigarettes, drinking instant coffee. It generally seems to be a winter night: the two-bar electric radiator glows at their feet.

One night, he recalls, he found himself looking at the door at the end of the sunroom. He'd scarcely noticed it before; now he asked Vincent where it led to.

'It's just a junk room.'

Vincent's tone had been clipped and dismissive, and Bradley had assumed that this was because a junk room was all it was. Had he been told that Vincent spent many hours of each week in there with Erika Lange, he would have found this hard to believe. That Vincent managed to compartmentalise his life, and to keep his acquaintances in ignorance of one another, Bradley already knew. What he scarcely suspected then was the extent of Vincent's dedication to secrecy.

Setting aside the 1969 diary, Bradley begins to examine some of the other material on the table. He returns to the folios containing *Ella of the Secret Service*: the 'adventure strip' that Erika and Vincent produced together, and which they'd apparently hoped to sell to the newspapers. He shuffles through some of the big sheets of art paper.

The story, Bradley assumes, was mainly composed by Vincent

– though he suspects that Ella herself was a character devised by Erika. Although she's the central figure, Ella shares the stage – and most of her Cold War adventures – with a male spy who is both her companion and lover. This is Dan Brennan, a handsome, dark-haired, athletic figure who is perhaps a daydream version of Vincent. Like Ella, he's given to wearing belted rain-coats. Their enemies are Soviet spies and agents, and Dan provides Ella with muscular backup when situations get rough. He frequently rescues her from KGB hitmen and other villains – usually dispatching them with his Beretta. But at times tremendous hand-to-hand combat takes place, with Brennan triumphing through his expertise in karate. He doesn't strip to the waist as frequently as Flash Gordon, but his muscular torso is displayed when he's captured by the KGB, and put to torture in a cellar.

Ella too falls into the hands of KGB interrogators at one stage, and is threatened with torment unless she betrays certain secrets. This is one of the occasions when she appears in her underwear. Tied to a pillar, she is interrogated by Colonel Petrovna, a female KGB officer with cruel, cat-like eyes and short-cropped black hair: a woman of obvious lesbian proclivities, who caresses Ella's body while explaining what exquisite pain she is about to inflict on her. Bradley is startled to come upon such an episode, and wonders what its influences were; then he remembers *From Russia with Love*, and decides that Colonel Petrovna owes a strong debt to Ian Fleming's Colonel Rosa Klebb.

Despite these touches of perversity, the general tone of the strip is romantic. Snatches of dialogue confirming this leap out at Bradley from the balloons; and again he seems to glimpse meanings in these banal and derivative exchanges that go beyond the surface story told in *Ella*: meanings which he doubts that the two collaborators could have consciously intended, and which give tantalising hints concerning their private fears and dreams. Juxtaposed with Vincent's diaries, these naïve passages of dialogue perhaps offer clues to the innermost natures of their creators.

ELLA: *They've signed our death warrants, Dan – but I don't care, as long as we're together.*
DAN: *That's how I feel too, sweetheart.*
ELLA: *You'll never own me, though. Nobody will. You know that, don't you?*

*

ELLA: *I don't want to die! I'm too pretty to die! My father always told me that.*
DAN: *Ella! Wake up! You're safe – don't you know me?*
ELLA: *Who are you? I don't know you. I'm not safe. I'm never safe.*

Putting *Ella* aside, Bradley now begins to look through some of the photographs Vincent printed in the Secret Room. He recalls Vincent saying that he acquired his old Speed Graphic camera in his first year at university: the year when he and Erika would have been secretly working on *Ella*. The Graphic was a news photographer's camera: state-of-the-art in the 1940s and '50s. Vincent had bought it cheaply, he told Bradley, from an ex-news photographer he'd met at the races, who was broke and had needed the money. It must have been then that Vincent built his little darkroom in a corner of the Secret Room.

Among the black-and-white prints are many shots of Erika, clearly intended as models for her drawings of Ella. These – and many of Vincent's other pictures – are striking, and their composition and lighting show Vincent to be a photographer of some talent. Erika looks precociously glamorous; but this glamour is mingled with a touching and sometimes amusing immaturity. The pictures were obviously taken in the Secret Room. An armchair and a table are in the background of some of them; in others the wardrobe with its long mirror can be seen. The pictures are made dramatic by the use of heavy shadow, and Bradley guesses that Vincent would have achieved this by using a single lamp, placed at a low angle. In most of these shots, Erika is dressed as Ella, in a belted raincoat and dark felt hat: very likely the hat that belonged to her school uniform, with the band removed. She holds a toy revolver, looking menacing. In one shot, she wears only bra and panties, standing in front of a chair with her wrists tied behind her back, tumbled blonde mane hanging across her forehead, glaring at the camera defiantly. Because of her youth, the effect is at once erotic and humorous. No doubt it was taken for the sequence with Colonel Petrovna.

But this can hardly have been so of the final picture in the set: one of the nude photographs dealt with in Vincent's diary. Bradley sits back, looking at it with the disquiet of a voyeur; but also with sadness. Erika's beauty – in which she took the solemn religious pleasure of the true narcissist – tantalised so many men, over her lifetime; yet she never seemed to see herself as provocative. She was *serious* about herself, Bradley thinks; and to encounter this image now is to contemplate something so perfect that he tells himself that Erika should never have changed; should somehow have been exempt from mortal decline.

Here she stands, in black and white, in the absolute beauty of her youth, posing for Vincent's Speed Graphic in front of the wardrobe mirror, looking at herself in the glass. So two figures are shown here. One – graphically real, seen from behind, and thus faceless – is almost childlike, with fragile, delicate shoulder blades and innocent round buttocks. The other (at which the first Erika gazes) is less real, having as it does a reflection's mirage-like quality. It's also far less innocent. There's no hint of constraint in its stance: instead, framed by the mirror's darkness, it's assured and faintly provocative. The eyebrows are raised, the closed lips touched by the smallest of smiles. Her hands are at her sides, most of her weight thrown on to her left foot, the other leg bent at the knee. Her back is slightly arched, her pelvis thrust forward. She is not a big girl, by current standards: around five feet four. But she's perfectly proportioned, with a long, narrow waist, and slender legs whose thighs already have a mature fullness. No adolescent fat: she was always athletic, and played a lot of sport, a discipline she'd continue with all her life. Her smile is both dreamy and wondering, and her brows seem raised in surprise at the sight of her own perfection.

I'll never be more beautiful than this, her expression says. *Who can blame me for taking a pride in it?*

Bradley puts the prints back in their box.

He decides now to skip the diaries for the next two years, returning to them later. He's curious to read the entries for 1972: a crucial year for Vincent. That was when Vincent was doing his M.A., before entering Foreign Affairs in the following year.

TWO

1

Vincent Austin's Diary

March 12th, 1972

SOME MONTHS AGO, Erika and I discovered the Tarot. It's been a revelation to us, and we've read all that we can find on it, in order to probe its secrets.

The cards, we've decided, are links to the invisible: doorways to the world of the spirit. Their little coloured pictures have a magic and a mystery that far surpass the comic strips of our childhood; they are guides to the whole of life's journey, with its hidden dangers and rewards: a mystical adventure strip from the Middle Ages. I'm sure Uncle Kenneth wouldn't have approved, bearing in mind the Tarot's links to Gnosticism, and the old pagan mystery religions. But I doubt that they're the Devil's cards, as the medieval churchmen believed. I find great wisdom in them, and can see many parallels to those archetypes that Carl Jung writes of.

Erika loves to dress up as the female figures in the major arcana, and I've photographed her in these roles. She's also made costumes for me to pose as two of the male figures – the Fool and the Magician – and has made very fine sketches of me. Last night she posed as the Star: the Naked Goddess, Mistress of Earth and Sea. Kneeling, she held a tilted water-jug in each hand: vessels that contained the Water of Life. Her eyes and her body's whiteness shone in the light; her lips were parted in joy; she signalled the approach of destiny and freedom. The Secret Room hummed with majestic transformation: we were now no longer ourselves. Far off, I heard a car go down Bay Road, in the other world.

Later, at Erika's request, I took out the cards for a reading. Whether they can actually foretell the future is something I remain uncertain about – although Erika is convinced they can, and loves to consult them. I don't rule out the possibility of divination – and neither, I find, does Jung, who links such systems to his theory of synchronicity. I'd lit some incense sticks, and the room was full of the scent of sandalwood. Erika put on her dark-blue robe, and sat down opposite me at the table. I took the cards from their square of purple silk, laid the silk on the table, shuffled the pack, and then gave them to Erika to re-shuffle – all as prescribed. She was the querent, since I was reading the cards for her: she wanted them to tell her tonight whether her life had reached a turning point. I arranged them in the Horseshoe Spread, face downwards.

The sixth and final card proved to be the Lovers, suggesting that Erika had a choice to make: one that might alter her life.

'That's true,' she said softly, and sat back, looking at me intently across the table. 'The Tarot's right.' She began to bite her thumbnail – always a sign of tension in her – and I asked her what she meant. What was the choice she faced?

'Whether or not to get out of here,' she said.

'And go where?' I asked.

'Anywhere,' she said. 'Abroad.'

Her eyes were blank and fixed as she said this, and her face seemed empty. But her lips had tightened in a way that indicated some serious emotion; and I was seized with a sudden fear. I know that she goes out with other men now, and I've learned to tolerate that; but the thought of being entirely without her is intolerable.

'You're not serious,' I said.

'I *am* serious,' she said, and fixed me with a blank, challenging stare. 'Come with me, Vin. We'll go away together.'

'You know I can't,' I said. 'I don't finish my M.A. until the end of this year. Then, if I get into Foreign Affairs, I should be posted abroad next year. Wait a little longer. What about *Ella*?'

'We'll never sell *Ella*,' she said. 'You know that.' She pushed out her lip, contemptuous of childish things, and a pain went through my heart.

'Surely you can wait until next year,' I said.

'No. That's too long,' she said. 'Don't you understand, Vin? I have to get out of this bloody little town. Do you think I can go on writing stories about these stupid local politicians, or who caught the biggest fish in the Derwent?'

She stood up, breathing quickly. She came around the table and stroked my cheek, smiling as though she'd been joking; as though I were a child who needed reassurance. 'It's all over now, Baby Blue,' she said.

She had spoken lightly; but the line from our favourite Dylan song keeps repeating in my head now like a warning.

March 24th, 1972

Last night I took Erika out to dinner and a film; then I drove her home in Connie's old Morris. Nearly midnight, and a dark, moonless night. I parked in a cul-de-sac on the eastern side of Lutana, and the lights of the Zinc Works pulsed and glared below us. Fierce stars.

We sat side by side in the dark, in the car's bucket seats. Michael Street was quite close by, but Erika will never let me drop her at her gate: she doesn't want me to encounter her father, she says; he often watches out for her. Since that one meeting with Mr Lange long ago, I've not met him again, and Erika has wanted to keep it this way. She prefers that we keep our friendship secret, she says.

'I'm leaving,' she said.

She'd spoken very suddenly, looking down at the lights. We'd been speaking of something else, and I stared at her.

'I mean I'm leaving altogether,' she said, and turned to me. In the half-light through the window (a street lamp; the glow of the windows of a house), her white face was strained and excited. 'In a week's time, I'm going abroad,' she said. 'I'll be flying to London.'

Something seemed frozen in my throat. Finally I said: 'I don't understand you. Is this a game?'

'No,' she said. 'It's real. I want to get a job on a paper there. I can't stay any longer, Vin. I did tell you that.'

I began to fire questions at her. How could she possibly hope to get a job on a London paper? She hadn't finished her cadetship; she didn't have a grading; she didn't have any money. How would she survive, in London? What did her father say about this? Was he going to back her financially?

'No,' she said. 'He doesn't even know. He'll only be told at the last minute. He'll try to stop me – but he can't. I'm nearly twenty-one. And I'm going with a colleague who's got contacts over there.'

Colleague. This is a term she savours; using it makes her feel professional. Twisting in my seat, I gripped her shoulder through her overcoat, bringing her face close to mine, willing her to look at me. She did so, and this time her expression seemed faintly alarmed. 'A colleague? What colleague?' I asked.

'He's on the *Mail*,' she said. She spoke rapidly now, in a tone that sounded absurdly official, as though she were making a report on something quite detached from her. 'His name's Geoffrey Baxter,' she said. 'You might have seen his byline. He's an A-grade journalist, with a lot of experience, and he's got a job lined up with Reuters. He'll show me the ropes there.'

'And how old is he?' I asked. 'Does he have a wife?'

'He's forty-two. He's divorced.'

'I see. Yes. And is he your lover?'

She looked away from me and smiled: a quick, light-hearted smile. 'No,' she said, 'but he's a man I know I can rely on.'

'I'm sure you can,' I said. 'He'll look after you and be a father to you. After all, he's old enough to be your father. And that's what you want, isn't it?'

At this, her head jerked around so that she stared at me directly. In the darkness of the car, her face had taken on an expression I'd not seen before, and she spoke almost in a whisper.

'What do you mean?'

'That you have to have a father,' I said. 'And this old man will be your new Daddy, as well as your lover. Won't he?'

'Don't you *dare* say that!'

'But I do say it,' I said.

She glared at me, her breast rising and falling fast. When she spoke again, it was still under her breath. 'What a filthy thing to say! Take it back, or you'll be sorry!'

'You seem to have forgotten,' I said. '*I'm* the one who has to look after you — isn't that what we've always said?'

She didn't answer this. Instead, her eyes filled with tears and she shook her head violently, so that her hair swung. Then she opened the door, jumped from the car, and ran away down the street, her overcoat flapping behind her, moving from light to light like a fleeing bird.

Head swimming, I started the engine. Below me, in the blackness, the stars of the Zinc Works pulsed: the lights of her father's citadel.

April 9th, 1972

Erika phoned at one o'clock this morning, when I was fast asleep in bed. It's only three weeks since she left for England. Fortunately, I've recently had a phone installed on my bedside table, and its ringing quickly woke me.

'Hello. It's me.'

She didn't identify herself; she never does, on the phone, and that deep yet childishly soft voice could never be mistaken for another. Across twelve thousand-odd miles, it was almost as clear as though she were calling from Lutana; but I seemed to hear the rushing of half the world's distance behind it.

'Where are you?' I asked.

'I'm in London. It's early afternoon here. What time is it there?'
'It's one in the morning.'
'Oh. Did I wake you?'
'It doesn't matter,' I said. 'Are you all right?'
'I'm fine. I've got a job on a little paper in North London. It's not one of the big metropolitan dailies, but it's a start. I love London – but half of me is missing. We're twins, Vin, remember? We'll never be apart for long.'

We talked for nearly half an hour. I wondered if the 'colleague' – whom she's sharing a flat with – was paying the phone bill.

April 21st, 1972

Erika and I call each other every week, now. These calls keep me bound to her, like a wire stretched across the world. What she says is true. We'll never be entirely separated.

May 22nd, 1972

This afternoon I had an interesting discussion with Professor Bobrowski. I see that I've made no reference to him in this diary until now, and it's high time that I did so.

Teodor Bobrowski is Professor of Political Science: the subject in which I majored when I took my B.A. last year. Now that I'm working on a thesis for my M.A., Bobrowski is my supervisor. He was my lecturer for nearly three years; he always seemed warmly disposed to me, and I've formed a deep admiration and liking for him. The subject of my thesis is revolutionary movements in nineteenth-century Europe – a topic in which Bobrowski takes a gratifying interest – and now that I have frequent sessions with him in his study on a one-to-one basis, I've come to regard him as my mentor.

He came here from Britain in 1954, having fled there from Poland after the Soviet takeover in 1945. He maintains the formal manners of pre-War Eastern Europe, but he combines this with an easy, low-keyed magnetism: a friendliness and charm that draw students to him outside lectures. He invites favoured members of his class to his home, where his wife gives them afternoon tea, and is often seen about the campus involved in animated discussion with a group of undergraduates – invariably on philosophical or political issues, since he has no time for small talk. I became one of this group in my second year.

Bobrowski is in his mid-fifties. His appearance, though pleasant enough, isn't conventionally impressive. Quite short – about five feet six – with the stocky, powerful build and broad chest and shoulders of a wrestler, he reminds one irresistibly of one of those cavern-dwelling dwarfs in European legend. His unusually large head is bald except for a fringe of sandy hair that has mostly gone grey, and his nose, like those of the dwarfs in illustrations, is broad and slightly up-tilted. His features are otherwise good: he has an expressive, sensitive mouth, a firm chin, and thoughtful grey eyes whose gaze is both steady and compelling. His face always seems to wear a calm expression, and he's invariably good-humoured. Life is constantly amusing, his expression seems to say: amusing and a little absurd. In both winter and summer he invariably seems to wear a shapeless, moss-coloured tweed jacket, collar and tie, and pale-grey trousers somewhat in need of pressing. In the streets he wears a beret, and carries a battered briefcase.

With senior students he respects, Professor Bobrowski relaxes his European formality to an extent where they are able to address him by his first name – which he renders in English as 'Ted'. By the time I reached third year, in 1971, I was one of these. And now that he's supervising my thesis, we seem almost to be forming a friendship.

In our sessions in his study, he is always conscientious in analysing the progress and direction of my work. But as well, he seems simply to want to talk to me, ranging over many subjects, but returning always to current international politics: his chief interest. It's almost as though he wishes to instruct me in matters outside the scope of my work. Perhaps his aim is to show me the outcomes in this century of those revolutionary theories and political movements that were the products of the previous one: these being the central subject of my study. But he often ranges far beyond this specialised channel, and I sometimes feel he's testing me in some way, or assessing my ability to respond to the ideas and information he throws up.

Whatever his motives, I grow more and more impressed with him: not only because of what he has to impart, but because of the style in which he does it. His European fluency and his control of language (given flavour by his Polish accent) fill me with admiration, as does the way in which every sentence that he speaks is as well-structured and rounded as though it's been set down in print. Such a man is not often encountered in provincial Hobart. Through him, I feel myself to be in touch with the far northern hemisphere; with shadowy old Europe; with the theatre of great events; with the future I long for. Sitting with him in his study today, I was able to forget my pain over Erika for a time. Pleasures of the mind! They are perhaps the only antidote to pain.

His study is on the first floor at the front of the main building. Through one of the tall casement windows, as we talked, we looked out over the sloping expanse of lawn and series of rose gardens by which the university is approached, here on its formal little hill opposite the railway station. The main building has always pleased me: a stone, three-storey Gothic structure, built by our colonial founders in the mid-nineteenth century, with buttresses and parapeted gables, covered with suitably ancient-looking ivy. I take a similar pleasure in Bobrowski's study, savouring its dark wood panelling, its high, encrusted ceiling and crowded bookshelves. Today, he came back to a favourite theme: the nature of the police state, and in particular the Soviet state. But he went into far greater detail than ever before.

'The inventor of the Soviet secret police was a Pole,' he told me. 'I am ashamed to say this, but it's true. And not only a Pole but an aristocrat. His name was Count Felix Dzerzhinsky. He was

typical of a certain type of intellectual who gave himself to
Bolshevism. The privileged son of landowners, who turned
against his class and his religion. A Catholic – and in boyhood he
intended to become a priest. Instead, he becomes the October
Revolution's Angel of Death.'

Smiling, letting this theatrical phrase hang in the air, he leaned
back in his aged swivel chair, his broad chest and shoulders only
just visible above the top of his desk. His gaze remained fixed on
me intently, as though to judge my responses.

'I've heard that Catholics make the best Communists,' I said.

'Alas,' Ted said, and sighed. 'Although I am a Catholic, I
acknowledge this. The virtues of Catholicism – devotion to
dogma, conscious submission to an entire spiritual and intellectual system – are turned upside down in such cases, and made
into a force for evil. As in witchcraft – yes? And this was the case
with Dzerzhinsky, who gave himself body and soul to the Revolution – who became Saint Felix, revered today by all good
officers of the KGB. His statue stands outside KGB headquarters,
like an icon to be worshipped. Iron Felix: he continues to strike
fear into people's hearts, as he did in life!'

He chuckled.

'So he was the KGB's founder,' I said.

'Of course. The Cheka, which he founded, was the ancestor of
the NKVD, and so of the KGB. After the October Revolution in
1917, it was Dzerzhinsky who built the police state for Lenin.
And why were the secret police necessary? Because the Bolshevik
Revolution was not a popular uprising, as so many suppose. The
Bolsheviks were *not* "the vanguard of the proletariat", as the
Communists like to claim. Or do you imagine that they were,
Vincent?'

No, I said. As I understood it, the Revolution had been a coup
d'état by a minority of activists.

Ted smiled, in the way that he used to do when one of us made
a telling point in a tutorial. 'They called it "the dictatorship of the
proletariat" – but this was a clever myth. It was the dictatorship

of a few fanatical intellectuals and terrorists. And when you do *that*, Vincent – when you set out to establish and maintain a dictatorship – there is only one way: through terror.' He paused, allowing the chill of this word, which he had pronounced with incongruous softness – almost with tenderness – to permeate his peaceful study. 'Yes?' He raised his eyebrows, his mild grey gaze fixed on me. 'I think so,' he said, and nodded. 'The facts confirm it. The Cheka, with Dzerzhinsky at the head of it, began immediately to secure Lenin's power – and terror was the term they themselves used: "Red Terror". This has had enormous historical implications – implications of which few people in this country, or in the West generally, have any real knowledge. I think they may interest you. I think you should be informed about them.'

Once again he paused to let what he'd said sink in; and something in his manner seemed to tell me that he had some definite reason for instructing me: a reason that was far more specific than the wish to simply transmit knowledge. Did I imagine it? Perhaps; yet I felt an odd and gathering anticipation. Before continuing, he dragged a packet of his powerful French cigarettes from underneath a folder. He passed one to me (they irritate my throat, but I wouldn't dream of refusing), and screwed his own into its holder. I hastened to get out my lighter, and lit his cigarette and then mine. He drew deeply, nodded in acknowledgement, and narrowed his eyes to look at me as he released the smoke.

'You have a fine mind, Vincent,' he said. 'I have high hopes for your thesis: I'm very impressed with the preliminary chapters you've given me. Your ideas about the dominance of the state in Socialist thinking, from Saint-Simon and Louis Blanc through to Moses Hess and Marx – these are quite penetrating. You have understood the fallacy that both the French thinkers and Hegel introduced: the paradox that says we will be freed by enslaving ourselves to the state. A great deal has followed from that, no?'

'Yet it began nobly,' I said. 'I've been most struck by Louis Blanc's writings. I'm sure he was a genuine idealist – with none of

Marx's ruthlessness. His idea that a sort of bargain could be struck – absolute power given to the state, and in return men would be given everything they could wish for, including happiness – it sounds so convincing, at first. Democracy as a sort of benevolent authoritarianism. I'm sure he believed it, and could never have anticipated where it would lead. To the National Socialism of the Nazis. To the Soviet dictatorship.'

Teodor nodded, the cigarette-holder jutting upwards from between his teeth, his eyes half-closed, listening with great attention. 'And also to the Soviet Empire,' he said, 'from which I had the good fortune to escape. You have heard of the Warsaw Rising? No? In 1944, as the Red Army marched towards Warsaw, the Polish Home Army launched an insurrection against the Nazis. But the Red Army, on the other side of the Vistula, had orders to do nothing to help us. Meanwhile, Stalin began a propaganda campaign to discredit us with the British and other allies. You know why? Because we were not only anti-Nazi, but anti-Communist. So a quarter of a million Poles were killed, the Home Army was destroyed, and this meant there would be no serious opposition to a Polish puppet government – the local Communists already being groomed by Stalin. And when Germany was defeated, the Russians sent in their secret police to purge all opposition. In exchange for Nazi terror we now had Soviet terror. So you see, Vincent, this is how I have come to have personal knowledge of the two most evil regimes of our century: Nazism and Communism. Poland was occupied by both. And I have learned that these two systems were exactly the same, liquidating people with the same dedication – though some of your scholars and opinion-makers still excuse the Communists, which is very puzzling.'

He shook his head, and then looked down at the sheets of paper in front of him: the latest section of my thesis, which I'd brought to him today. For some moments he sat motionless: staring, I knew, into a past I could barely imagine. Then he said:

'You seem to have gained a fair knowledge of the history of modern totalitarianism. You make some telling points about its roots in the early nineteenth century's revolutionary thought. Which brings me to something I'd like to discuss with you, Vincent – something that goes a little beyond the matter of your thesis. You clearly know most of the facts about the Russian Revolution, and you know something of Leninist and Stalinist rule. But what I think you know little or nothing of is the history and nature of the Comintern.'

'You mean the Communist International?'

'Yes – that's its other name. This is the great missing piece in a true understanding of Soviet Communism and its impact on the West. And ignorance of this piece is what allows so many people to entertain delusions about the Communist parties of the West. I'm not saying this is necessary to your current study, Vincent. I'm speaking of a wider knowledge that may be useful to you in the future.'

He looked out the window over the lawn and seemed to muse for a moment. He ran a hand over his large bald head, and smoothed into place the remaining grey-blond hair at the sides.

'The Comintern,' he said softly. 'What a remarkable instrument it has been! It was set up by Lenin as a means of establishing the Revolution worldwide. It did so by controlling the Communist parties in the West – which it supplied with funds – and by influencing the thinking of those in the West its leaders described as "innocents". I think you know how well this has succeeded – but you don't know *how*. Do you?'

I suggested through propaganda.

'Of course. But the means, Vincent, the weapon? I will tell you: a combination of deception – and secrecy.'

'You mean espionage?'

My tone must have been eager, because he smiled at me with amused indulgence.

'This interests you? Espionage in the broad sense, yes,' he said. 'Lenin and Dzerzhinsky called it "secret work" – and they saw it as glorious. They were liberating humanity through this means, they said – and eliminating the Revolution's enemies. But the word "espionage" does not entirely describe it. They have used both legal and illegal means; they have used a mixture of truth and lies; they have operated as today's publicists do; and in these ways, and through their secret agents, they have succeeded in influencing the world-view of many highly influential people in the West. I mean writers, artists, journalists, film-makers, politicians. The Comintern had its own propaganda network, its own secret service, its own journals and film companies through which to spread lies and half-lies. In this way, the mass arrests and torture by the secret police, and the deaths of millions through massacre and starvation, were cloaked and hidden from the West.'

He spun around in his chair, got up, and crossed to a filing cabinet. He rummaged there for a moment, and then came back with three black-and-white photographs, which he laid on the desk in front of me.

'After it was set up by Lenin in 1919, the Comintern spread its message mainly through the efforts of these three men, who served Lenin and Dzerzhinsky from the beginning, and then Stalin. I would like you to learn something about them.'

He pointed first to a bald man with thick spectacles and pale, world-weary eyes: a man, I thought irreverently, who bore a certain resemblance to Bobrowski himself.

'This is Karl Radek,' he said. 'Lenin's most faithful protégé. Another Pole, I'm afraid – a clever literary intellectual who acted as a sort of publicist for the Revolution. He cultivated journalists, and planted the information, both true and false, that the Party wanted published in the West.'

He pointed to the second picture: that of a man in his thirties with dark, tousled hair, a shrewd, tough-looking face, and a humorous, remarkably intense gaze.

'And here is the true leader of the secret work of the Comintern: a German Communist called Willi Münzenberg. He was in my opinion a genius: the most brilliant propagandist and most remarkable secret operative of modern times. Few have heard of him – yet this man moulded the opinions of millions, and has literally changed history. Through his agents, his networks of fellow travellers and his committees, Münzenberg spread Stalin's propaganda throughout the whole of Europe and the United States. Many of his agents led double lives: even their close friends never knew their true identities. Münzenberg, in this way, has set the course of Western left-wing thinking and activism from that day to this. It was Münzenberg who used the term "innocents" for the writers and artists and intellectuals he duped and recruited to the cause.'

He pointed now to the third photograph in front of me: that of a big, handsome man with dark hair, a trim moustache, and large, soulful, heavy-lidded blue eyes, looking like an old silent film star.

'This is the greatest illegal agent of them all,' he said. 'Theodore Maly – nicknamed "der Lange: the tall fellow".'

This name caused me to flinch, but Ted went on without noticing.

'It was Maly who recruited and ran as agents some of the most sophisticated young men in England: the Cambridge spies, whom I'm sure you will know about: Philby; Burgess; Maclean. He had great charm and intelligence. Maly was Hungarian by birth, and was actually an ordained priest. Yes, another one! He served as a chaplain in World War One, and its horrors made him turn to Communism. Unlike his colleagues, Maly seems to have been a man of genuine compassion and sensitivity. Yet in the end, he had to try to close down that sensitivity as he witnessed the liquidation of the Russian peasantry, in the name of collectivization.'

He grimaced, sighed briefly, stubbed out his cigarette, and gathered up the photographs. Looking up, he rapped on the pictures with the nails of his left hand.

'Brilliant, extraordinary men, Vincent! Even though they served the Devil's party. Everything begins with these men, and continues to affect us today. I would like to lend you some papers on the subject of the Comintern and its agents: papers I have written myself. Would you be interested?'

I said I most certainly would, and Bobrowski stood up, smiling, indicating the end of today's discussion.

'Good,' he said. 'I think you will benefit, Vincent. Who knows? It is a subject that may even influence your future course in life.'

May 25th, 1972

I'm at last learning about the great spies: those of the Devil's party, as Ted Bobrowski calls them. The material he's given me to read has been a revelation.

Karl Radek! Willi Münzenberg! Theodore Maly! These were more than mere spies, I see now. A priesthood serving the religion of state terror, covert missionaries for a monstrous system, they seduced both the gullible and the brilliant; they altered the course of the world. One could almost begin to admire them, were it not for the cause they served.

Sitting here, looking at these faces and then at the humble objects on my desk (my brass owl paperweight, my jar of pens and pencils), and at the faded, varnished frame of the dear old sunroom window that has for so long been my vantage point, I wonder is it possible that I – a native of this small provincial island in the world's ultimate south – will ever take the field against the descendants of those masters of the art of espionage? Will I, Vincent Austin, some day be part of the clandestine struggle that dominates our age?

June 2nd, 1972

Something extraordinary has happened. It seems possible that the very wishes I expressed in the entry above may be granted. Visiting Professor Bobrowski today, I told him as soon as I arrived in his study how fascinating I'd found the papers he'd lent me, and how profoundly they'd added to my understanding of international Communism. He made no specific response – merely nodding, smiling broadly, and studying me. (How he *studies* me lately! Do I imagine it?) Then, instead of resuming our discussion on my thesis, or on the Comintern and its agents, he became unexpectedly personal.

'If you will forgive my curiosity, Vincent, may I ask which religious denomination you belong to? I assume you are Anglican?'

Yes, I said, but I was Presbyterian on my mother's side. My aunt Connie, who had been my guardian, was Presbyterian, and had occasionally taken me to their services when I was young. But Connie wasn't a great church-goer now, and neither was I – not being attracted to organized religion.

'Ah,' said Bobrowski, 'then you are of Scottish descent on your mother's side?'

I said I was.

'I see. Yes, one sees it now. You may not practise, but one detects in your character and outlook the influences of Calvin, John Knox, and *The Book of Discipline.*' He held up his hand, continuing to smile. 'I do not say this disparagingly, and I do not brand you as a Puritan. I merely say that you exhibit a certain rigour and definiteness on questions of right and wrong. I have never noticed that you tolerate any blurring.'

I said I supposed that this was so.

Bobrowski nodded. 'That is your spiritual inheritance – and no bad thing, of course. You don't mind my asking you these questions?'

'Not at all,' I said.

He sat back in his chair, head on one side, regarding me now with a ruminative expression. 'You see, Vincent,' he said, 'as I get to know you better, I grow more and more curious about you. You are very much an exception among your fellow students: something of a heretic.' He laughed. 'You look shocked; but you will surely agree that in our time it is the conservative who is the rebel and non-conformist? And that is what you are. Most other undergraduates on this campus – including your friend Derek Bradley – entertain left-wing convictions of some kind. Well, this is natural: they are young, and full of generous idealism. I went through that phase myself as a student in the 'thirties – until I had the privilege of seeing the face of totalitarianism at close quarters. So I ask myself: since you have *not* had that experience, Vincent, what is it that has made you different?'

I stared at him, trying to formulate an answer.

'Let me be more precise,' he said. '"Conservative" is a term of abuse in the fashionable lexicon – you know that. So I am asking: what has made you a conservative?'

I thought for a time. Then I told him that I preferred the term 'traditionalist'. I had read history from a very early age, I told him. Having been a good deal on my own, I had had plenty of time to read, and my reading had made me value tradition and custom above everything. Without it, in my view, there could be no continuity. And without continuity there could be no genuine civilization. My reading had also convinced me that the most civilized and tolerant societies had been those that refused to smash tradition and order – however many reforms they might have made.

'Most would agree with that,' Bobrowski said. Expressionless, he continued to watch me. Then he asked: 'And when did you first begin to dislike revolution?'

'It began as a schoolboy,' I said, 'when I read *A Tale of Two Cities.*'

He smiled. 'Ah yes,' he said. 'Your beloved Dickens. An entertaining melodrama.'

'It woke my interest in the French Revolution,' I said. 'At first it was just a boy's fascination with the Terror. How could a civilized country descend into such barbarism? That was what I wanted to know. It was only when I came to read serious histories that I began to understand that the Terror had not simply been a descent into senseless violence, but a deliberate mental perversion: a horror born of the mind.'

Bobrowski smiled faintly, and waited. I felt that I was being put to some sort of test.

'I remember you once pointed out that the Jacobins were running Europe's first totalitarian dictatorship,' I said, 'with the Committee of Public Safety as their instrument. True; and what I find most horrifying is that as Robespierre and Saint-Just ordered more and more executions, and called for more and more blood, they claimed that they did so in order to *purify* society – to create ultimate happiness for all. Those men were truly monsters – of a new kind.'

'Monsters indeed,' Bobrowski said softly. But he continued to wait, one hand cupping his chin.

'Then I saw the parallel with Soviet society,' I said. 'Both groups killed in the name of a social philosophy. Both promised that Paradise would come when enough traitors and undesirables had been liquidated. And I began to understand how close to us the Jacobins are. They injected a poison into Western society that is still with us.'

'Stalin's bill was heavier,' Bobrowski murmured. 'To begin with, five million peasants sent to Siberia, and a million more murdered. But I grant you, the Jacobins set an impressive example. And yes, they are still with us.'

'What affected me most,' I said, 'was when I read Edmund Burke on the Revolution. Burke influenced my entire outlook.'

Bobrowski narrowed his eyes. 'Really? Can you be particular?'

'Burke praises liberties and the English constitution as an *inheritance*,' I said, 'and he claims that this follows nature: that it's in symmetry with the order of the world. You remember what he says? "People will not look forward to posterity, who never look backwards to their ancestors." That seems to me profoundly true. By contrast, Burke says, what happened in France, through violent revolt, was that in one grand explosion all the examples of antiquity and all precedents were destroyed in the name of "the rights of men". How does he put it? "The decent drapery of life was rudely torn off." Regicide, parricide, sacrilege: all were permitted, since revolutionaries harden themselves against mercy, and pervert their natural sympathies. And the greatest mistake of the Jacobins, he says, was to imagine that rights can be *imposed* on a society. Society is an organic whole, a partnership – and men can't simply claim any rights that take their fancy. I also like what Montesquieu said: "Liberty does not consist in doing what one pleases. Liberty can only consist in being able to do what one ought to do."'

I stopped. I'd grown somewhat carried away, at this point; now I sat back. For a time, Bobrowski was silent, regarding me with a mild and thoughtful expression. Then he smiled, and said: 'You make a convincing case for your beliefs. Well, you are right in seeing a direct line from Jacobin France to the Soviet Union. There is also a connection between Communism and the Enlightenment, as you may have realised. Marxism lays claim to the ideals of the Enlightenment – but it perverts them. Many are fooled, and fail to see this – which is why anti-Communism is so unpopular. Middle-class opinion-makers will happily blaspheme Christianity and reject much of Western tradition, blaming both for all our ills – but they will seldom blame any aspect of the Enlightenment. The Enlightenment's ideas are sacred – and those of the Marxists are made to look charmingly similar. So how can the fashionable disagree? And so much of this we owe to Willi Münzenberg and his friends.'

He got up from his desk and moved across to the window, where he stood looking out over the lawn and the rose gardens. Screwing another cigarette into his holder, he seemed to ponder, and a silence fell which I decided not to break. Lighting the cigarette, squinting through the smoke, he appeared to be debating something in his mind. A ray of late, dusty sunlight fell on him, lighting up his large, balding head; turning him into a grave, wise dwarf, sent to me as a guide.

He turned from the window and looked at me for a moment. It was a look of unusual keenness, quite different from his usual easy grey gaze: only his snub nose, which I have always found a little comical, prevented him from appearing intimidating.

'Civilization's enemies appear in every age,' he said. 'They have different names – but as you and I seem to agree, Vincent, they are always essentially the same. What is going on at present is a secret war against them. It is a secret war because Münzenberg and his colleagues made it so. And our only hope is to fight it more cleverly than their descendants do.'

He moved from the window to stand in front of me, leaning against the desk and looking down on me, drawing on his cigarette. Because of my height and his stockiness, he did not have to look down very far, and was almost uncomfortably close. There was a cut under his nose from shaving.

'You say that you intend to apply to enter Foreign Affairs next year,' he said. 'I have little doubt you will succeed. You will certainly gain your M.A., and your mastery of Russian is impressive: you speak it now almost as well as I do. You get on easily with other people. So you have all the qualifications the Foreign Affairs people look for. I will be happy to provide what help I can, of course, in the form of a recommendation.'

I began to thank him; but he held up his hand.

'However,' he said, 'let us return to the subject of the secret war. You could help fight this war, Vincent. Do you understand what I'm saying?' Without waiting for a reply, he said: 'I see that you do. I have also noticed how your face lights up when we speak of it.' He chuckled, scanning my face. 'I think that you would like to be involved,' he said. 'Please make no comment, but simply listen to me. You *could* be involved, and it need not be incompatible with your career in Foreign Affairs. But in speaking as I am going to do now, I have to ask you first to keep a serious confidence. Can you do that? Do I have your solemn word?'

I said that he did, and he held out his hand, his expression absolutely serious. I took it, and we shook hands. I was now growing very tense: tense in the wonderful way that I am just before the start of a race, when I've put far too much money on a horse I think is a certainty.

'I should not be telling you this directly,' Bobrowski said. 'I'm taking a risk in doing so – but I feel I can trust you. I will simply say at this stage that I know people who might help you: people

who are looking for young men of your special qualities and abilities. If you wish, I will speak to them. Do you wish it?'

I said I did, and we stared at each other for a moment. Then
his smile came back. 'Good,' he said. 'I'll get back to you about
this matter very soon.' He looked at his watch. 'I had better be
getting home to dinner, or my wife will be angry. She cooks my
favourite beef stew.'

There was a swaying in my head as I stood up from the chair:
I was drunk with incredulous hope, and I found that I was
thinking of Erika.

June 5th, 1972

Today Ted Bobrowski called me on the phone, which he's never
done before. He sounded different from his usual self; he spoke
almost like a businessman, with brisk directness.

'I'm phoning to ask whether you are free tomorrow evening,
Vincent. You are? Excellent. An acquaintance of mine is coming
over from Melbourne especially to meet you. He'd like to take
you to dinner at a restaurant in town, in order to discuss the
matter we spoke of. He will phone you this evening, to settle
the details. Please wait for his call at eight o'clock.'

I asked for his name.

'His name is Paul,' Ted said. 'That is the only name he will give
you.'

When I put the receiver down, my body was filled with a
strange tingling. It told me my new life was beginning.

June 6th, 1972

Just back from my dinner with Paul. I write this at midnight, a
little drunk, but in no way tired. I doubt that I'll sleep much
tonight.

We dined at the old Savoy Grill in Macquarie Street: a strange
choice, I thought at first, since there are now much livelier

restaurants in Hobart, and the Savoy, which must date back to the Great War, has become rather sad, despite the fact that its food and service are kept to a good standard. Respectable and sombre, with dark wainscoting, sporting prints on deep-pink walls and immaculate, starched tablecloths, it's favoured now by the elderly, and people from the country – rather like those good hotels that have seen better days. But then I realised that Paul had probably chosen it for this very reason: it was the sort of place where we could talk quietly, without competing noise, and with little chance of meeting people of my generation: that is, people who might know me.

We sat at a table in a corner, under a dim indoor plant in a brass pot. The big, carpeted room had the hush of a funeral parlour; only about half-a-dozen other tables were occupied. Well, it was a Tuesday night.

'I'm told the fish is good in Hobart,' Paul said. 'Should I order fish, do you think?'

'An excellent idea,' I said. 'I'd suggest the grilled trevally.'

'I'll follow your advice,' Paul said. 'Will you join me? Or would you prefer something else?'

I said I'd have the trevally too. Paul was scrupulously courteous, but there was an air of authority about him that made me feel it would be wise to follow his suggestions. He was somewhat intimidating, in fact, perhaps because he seldom seemed to smile, and I also left it to him to order the wine. As he frowned over the wine list (he chose an expensive South Australian riesling which turned out to be the best I'd ever drunk), I was able to stealthily observe him. Tall and thin, somewhere in his early forties, he wore a well-cut, dark-grey suit and striped tie, and somehow suggested a military officer in civilian dress, probably because of his military-style moustache. He also (through a somewhat juvenile process of association) reminded me of Ted's photograph of the master spy Theodore Maly, being dark-haired with contrasting, bleak blue eyes. Was he an intelligence officer? Or some other kind of public servant? I thought it better not to ask.

When the trevally came, delivered by an aged waiter in a long white apron who might have stepped out of *Pickwick Papers*, Paul took a careful mouthful, and then looked across at me and smiled briefly. 'You were right, Vincent,' he said. 'This is first-rate. I've seldom found fish as good as this in a Melbourne restaurant.' He dabbed his mouth with his napkin, raised his glass, and held it towards me. 'Cheers,' he said. 'To your future.'

My heart jumped, as I reached out to touch my glass with his. I expected he might now reveal the purpose of our meeting, but he delayed it, and our conversation over the main course proceeded along neutral lines. He asked me about my background, learning that I came from farming people, and had been orphaned early. He asked me a good deal about myself, including whether I kept myself fit. He seemed pleased when I told him I captained the university tennis team. He already knew about my private study of Russian, and asked me why I'd chosen to do this; I told him I hoped it would help me to get into Foreign Affairs. We then discussed current events, and he asked me what I thought of President Nixon's recent visit to China. To what degree would it really alter the course of US–Chinese relations? From this he turned to Vietnam, and the renewed American raids on Hanoi. Did I think these would check the North Vietnamese pressure on South Vietnam – or was the war being lost? I answered at some length, aware that I was being tested, and he listened with flattering attention.

When the main course was cleared away, and sweets and coffee had been ordered, Paul leaned forward, refilling my glass. I was drinking slowly, knowing it was important to keep a clear head. He put the bottle down, his stare fixed and deliberate. 'So you want to work for your Government overseas,' he said. His tone had subtly changed: it held a note of gravity, almost of challenge.

I said that I did.

He nodded. 'Professor Bobrowski speaks very highly of you,' he said. 'He believes you'd go far in the Service. Ted's a brilliant man: I take his opinions very seriously, and I have the impression he may be right about you.' He drank off his wine, put the glass down, folded his hands, and leaned forward. 'I believe you may be one of those people who can serve his country in a particular way,' he said. 'But I must ask you to assure me now that what I say next will be repeated to no-one. Can I trust you, Vincent?'

I said that he could.

'Good,' he said. 'In that case, I'd like you to fly to Melbourne this weekend, to go through a psychological screening process. Your ticket is already booked. Don't tell anyone where you're going – make up a story for the people close to you. I'll meet you at Melbourne airport, and your screening will start next morning. I'm confident about the qualities that Professor Bobrowski and I see in you, and I think you'll come through with a positive report. Then we can look at getting you into the Service. Are you interested?'

'You mean the Diplomatic Service?' I knew that the question was a stupid one, but I wanted him to declare himself.

He raised his eyebrows. 'No, no. I thought you understood, Vincent. I'm the senior recruiting officer for ASIS – our overseas Secret Intelligence Service.'

The little door behind the curtain had opened, and my heart was beating hard; but it was time for me to be on my mettle, I thought. I lowered my voice, conscious that a middle-aged couple at a nearby table were glancing at us. 'Can I get this clear?' I said. 'You want me to be screened with a view to becoming a spy?'

He closed his eyes briefly, as though I'd used coarse language. When he answered, he lowered his own voice.

'Of course. How else did you think it happens? By the way, I'd prefer we use the term "intelligence officer". And in a sense, you *will* be working for Foreign Affairs – but I'll deal with that later. I'll ask you again: are you interested?'

'Yes, I'm interested,' I said. 'Very.' I was smiling broadly, unable to help myself, and Paul gave me a small, bent smile in return.

'I'm delighted to hear it,' he said. 'I'll confirm your flight, then. We should be able to tell you by Tuesday whether you've been accepted.'

'What will the screening entail?'

'It's very simple, really,' Paul said. 'We have to find out that you've nothing nasty hidden.' He smiled again. 'Don't worry. I'm sure you haven't.'

We came out into Macquarie Street and walked towards the Post Office corner, where I'd catch my tram. Paul was staying at a hotel in the city.

A clear, cold night, with little cloud. We had both put on our overcoats.

'Antarctic weather,' Paul said, and briefly laughed and shivered. 'I'm used to warmer climes.'

We walked in silence, after that. Stars were visible above the high Victorian parapet of the Supreme Court building, next to the lit-up oaks and elms in Franklin Square. The sudden siren of a ship, coming from down in the port, was like a warning. I was tipsy, I found, as I breathed the icy air; but it was Paul's revelation, not the wine, that had caused this. When we reached the corner of Elizabeth Street, everything looked as usual and yet not, on this brink of my new life. Changed and portentous, the yellow-glowing Post Office clock in its ornate, Edwardian stone tower, showing five past ten. Portentous, the two waiting trams that sat humming here: one of them mine. But I knew I'd miss it, since I sensed that Paul had more to say.

'You're in no hurry?' he asked.

No, I said; it was early.

'Good,' he said. 'I won't keep you, but before we part, I'll briefly outline the course of action I have in mind for you. It's one that MI6 in the UK sometimes follows – but it's never been done here before. So you'll be rather special, Vincent.' He looked at me in a way that was probably intended to be encouraging. 'Once the screening's done, and once you've completed your M.A., you'll be provisionally accepted – assuming that you're passed as suitable, that is. Then, in the new year, you'll come to us in Melbourne and we'll give you three months' training there. After that, you'll go to

London for training with MI6. But when you get back to Australia, things will take a different course from usual. You'll then apply for a Foreign Affairs traineeship.' He smiled at my look of surprise, as though at a private joke. 'So you see, Vincent, you *will* go into Foreign Affairs, as you planned. You'll go to Canberra as a trainee diplomat, in the normal manner.'

'I don't understand,' I said. 'What if they don't accept me?'

'They will. We'll arrange it. That's the whole point,' he said. 'It's greatly to our advantage, as well as yours. Only the most senior officers in Foreign Affairs will know your true status. Your colleagues never will. It means we'll have an ASIS man working as a full-time Foreign Affairs officer, under full diplomatic cover. Do you see?'

I said I did, trying to absorb the implications.

'Let's see you clear the hurdles first,' he said. 'And now I should let you get home to bed. Before I do, though, let me ask you: are you sure that this is the work you really want to do?'

I told him I'd wanted to become a professional intelligence officer for many years.

'It's not an easy profession,' he said. 'We tend to be loners. It can sometimes be ugly. Marriages don't survive well. Most people despise us. And some of us end up having an identity crisis.' He paused, looking away over the road at the Post Office. When he resumed, his voice had grown very quiet. 'A man wakes up one morning,' he said, 'and looks for his inner self – and he finds he's mislaid it. So few people know who he actually *is* – do you understand? So how can he be sure himself? What follows can be a nervous breakdown. Sometimes, suicide. Can you be sure you're made of the stuff to avoid that?' He turned and looked at me directly, his bleak gaze neither challenging nor aggressive, but coolly concerned. In that moment I felt that I liked him, and sensed a sort of melancholy in him.

'I believe so,' I said. 'I've always been a loner. I'm good at it.'

'I hope so,' he said. 'Good night. I'll see you in Melbourne, Vincent.'

We shook hands and he turned away abruptly, and set off across the road.

It's two in the morning; now I must try to sleep. I wish I could phone Erika, but know it's unwise. My life of deception begins.

2

BRADLEY SITS BACK in Vincent's chair, pinching the bridge of his nose and pushing aside a pile of binders: the diaries covering the period from early 1973, when Vincent joined Foreign Affairs, to the end of 1981. He's finished reading them all, and they've seldom failed to engage his interest, these records of a double life. What remains to be read are those of the last three years: from 1982 to the end of 1984. He'll start on those tomorrow.

It's late afternoon, with soft, misty rain outside; time to go downstairs and make up the fire for Connie. But he lingers for a few minutes more, wearing a faint, unconscious smile, his heavy-lidded eyes staring out at the rain with an expression of incredulity. Vincent! This eccentric friend of his student days, this former Foreign Affairs colleague – whom he once viewed with an affectionate amusement which had an element of condescension in it, and whom he saw as brilliant but unworldly – has turned out to be someone he scarcely knew at all. True, he discovered this to be the case two years ago, in China; but the full extent of Vincent's dual existence has only emerged in the diaries. Staring at the rain, Bradley summons his friend up, studying the long, well-remembered face for clues to his duplicity. And Vincent looks back at him, laughing softly with his mouth closed, in a way he had – making a resultant humming that sounds like a comment on life's absurdities. (*'Hm – hm – hm.'*) His deep-set hazel eyes, alight with private amusement, regard Bradley fixedly from behind their glasses; but is it only amusement that glints in them now? Is there perhaps a cunning evasiveness? The hard light of deceit?

Until they both served in China, Bradley had no idea that Vincent was an ASIS officer under cover, and the double life that the diaries describe is one that he never even suspected. He'd not had much opportunity to do so, since Vincent and he hadn't been appointed to the same embassy together until 1982, when Bradley was posted to Peking.

He had joined Foreign Affairs a year after Vincent, early in 1974. When he'd arrived in the Department in Canberra, Vincent had still been there, working on the Southeast Asia desk; but Vincent had left soon afterwards to take up his first posting, as Third Secretary in New Delhi. Those few months in Canberra would be the last time they would see each other for the next eight years, since Bradley would serve in Rome, London and Bangkok, while Vincent's postings after New Delhi would be Jakarta and Singapore. So their paths had not crossed. Now, reading the diaries, Bradley has finally learned the details of Vincent's hidden life – a life which it seems reached a peak of success in Singapore, where his ability to recruit agents yielded some valuable results for the Government, and earned him high praise from his superiors.

His career had in fact made a steadily upward arc until 1982, in China.

PART TWO

The Eastern Wall

ONE

1

ON THE CAAC flight from Hong Kong to Peking, Bradley sat
with his Post Report in his lap, idly flicking through it. Issued to
him in Canberra before he left, it supplied all the essential facts
that the Department thought he needed to know about the
country to which he was being sent for the next two to three
years: governmental structures; recent political developments;
local customs and taboos; the sort of clothing suitable for the
climate. He read a little of the section on China's new 'open door'
policy, which told him that the People's Republic was no longer
an entirely closed country, but was still one where permission
would be needed for almost any move he might wish to make.
Then he grew bored, and closed the Report on his lap.

It was a fine afternoon in May, and his face was bathed in sun
coming through the window beside his seat. A pretty Chinese
flight attendant in a sky-blue suit had brought him a cup of
green tea, a bar of chocolate and a paper fan; now Bradley
shaded his face with the fan, gazing down on China: an antique
quilt of cultivation, olive and brown, stitched with the long
silver ribbons of its ancient canals. He'd stayed overnight in
Hong Kong after the flight from Sydney; he was rested, and had
a sense of unusual lightness and wellbeing, perhaps because his
life was entering a new phase. The cabin was only half-full: not
many Westerners were yet venturing into China, despite the
new policy of encouraging visits by highly supervised foreign
guests. A group of them sat across the aisle from him: elderly

American tourists exchanging elated banter, like children on a treat.

The plane had already passed over most of the country, from the south to the north. Flooded rice paddies, calm in the sun, carried the aircraft's shadow, and the bends of China's great rivers unwound in succession, their names resounding in Bradley's mind: the Pearl; the Yangtze; the Yellow River. Soon, they would arrive in Peking, and Bradley found himself nursing a vast expectancy. The fact-based political briefings he'd been given in Canberra faded from his mind, and he began to listen instead to the voice of the child inside him – something he still indulged in, on the edge of his thirty-first year. This voice told him that however repressive the current regime might be, and however harsh today's facts, he was about to enter a nation which very few people in his generation had seen, and which might still contain a second, secret country, preserved inside the Marxist republic: some remnant, perhaps, of the China of Tu Fu and Li Po and Po Chü-I – those poets of the T'ang whom he and Vincent Austin had savoured in their undergraduate days – an ideal China, unlikely as legend, with lutes on the river, pearl blinds, lights through gauze curtains, and devoted friendships between poet scholar-officials. Or so it pleased Bradley to imagine, as the aircraft began to lose altitude.

Preparing to land, it dropped down over the North China Plain, and his thoughts turned to Vincent, who would be meeting him at the airport, and who was now a Cultural Attaché with the rank of First Secretary. The American tourists were clicking their seatbelts shut, their voices sonorous with anticipation. In their minds and Bradley's the plane might have been landing on the moon. It dropped lower, and an entirely rural landscape opened up: a country of pastels, light-green, yellow and ochre, extending to pale-blue mountains far out on a rim, peaked like those in Sung paintings. The runway extended between fields of wheat and vegetables. Building materials lay about. No sign of Peking, which was apparently miles away: just some low, red-brick buildings, casual and crude as outhouses. Even the airport's control tower proved to be of red brick, like a tower in a child's story book: humble and strange and rather charming, after its sleek white counterparts in the airports of the outside world. And around the edges of the tarmac, the anticipated guardians of the People's Republic could be seen, in their green military fatigues, the red stars of Communism on their caps.

The terminal building was small and basic, reminding Bradley of a country airport in Australia. Vincent was waiting for him in the arrivals area, grinning as though at a joke that he and Bradley would soon share, a red disc hung around his neck to indicate his diplomatic status. He wore a formal navy suit and tie, and looked very much the senior Foreign Affairs officer, Bradley thought. He hadn't changed in the eight years since Bradley had last seen him; having looked older than his age in his twenties, he promised to remain changelessly youthful into middle life. Reaching for Bradley's hand, he seemed filled with delight. His grip was surprisingly strong, his rapid voice was charged with all its old enthusiasm, and his archaic Wodehouseisms were still intact.

'What ho, Brad! So good to see you. Let's get you processed, and out of here.'

They moved through a gate reserved for air crew and diplomats, and Bradley presented his diplomatic passport at a desk. It was studied by a blank-faced official in a blue cotton Mao cap, who stamped it quickly and waved them both on.

At the carousel where the luggage revolved, a tall Chinese chauffeur in a grey uniform stood waiting for them. Since Bradley was immune from any customs check, they moved immediately out the doors, the chauffeur following behind with Bradley's bags. The Embassy's white Mercedes was parked by the steps.

It was spring, here in North China; the air was light and dry and delicate, and fields of young green wheat came to the edges of the road. There was very little traffic on this road from the airport to the city, which ran through level countryside. Poplars and pruned willows lined the way, reminding Bradley of Lombardy: a land-scape that seemed at first to be more European than Chinese. But then, like a herald, a small, lone cyclist passed, pedalling along in the shade of the poplars in blue cotton jacket, trousers and cap: the uniform of the People's Republic.

Bradley turned to find Vincent studying him, his hands folded in his lap, his long, pallid face wearing an expression of amused gratification. 'So,' Vincent said. 'You're finally here, Derek. At last we serve in the same embassy. Excellent. *Ex*-cellent.' He savoured the word like a sweet, parodying himself in the way that Bradley remembered. 'Congratulations, by the way. It didn't take you long to make Second Secretary. But I gather from your letters you weren't enchanted with Thailand?'

'It was fine in the Thai countryside, but Bangkok's hell. Busting at the seams, and the traffic's permanently gridlocked.'

'Really? Well you won't find any gridlock here – there are practically no private cars, as I'm sure you know. But the crowds are another matter. After a while, one longs for space and privacy. We are either watched or eavesdropped on – or both.' He glanced quickly at the Chinese driver, silent at the wheel in front of them. Then he took off his glasses and polished them, and his high, white forehead, with its prominent, knob-like frontal bones, was suddenly made more prominent. 'There's a lot to tell you,' he said. 'But that can wait until this evening. Meanwhile, I have a bit of bad news. Your flat in the compound isn't ready. Your predecessor, Harrison, left the place in a bit of a mess. It needed a thorough cleaning, and the Ambassador ordered it to be repainted. You've been booked into a hotel for a few nights.'

'I can stand that,' Bradley said. 'As long as the plumbing works.'

'It won't be that bad,' Vincent said. 'This is one of their tourist hotels, catering for foreigners. They make sure the amenities are adequate. I'll have to drop you there and dash back to the Embassy. The Ambassador's demanded that I confer with him at five o'clock. We have a trade delegation from home arriving here tomorrow, and we have to hold their hands.'

'Shall we meet for dinner?' Bradley asked.

Vincent looked regretful. 'I'm sorry,' he said, 'I think the Ambassador will insist that I eat with him, in order to prolong our discussion. But I'll get away afterwards, and come to your hotel. Have your dinner there, Brad – it's the best option anyway, since there are precious few good restaurants in Peking. I'll phone your room at eight o'clock, just to confirm. Then we can prowl about the city.' His voice dropped, and became confidential; he glanced once again at the driver's spiky black head in front of them. 'The Ambassador's fussing about this trade delegation. You wouldn't believe how crass some of these people can be. They so easily drop gross clangers, and offend Chinese sensibilities.'

'Oh dear.'

Vincent sighed. 'You may smile, Brad, but I'm sure by now you've experienced the Australian politician abroad. The ones who come here are dreadful. This Fraser Government's no better than Whitlam's, in that regard. Would you believe that they expect us to pimp for them? And the businessmen are the same. They want *girls*, here in the most puritan society on earth! They don't come right out with it, of course. I had a Minister here recently who said to me: "You know, Vincent, I've never seen an Asian girl naked." "Really, Minister?" I said. "You'll have to go to Bangkok for that."' He began to laugh with his mouth closed, his long, well-shaven chin with its permanent blue shadow of beard thrust sideways.

The road had become wide now, and was lined with plane trees and low brick cottages. It was no longer empty. Swarms of black bicycles surrounded them, ridden by a horde in the same blue Mao jackets and caps as those of the first little cyclist. Occasionally a white shirt or a khaki jacket or a red-starred khaki military cap broke the pattern; otherwise, there was no variation, and their sheer numbers made the cyclists faintly alarming. Men predominated, but women wheeled by as well, shapeless and sexless in their humble blue cottons. All rang their bells constantly; in response, the silent chauffeur steadily sounded his horn. But the cyclists took no notice; sometimes, one would glide dreamily across the front of the car. The only other cars here were occasional Red Flag limousines: huge Chinese luxury vehicles whose drawn tulle curtains hid important officials, remote from the people as their imperial predecessors had been.

Progress grew slower and slower, until finally the Mercedes came almost to a halt, obstructed by a slow-moving cart piled high with cabbages, drawn by two little ponies, its driver a very old man in a wide straw hat who appeared to be fast asleep. The chauffeur muttered to himself but made no attempt to pass, and the car proceeded at walking pace. Vincent turned to Bradley with an expression of sardonic forbearance.

'In spite of all Deng Xiaoping's efforts to reform the economy, the twentieth century hasn't really taken hold yet,' he said. 'Adjust your mind to life in the Middle Ages, Brad.'

The Peace Hotel was in Jinyu Hutong, or Goldfish Lane.

Goldfish Lane proved to be a narrow alleyway lined on both sides with walled, blank-faced buildings. All was grey here: dim grey brick and stucco, and crumbling grey tiles on roofs and along the tops of the walls. It was the grey of dirty water, and the lane smelled of drains. The buildings were dim and dilapidated. Dark, arched doorways occurred in the walls at intervals, leading to forbidding, half-glimpsed courtyards. Between two of these aged buildings, the tall, square gates of the hotel rose with Stalinist severity. Made of ferroconcrete, as the hotel itself was, they were topped with Chinese lanterns, also fashioned from cement. The cube-like eight-storey building with its small steel-framed windows looked rather like a cheaply built office block in a provincial city; but Vincent had told Bradley that for most Chinese it represented unattainable luxury.

The dining room recalled country hotels of the kind that Bradley had encountered as a child. Entered from the lobby through frosted glass doors, it was long and narrow and furnished with a dozen or so round tables covered with starched white cloths. The straight-backed chairs had lace antimacassars, and there were lace curtains on the windows, giving the place a look of needy respectability. Most of the tables were empty, but a few were occupied by Europeans of various nationalities, all of them male; he heard German spoken, and what sounded like an eastern European language, but no English. He'd been followed in through the doors by a small, thin man who proved to be the only Chinese diner, and who sat by himself in a corner. He wore an outfit that caught Bradley's attention, since it broke with the pattern he'd seen until now: a neat, dark-grey, military-style jacket with patch pockets, buttoning to the throat, and matching knife-edged trousers. He was a sober-looking little man, with a rather long nose for a Chinese, and the material of his well-pressed suit – a sort of gaberdine – was clearly of far better quality than the cheap, rumpled cottons of the masses. Bradley had found already that in a land of people in uniform, small variations of dress become interesting, and he decided that this man must be an official of some kind. Vincent was right: People's China recalled Europe of the Middle Ages, where it was forbidden to wear any other clothing than the costume which denoted your rank and occupation.

The two waitresses here were also in grey: long grey cotton dresses reaching well below the knee. Their expressions were severe. One of them handed Bradley a menu, in absolute silence. It proved to be in Chinese and a number of European languages, including English, and he ordered a chicken dish, anticipating something similar to the Cantonese cuisine he was accustomed to in the restaurants of Australia and Southeast Asia. But that of North China proved to be different. He found himself dealing with a very tough chicken which was accompanied by its feet. The only other accompaniments were leek and steamed buns. Pushing the feet aside, and trying not look at them, he did what he could with the chicken, and filled up on the steamed buns. At one point, he had glanced up and found the Chinese man in the grey uniform looking at him with an expression that was difficult to read. Sympathy? Or sardonic amusement?

At eight o'clock he sat reading a magazine in an armchair in his room, waiting for Vincent's call. It was a clean room, with an adjoining bathroom that was also moderately clean, but the fittings seemed to date from the 1950s. The cream paintwork on the walls and doors of the room was roughly applied, needing a second coat, and the furnishings were basic and old-fashioned. Bradley sipped his third cup of tea, struggling against a sense of discouragement.

At eight-fifteen, the phone finally rang: an extremely loud ring, making him jump. Picking it up, he heard Vincent's voice, but it came to him muffled and broken, as though through static. At the same time, there was a series of clicks.

'Vincent?' he said. 'This is a very bad line.'

'Yes, that's perfectly usual,' Vincent said, his voice becoming clearer. 'Just wait a moment, Brad. Give our friends time to adjust their equipment.' He paused, letting this sink in. 'Go down to the lobby,' he said. 'I'll meet you there in ten minutes.'

They set off down Goldfish Lane, going deeper into the networks of the hutongs: the little grey alleyways that lay behind Peking's main avenues. Although the traditional transcriptions for Chinese names had recently been replaced by Pinyin versions, and Peking was now Beijing, the old name was still hanging on among English speakers, and the district through which Vincent was taking them was still essentially the old Peking: a medieval city whose avenues were as wide as those of Paris, but where very few buildings were above four storeys, and where most of the people lived in the hutongs. In every lane, crowds shuffled by in the proletarian uniform of blue cotton Mao jacket and trousers, and Bradley found himself viewing them through an amber twilight; electricity was rationed, and street lamps burned with a sullen dimness. There were still very few Westerners here, and he and Vincent were stared at with frank and intense interest. The people were ethnically mixed: many were of the small-boned Han type, but most were the tall, strongly built Mongols of the north: flat-faced, big-boned and handsome. The girls were often beautiful, with broad cheekbones, fair skin and wide-set eyes, which they lowered, as they passed, with old-fashioned modesty. All of the women wore trousers, but there were occasional touching attempts at individuality: a tight-waisted jacket with a pin-stripe, like part of a suit from the 1940s; a linen sunhat with a flower pattern on it. Here and there, the graceful, curving eaves of old China rose above the walls, and they passed three-storeyed houses with ornate balconies, and old gateways carved with stone lions. But most of the hutongs consisted of row on row of tiny, single-storeyed cottages with thatched or shingled roofs, grouped around central courtyards. They had entered a village world.

Through open doorways, Bradley glimpsed the few possessions of its inhabitants: a table and a tin washbasin; a curtained bed; a singlet hung to dry on a line that stretched across the room; a bicycle propped against a chair. The spectral odour of drains followed them constantly; the houses had no running water or lavatories, Vincent told him, and a communal toilet block must serve a whole lane.

'You're looking at the fruits of Mao's revolution,' Vincent said. 'His final two decades of insanity kept China in this condition. The question now is whether Deng Xiaoping and his modernizations can begin to repair it.'

'Talk like this could get you purged, comrade. After all, my phone was tapped,' Bradley said.

'Of course,' Vincent said. 'They do it all the time. They're so clumsy about it, it's a joke. You'll be watched and listened in on constantly – so remember, never say anything that could offend official sensibilities. Welcome to life in the Middle Kingdom.' He chuckled, and took Bradley's arm affectionately. 'And welcome aboard,' he said. 'It's so good that you've come, Brad! I hoped against hope that you'd get this posting; I'm delighted that the friend of my youth has joined me here. I hope you won't regret it, old chap. China can be a somewhat grim posting: we're cooped up in the compound most of the time, and kept from any real contact with the life of outside. But it has its interesting aspects. For me, to see a Marxist dictatorship at work is endlessly fascinating.'

'It confirms all your worst fears, Vin, I'm sure.'

'It's actually become much better, since the fall of the Gang of Four – as you no doubt know. A lot of unfortunate intellectuals and scholars have been let out of prison, and the more insane repressions have gone. But don't be deceived by the official line on freedom: the iron hand is still there.' He glanced quickly at Bradley. 'What interests *me*, Derek, is this. Here and there, just occasionally, one meets educated Chinese who are survivors in spirit of the old *shen-shih*: the scholar gentry. Mao murdered most of them, but one or two are left, surviving in holes and corners, or wearing masks and spouting the official line. The sort of people, for instance, who teach classical Chinese literature in the universities, while their time-serving colleagues teach propaganda. During the Cultural Revolution, and under the reign of Mao's monstrous wife, most of them were sent to prison camps. But now they're back; and if you approach them gently, they'll lose their nervousness enough to have a conversation with you. I've become friendly, for instance, with an elderly professor at Peking University who's an expert on T'ang poetry. Back in the mid-sixties, when the universities were shut down, he was tormented by the Red Guards, and he and his wife were put to labour on a commune. Can you imagine? Professor Liu is a most sensitive and intelligent man; he and I share an enthusiasm for Waley's translations of the old songs of the second century. You remember, Brad?' Circumnavigating a man carrying a crate with two chickens in it, he threw his head back, and recited:

'The Eastern Wall stands high and long;
Far and wide it stretches without a break.'

'What a memory you have,' Bradley said.

Vincent laughed. 'You remember those late nights in my study, when we'd read our favourite poems aloud? I miss those days in New Town, don't you? The times when I'd come to your parents' home for dinner, and your mother would have made her wonderful chocolate cake? When we'd walk and talk for hours at night, roaming out through Glenorchy, never growing tired. Wonderful times, Derek! We were so *alive*!' He gazed over the heads of the crowd, and a small, reminiscent smile touched his lips: the smile of a man who had lived in Arcady.

Bradley smiled indulgently. It had seemed a very ordinary suburban youth to him; but in Vincent's private world it was clearly something else altogether. He was still a very sentimental man, Bradley thought: sentimental in a style that went out with the Victorian era. Yet the things Vincent grew sentimental about were odd: not quite the things that most people would have seen as subjects for nostalgia. And he somehow combined this with a capacity for incisive thinking, and even a cold realism. As he walked, blindly smiling, holding Bradley's arm in the amber twilight, many almond eyes looked Vincent up and down, but he was quite oblivious; instead, he exuded a sort of proprietorial joy.

They stopped in front of a bakery, open on to the lane, where men in white cotton caps tended brick ovens, shovelling the pale, steamed bread of North China onto trays. As they stood watching, Bradley glanced back up the lane and caught sight of the grey-suited Chinese from the hotel dining room, standing next to a gateway. For a second, the man met his gaze; then he turned away and began to study the crowd that streamed past him.

'We're being followed,' Bradley said, and jerked his head.

Vincent sighed. 'Yes, of course,' he said. 'A goon from the Ministry of State Security, checking you out. They don't like us roaming about in places like this. They're terrified we'll *talk* to people. They're very paranoid about that.' He glanced at his watch. 'Come along,' he said. 'We'll go to where the shops are. I'll take you up to Wang Fu Jing Street.'

*

Wang Fu Jing's wide avenue proved also to be half-medieval. Between its four-storeyed Stalinist buildings of stone and stucco, little wooden cottages of a more human era still crouched, and humble household goods spilled out on to the pavement. Washing-lines were slung between locust trees, whose leaves glowed pale-green in the street lamps. On the road, carts trundled by among the bicycles, coming in from the communes with loads of bricks and vegetables, most of them drawn by horses or donkeys, some pulled by men in ragged headcloths. Dusty windows displayed goods that seemed to have been spirited to Peking from some universal underworld of second-hand: out-of-date refrigerators and electric fans; male European dummies with simple-minded smiles, wearing the suits and waistcoats of forty years ago; hats that Bette Davis might have worn. The human streams that flowed along these broad pavements had a density Bradley had never encountered before, even in Southeast Asia, their blue cotton uniforms making them resemble an advancing army.

'I think our tail has given up,' Vincent said. 'He'll be happy that we're out of the back alleys and on a respectable street – one where they like us to go. Most foreigners shop in the Friendship Store here, which is all for our benefit. But I'm not taking you there.' He glanced at his watch. 'We're going to the Foreign Languages Bookstore.' He chuckled. 'Don't worry, I'm not expecting you to browse. We're meeting someone outside, at nine o'clock. A surprise for you, Brad.'

'Yes? Who is it?' A sudden wave of travel-weariness had overtaken Bradley, and he wasn't in a mood for mysteries.

'A member of our mission,' Vincent said. He paused, turning his head to peer at Bradley as they walked. 'It's Erika Lange,' he said.

Bradley was startled enough to stop and stare. Vincent halted too, and the remorseless blue crowds flowed around them. 'Erika? Here at the Embassy?' Bradley said. 'I thought she worked in journalism.'

'She still does,' Vincent said. 'Over eight years ago, she joined the Foreign Affairs Information Service as a press officer – and in 1980 they posted her here. So when I arrived last year, she was here to greet me.'

'She never married?'

'No,' Vincent said briefly.

'So you and she are back together?'

'You might say that,' Vincent said. 'But simply as colleagues and friends.' His tone had become formal, discouraging further questions. 'Come on,' he said. 'I thought we three would have a drink in the foyer of the Peking Hotel – just around the corner, in Chang'an Avenue. It's one of the few places in the city where foreigners of all kinds can mix.'

A few minutes' walk brought them within sight of the display windows and posters of the Foreign Languages Bookstore; but there seemed at first to be no sign of Erika Lange. Then Bradley noticed that in the crowds flowing towards them, many eyes were turning to the left, in the direction of the kerb, where a locust tree grew. Following these glances, he discovered Erika standing under the tree.

The interest she was attracting wasn't surprising: there were no other Western women to be seen, and her looks would have drawn attention even if there had been. Her hair shone gold in the light from the bookstore window, and her face, in contrast to the tan Chinese faces flowing by, seemed dramatically pale. She wore a navy-blue lightweight woollen overcoat, cut very full, reaching almost to her ankles like a cloak, hanging open over a moss-green dress. It was an outfit that was clearly expensive, and she was slim enough to wear it well. As Vincent and Bradley approached, she turned and stared at them, but didn't smile. She must be thirty or so now, Bradley thought, but she'd become even more attractive in her maturity than she'd been as a girl, looking more like a model than a journalist. Her wide-set, light-blue eyes held the cold, lost blankness that he remembered, even after so many years; and he could no more read them now than he'd been able to do on the occasion of that single brief meeting when they were young.

He and Vincent halted under the tree. 'Erika, you remember Derek Bradley,' Vincent said. His face glowed with incongruous pride, as though he were bringing her a gift. 'You two met in Hobart, when Derek and I were students.'

Erika extended her hand to Bradley, her face still blank, her full lower lip thrust out in a way that looked faintly pugnacious. 'I remember,' she said. Her voice was low, and almost toneless. 'You still look like a student, Derek. But better dressed.'

Vincent gave a shout of laughter. 'It's true, Brad. You've scarcely aged at all.'

Erika released Bradley's hand, her eyes continuing to hold his. Then she smiled, and the smile startled him. It changed her entirely, filling her face with a warmth that had not seemed possible; with a mysterious delight; with a humorous, irresistible flirtatiousness that caused her light eyes to dance, as water dances with sun on it. It told him that life was an adventure, and invited him to share it; and then he remembered. This had happened before, the first time he'd met her, at nineteen.

2

TWO DAYS LATER, at ten in the morning, Bradley sat at his desk on the top floor of the Australian Embassy, a stack of papers and documents in front of him.

The Embassy was a temporary one: a three-storey building of faded beige stucco, set back from the street, with Chinese elms and an Australian flag planted in the driveway. The walled compound, together with a number of others, was located in San Li Tun, a new diplomatic district on the road to the airport. Its gates were guarded twenty-four hours a day by soldiers from the People's Liberation Army – whose main purpose, according to Vincent, was to make sure that no unauthorised Chinese citizens got inside. Bradley's office, like that of the other diplomats here, was in the Embassy's Political Section, which was designated as a secure area. No foreigners were admitted, and other Embassy staff had to punch in a number on a door downstairs to get in.

His office was pleasant enough, but had little charm. Its polished timber desk, as well as its other furniture, was imported from Australia, and strictly functional. The executive chair he sat in was of black vinyl, and there were two chairs for guests, upholstered in navy fabric, opposite the desk. An original painting by an obscure Australian artist hung on the wall: a stylised figure on horseback in a desert, heavily influenced by Sidney Nolan. Only the Ambassador rated a painting by an artist of any fame: his office featured a Brett Whiteley. Bradley had taken off the jacket of his pale-blue summer suit, loosened his tie, and had swivelled his chair around to stare out the window. Across the walls of the compound, drab workers' dormitories could be seen, beyond which lay pale-green wheat fields, in the same rural countryside he'd come through on his arrival: a countryside which Peking was devouring. Gazing, sitting quite still, his left hand cupping his chin, he sat in an attitude of waiting.

He would move into his apartment in the compound tomorrow; this evening would be his last at the Peace Hotel, where he'd face one more of its alarming meals. Yesterday, Vincent had gone off on official business to Shanghai for a week, and although Bradley's five other diplomatic colleagues at the post had proved friendly enough, they were busy and abstracted, and he'd so far received no invitations to socialise – other than to be informed that there was a German Embassy reception next Tuesday. Meanwhile, Peking had its compensations. Spring and autumn were the best seasons of the year here, his colleagues had told him – the summers being too hot and the winters freezing. And certainly the weather at present was inviting. Elated by the light, dry air and the young green leaves on the trees, Bradley found himself filled with a formless sense of expectancy as he moved about the streets: an electric, un-directed energy which continued to affect him. His spirit had responded to the flat, austere spaciousness of this region of the North China Plain, with its level fields, distant hills and lines of willows and poplars, glimpsed in occasional vignettes beyond the city limits. This was the dreamlike landscape celebrated by those classical poets whom he and Vincent had been so fond of in their youth: a haunted, ancient, deceptively mild countryside receding towards the Great Wall, where the horns of the barbarians had once sounded on the wind.

He had not yet had much time to visit Peking's historic sites, beyond a visit to the Forbidden City. Walking with the swarms of tourists through the vast Meridian Gate, breathing the ancient, tomb-dry air of the Ming Dynasty, he'd experienced an odd mingling of awe, delight and melancholy; and in fact, the weight of a huge melancholy seemed to Bradley to hang over the whole northern capital. Or perhaps it was simply the weight of the past: the immensely strange, forbidding past of China. Meanwhile, a feature of the modern city that had begun to trouble him was the absence of the pleasures and amenities that were taken for granted in most towns in the world, and which he'd been used to in Bangkok: good restaurants; bars; nightclubs; varieties of shops. He'd even begun to miss the sight of advertising signs. It appeared that there would be little for a single man to do, in this strict Communist metropolis – and this, together with a continual sense of being watched, was beginning to create in the usually optimistic Bradley a certain disquiet. Twice, in Goldfish Lane, he'd passed his grey-suited follower from the intelligence service, who had stared at him with open and insolent interest; and he began to think that his room in the hotel was being searched when he was out. His personal possessions were moved about in a way that seemed suspicious.

He swung back to his desk now, shrugged to dismiss his thoughts, and began to shuffle through the pile of papers and documents, preparing himself to begin on a project the Ambassador had assigned to him. This was to monitor China's relationship with the United States, with particular reference to President Reagan's policy of continuing arms sales to Taiwan, and the responses to this of the Chinese Government. Bradley had begun by making contact with the Embassy's translation staff, asking them to bring him anything in the Chinese newspapers relating to these topics, and already a small batch of typescripts had been delivered to his desk. He picked them up and began to read.

Some five minutes later, there was a knock on his open door. At the same time, a low female voice said: 'Knock-knock.'

Before he looked up, Bradley knew who it was; it was a very distinctive voice, being deeper than those of most women, with a certain odd flatness about it. He stood up. 'Erika,' he said. 'Come in.'

She walked towards his desk, her brows raised as though in pleasant surprise. Her fair hair hung from one side across her forehead; as she came, she pushed it back with a gesture he guessed to be habitual. Today she wore a white silk blouse with full sleeves caught in at the wrists, and dark-blue slacks.

'Hello,' she said. 'I thought I'd see how our new Second Secretary is getting on. So I crashed the secure area. Do you mind? Am I interrupting your work?'

'Of course not. I'm glad of the company.' Bradley moved quickly from behind his desk, and pushed one of the visitors' chairs towards her. 'Please,' he said. She sat down, and he took the other chair, so that they faced each other.

'Is that how it is? Glad of some company? You sound a bit adrift,' she said.

Her tone was engagingly whimsical, and he found himself listening to her accent, which had stirred his curiosity during their previous meeting. It wasn't really Australian; it was oddly neutral, almost like a trans-Atlantic accent. He remembered that Vincent had told him that her father was German, which perhaps accounted for it. She smiled as she spoke, examining his face with a questioning directness. It was the same smile that had affected him so strongly outside the bookshop, making him decide that she was an entirely different woman from the one he'd imagined her to be. Her pale yet vivid eyes, in which the light from the window set up a distracting glitter, were in no way cold today: they had an intimate warmth that somehow seemed to imply that he and she had once enjoyed a special, mysterious friendship: a friendship they were about to renew. Bradley found this odd, but agreeable. When he and Vincent had sat with her over drinks in the foyer of the Peking Hotel, the conversation had been general, dealing mainly with Foreign Affairs gossip, or with the difficulties of life in China. She'd remained impersonal; almost distant. Now, it seemed, she'd changed.

'Adrift?' he said. 'No, I wouldn't go that far. But I don't get the impression there's a lot going on here socially.'

'There are endless receptions, of course.'

'I'm sure. The bane and necessity of a Foreign Affairs officer's life.'

'Yes, they can be a bloody bore: but they're useful profession-ally, aren't they? And as you've gathered, we don't exactly lead a swinging private life, here in the People's Republic. It's not possible. The Peking Hotel foyer is the trendiest spot in town: does that show you the extent of the problem? So we have to make our own fun. We do that here at the Embassy every Friday night, in the Down Under Bar. It's set up in the basement. The Foster's flows freely, and most of the Australian journos in town turn up – which I'm always glad of. You should come, Derek.'

'I will. You'll be there?'

'I'll make a point of it. Vin won't be back until Sunday, so you can be my escort.' She paused, and smiled again. 'And how are you getting on with the other FAOs?'

'It's too early to tell. I scarcely know them. None of them were in my intake, so there are no old friends here.'

'Except Vincent. You've no idea how he's looked forward to your coming. He regards you as the best friend he has – did you know that?'

'Well, we've been friends a long time. But you know, since we graduated, we've only been in the same place once: in Canberra, in 1974, when I first joined the Department.'

'Tell me,' she said, 'what should I call you? Derek, or Brad? Vincent always calls you Brad.'

'Most people call me Brad.'

'Yes. I like Brad. Derek is so stiff. Doesn't go with your looks.'

'You think names and looks have to match?'

'They ought to. Anyway, you're a Brad. The reliable type.'

'Ouch.'

She laughed, and he joined in, wondering why she was flirting with him. Erika was the sort of woman who flirted with her eyes, in the sidelong, mischievous, innocent way that some small girls did. He guessed that she did it indiscriminately, without expecting to be taken seriously.

Without warning, she stood up, and Bradley did the same. 'So. I'll see you on Friday night,' she said.

She turned, raised her hand, waggled her fingers, and hurried out without speaking further.

3

BRADLEY WOKE SLOWLY this morning, inhaling a smell which he knew to be Great Leap Forward floor polish: a Chinese solvent used by Mrs Hong, the housekeeper. She had been cleaning the parquet floors of his apartment; he'd moved into the compound yesterday, and he contemplated this fact with a sense of well-being. Now he had privacy, and room to spread himself. And for no rational reason, as sleep's last traces lingered in his brain, he was conscious of the imminence of some strange and unpredictable event lying in wait for him today, its essential odour resembling that of the floor polish.

He'd been dreaming: one of those dreams that obliterated the present, and was more intense than waking life. He'd been a boy, back in New Town, and the dream had been one of bleached paling fences, warm and reassuring in the sun; of flowering gardens in the island's mild summer, filled with the lovingly tended plants of the northern hemisphere; of radios at open windows, sleepily discharging the pop tunes of those days; of calling children's voices, coming across the roofs of the safe, drowsing neighbourhood: wild, happy voices that appealed to him to join them, and still called in his head. Like absolute safety, like unquestioning happiness, like childhood itself, they'd never be found again; so why had he dreamed them? And why had he woken to a mingled sense of pleasure and regret?

Then he remembered: somehow Judith had come into the dream. She'd wandered with him down a road which eventually became teeming Silom Road in Bangkok. They'd met, as always, at the entrance of the British exporting firm she worked for; now they walked into Oriental Plaza and sat over lunch in an outdoor café there. In the dream, in languid, humid Bangkok, she smiled at him across the table, eyes narrowed against the glaring sun, chopsticks poised over her bowl. Judith: waving brown hair; large and humorous blue eyes; a wide, full mouth. They never ran out of things to say, they always laughed a lot, and their lovemaking had been sensual and unfailingly satisfying. They'd been happy, for nearly three years. Why hadn't he married her, as she'd wanted? This morning, coming out of his dream, finding himself alone in austere Peking, Bradley could give himself no satisfactory answer.

It was Friday, and nothing special was scheduled for him: merely an appointment at the Chinese Foreign Ministry. But this evening, he recalled, he'd be meeting Erika Lange in the Down Under Bar, in the basement of the chancery building. Since her visit to his office, she'd hovered in his mind. She came there un-invited, and was constantly dismissed; but she always returned.

Showered, shaved and dressed, Bradley sat over coffee in his tiny kitchen, gazing out the window at the pink-walled Embassy of Singapore next door. When Vincent got back, he decided, he'd try to lead him into confiding a little more about his true rela-tionship with Erika. Vincent's claim that it was a platonic friendship was difficult to believe: Bradley was more inclined to think that she remained the love of Vincent's life, even after all these years.

The Down Under Bar was similar to the one Bradley had attended regularly in the Australian Embassy in Bangkok. Most embassies maintained such informal entertainment areas some-where in their chanceries: places to forget the cares of the post each week, and to let off steam with selected fellow expatriates: journalists; business people; international airline crews. The basement of the Peking chancery, which housed such necessities as the generator and a room for the cleaning staff, was painted battleship-grey. One end had been cleared to create the bar, into which some forty people were crowded, most of them standing, a few sitting on chairs around the walls, their talk and laughter echoing off the ceiling, where conduits for the airconditioning, water and electricity ran overhead.

Bradley pushed his way through the crowd, smiling and nodding to other members of the mission. He was making his way towards a small, horseshoe-shaped bar at the far end of the room, where a young Third Secretary wearing a pink shirt and bow tie was this evening's barman. Erika Lange and a young woman with thick black hair pulled back in a ponytail leaned against the bar, drinks in hand. They wore similar dark cocktail frocks. As Bradley approached, Erika turned and looked at him, her eyes catching the light in a way that appeared almost baleful. Then her face showed recognition, and she smiled.

'Derek, this is Moira Paterson,' she said. 'Moira's a correspondent with the Sydney *Courier*.' She turned to Moira. 'Derek Bradley's our new Second Secretary.'

Moira extended her arm at full length, and Bradley took her hand. She was narrow-faced, and her large eyes were an arresting green. 'Hello Derek,' she said. 'Are you also Erika's new toy?'

Astounded, Bradley stared at her for a moment. 'Nothing so fortunate,' he said. 'I'm just the friend of a friend. Does that satisfy the *Courier*?'

'Moira, you're being bloody crass,' Erika said. She looked at Bradley. 'She's had a long hard day at the Chinese Foreign Ministry.'

'Trying to get permission to travel to Canton,' Moira said, addressing the air. 'It's like pulling teeth, with these bloody people.'

She began a recital about the difficulties of reporting in China, in which Erika joined. After a time, Moira peered across the heads of the crowd and said: 'There's Tom Wall from the Melbourne *Globe*. You wanted to meet him, Erika. Come on, I'll introduce you.' She looked at Bradley. 'Will you excuse us for a moment?'

Turning back to the bar, Bradley asked for a beer. Picking it up, he found himself standing next to Arthur Chadwick, a First Secretary in his forties who had briefed him on his arrival. In appearance and style, Chadwick somewhat resembled a former Air Force officer: shaggy fair hair, a clipped moustache and a good tweed suit. 'Cheers,' he said, and raised his glass. 'How are you settling in, Derek?'

Bradley told him he was settling in well.

'Hit it off all right with the Ambassador?'

'He's been very helpful,' Bradley said.

'Good. Charles is quite a decent chap,' Chadwick said. 'Very capable, with quite a knowledge of Chinese culture. But if he gets a set against someone, he can really shut all the doors. There was a Third Secretary here – he's moved on now – who was a bit of a pain, and got up the Ambassador's nose. The old man cut down his travel budget, and wouldn't let him spend on repairs to his apartment. Even dried up his supply of pencils.' Bradley laughed, and Chadwick extended his whisky glass towards the young Third Secretary. 'Norman, old man, I wonder if I can trouble you for another Scotch. And one for my friend Bradley.'

As the whiskies were being poured, Bradley glanced quickly across the room. Erika and Moira were talking animatedly with a tall, big-bellied man in thick-framed glasses; Erika was laughing at something he'd said, bending a little at the waist. They showed no sign of returning.

Chadwick had followed his gaze. 'I see you've already met Vincent Austin's lady friend – our glamorous press officer. She's certainly pretty, that one. And a great flirt – flirts with everyone. But that's as far as it goes, I think.'

'Really? I hadn't noticed.'

Chadwick glanced at him. 'Just remembered – you're a friend of Vincent Austin's, aren't you? Erika's Vincent's romantic interest, I'm told. Hope I haven't spoken out of turn.'

'Not at all.'

'As a bachelor, you'll be glad of any attractive female company after a while,' Chadwick said. 'You'll miss the fleshpots of Bangkok, I imagine. No denying that Peking is a hardship post – especially if you're single. Because of the way we're segregated by this paranoid regime, there's simply no contact possible with the local people – except for the hired help. We're living in a ghetto. I can tell you, one gets very bloody tired of watching imported videos in the evenings. People even have fights over copies of the Australian newspapers. My wife and I would go mad without our little trips to Hong Kong. Make sure you get some Hong Kong R and R yourself, now and then. It's essential to one's sanity.'

'Thanks for the tip,' Bradley said.

He looked across at Erika, but could not catch her eye. He decided to leave fairly soon.

When he got back to his apartment, he was slightly tipsy. He'd made a circuit of the basement room, talking to other members of the mission, and had been introduced to two Australian businessmen who'd launched into a harangue about the Byzantine labyrinths they'd been forced to enter in order to set up a clothing factory in Shanghai. Deeply bored, Bradley had continued to drink whisky to make the discussion endurable. Finally he'd made his escape.

He moved down the little hallway that led into the living room, took off his jacket, and threw it on a chair. He turned on a standard lamp in a corner of the room, leaving the main lights off, and sat down on the couch, pulling off his tie. The lounge suite here, brought from Australia, was in the same minimalist style as his office furniture: Swedish-style blond wood, upholstered in mustard-coloured fabric. There were scatter rugs on the parquet floor, and the walls were stark white, made less harsh by the soft light of the lamp. His predecessor Harrison had left a single picture on the wall: a Chinese scroll painting of pine trees and distant mountains. He had also left a video machine under the

TV set, and a collection of aged videos. A cassette-player which Bradley had brought from Bangkok, together with his collection of music tapes, stood on the coffee table. Music sustained him. He pushed the play button now, and leaned back, listening to the opening of Rimsky-Korsakov's 'Antar', at low volume. He thought about making a coffee, but didn't.

There was a light knocking. Moving quickly down the hallway, he opened the door to find Erika standing outside. She looked up at him with an expression that startled him, her eyes wide and fixed. It was the expression of someone who'd come with alarming news, or who had been given a violent shock. Or else (he couldn't be sure), it was a look of accusation. In contrast with her dark-blue cocktail frock, her face seemed paler than usual.

'I'm sorry,' she said. She had spoken very fast under her breath, so that he only just heard what she'd said.

'I don't understand,' he said. 'Sorry for what?'

'For deserting you like that. I'd like to explain.'

'You didn't desert me,' he said. 'There's nothing to be sorry for.'

'Yes. Yes there is,' she said.

'Look,' he said, 'why don't you come in? I'll make us a coffee.'

He stood aside, and gestured. For a moment she continued to examine him; then she moved forward, and preceded him in silence down the hall. As they came into the half-light of the living room, there was a swelling of brass and strings: the first movement of 'Antar' was nearing its end, and Gul Nazar had promised Antar the three great joys of life. Erika came to a halt and swung around to look up at Bradley again. She seemed suddenly quite small.

'I didn't intend to leave you high and dry,' she said.

'You didn't,' he said. 'We're there to circulate. I circulated. Think no more about it.'

'But I said I'd be with you there tonight – and you're new to the post. It was rude of Moira not to suggest that you join us. She's very possessive; wants all my attention. And when I finally got away I found you'd gone.' She spoke at normal volume now, but her voice had a flat dryness only slightly less unnatural than her whisper had been. She went on very rapidly, as though reciting something pre-prepared. 'The thing is, I wanted to meet Tom Wall from *The Globe* because he's new, and I hope he'll place more of my press releases there. *The Globe* hasn't been giving us much space, and the Ambassador's fussing about coverage for a trade delegation arriving next week. Canberra's breathing down his neck. It would be a big plus if *The Globe* gave it some play. So buttering up Tom Wall was an opportunity I had to grab. Do you see?'

'Of course. I really do understand,' Bradley said. 'Would you like that coffee?'

Her mouth, still tight, bent in a smile that was like a wince, and she looked at him slyly. 'Have you got anything stronger?'

'Only Scotch.'

'That would be fine. Straight. No ice.'

Side by side on the couch in front of the coffee table, they touched glasses. 'Cheers,' Erika said, and they drank. The light from the lamp in the corner put shadows under her cheekbones, which Bradley noticed now were more prominent than he'd remembered. The whisky, on top of those he'd already had, was nudging him towards drunkenness, and Erika's face had taken on a deceptive quality: a face he knew and yet didn't. There was only a small space between them, and the physical appeal she emanated was so strong that it was difficult for Bradley to keep his expression neutral.

She turned away now and looked at the cassette-player, cocking her head. 'What's that music?'

'Rimsky-Korsakov.'

'I don't think I know this piece.'

'It's about an Arabian prince who goes out into the desert, and meets Gul Nazar, the Queen of Palmyra.'

Erika's expression became solemn, like that of a child expecting to hear a story. 'And what happens?'

'She's a supernatural being, and she grants Antar all the joys of life. They fall in love, but she tells him he must kill himself if he ever feels his love for her is fading.'

'And is that what happens?'

'I'm afraid so.'

She nodded, staring into her lap. In the dimness, she looked very young. 'That's sad,' she said. 'But she was right to make him promise it. You must be fond of music, Brad.'

'One of life's joys. It will help to get me through, here.'

'Poor Brad. Here you are in this standard-issue Embassy apartment, just like mine, with music to get you through the evenings.'

To Bradley's amazement, she reached up and placed her hand on the back of his neck; then she began gently to massage it. 'It must be hard, getting adjusted here,' she said, and leaned forward to smile at him sideways. It was a friendly, sympathetic smile, and made what she was doing seem natural.

Bradley sat very still under this light, soothing hand. It continued to move to and fro, while his thoughts moved with alcoholic ponderousness, and his pulse quickened. The blatancy of her action was both comical and charming, but he knew that he must cut it short – not just out of loyalty to Vincent, but because instinct told him he was being drawn towards a border that was both easy to cross and deeply equivocal. Erika attracted him to a degree he found it difficult to resist; but aside from his wish to be loyal to Vincent, there was something about her that warned him of extremes; of unpredictable possibilities. He sat back, and her hand fell away.

'Can I top up your drink?' he asked.

She continued to smile and to hold her pose, still leaning forward to peer sideways into his face; but now her smile was coloured by an open, artful amusement. 'Better not,' she said, 'or I might get smashed. I've had rather a lot, tonight. That's what you're thinking, isn't it? That I've had rather a lot.'

'It doesn't show.'

'You're so polite. I'm bloody smashed, and you know it. Do you want me to go?'

'Not if you want to stay.'

She laughed. 'You're a very careful man, Brad, aren't you?'

'Part of the stock in trade. And I'm thinking of your friendship with Vincent.'

She frowned. 'That's all it is,' she said. 'A very close friendship. Nothing more.'

Having said this she fell silent, head bent, swirling the drink in her glass as though something had begun to preoccupy her: something that had removed her from the present situation. Her moods were certainly mercurial, Bradley thought; they changed as you watched. And he began to suspect that there was another personality here, inside that of the self-possessed young woman she usually seemed to be: one of those personalities somehow permanently linked to very early youth. It caused him to remember again the encounter he'd had with her and Vincent in student days, in front of the Post Office in Hobart, when they'd looked at him from inside that bubble of theirs: that territory all their own.

Suddenly she looked up again, seeming to read his thoughts. Her gaze held his, fixed and oddly imploring. She said nothing, scanning his face, and the full lower lip which sometimes appeared truculent was now both inviting and tantalising. He took both her shoulders in his hands.

As they kissed, and her mouth opened under his, he felt her whole body turn and arch to meet him, with a consent which had a hint of violence in it. Even in this, there was a sort of warning; but Bradley no longer cared.

In the middle of the night he woke, and found himself lapped by a zone of strangeness. There was only a faint light through the bedroom window, and he could just make out the outline of Erika's body under the sheet that covered them both. A sheaf of her hair lay across the pillow, and her face, half-turned towards him, was a pallid oval, its features undefined, its eyes closed and blind. He could detect no sign of breathing: her sleep resembled its sombre counterpart. The more he looked at her, the more she became a chimera: a woman he didn't recognise.

Locked in lovemaking, she had swung between two poles: affectionate submission, and a sexual aggression that had curved into abandon, ending in a descent into wild, abject abasement. This had been an amatory style quite unlike anything Bradley had experienced before, thrilling his nerves and leaving him shaken. Certainly it wasn't what he'd anticipated, since nothing in Erika's daytime self had hinted at it. Despite her mood-swings, the essential impression she gave was of innate coolness, backed by a brittle self-discipline. The way in which Vincent had spoken of her long ago had reinforced this notion in Bradley's mind, and he'd prepared himself for a lapse into coldness; perhaps even frigid withdrawal. But the reverse had been the case.

They had talked, during the night. Propping herself on one elbow, she had peered into his face through the dark with a fervent, challenging intensity: an intensity which was partly diluted by a hint of humour in her voice, and in the corners of her eyes. But she was full of such contradictions.

'I was attracted to you from the beginning.'

'What beginning?'

'When we first met in Hobart. You remember? You were an untidy student, and I was a cub reporter. I could see why Vincent doted on you. He'd talked about you so much I felt I knew you. I liked your looks: you were handsome without being vain. A handsome, happy boy. And you looked serene: you still do. I like a man who's serene; you know he'll never fuss, and will keep things on an even keel. I hoped we'd meet again — but it didn't happen.'

'Well, now it's happened. I thought you were beautiful then. You're much more beautiful now.'

'Thirty-one next month. I won't be pretty much longer. We're the same age, did you know? I found that out from Vincent.'

'Vincent. What are you going to do about him? What am I going to do about him?'

'What do you mean?'

'He's my friend. And we've both been disloyal to him, haven't we?'
'Have we?'
'Come on: he's in love with you. So what are you and I doing?'

For a few moments more, she had continued to stare at him. Then she had rolled away onto her pillow, lying on her back and staring upwards in silence. The night was warm; she had thrown the sheet off them both and lay naked, one slim leg bent, the other outstretched. The movement had caused her small, firm breasts to tremble slightly; in the dark, the areolas of the nipples had looked black. Finally she had spoken again, in the flat, almost toneless voice she seemed to use when she was dealing with something that troubled her, or something she thought serious.

'You've got it all wrong. Vincent and I aren't lovers. I thought you knew that, Brad. Vincent is like a monk: he doesn't get involved with women. I'm the only woman he cares about, and he cares about me as a friend. I got a posting here after a lot of trouble in my life, and I was very glad when he arrived the following year. He and I will always be close. But not in the way you think.'

She moved again then, throwing herself on top of him to nuzzle his neck, and her tone changed to one of light-hearted amorousness.

'I'm terribly attracted to you. I knew this would happen.'
'I didn't. Why are we attracted to each other, do you think?'
She had chuckled, her face still buried in his neck.
'It's the pheromones.'
'The what?'
'Something I read about. Human beings secrete some sort of chemical that gives off a scent. If a man and a woman have the right pheromones, they fall for each other.'
'Is that what's happened with us?'
'Don't you know?'
'I suppose I do. What are we going to do about Vincent? He'll be back on Sunday.'
'That depends.'

'On what?'
'On whether you're serious about me.'
Startled, Bradley had fallen silent for a moment. He had not
anticipated a request for seriousness – if that was what this was –
and his response was guarded.
'Would you want me to be serious?'
She was still lying on top of him; his hands moved over her
back and firm buttocks. She had raised her head so that she could
bring his face into focus, and her deep, low voice had held a
baffling blend of mischief and gravity.
'What do you *think, mister?'*
They stared at each other; again he had made no answer, but
had drawn her head down and kissed her. Then they had ceased
to talk.

When he woke again, she was gone, the sheet flung back.
Morning light was coming between the curtains of the bedroom
window; there were footsteps in the corridor outside, and the
radio alarm clock on his bedside table read 6.45. Staring at it, he
found himself looking at an unfamiliar sheet of paper lying next
to it. He picked it up, blinking at the neat, pleasing handwriting.

*Maybe it was the pheromones. Maybe it was a mistake. If it was,
we can walk away now, and no hard feelings.*

E.

Sitting on the edge of the bed, Bradley re-read this message a
number of times, as though working to crack a code. It was
Saturday today, and neither of them had commitments; they
could have spent the day together. So why had she left? His heart
beating unevenly, he tried to decide whether she wanted to see
him again or not – and was disconcerted to find that he dreaded
to discover that she didn't.
Then he remembered that he'd not really answered her
question: he had not told her that he was serious. Was this why

she'd crept away without waking him? But that was ridiculous, he thought: they barely knew each other. He tried to be amused, and told himself to be rational: to step back. But he found to his dismay that he could not step back. In all of his involvements with women in the past, Bradley had been able to do so, preserving what he thought of as emotional balance – which meant that if necessary he could 'walk away', as Erika had put it. But he had not been involved before with a woman of Erika's beauty: a beauty that was followed everywhere by glances of furtive yearning, and which seemed to secrete the mystery of perfection. Having been sought out by such a woman resembled the arrival of great good fortune; one did not have the option of stepping back, Bradley decided.

Addiction had already begun. Surrendering to it, he had a quick, heady sense of recklessness.

But some minutes later, standing under the shower, he began to grow sober again. His reflections had been absurd, he decided; his detachment would be maintained. Nevertheless, he came to a decision which was very like succumbing to temptation. Her apartment was on the floor below, and he knew its number; he'd go down there as soon as he'd dressed, in the hope that she was in, and discover why she'd left.

When he knocked on her door, she opened it almost instantly, wearing a pale-green dressing-gown of Chinese silk, her hair damp from the shower. She stared at him solemnly, as though he were a stranger.

'I came down to wish you good morning,' he said.

She made no answer, but simply opened the door wider, her face blank. As soon as he was in the narrow hallway, she shut the door and threw her arms around his neck, her lips against his ear.

'Good morning. I'm so glad you came.'

They stood holding each other, and Bradley experienced a mindless surge of gladness. Her grip was tight; almost urgent. She felt very slight, through the gown. 'But why did you leave?' he asked.

She leaned away a little in his arms, and looked at him. 'I needed to freshen up,' she said. She ducked her head; then looked up again. 'No: that was a lie,' she said. 'I wanted to see if you'd come to me.'

'You wanted to see if I was serious.'

'Yes. That's why.'

'I'm serious.'

She scrutinised his face, as though looking for clues to his integrity. Then she smiled and nodded, and kissed him on the mouth.

'Good. That makes two of us,' she said.

'So what now?' Bradley asked. His tone was light. His premonition had been accurate, it seemed: everything had changed.

'What now?' Her eyes held their joking light. 'Now I'll make us breakfast,' she said.

4

AT SIX O'CLOCK the following evening, Vincent knocked on Bradley's door.

'What ho! Here I am back!' he said. Framed in the doorway like a large, flapping bird, he reached out and pumped Bradley's hand, beaming as though he'd been gone for a month. 'At last we can catch up on things,' he said. 'Come down to my apartment in an hour. We'll put on the nosebags and share a Hunter River red. How does that sound, old chap?'

Vincent had decorated his apartment himself, and had bought some Chinese furniture and curios, so that it had far more individuality than Bradley's, and was almost cosy. A large, handsome silk rug hung on the wall of the room where they ate: it was patterned in swirls of blue and white. When Bradley admired it, Vincent surveyed it with complacent pride. 'A traditional Chinese design,' he said. 'The Cloud Pattern. Superb. I'll be taking it home with me.'

Their dinner was prepared by Mr Wang, one of the Embassy's cooks. He also cooked Bradley's evening meals; neither he nor Vincent had any enthusiasm for cooking for themselves. During the meal, while Wang came and went from the adjoining kitchen, they were somewhat constrained. He was a smiling, middle-aged, broad-faced northerner who had an engaging friendliness; but they had to assume he would be compelled to report anything in their conversation of political interest.

When he'd gone, and they were sitting in armchairs over coffee,

Vincent leaned forward with an expression Bradley knew well: he was about to confide something.

'I have a social engagement tomorrow night that might interest you,' he said. 'I hope you can accompany me, Derek. I'm visiting Professor Liu Meng and his wife Dorothy, at their home. I spoke about him to you, didn't I? He's a remarkable person: a scholar who truly loves the classical poets; an expert on the T'ang; a survivor from the old Chinese gentry. His father was a mandarin, and sent him to England before the War. He's an Oxford graduate. Met his wife there when they were both students.'

'They must be quite old,' Bradley said.

'In their seventies,' Vincent said. 'After they graduated, they got married, and eventually came back to China in the period of the Nationalist Government at Nanking. Little did they know what lay in store. But they've cast in their lot with the Communists and have never left. They both love China. Meng is a true patriot.'

'His wife's English? You told me once they were sent to a labour camp in the 1960s. She can't have been young, even then. How did she survive it?'

'She survived it, and so did he. They're both very tough people. Tougher than we'll ever be, old chap. Their backgrounds make them suspect, of course, but they're Communist Party members nevertheless – and Liu Meng has an international reputation as one of China's most distinguished scholars, who's published English translations of Tu Fu and Po Chü-I. So the Party bosses really don't like to touch him now – and of course he toes the Party line in public. He and Dorothy look forward to meeting you. I've become quite close with them – and I told them you're the friend of my youth, and someone they must meet.' He smiled, nursing his coffee cup and saucer, his eyes narrowing, head cocked on one side in a way that was both droll and affectionate, reminding Bradley of the old days in the sunroom at Bay Road.

'I'll look forward to it,' he said.

'Good. Now tell me: were you able to entertain yourself in my absence? I hope you aren't suffering from Peking boredom yet.'

'Not at all,' Bradley said. 'Erika's been kind to me. She showed me about the city, yesterday.'

Vincent's smile remained unchanged; but his gaze, resting on Bradley's face, seemed to become a little more fixed. 'I'm very pleased to hear that,' he said. 'I was hoping that you two would get on well. I'm assuming you *did* get on well?'

'Yes. I like her very much. I hope you don't mind our going out together?'

'Not at all, old chap. Why should I mind?'

They were both sitting very still now, holding their coffee cups and saucers as though frozen into position. Instead of answering Vincent's question, Bradley put one of his own.

'I used to assume you were in love with her, Vin. You say it's just a friendship now, but I've been wondering what that really means.'

Vincent looked quickly aside, as though searching for something. Then, frowning a little, he leaned forward and put his cup and saucer on the coffee table. Finally he looked up at Bradley again.

'I'm not sure that I ever used the cliché "in love" concerning my relationship with Erika,' he said. 'It's not a term I'd employ: it's not a phrase that's adequate to describe our association.'

There was an awkward pause. Finally Bradley said: 'I don't think I really understand.'

Vincent ran his hand through his thick brown mane, which was glossy as always with hair cream. 'No,' he said, 'of course you don't, since I've never spoken of it to you. Let me put it this way: ever since we were children, Erika and I have had so much in common we might easily be brother and sister. That's still the case.' He sat up straight, and spoke with great emphasis. 'The bond will always be there, do you see?'

'If you say so. Not that it's really my business.'

Vincent smiled. 'But of course it is,' he said. 'Because you and she have fallen in love with each other.'

Bradley laughed: a laugh expressing embarrassment rather than amusement. 'Come on, Vin – that's a bit premature,' he said.

Yet as he spoke, he realised that it was true. He was not just involved in a physical affair with Erika; he was already in love with her, in the sense that she was hardly ever out of his mind, that he was missing her even at this moment, and that the whole external world was leached of its meaning when she wasn't present. He had recognised this quite suddenly, as though Vincent's words had forced him to confront it, and it caused him a vague alarm. He'd not been affected in this way since adolescence, and he suspected already that it would greatly complicate his life, and might even bring him grief. And yet he didn't care. Instead, he now experienced a surge of that fatuous and reckless joy which accompanies the early stages of infatuation, making him want to openly admit that what Vincent had said was true – thus having an excuse to talk about Erika further, which was all that he really wanted to do. But he retained his self-possession and sat silent, watching Vincent's face.

'It's not premature,' Vincent said. 'I happen to know how attracted Erika is to you. She's already spoken to me, in fact. If you're not in love with her yet, Derek, you will be. I only hope you won't be sorry. And what you have to realise is this: that any relationship with Erika is also a relationship with me.'

Bradley stared at him. This remark was so bizarre that he could find no way of answering it, and didn't attempt to do so.

Vincent sat back, his hands folded on his chest. When he spoke again, his voice was softer than usual, and had taken on an odd, indulgent tone. 'Dear old Brad. I wonder whether you remember our talks of undergraduate days? If you do, you'll remember that I'm very old-fashioned in my philosophical ideas: that I remain a disciple of Plato. I believe in those Platonic Forms that modern metaphysicians think they've proved invalid. What fuckwits they are! No philosopher has ever succeeded in dismissing the Forms! And for me, they still exist: eternal, supreme, actual, yet outside the material world. The Platonic archetypes are true: particularly the archetype of Beauty.' Seeing Bradley's expression, he held up his hand. 'Bear with me, Brad. This is relevant to the question you've asked. You remember Plato's concept of Eros? That the Good, the True and the Beautiful are one? When we admire a beautiful object, or a beautiful human being, we're experiencing Beauty itself, as though seen through smoke, or mist. The beloved is Beauty's instrument – and that's why we give ourselves to her.' He paused, his bony, gesticulating hands upheld; then he dropped them to his chest again, and folded them there. 'There are some particular women who are truly incarnations of Beauty,' he said. 'In them, consciously or unconsciously, we see Aphrodite manifest. That's why they fascinate people. For me, Erika is one of those women.' He had begun to twist his interlaced fingers together, his gaze never leaving Bradley's face. 'But all this doesn't mean that I'm in love with her,' he said. 'Not in the usual banal sense of that term. So why should I mind if you and she – my two most treasured friends – find that they love each other? It's possible you may be intended for each other – and if that's so, I'm truly glad of it.' Sitting back, he smiled his widest smile, his eyes narrowing with a sort of affectionate cunning behind their glasses.

Bradley stared at him, gratified yet embarrassed, trying to summon up a suitable reply. Before he could do so, Vincent stood up, and his tone became brisk and reassuring. 'It's late, old chap. I'll let you get to bed. Remember: tomorrow evening, we go to Professor Liu.'

5

A TAXI WITH a silent, hunched driver carried them towards the suburbs. The night was dark, with an overcast sky, the street lighting faint and ghostly. When they arrived at the building where Professor Liu's apartment was, Bradley had no notion as to what part of the city they were in. Somewhere in the west, Vincent had said. Each of them carried a bottle from their hoard of duty-free Scotch, which Vincent said Liu Meng and his wife both doted on, and which was largely unobtainable in the People's Republic.

They got out; Vincent paid the driver, and Bradley looked about him in sober surprise. They'd been brought to what appeared to be a wasteland, or a place that had recently been sacked: a deserted, silent district where a gritty wind was blowing, and whose dominant colour was the silver-grey of mould. The taxi's red tail-lights, racing off into the dark, were leaving them on a road which was empty except for a group of staring boys, a scavenging dog, and a man in a worn cotton jacket of the same dispiriting grey as everything else here, pedalling by on a bicycle. There were no other cars in sight, and Bradley had a sense of being marooned. Rows of apartment buildings of two and three storeys stood against the sky, Victorian in their grimness. Vegetable smells hung in the air.

This was Bradley's first visit to a private home in Peking, and he'd not known what to expect; but he'd not anticipated that a professor at Peking University would be living in a district like this. He said so, and Vincent looked at him knowingly.

'Not exactly charming, is it? But I can assure you, Brad, that the Lius are living in comparative luxury, by Peking standards. They even have a telephone, which puts then in a very favoured category indeed.' He broke off, waving and smiling. 'There's Liu Meng waiting for us now,' he said.

A white-haired figure stood in front of an arched entry to one of the apartment blocks, waving back at Vincent: an old man wearing a single-breasted, charcoal-grey jacket with patch pockets, buttoned to the throat, of the type common among Party cadres. They hurried across the road towards him, clutching their bottles, and Vincent began to speak even before they reached him, his voice eager and rattling.

'Meng! How kind of you to wait for us! Here's my friend Derek Bradley to meet you!'

He performed introductions, and Liu Meng held out his hand to Bradley.

'I am so pleased to meet you, Derek. May I call you Derek? You must call me Meng.'

Oxford had left its mark: he had the faintly drawling delivery of the old English upper class, with only a hint of Chinese accent. He was a thin, stooped old man, and his white hair was sparse and wispy, but his grip was surprisingly strong, and his gaze, meeting Bradley's, was keen and curious. His dark almond eyes had heavy lids, but they shone with humorous alertness. He had a long face, with fine features, the skin a pale parchment colour. The face of a mandarin, Bradley thought.

Liu Meng looked at the bottles of whisky, and smiled slyly at Vincent. 'I see you have brought me my favourite medicine. That is really very kind of you, my dear. Come along, then: Dorothy is looking forward to seeing you.'

Shuffling, he led them through the archway into a gloomy, cobbled yard where building materials lay about, and on into a foyer smelling of drains, its high walls coated with layers of grime. A group of young men in the universal blue cottons stood looking at them here, and murmuring. One laughed; but Liu Meng ignored them and shuffled on. 'This way, this way.' Vincent and Derek followed him now down a dark, arched passageway, into deeper and deeper gloom; it was as though he led them into a catacomb. Finally, turning a bend in the corridor, the old man brought them to a tall, heavy door of dark-stained wood. Opening it, he smiled at them with an almost wistful encouragement, and gestured.

'Please,' he said. 'Do come in.'

As they crowded inside, Bradley had the impression of going back in time. They were now in the small, threadbare, high-ceilinged sitting room of an indigent Oxford scholar from fifty years ago: sombre and feebly lit, like the desolate streets outside, with a dim Persian carpet, worn leather chairs and a small leather sofa, and a library of books filling three of the walls to the ceiling – most of them, so far as Bradley could see, in English. A round, polished table stood in the centre, on which stood a Thermos flask, lidded Chinese mugs, plates, and a large dish of little cakes. An antique-looking, leather-topped desk with a swivel chair was set against the far wall; on it sat the black, important telephone. Through a half-open door next to the desk, a room was visible which appeared to do duty as a dining room and bedroom: a dining table and chairs could be seen, and beyond that a double bed with a pale-blue coverlet, on which a white kitten lay asleep. A clothes line was strung across this room, with a number of shirts and blouses hanging from it, and Bradley guessed that some sort of kitchen would be the only other room the apartment had. The books gave the sitting room a civilized air, but the shabbiness of the apartment shocked him, and he felt a stab of pity. Here was the kind of courageous, self-respecting poverty that had almost vanished in the West; yet this was the home of one of the most eminent scholars in China.

There were two people here: a young Chinese man, peering at them from one of the armchairs, and an elderly, white-haired Englishwoman in a long, sky-blue cardigan, frilled blouse and tweed skirt, standing in the middle of the room. Bradley had the impression that she'd been in this position for some time, watching the door. Her expression was cautious; almost challenging. But now she came towards them, smiling, and her face was transformed. Despite her age, Dorothy Liu was an attractive woman. Thick, waving white hair framed her face like two outspread wings, and her skin had an almost golden tinge. As she advanced, stooped a little, looking up at them from under her brows, her eyes searched the faces of her visitors. They were a brilliant sapphire blue, and almost almond-shaped; together with her golden skin, they made her look faintly Chinese.

'Vincent! How nice to see you,' she said, and stretched out her hand to him. Her accent, like her husband's, was from the pre-World War Two British upper class; but her delivery was sharper: authoritative and peremptory. 'Now introduce your Australian colleague,' she told Vincent, and looked at Bradley.

But Liu Meng intervened. 'My dear, this is Derek Bradley – another young diplomat,' he said. 'And now I must introduce our friend Mr Yang Wenfu.'

While they had been speaking, the young man had got up from his chair to stand at the edge of their circle, looking from one to the other. His gaze seemed to Bradley to be intensely curious. He had thick, back-swept hair, and wore a crisp white shirt and dark trousers.

'Yang Wenfu is one of my graduates,' Professor Liu said. 'He is working as an English translator with our Public Security Bureau. He has also translated a number of English novels into Chinese.'

Yang murmured greetings in English in a low voice, shaking hands with Bradley and Vincent in turn, his eyes examining them with an analytical interest from which warmth seemed to be absent. 'Professor Liu has spoken about you,' he said to Vincent. 'He says you have a great knowledge of our ancient poets.'

'An exaggeration,' Vincent said. 'Professor Liu is too kind. My knowledge is mainly restricted to English translations, since my Mandarin is pretty basic. But it's true I'm devoted to the T'ang poets – Tu Fu, Li Po and Po Chü-I in particular.'

'That is unusual,' Yang said. 'Few Westerners read them, I believe.'

'And fewer Chinese,' Vincent said briskly. 'Most of them these days have not even heard of your classical poets, I find. One of the less happy effects of the reign of the Gang of Four.'

Yang's eyes widened a little, and he looked at Vincent in silence.

'Come, everybody,' Liu said, and made a languid gesture at the room. 'Let us not stand about. Do make yourselves comfortable.'

'Yes, everybody please sit down,' Dorothy said. Her smile had become a little fixed, Bradley thought, as her eyes went from Yang to Vincent. 'We have tea and cakes,' she said, and moved across to the table. She glanced at Bradley. 'Probably more basic than anything you're used to, Derek.'

'Not at all,' Bradley said. 'Your cakes look very inviting.'

'How polite you are. They're moon cakes,' Dorothy said, and began to distribute them on to individual plates. 'They're eaten at the time of the mid-autumn festival, when our family reunions take place. But Meng and I are very fond of them, and eat them all the time – perhaps because we're in the autumn of our lives.' She handed the plates about, beginning with Bradley, who had sat down in one of the deep leather chairs, then moving across to Vincent and Yang, who sat side by side on the sofa, knees together, looking like men on a bus. Vincent bit into his cake and chewed. 'Delicious, Dorothy,' he said. 'Your moon cakes are always first-rate.'

'I'd like to say they're mine,' Dorothy said. 'But they're made by our *ayi*: she's a far better cook than I am.'

Going back to the table, she began spooning tea leaves from a canister into the mugs. She picked up the Thermos of hot water, and looked about the room. 'You'll all take tea, I hope?'

'Perhaps not, my dear,' Liu called. He had gone across to a small occasional table by the desk, where a set of whisky glasses stood. 'I prefer Scottish tea. Vincent and Derek have brought Johnnie Walker Black Label, and I propose to open it immediately.'

He looked across at Vincent with a conspiratorial air, and Vincent grinned. 'Excellent idea, Meng.'

But Dorothy Liu frowned. 'First we should have some tea, Meng, don't you think?'

'*I* will not, my dear.' Liu uncapped one of the bottles and began to pour the whisky into a glass.

Raising her brows with a resigned expression, Dorothy looked at the others. 'Will anyone else have tea with me?' All three murmured that they would, and she began to pour hot water into the mugs, afterwards putting on their lids to allow the tea to draw. Then she passed them to Bradley, Vincent and Yang, and sat down with her own tea in one of the leather chairs.

Liu came across and sat on a straight-backed chair beside her, his smile mischievous, his hooded eyes playful. 'Come: you must all drink a toast with me in *tea*,' he said, and raised his glass of whisky.

Dorothy cast up her eyes; but she lifted her mug, and the others followed suit.

'Good health,' Liu said. 'You are all very welcome.' He drank off some of the whisky and gave a sigh of satisfaction, smiling and nodding at Vincent and Bradley in turn. 'This excellent Scotch makes you doubly welcome,' he said. 'A great luxury for us, as you know. Dorothy loves it as much as I do, but she makes herself wait: a pleasure postponed is more intense, isn't that so, my dear?'

Vincent had removed the lid from his mug, and leaned forward to place it on the table. He sipped the hot tea gingerly, and then turned to Yang. 'So tell me, Mr Yang, which works in English have you translated?'

'Both were American. John Steinbeck's *The Grapes of Wrath*, and Ernest Hemingway's *For Whom the Bell Tolls*.'

'Ah yes,' Vincent said. He was wearing what Bradley thought of as his clergyman's smile: finicking, and accompanied by a sort of dainty blinking. He was also using his clergyman's voice: a sonorous, slightly chanting delivery he'd used in their youth for humorous effect – not so exaggerated now as to be openly frivolous, but recognisable to Bradley nevertheless. 'Both novels would be approved of in China, I'm sure,' Vincent said. 'Their political positions are beyond reproach, I imagine.'

Yang looked sideways at Vincent with an uncertain expression, as though trying to decide in what way this was meant. 'These novels are greatly admired,' he said. 'Steinbeck in particular. He tells us much about the sufferings of the poor in America.'

'Of course, of course. Even though the Depression ended fifty years ago. But tell me, Mr Yang: have you perhaps thought of translating other American writers of that period? William Faulkner, perhaps – or Scott Fitzgerald?'

'Faulkner we find too difficult: it is unclear what his view of life is. It may be a reactionary one, perhaps. Fitzgerald does not seem worthwhile. He is just a social butterfly, with no consciousness of important issues.'

Professor Liu had been watching Yang and Vincent with his weary-looking, heavy-lidded eyes. Now he drawled suddenly: 'Fitzgerald does not sufficiently reflect the people's struggle, you see, Vincent. He only deals with the struggles of individuals.' His smile remained playful and pleasant, but his tone was languidly ironical. Yang glanced at him quickly, with what looked like a flash of suspicion.

'Poor butterfly,' Vincent said lightly. 'One hasn't heard that expression for a long time. Poor old Scott.' And he and Liu exchanged looks that held a humorous complicity.

Remembering what Erika had told him about the nature of Vincent's interest in the professor, this look of complicity caused Bradley to begin to grow uneasy. He assumed that Mr Yang was an orthodox Marxist, and a faithful son of the Party; if this was so, it seemed unwise for Professor Liu to be speaking as he was doing. On the other hand, perhaps Yang was not as orthodox as he seemed, and was someone Liu trusted: it was almost impossible to judge such things here. He glanced at Dorothy; her face was blank, her eyes fixed on her husband.

Vincent now turned towards Yang, dropping his mock clergyman's tone. 'But suppose I were to tell you, Mr Yang, that many people in the West today see Fitzgerald as one of the great writers of the century – a far greater writer than Hemingway, who deals in spurious emotion and gross sentimentality? Suppose I were to say to you that Hemingway rings false, and Fitzgerald rings true? And that *The Great Gatsby* survives as a masterpiece, while *For Whom the Bell Tolls* is far less likely to do so? What would you think of that?'

Yang stared at him, his lips parted. 'I would find that hard to believe, Mr Austin,' he said. 'I would have to wonder if you are a little bit reactionary, perhaps, in your literary opinions.' He smiled, apparently intending to take the edge off what he had said; but the smile was a grimace, betraying barely suppressed hostility, and he leaned away from Vincent as though their close physical proximity began to make him uncomfortable.

'Come, Wenfu,' Liu murmured. 'This is not a term you should apply to our guest.'

'I speak only of his opinions – not of him,' Yang said. But he looked in no way abashed.

'Reactionary,' Vincent said, in a musing tone. 'Reactionary.' He tasted the word, looking at Yang. 'I'm not offended, Mr Yang, I assure you, since this is a word that has no meaning for me. It's a jargon word, and such words have no real power. But let me try to explain. In the view of those Westerners who are not Marxists, propaganda is not literature, you see. Literature is finally about beauty. Such an old-fashioned word! But no other will do. When we come to the final paragraph of *Gatsby*, for instance, beauty is what we find.' He raised his long hands, the fingers crooked like claws, and Yang stared at them uncertainly, as though wondering what he would do next. 'It rises,' Vincent said, lifting his hands slowly to the level of his face. 'Rises! And suddenly we are in the presence of beauty, of poetry, and of the great dream of life.'

'"So we beat on, boats against the current, borne back ceaselessly into the past."' Liu Meng, in his soft drawl, had recited the novel's last line. Now he gently clapped his hands. 'Well said, Vincent. Without beauty, writing is merely dross.' He looked at Yang. 'That is why we must value our ancient Chinese poets. All of them celebrate beauty.'

'They do indeed,' Vincent said. 'When Derek and I were students, it was their beauty that captivated us. Derek's favourite was Po Chü-I. Mine was Tu Fu.'

'Ah yes,' Liu said. 'Of all poets, our greatest.'

'One good quotation deserves another,' Vincent said. Looking across at Liu with a small, affectionate smile, head tilted back, he half-closed his eyes and recited:

'By Yangtse and Han the mountains pile their barriers,
A cloud in the wind, at the corner of the world.
Year in, year out, there's no familiar thing,
And stop after stop is the end of my road.'

Nodding, Liu smiled back, his heavy lids lowered so that his eyes were just visible. 'Very fine,' he said, and there was no irony in his voice now; instead it held deep pleasure, and a note of yearning. 'The A.C. Graham translation, is it not?' When Vincent nodded, he went on: 'There are no better translations in English. Professor Graham is a remarkable scholar, with a great poetic gift. His feeling for the pathos of the late T'ang is profound.' He looked politely at Yang. 'I am not sure whether you recognise the poem from which Vincent has recited, Wenfu. It is one of Tu Fu's last works, written in exile and sadness, when he was forced to flee to K'uei-chou, on the Yangtse. His last works coincide with the decline of the dynasty: the twilight of the T'ang.'

'You sound as though you regret the fall of this dynasty, Professor Liu.' Yang's upper lip was faintly curled, and he seemed almost to sneer. 'But what is there to regret? We are speaking of a feudal empire in which a small, privileged aristocracy ruled over the starving and suffering masses. And Tu Fu was one of that privileged class, and the servant of those rulers, I think.'

Dorothy Liu said sharply: 'My husband was speaking of poetry. Not of feudal rule.' Her eyes were fixed on Yang, and their arresting blue had taken on a gleam that looked like anger. But they contained something else besides anger, Bradley thought: not fear, perhaps, but a concern that was fear's first stage.

Yang's steady stare was almost insolent. 'Of course,' he said. 'I understand this.' He turned back to Liu. 'But if Tu Fu's poem is one of regret for the decadent Empire, what is the value of the poem? This I don't understand.'

Professor Liu's face had become expressionless, but its lines seemed to have deepened. He appeared to consider his words before he answered; when he did, his voice was soft. 'Since the fall of the Gang of Four, the Party has declared that we are all permitted to respond to writing that expresses the hopes and joys and sufferings of individuals – not just didactic works that deal only with the problems of society. You are aware of this, Yang Wenfu?'

'I am aware.'

'Very well. Tu Fu's last poems are like that. They express his sadness in exile, as he nears the end of his life. They also express his wise resignation, as he realises that his world is being swept away. And so we experience these emotions ourselves – emotions that many have felt, in many different ages and places, and for different reasons. That is why these poems are great, and why our two friends have understood them, on the other side of the world. That is a wonderful thing, surely.'

But Yang merely stared, and made no reply. He seemed to sulk.

If Liu registered this rudeness, he gave no sign. His face remained bland, and he added: 'In many of Tu Fu's poems, too, you will find pity for those who die in war, and indignation that villages are laid waste as a cost of expanding the Empire. No doubt you would approve of those sentiments.'

'No doubt,' Yang said. 'But most of those old poems of the T'ang, on which you spend so much study, are written merely to paint pretty scenes, or to discuss private emotions. And because of this, I think, they are not worth a penny.'

Professor Liu blinked; it was as though the young man had struck him, but he made no other sign. Tension entered the room, adding itself to the weak, gloomy light. Then Vincent spoke, leaning forward on the couch to peer sideways into Yang's face, and employing his clergyman's smile.

'But good poems aren't written for pennies,' he said. 'Very few poets are capitalists, Mr Yang.'

Yang refused to look at him, staring instead across the room towards Liu and Dorothy. Dorothy looked at nothing, her mouth set, her face grim.

'The pursuit of beauty is a difficult one,' Vincent went on, 'as most of us know. And the only rewards are responses from people of spirit and imagination. So perhaps we shouldn't enquire as to a poem's monetary worth. It's either worth nothing, or it's priceless. Wouldn't you agree, Mr Yang?'

Yang merely shrugged. There could be no mistaking his hostility now, and a silence fell.

Professor Liu turned to Bradley, his expression as bland as ever. 'Vincent says that you prefer Po Chü-I to Tu Fu, Derek. That is interesting. On what do you base this preference?'

'Perhaps because the detail in Po Chü-I's work seems more vivid,' Bradley said. 'Tu Fu gives us perfect small moments, but Po gives us a whole canvas. And there's so much that's personal and good-hearted in his poems, isn't there? His feeling for old friends, such as Li Chien. His sadness over the lost slave girl. The way he loves his flowers and bamboos. His pity for the misery of the peasants, toiling in the fields while he lives in comfort. Mr Yang might approve of that side of Po Chü-I.'

He glanced across at Yang, who remained silent and expressionless. But Liu looked delighted, and turned to Dorothy. 'You see, my dear? An Australian who has truly read Po Chü-I! Derek is familiar with our old poets, just as Vincent is!'

He reached across to Bradley, and took his hand. He held it for many moments, peering with great warmth into Derek's face. He was clearly moved to an unusual degree, and for a moment

Bradley was startled and mystified by this open display of emotion – a display that was fuelled, perhaps, by the benign fumes of the whisky. But then, looking into the old man's shrewd, infinitely cautious eyes, he had a sudden surge of understanding. For years, in this watchful totalitarian state, with its doctrine of literature as an ideological tool, with its terrible penalties for heresy, and its rejection of ancient China's traditions, a scholar like Liu from the old gentry class would have been deeply suspect; even more so, presumably, when his chief scholarly interest was in the poetry of China's golden age. Then, when the madness of the Gang of Four had taken hold, this enthusiasm had become an actual offence, causing Liu Meng to be degraded, imprisoned, and set to labour on a commune. And even now, with the fanaticism of the Gang of Four rejected, and with lip-service being paid to the country's heritage, Liu would have few fellow spirits. A policy of increased intellectual freedom had been declared, but in practice it was a very limited freedom indeed, and the pitfalls of heresy against Marxist doctrine were almost as numerous as ever. People like Mr Yang remained the chosen ones of the Party, their disapproval of Professor Liu's enthusiasms more veiled and restrained than before, but probably as real as ever, ready to appear at any time in the form of accusations of bourgeois decadence – even of disloyalty to the state. How lonely it must be, Bradley thought, to be a scholar from the old culture here, and a truly cultivated man! How few people would Liu ever meet who were lovers of the T'ang poets! He understood now why the old man had held his hand: it touched him, and he hoped that Liu Meng saw that it touched him.

'There is often a note of regret, in Po Chü-I,' Liu said now. 'I'm sure you have noticed this, Derek. That is why he's been called an autumn poet – whereas Tu Fu is a summer poet. Po Chü-I has an autumnal spirit: soothing and quiet and melodious, but always with melancholy underneath, knowing that things will soon die. Is that what appeals to you, Derek? Is yours also an autumn spirit?'

'I think it must be,' Bradley said. 'I like tranquillity and wist-fulness, and I always like sad songs. I'm a blues man.'

'Blues?' Liu looked puzzled for a moment; then he laughed. 'Ah yes, the blues. Dorothy and I used to listen to blues records at Oxford, when we were young.' He drank off the last of his whisky. 'I, on the other hand, am a lover of spring,' he said. 'Even though I'm old, I love the mad spirit of everything bursting into life. I like a little madness.'

'You like too much of it,' Dorothy said.

Her face remained set. From the couch, Yang watched them in silence, while Vincent smiled benignly.

'Perhaps I do,' Liu said. 'But one cannot help one's nature. So Li Po is my poet – mad, drunken Li Po, the poet of spring and joy – who died when he tried to embrace the moon's reflection in the river, and fell in and was drowned. No doubt he was sozzled at the time.' He chuckled, and stood up. 'This reminds me – it is surely time for you all to take a whisky with me.'

By eleven o'clock, the first of the two bottles of Scotch had been emptied, and Liu had opened the second. Mr Yang had left some time ago, after drinking only one glass; he had made a polite farewell speech to the Lius, thanking them for their hospitality, but there had been no warmth in his face. As soon as he'd gone, the conversation became easier; only Dorothy remained subdued.

Like his cherished Li Po, Liu Meng proved to be an enthusiastic drinker. To Bradley's surprise, Dorothy was just as dedicated, matching her husband glass for glass. They both drank their whisky neat, while Vincent and Bradley added water from a jug on the table – neither of them attempting to match the pace set by the old couple. Except for a slight slurring in his speech, and occasional boisterous laughter, Liu seemed unaffected; but Dorothy's eyelids drooped a little, and she sometimes swayed in her chair.

'Do you ever return to England?' Bradley asked her.

She looked at him, and the blue of her eyes grew bitter. 'We did, not long ago,' she said. 'Now that Meng is a Party member, it's easier to get Government permission to travel. But there's not much point: we have too little money. I've no wish to depend on charity from friends in England.' She threw down the remainder of her whisky and held the glass out towards Liu, her arm extended at full length.

Getting to his feet, Liu re-filled the glass. As he did so, he said: 'Well, my dear, this is our home. Our children and grandchildren are here. Even though Peking is not as it was.'

'Meng is a native of Peking,' Vincent told Bradley.

'Of a different Peking from this one,' Liu said. 'The old Peking that is lost. My father was a scholar. We had a small property outside the city. When I was nineteen, in 1928, Peking became Nationalist Peiping, and my father served as an official. In that time, before the Japanese made full-scale war on us, China became very Westernized, and my father decided to send me off to Oxford.' He smiled reminiscently, and looked at Dorothy. 'There I met the love of my life, and we married.'

Dorothy had been looking into her lap, sitting very still, her glass suspended in her hand, as though trying to solve a problem. Now she looked up at Liu Meng; she said nothing, and her eyes were utterly bleak. But she reached out and briefly touched his hand. Liu picked up the bottle from the table in front of him, and poured more whisky into Bradley's glass; his hand, Bradley noticed, was a little unsteady.

'When Dorothy and I came back here, after some years in England,' Liu said, 'the Japanese occupation of North China was already quite advanced. When Peking fell to them, they set up a puppet government. Still my father survived as an official, and I was given a teaching post at the university. The Japanese needed officials and teachers.' He sighed. 'All these things my father survived. He would not have survived the government of Chairman Mao, since all of his class were purged. But he died, fortunately, during World War Two, and my mother died soon after. Our property of course was seized; but I continued to occupy my post at the university.' He smiled. 'I have been fortunate. The Party has been quite tolerant of me, considering my origins as a scholar. Of course I have become a good Marxist.' It was impossible to tell whether he said this ironically or seriously; his face told nothing.

'Why do you speak so freely?' Dorothy had turned to him suddenly, her expression almost fierce.

'Freely, my dear? I have told them our story, that is all. And these young men are friends.'

'Of course we are,' Vincent said. 'You can trust us absolutely.'

'Perhaps,' Dorothy said. She turned to Liu again. 'But I doubt that you can trust Mr Yang.'

'He is young, and a zealot,' Liu said. 'I did not know that he was so limited. To ask him to meet our friends was a mistake. But he can do no harm.'

Dorothy closed her eyes and took a deep breath. 'We must hope that you're right,' she said. She finished her glass of whisky in a single gulp, throwing back her head. Then she looked at Vincent, and her expression was severe. 'I wish you had not been quite so clever with Mr Yang,' she said. Her speech had become slurred, and she seemed to pick her way from word to word. 'You have the luxury of free speech in your country, Vincent – but perhaps you don't understand what can happen if opinions are expressed too openly here.' She pointed at her husband, swaying more than ever in her chair. 'Meng says he has been *fortunate*,' she said. She almost spat the word, and her eyes shone with an extraordinary anger. 'But in the Cultural Revolution, the Red Guards paraded him through the streets with a dunce's cap on, and punched him and spat on him.'

'Now, now, my dear,' Liu said. 'Vincent and Derek do not need to hear this. That time is over long ago.'

But Dorothy continued as though he hadn't spoken. 'He was fortunate in one way,' she said. 'A number of his colleagues died in prison cells, lying in their own filth. And Meng and I were lucky in being assigned to cart shit on a commune, and eventually being allowed to come back here to our home. When we walked in here, we found everything smashed up, and our whole library gone. The Red Guards loved burning books. We were sitting here in the middle of the mess when there was a knock on the door. It was one of Meng's favourite students. He held out a book. "They burned all your books," he said. "But we saved this one."'

'Dear God,' Vincent said.

Liu waved his hand at the bookshelves. 'I have managed to replace a good many,' he said mildly. 'Some of course could not be replaced.' He stood up suddenly, rocking a little, and smiled at Vincent. 'My labours on the commune made me strong,' he said. 'That was one good result. I can always beat Vincent at arm-wrestling – isn't that so, Vincent?'

'Every time,' Vincent said, and grinned.

'Come,' Liu said. 'Perhaps tonight you will win. Derek must be referee.'

He and Vincent pulled two hard-backed chairs up to the table, and sat down facing each other. Both rolled up their sleeves; then, propping their elbows on the table, they locked hands and began the contest, watching each other, grimacing and breathing hard. Liu, Bradley saw, had remarkably developed biceps for so old a man. For some moments, their arms remained upright, trembling with effort. Then Vincent's arm began to waver, and Liu forced it inexorably backwards. When he had pushed it to the table, he shouted with laughter, and Vincent and Bradley joined in.

'You see, Derek?' Liu cried. 'He is much younger, but not so fit as I am.'

When their laughter had died away, Liu said: 'It is time for us to drink some *mao-tai*. What do you say?'

'No.'

Dorothy had spoken, and her slurred voice was loud. Her swaying had become more pronounced, and Bradley was shocked to see that her face had changed to a drunken, angry mask. Her eyelids drooped more heavily, and her features had gone slack.

The liquor had suddenly overwhelmed her. 'Our guests will be tired,' she said. 'Tired. They should go home. I'll call a taxi.'

'No, no, first they should have some *mao-tai*,' Liu pleaded.

'*No!* They must go! I'll call a taxi.'

Dorothy got up and lurched to the desk, collapsing into the office chair. Hunched, she picked up the receiver of the antique black telephone, and began to try to use the rotating dial, poking at the holes with her fingers. But this proved too much for her, and she sat over the phone as though in meditation, motionless as a statue.

Liu smiled at Vincent and Bradley, who stood in awkward silence. 'She is too sozzled,' he drawled. 'It can't be helped.'

He turned, and walked to the desk. 'I will do it, my dear,' he said, and took the receiver gently from her hand.

6

'ONE HAS TO tread so bloody carefully,' Vincent said. 'People here are always looking over their shoulders. Anything they think could give them aggravation with the authorities sends them running for cover. Then all one's work in building goodwill is undone.'

'That did seem a possibility last night,' Bradley said.

They were walking through Beihai Park, late in the afternoon. Both had found themselves free of commitments, and had escaped from the Embassy early, intending to have dinner in the city. The waning sun was mild, and a lemon-hued light held the ancient imperial gardens, muting the voices of the crowds of Chinese tourists from the provinces. Bradley and Vincent paused beside a carved stone balustrade that skirted the central lake, and stood looking towards an island in the middle with an artificial hill, topped by the bell-shaped tower of the White Dagoba.

'Meng was okay,' Vincent said. 'But I'm afraid Dorothy was bothered by our exchange with Mr Yang.'

'With good reason,' Bradley said. 'You really wound him up, mate, didn't you? He'll report you as a dangerous reactionary.'

He'd intended this lightly, but Vincent pursed his lips. 'Let him, dear boy; let him. If the regime is going to pretend it has launched a new era of cultural freedom here, it will have to get used to hearing people like me blaspheming things like literary dogma.' He pulled a packet of cigarettes from a pocket of his navy-blue blazer and lit up, bending his head sideways and frowning. Bradley had given up smoking years ago, and Vincent had attempted to do so; but he had sporadic lapses, and was apparently going through one now. He snatched the cigarette from his lips with nervous speed, releasing a long stream of smoke into the peaceful air. 'You're right in one way,' he said. 'What Dorothy is afraid of is that my heresies will reflect on Liu Meng. Meng's not afraid, of course – he has too much guts for that. But I don't want Dorothy discouraging my friendship with him. That's the last thing one wants.'

'He's a marvellous old bloke,' Bradley said. 'What a survivor.'

But Vincent appeared not to be listening. Drawing on his cigarette, he continued to stare out over the lake. Almost under his breath, as though speaking to himself, he said: 'The question is, why was the odious Yang there at all? A creature from the Public Security Bureau?'

'Why not? The Bureau employs an army of cultural bureaucrats, doesn't it? Since Yang's presumably one of them, he'd be interested to meet our Cultural Attaché.'

For a moment, Vincent continued to stare at the lake and the white Buddhist tower on its island. Then he turned and looked at Bradley, his expression unusually sober. 'You must surely know what else the Bureau does, in addition to its cultural activities. It maintains social order, as they put it. It runs the correction camps and the police. In other words, it's one of the main arms of the police state.'

'But that doesn't mean Yang's a spy. He's probably just what he says he is – a translator.'

Vincent seemed not to have heard him. Cigarette between his lips, he stood frowning at the ground in silence, as though trying to solve an equation. Then he said: 'Perhaps. Even so, why would Liu Meng introduce us to a bloody Marxist puritan like that one? He's not the sort of person Meng could possibly like – one-time student or not.'

'Maybe Meng was told to invite him,' Bradley suggested. 'Have you thought of that?'

Vincent looked up. 'What do you mean?'

Bradley hesitated. He was beginning to sense that this discussion might lead them into areas that would prove to be troublesome: a premonition that seemed to be coloured by the late lemon light in the park, which grew more and more intense as it deepened into twilight. 'Maybe there are trade-offs that Meng has to accept,' he said, 'in order to lead a quiet life. Maybe the Bureau told him to introduce Yang to you, and he had to do it. You arrange cultural exchanges, Vin: it's possible Mr Yang wants a junket to Australia, and he hopes you'll set it up for him. Right? Or maybe they assigned him to report on your friendship with Liu Meng.'

Vincent stared at him. 'You haven't taken long to tune in to the situation here, have you, Brad? You're saying now that Yang may be a spy after all.'

'Just thinking aloud. I'm not an expert. You'd be a better judge of that than I am.'

Vincent took the cigarette from his lips and examined it carefully, as though for blemishes. When he spoke, there was a marked tension in his voice. 'You see me as an expert on espionage, do you, old fellow?'

'I see you as an expert on most things,' Bradley said.

'Ah. You have too high an opinion of me, Brad.' Vincent's words sounded friendly enough, but the warmth to which Bradley had long been accustomed was absent from his voice.

'We should be going,' Bradley said. 'They'll close the gates soon.'

Abruptly, Vincent swung around to face him. He dropped his cigarette to the ground and crushed it under his shoe. 'Erika's told you,' he said. 'Hasn't she?'

'Told me what? What are you talking about?' Bradley looked at him in open surprise.

For some moments, Vincent didn't answer; he looked back at Bradley with a severe expression. When he did speak, his voice was so low that Bradley had to strain to hear it.

'That I'm with ASIS,' he said.

Bradley laughed. 'You're joking, Vin.' But Vincent maintained his look of severity, and Bradley stopped laughing. 'You're not joking,' he said. 'Jesus, Vin. With ASIS. And all these years you never told me.'

Vincent's eyes dropped to the ground, as though in search of something. 'So you *didn't* know,' he said. 'This is unfortunate. I shouldn't have mistrusted Erika.' When he looked up, his eyes held a pained appeal. 'I would have told you eventually,' he said. 'But it's absolutely forbidden, Brad. You must know that.'

In spite of himself, Bradley continued to smile. His amusement had partly been brought on by surprise, and partly because Vincent's demeanour seemed absurdly melodramatic. But now, seeing Vincent's face harden, he adopted a sober expression. 'Of course,' he said. 'I understand that. And how long have you been with them?'

'From the beginning – from when I first joined the Department.'

'But that's against every policy of the Department,' Bradley said. 'Who knows about it?'

'Only the ambassador, in each post I go to. And Erika, of course.'

'Well, congratulations,' Bradley said. 'You certainly fooled me'

'I promise you, I would have told you when I was able,' Vincent said.

'Really? I can't help doubting that, mate.'

'Don't doubt it,' Vincent said. '*Don't* doubt it, Derek. I *couldn't* tell you – even though you're my dearest friend. That's because I'm not attached to the Embassy in the way that an ASIS operative normally is – and I'm forbidden to identify myself even to my closest colleagues.' He paused, watching Bradley's face. 'Do you see? I'm under deep cover, and always have been. That was the condition of my recruitment. Do you remember Ted Bobrowski?'

'Of course.'

'Ted recommended that they recruit me, and that I join

Foreign Affairs. Only the head of the training course knew that I was actually with ASIS – and after that, only the most senior officers were told. That's the way it still is – or has been until now. Now *you* know, old chap.'

'Yes. But it's your affair, Vin – you aren't obliged to tell me anything more.'

'Of course I'm not obliged to. But because of our friendship, I've always wanted to. I'll live a lie with most people, for the sake of the Service – but I'd rather not have done it where *you* were concerned. That's what I want you to understand.'

'Okay, Vin. I understand.'

Apparently satisfied with this, Vincent let his angular body relax into an easier pose. 'I'm glad you do,' he said. 'And I trust you to protect my cover. I know I can.' He glanced at the strolling crowds, as though suspecting a hidden observer among them. 'Let's go, shall we?'

With a quick, jerky movement he took Bradley's arm, drawing him away from the balustrade and compelling him to walk along the path. As they went, he spoke towards Bradley's ear with a soft, compulsive urgency.

'Now that you know my situation, Brad, there's so much I want to tell you. Do you know what the intelligence game does to people like me? It's like a dream you can't wake up from. You play a part for so long, that there are times when you begin to wonder what's happened to your inner self. You even begin to be afraid that it's lost. Sometimes I'm not sure who I *am* any more.'

He gave a quick, snorting laugh, then abruptly checked it, his face becoming solemn again, his sideways gaze insistent, his grip on Bradley's arm tightening. He seemed to be reciting a speech he'd long prepared, or had long bottled up, and his hushed, theatrical tone made him seem like a caricature of a spy, causing Bradley once again to suppress a smile. Yet Vincent's disclosures were almost certainly sincere, he thought. He had lived so much in books and in his head, and had so long been solitary, that he probably experienced even the most intense emotion at one remove, and a theatrical response to it was the one he believed to be appropriate.

'One is always required to manipulate people,' Vincent was saying. 'There are no normal relationships, except with one's colleagues in the game. Do you see, Brad? After a time, one desperately needs to be with just one or two people who know who one really is, and with whom one doesn't wear a mask. I've always wanted *you* to be one of those people.'

'Well, now I am, it seems. And the other's Erika.'

'Ah, yes. Erika. In all these years, she's never betrayed me to anyone. I shouldn't have suspected her now – but the situation between you two is somewhat special, isn't it?' He darted a humorous, sly glance at Bradley. 'One thing more,' he said. 'You have no conception of what is at stake in my relationship with Liu Meng. I'll just tell you this, and I depend on you utterly to keep silent. Meng longs to escape this regime, and I believe I may be able to help him. I may get him and Dorothy out to Australia. This is what I'm working on. They could attend one of our cultural festivals – and defect.'

'For God's sake. Would Canberra buy this?'

'I believe so. Liu has very high connections, and would bring invaluable information with him. Quite a feather in my cap, by the way.'

'Don't do it,' Bradley said. 'The Lius are old; too old to make a jump like that. They've got family here, and I can't see Dorothy agreeing. And if it backfires, you could end up in a Chinese gaol.'

Vincent smiled calmly. 'Don't worry,' he said. 'I have it all worked out. I can't tell you more, Derek, and I ask that you forget we ever had this conversation.' Abruptly, his tone changed; he became once again the genial Vincent of archaic mannerisms whom Bradley had always known. 'I'm getting hungry, old chap: it's time to seek out a restaurant, don't you think?' His voice took on a tone of hungry relish. 'Tonight we should sample the classical Peking *Duck*. What do you say?'

They walked on, through a deepening twilight in the park which matched Bradley's new unease.

'I believe Erika's attending a big dinner tonight,' Vincent said suddenly. 'The one for the trade delegation. I had to deal with our illustrious business leaders this morning, and I'm very glad I got out of the dinner: a little of those people goes a long way. The Chinese are giving them a banquet in the Great Hall of the People, which delighted our Ambassador, of course. Morton has ordered Erika to attend, so that she can do yet another press release – and also, I imagine, because she's decorative, and titillates the businessmen. There's a red-faced fellow from the mining industry who's already infatuated with her: no doubt she'll be sat next to him.' He smiled slyly. 'Don't worry, old chap, he won't get her back to his hotel room – though he'll try.'

At nine-thirty, Bradley was back in his apartment.

Vincent had suggested a nightcap, but Bradley had excused himself, saying that he was tired. This was untrue. His real reason was that Erika had promised to come to him as soon as the banquet was over, and had told him that she expected to get back to the compound by ten o'clock. He was to wait for her knock on his door.

Once again he sat on the couch in the half-light, with music coming from the cassette-player on the coffee table. It was the Bruch Violin Concerto, turned down low, and he was only half-listening. He was unaccountably tense and restless; from time to time he would get up and pace about the room and then sit down again, and Bruch's romantic storminess began to be oppressive. Absent, Erika seemed to have the quality of making her reappearance doubtful; to somehow have become ephemeral. Ten o'clock passed, and ten-thirty, and her knock failed to sound on the door.

When eleven o'clock came, Bradley decided that she certainly wasn't coming, and got up to go to bed.

As he was undressing, the phone beside his bed rang. Picking up the receiver, he held it to his ear without speaking.

'*Derek? It's me. I'm calling from the lobby of the Peking Hotel.*'

The low, intimate voice thrilled him. It was the first time he'd heard it on the phone, and the line seemed to exaggerate its boy-like depth – as well as that flatness which, instead of being monotonous, somehow made it sexually tantalising.

'*I wanted to phone you before,*' she said, '*but I couldn't get away. I'm calling from the reception desk: I've had a terrible time getting the use of a phone. You know what they're like about phones. After the big dinner, the guys in the delegation wanted more action, and asked us all to come to the Peking Hotel lobby for drinks. They kept ordering more and more rounds, and we had to keep them happy. A heavy from the mining industry has been making a play for me – but I've managed to fend him off. Arthur Chadwick and Norman Cunningham have the use of an Embassy car, and I want to ride back with them. I really don't want to start looking for a Peking taxi. What are you doing?*'

'I'm about to go to bed.'

'*I'll come and join you there – shall I?*'

'Sounds like a good idea.'

Her voice dropped lower. '*I want you all the time; I can't stop thinking about you.*'

'I have the same problem about you.'

'*I'm glad. You've got a very nice voice on the phone, Mr Bradley. I like talking to you on the phone.*'

'I'll leave the door off the latch,' Bradley said.

He lay in bed with the light out. Vincent and he had drunk a bottle of wine with dinner, and he found himself growing sleepy. He closed his eyes; Erika's voice repeated itself in his head, and he began to consider now how little he actually knew her – despite the fact that she originally came from the same small city as himself, and the same suburb. And this was odd, he thought. He had never even passed her in the street at home, so far as he knew. Yet suddenly he seemed to remember a very pretty girl of twelve or so, walking past his parents' house in Pirie Street when he was the same age, perhaps on her way to visit Vincent in Bay Road: a girl in a loose green sweater and jeans, whose thick fair hair hung over her forehead. The day was sunny, and there were bees buzzing in the lavender in his mother's front garden. It was a single, elusive image, quickly gone. Perhaps it had been Erika; perhaps not. It was difficult to believe that she'd grown up in New Town: she seemed too foreign, and somehow without nationality. Possibly this was explained by the fact that her father had been German; or more likely it was because she'd lived abroad for most of her adult life, from the age of twenty until now. He'd learned in their talks that she had worked on newspapers in London for two years; then, when she'd joined the Department's Information Service, she'd been posted for a time to New York, then to Jakarta, and now here. Her only relative in Australia, apart from a sister of her late mother's who lived in Melbourne, had been her father – and he had died five years ago, and their house had been sold. Other than to tell Bradley this, she never talked about her father. So in fact, she was without roots, without any fixed location, without connections, without a place she could now call home. She was somehow in a different dimension from other people, Bradley thought – almost as though she had no solid attachment to the normal world.

There are few things more seductive than the alien mixed with the familiar. We are beckoned by the first into the unknown, while the second puts out its cords to entwine and reassure us. This, perhaps, accounted for the hold that Erika was starting to exert over Bradley's imagination: a hold that he was trying to resist. He had never lost his balance in emotional involvements, and didn't want to do so now; but something almost below the level of conscious thought was warning him that his balance was already being lost. He tried to draw back: he reminded himself of Erika's disturbing mood changes, and tried to recall any physical imperfections she might have, in an effort to see her through a lens of realism. Her body was perfect, defying any such effort; and her face was captivating. But her lips, he thought, might be considered a little too thin, drawn downwards in repose in a way that suggested a capacity for cruelty. Perhaps he should be warned by this.

It was useless; he longed for her to come, and fell into a doze.

He heard his name being whispered. It seemed to have been repeated a number of times, and he rose through fathoms of unconsciousness.

'Derek?'

There was a smell of expensive perfume. She was leaning over him in the darkness, her face close to his, and her formal evening gown made her unfamiliar: the colour of red wine, it left her shoulders bare. It seemed to him that he dreamed her, since darkness made her face chalky and mask-like, as faces in his dreams often were; she brought strangeness into the room. He blinked, raising himself from the pillow, and made out her whimsical smile.

'Wake up mister,' she said. 'There's a woman in your room.'

TWO

1

BRADLEY STOOD ON the fifth-floor balcony of his room in the Lake Hotel, contemplating the world of the Willow Pattern. It was eight in the morning – time to go down to breakfast in the dining room – but he lingered, leaning on the yellow stucco of the balustrade.

He'd been told that the West Lake was beautiful, but had not expected beauty like this. Peking had made him pessimistic about ever encountering the unsullied China of his imagination; now, however, it lay in front of him. Immediately below the balcony, treetops receded in wave after wave – locusts, planes and trees of heaven – and from their midst rose a single, feathery young pine, almost close enough to reach out and touch. On his right was Solitary Hill, a tree-covered island a few metres offshore, a tiled pagoda rising from its top. In front of him were the glassy, blue-green distances of the lake, with islets and pagodas and pleasure boats and humpbacked stone bridges, veiled in early haze. Green wooded hills surrounded it, and on its far side stood an ultimate line of pastel-blue mountains. Lotuses floated at the nearby water's edge, and little groups of Chinese strolled on a pathway around the lake.

The day was very still: the summer heat was gathering, like a wave rolling lazily towards him, and the only sounds were the cheerful voices and hammerings of invisible Chinese tradesmen, coming up through the canopy of leaves. On the eastern shore of the lake, the buildings of Hangchow could be made out: the ancient capital of the Southern Sung which had dazzled Marco Polo. Solitary Hill was linked to it by the Bai Causeway, whose long, thread-like road emerged from the far side of the island, crossing a humpbacked bridge to run across the lake into the distance – its willows and pedestrians and blue-clad cyclists mirrored in silver. Bai Causeway, Bradley had discovered, was named after Po Chü-I (now rendered in Pinyin as Bai Juyi), who had caused it to be built when he was governor here, in the ninth century. This made him contemplate the scene with extra pleasure, and he lingered for a few minutes longer. Soon, he would have to be ready for the morning session of the Conference.

It was the first week of June. Two days ago, the Ambassador had called Bradley into his office and had informed him that the Chinese Government was hosting a conference for an American business delegation, to discuss the expansion of trade links. The hotel on Hangchow's West Lake had been chosen as the venue.

'I don't need to emphasise how important this conference is to the Chinese,' the Ambassador had said. 'Its political implications are vital. Since President Reagan sent the Secretary of State here last year, I understand Washington is hinting at a more even-handed approach on the Taiwan issue. So this conference will be about more than trade, under the surface. You do see that?'

Bradley said that he did, and the Ambassador smiled. 'Of course you do,' he said. 'The reports you've been preparing for me on China's relations with the United States have been really informative, Derek. Canberra told me you were good value, and they were clearly right.'

Bradley thanked him. They were sitting in two of the green leather armchairs intended for guests. There was a faint smell of pipe tobacco: Charles Morton (as Vincent liked to point out) was one of the few surviving men in the world still smoking a pipe. In his early sixties, Morton was an Australian diplomat of the old school, now vanishing: very much on the British model, his accent just a few shades off upper-class English, his voice unctuously soothing, with a tendency to moo. Tall and lean, he wore his tailored business suits well: today's was silver-grey, and double-breasted. Lying back in his chair, one hand in his jacket pocket, he contrived to look both informal and elegant, like royalty at ease. His thick grey hair was parted on one side, and fell boyishly over his forehead; his tanned face was benign, his small brown eyes guarded. He spoke fluent Mandarin, and in previous interviews with Bradley had displayed considerable knowledge of China. Usually calm and measured, he became almost excited when straying on to the topic of Ming painting: his special interest. A silk scroll copy of a fifteenth-century painting by Wu Wei, showing a scholar reading under a pine tree, hung on the wall near an explosive blue impression of Sydney Harbour: the Brett Whiteley.

'How are you settling in?' Morton asked Bradley now. 'Well? Good. Good. My wife and I have been intending to ask you to dinner – you must certainly come to us when you get back from Hangchow. I've been wanting to invite you before, but one gets so dreadfully snowed under.' He brushed his grey forelock back, with an air of being briefly overwhelmed. 'But your friend Vincent Austin has been filling you in on the Peking scene, I gather? Excellent.' He brightened, head on one side, studying Bradley's face. 'A brilliant fellow, Austin. Quite brilliant. And amusing. Very amusing.' He perhaps expected a comment, but Bradley made none.

The Ambassador sat up, folded his hands and leaned forward. 'Now then, in regard to the Conference. I want you to prepare me a report – a detailed report. I don't just want to know about issues discussed and agreements made – I want to know about the relationships between the delegates. I also want to know about anything you can pick up regarding the Chinese–American relationship beyond the trade level – particularly in regard to any shift over Taiwan. Taiwan will be the big bargaining chip in regard to trade, as I'm sure you've realised.'

Bradley said that he had.

'Good. I've been wanting to send a think-piece to Canberra on where the US–Chinese relationship might go in the next few years. If your report is substantial, it could well provide a basis for my piece – in which case I'll do a despatch, and add your notes.' He smiled benevolently.

A despatch was the highest level of communication with Canberra beyond day-to-day reporting; the Ambassador was offering Bradley something of an honour, and Bradley had tried to look suitably grateful.

He had made the two-hour flight from Peking to Hangchow yesterday evening, arriving at nine o'clock. Erika was to come here the next morning, and they hoped to meet in the lunch break, after the first session. A shuttle bus for embassy officials had brought him straight to the hotel, where he had gone up the steps into the lobby to register. The night was dark, and he had only caught a glimpse of the lake, with its dim lamps curving away at intervals around the shore.

The Lake Hotel was pleasantly old-fashioned, probably dating from the 1930s; the lobby had wood-panelled walls, decoratively carved, with wooden Chinese lanterns suspended from the ceiling and azaleas in glazed blue-and-white pots standing by the reception desk. Resonant American voices boomed through the lobby: the area was crowded with delegates, Western journalists, and officials from many of the embassies in Peking. As Bradley approached the desk, a smiling, solidly built Chinese stepped into his path.

'Mr Bradley?'

Bradley confirmed his identity, putting down his overnight bag. The man smiled more broadly; he had a jovial expression, as though at a joke they were about to share. 'Good,' he said. 'Welcome to Hangchow, Mr Bradley. I am Lao, from the Foreign Ministry.'

Somewhat puzzled as to why he was being met by a Government official, Bradley greeted him politely, and waited. Lao was perhaps in his late thirties: round-faced and broad-chested. His shock of high black hair was swept straight back, with stray wisps escaping. He reminded Bradley more of a bodyguard than a bureaucrat; but his English was good, and he wore the dark-grey, military-style jacket with patch pockets that was the unofficial uniform of a Party cadre. His trousers were somewhat creased and rumpled.

'While you are here, I hope that I can be of help to you,' Lao said. 'The Ministry has set up a Secretariat in Room 12, on the second floor. We will be here for the duration of the Conference, at the service of delegates and Foreign Service officers. If I can assist you, or give you information, please call on me.' He produced a business card, and held it out to Bradley. 'Here is my card. The room number is written on the back.'

Bradley thanked him, and began to pick up his bag; but Lao still stood planted in front of him, his feet apart, his expression somehow expectant, as though they were destined to begin a friendship. Then he asked: 'This is your first visit to Hangchow?'

Bradley said that it was.

Lao nodded. 'Then I hope you will have time to explore,' he said. 'Industrial development has done damage to our country's beauty – and the city of Hangchow is just an industrial town these days. But the West Lake!' His smile now expressed delight. 'The West Lake region is another matter. This is unspoiled: the loveliest place in China. Do you know our saying? "There is Heaven above, and Hangchow below."'

'Then I look forward to seeing a bit of Heaven,' Bradley said.

Lao laughed loudly, as though at a choice witticism. 'Good! I hope that you do. Perhaps I can join you at some stage: we might get together for a meal or a drink. Meanwhile, remember I am here if you need any assistance.'

He moved aside, raising his hand, and Bradley picked up his bag and moved towards the desk. It was only when he got into the lift to go up to his room that he had wondered how Lao had known who he was.

Released from the morning session, the delegates and special guests flowed out the double glass doors of the hotel ballroom, where the Conference had been set up. Bradley was one of the first to emerge, and looked about for Erika. Journalists had not been allowed into the opening session, which was why she'd decided not to fly into Hangchow until late this morning.

He saw her straight away: one of a group of foreign correspondents standing on the far side of the foyer, next to a row of the tall glazed blue-and-white pots with their flowering azaleas that were everywhere in the hotel's public spaces. She was laughing with a dark-haired young woman standing next to her, and Bradley recognised Moira Paterson from the *Courier*. As he made his way through the crowd towards them, Moira looked across at him, raised her eyebrows, and said something to Erika, who turned her head quickly to seek him out. She seemed at first to look startled; but then she smiled.

'Here he is,' Moira said, 'our man from the Embassy.'

Erika's gaze, fixed on Bradley, flickered for a moment at this, going uneasily to Moira. Then she looked back at him. 'Hello,' she said. 'How was the session?'

'Pretty boring,' Bradley said. 'You didn't miss much. Tariffs. That sort of thing.'

'Really? You surprise me, Derek,' Moira said. 'My contacts tell me that something quite big is on the agenda.'

'And what might that be?'

'You're the diplomat. You should know.'

Bradley looked at her, trying not to grow irritated, surprised again by her barely veiled hostility. Her thin, fine-featured face could have been attractive, but ill-will seemed to give her a permanent sneer, and her large, deceptively limpid green eyes held a look of accusation. Remembering what Erika had said about her, he wondered briefly whether some sort of jealousy could be the cause of Moira's resentment. He found the idea bizarre.

'Come on, Moira,' Erika said. 'Stop being a journo for a moment. Derek doesn't have to tell you everything.' It was a mild reproof, but she was smiling at Moira as she spoke, and the smile seemed affectionate.

Moira continued to stare at Bradley. 'What I hear is this,' she said. 'There's a big deal with Boeing that will go on the table. The Government's set to buy a whole lot of aircraft from them for CAAC. I would have thought that would ring a few bells – even with a diplomat.'

'I suppose it would,' Bradley said. 'But they didn't ring this morning.'

Erika tucked her hand into the crook of his arm. 'Enough of politics. You said you'd take me to lunch, Brad. I'll see you later, Moira.'

'Yes. I'll look forward to that, sweetie.' She smiled at Erika, ignoring Bradley.

'"Heaven above, and Hangchow below",' Bradley said. He gestured at the lake, the deep green hills, and the far blue line of mountains.

'That just about describes it,' Erika said. 'Is that from one of your old poems?'

She had taken to referring to the classical Chinese verse he and Vincent quoted as 'your old poems', and she looked across the table at him now with an indulgent expression. It was very hot and still, and although there were electric fans revolving in the ceiling of the teahouse, she flapped a little paper fan beside her face. She seemed not to perspire, and looked cool and relaxed in a beige cotton dress with a large, spread collar.

'No,' Bradley said. 'It's a Chinese saying about old Hangchow. A Government official quoted it to me last night.'

They had come to Solitary Hill on foot from the hotel, crossing a small stone bridge that linked the island to the shore. The open front of the teahouse looked out over West Lake, and their table was next to a long wooden balustrade: they might have been on the deck of a ship, suspended above the lake. They had finished their lunch, bowls and chopsticks pushed aside, and were drinking the local Dragon Well tea from little cups. Close by, the long straight ribbon of Bai Causeway stretched across the water, with its lines of willows and peach trees and its endlessly moving, blue-clad pedestrians and cyclists. On the far eastern side of the lake which was the causeway's destination, the industrial chimneys of Hangchow shimmered and smoked like a mirage, remote from the West Lake's beauty. Power boats with canvas awnings carried tourists out to the islands and their pagodas in the centre of the lake. Close to the shore, four young Chinese girls paddled a canoe-like skiff through flat water. A white magnolia was flowering just below the railing, and Bradley seemed to catch its scent. In the hot stillness, voices from other tables and the clatter of crockery came to them as though through a screen; cicadas whirred, and a single bird made a repeated, hypnotic call: *zinc; zinc; zinc.*

Erika sipped her tea, looking at him over the rim of her cup. 'Yes, it's heavenly here,' she said. 'You love places like this, don't you, Brad? The way you love your old poets.' It was a flat, matter-of-fact statement, made in her toneless voice.

'Yes,' he said. 'I wish we could stay here. I wish there was no bloody conference.'

'But there is,' she said, 'and we both have to cover it.' She continued to study him. Then she said: 'Everyone says you're first-rate, and on your way up. But you don't really like Foreign Affairs, do you?'

'What makes you think so?' He was startled; she had never hinted at knowing this before.

'Lots of little things,' she said.

Bradley laughed. 'You're very clever.'

'Tell the *truth*,' she said. She spoke on a facetiously commanding note, like a small girl playing a game. 'You have to tell me the truth.'

'I like the Service,' Bradley said. 'It's given me an interesting life. But lately I'm bored. Peking's not an easy post.'

'No, it's not. We've got a long haul in front of us, cut off from the things that make life fun.' She paused, still studying him. 'I wonder if you'll leave the Department. Has it come to that?'

'Not immediately – but eventually.'

'Really? Well, if that's what you want, you should do it. And maybe you shouldn't wait.'

'What do you mean?'

She grinned at him, cocking her head on one side, her expression mischievous. There was an odd light in her eyes, whose blue seemed to reflect the spaces of the lake, and whose pupils had grown very small – as though she'd been drinking, he thought, or smoking dope. 'Let's run away,' she said suddenly.

He laughed, sensing that she'd spoken without thinking. 'What?'

'I mean it,' she said. 'Let's run away.' She was speaking very fast, and her voice had grown breathy. The words seemed to intoxicate her.

'You are joking, aren't you?'

'Let's just quit and go,' she said. 'Fly out to Hong Kong and disappear.'

'Now I know you're joking.'

'Not entirely.' She looked out across the lake, and said softly: 'It's what I'd like to do.'

'And why would you want a thing like that?'

She turned back to him, and now her face had grown serious. 'Because I'm in love with you,' she said.

Bradley sat still, watching a smiling Chinese waitress in a green cotton uniform collect bowls from a nearby table; hearing the bird say: *zinc; zinc; zinc.* These words had not been spoken until now: not even in the throes of lovemaking, despite their mutual declaration that they were 'serious'. And his inward response was disconcerting. An instant flaring of delight was followed by something else: by that formless apprehension that had touched him before, on the night when he'd waited for her to come to him from the banquet. Why this was, he couldn't have said, except perhaps that it had something to do with the unpredictable expressions that played across her face, sometimes succeeding each other within minutes. *I still don't know who she is*, he thought.

He reached across the table and took her hand. 'And I'm in love with you,' he said. 'As you've probably guessed.'

She smiled quickly, again with a hint of mischief. 'I had some idea,' she said.

'Maybe you're right: maybe we should run away,' he said. The idea was absurd, yet intoxicating.

'That's up to you, mister. I'll come with you anywhere,' she said.

They looked at each other in silence; then the playful expression left her face, and she glanced at her wristwatch. 'We have to go back. The session starts at two-thirty.'

'What time shall I see you for dinner?'

Erika's eyes shifted to the lake. 'Brad, I'm sorry,' she said, 'but something's come up. I have to go to dinner with the press corps.'

He stared at her, trying to conceal his disappointment. They had told each other in Peking that they would spend their free time here together; and since the Conference ended tomorrow afternoon, there would be little time left after tonight.

Erika looked at him again. She spoke hurriedly now, as though to dispose of unwelcome business. 'All the journalists are going to dinner at a restaurant in the city. The contacts I'll make will help me place my story on the Conference. So I have to go. Can you understand?'

'Sure,' he said. 'Maybe we can meet again tomorrow at lunch, before we leave.'

She looked shocked, and a sort of panic crossed her face. 'No. *Tonight*. You know I want to be with you tonight. I'll leave the dinner as early as I can: I'll come to your room by nine. Will you wait for me?'

'If you want. I'm not going anywhere.' Saying this, he smiled, but she continued to look at him doubtfully.

'It's all right?'

'It's all right.'

They walked back across the bridge, and around the lake. They said little more; a heaviness hung over them, and their few remarks mingled with the dinning of cicadas, and the endless ringing of bicycle bells.

At seven o'clock, Bradley went down to the hotel dining room and headed for an empty table. But two political officers from the British Embassy waved to him, and beckoned him to join them. They were men he'd met at a recent reception and had got on well with, and he was glad of their company; he'd expected to eat alone.

At a little after eight, with dinner over, he said good night to them, making the excuse that he had notes to write up. This was true; but he wanted first to take a solitary walk.

He strolled along the path by the lake shore, breathing in a coolness that had come with the dark. Out on the spaces of West Lake, many little lights had come on, weaving that prospect of mystery that lights on water always do. Some winked on the islands; others glowed on boats that moved slowly through the dimness as though on a search. The path was still thronged with people, most of them Chinese; it was never possible to be alone in China, except inside a room, but there was a quietness here that resembled privacy. Walking slowly under the trees through successive pools of light cast by the street lamps that curved around the lake, Bradley was attempting to analyse his relationship with Erika. The exercise was well overdue, he told himself, since he seemed to be slipping into an involvement whose ultimate destination was dubious.

This state of mind had been triggered by their aborted dinner. Despite his efforts to dismiss his response to this as petty, he found himself reflecting that this evening was somehow a repetition of the evening of the trade delegation banquet. Once again, Erika had created a situation where he must wait for her, as the evening slipped away. She was not with him, yet neither would she release him: connected to her by a tantalising thread, he must hope for her eventual reappearance, and Bradley began to wonder whether this was a deliberate pattern: an odd quirk in her make-up.

'Mr Bradley!'

The voice had spoken from behind him. When he swung around, trying to locate its owner among the crowd of Chinese faces, he recognised Lao, the man from the Foreign Ministry, smiling with a warmth that still seemed to assume that a friendship was budding between them. As Bradley came to a halt, Lao hurried to catch up with him.

'I thought that it was you, Mr Bradley, but wasn't sure,' he said. 'I left a message for you at the hotel desk – did you not get it?'

'I'm afraid not – I didn't check for messages,' Bradley said.

'Ah – a pity.' The wide smile never left Lao's face, and he smoothed his shock of thick, untidy hair. 'I was hoping we might dine together,' he said. 'I know a very good restaurant on the island, and would have enjoyed taking you there. Never mind – so now you are having an evening stroll. May I join you?'

'Of course.'

They walked on together, and Bradley said: 'You were right about the West Lake.'

Lao, who was smoking a cigarette, took a deep drag on it and exhaled, looking about him quickly as though to verify what Bradley had said. 'Yes – all Chinese love it here,' he said. 'I'm glad you enjoy it too. And your friend Miss Lange – does she also like it?'

Bradley looked at him, letting his surprise show before he answered. 'Yes, I believe she does,' he said, and his tone was intended to discourage further enquiries. It seemed that he and Erika were being watched; he resented it, and also began to grow wary. The attention this Foreign Ministry official was giving him could scarcely be usual, given the fact that Bradley was merely at the Conference as an observer, and he began to ask himself what Lao actually wanted.

Lao continued to smile, apparently unaffected by Bradley's sudden coolness. 'It must be a very nice change here from Peking,' he said. 'How do you find it in the capital, Mr Bradley? A little different from life in Australia, I guess.'

'I like it well enough,' Bradley said. 'But Peking's a little restrictive, in some ways.'

Lao nodded. 'It's difficult for you to meet Chinese people, I think, and to have free discussions. Our Government has set out to make things more free, and it's true this is happening in many ways – but the authorities are cautious. Very cautious.'

He stopped, causing Bradley to stop too, and threw his cigarette end into the lake. Then he tugged a packet from his top pocket, and offered a cigarette to Bradley, who shook his head. Lao put a fresh one in his mouth and lit up, his big, fleshy face reflecting the flame in the dark. Like so many Chinese, he was apparently a chain smoker. Exhaling, he faced Bradley directly, and for the first time, his smile had vanished.

'The difficulty is,' he said, 'that foreign friends are sometimes not clear where the boundaries are. I want to give you some good advice, Mr Bradley. You should be very careful who you mix with, and what you say to them. Perhaps you will understand what I mean.' He paused, no longer affable, his face hard, his gaze fixed on Bradley's. The transition was both surprising and threatening, causing a chill to go across the back of Bradley's neck. Lao was clearly not what he'd claimed to be, he decided. He was probably from the Ministry of State Security: China's intelligence service.

'I'll try to remember that,' Bradley said.

Lao nodded. 'It would be sensible to do so,' he said. 'Westerners are very frank, and I understand this. But some of our people don't appreciate this frankness – and it can sometimes be dangerous. Your Cultural Attaché is unusually frank, isn't he?'

'He's very open, if that's what you mean,' Bradley said. He adopted a tone that was deliberately sententious. 'Mr Austin's a valuable member of our mission. He does important work arranging cultural exchanges between your country and ours – and in cultural matters, free discussion is healthy, don't you think?'

For a moment, Lao said nothing, looking at Bradley, his cigarette between his lips. His heavy lids drooped against the smoke, and his glinting dark eyes were just visible. 'Perhaps so,' he said. 'But nevertheless, he really should be careful, or it might create trouble. I hope you will tell him that.'

'I'll pass on your remarks,' Bradley said. He had begun to grow angry, and would have said more, but he reminded himself of the monolithic structure that stood behind Mr Lao, and refrained. 'And now I must get back to the hotel,' he said. 'Will you walk back with me?'

'I think not,' Lao said. 'I must walk around the lake a little more, for exercise. I need to keep fit.'

He raised a hand in farewell, and his smile reappeared, jovial as before.

When Bradley got back to the hotel, it was a quarter to nine. He didn't imagine that Erika would be here yet; she had promised to be back by nine, but he fully expected her to be late, as she had been on the night of the banquet. He went to the reception desk, and asked for messages.

The young Chinese woman there handed him two folded slips of paper. The first that he opened was from Mr Lao, giving the time of writing as five o'clock, and was typewritten. It stated that he would very much like to take Bradley to dinner, and asked that he contact him in Room 12. Bradley crumpled it up, and opened the second. It was from Erika, and was handwritten.

Room 45. 8.30 p.m.

Dear Derek,
   I'm back. Where are you? Please come to my room.
                                        Erika

He took the lift to the fourth floor and hurried along the corridor. When he knocked on her door it opened instantly, as though she'd been standing behind it. He came in, and she closed the door behind him without speaking, turning to look at him with a set expression. The room, which was almost identical to

Bradley's, was in semi-darkness. The only light came from an old-fashioned lamp on a table beside the bed, with a green, tulip-shaped shade. Like the Lake Hotel itself, the room was a capsule from the 1930s: pale-green walls, dark-brown carpet, a double bed with a striped, green-and-mustard spread, a mosquito net hanging like a dim cloud above it, an antique cradle phone on the table beside it. Some of Erika's clothes had been flung there, and on an easy chair nearby. A fan in the ceiling hung still. Multi-paned doors of dark-stained wood stood open on to an individual balcony like his own, framing the warm dark.

Erika was still wearing the beige cotton dress with the spread collar; it was creased a little, and she didn't look as fresh as she'd done at lunchtime. There was an appearance of strain and fatigue in her face; she was apparently in the grip of a suppressed anxiety, her eyes wide. Perhaps, Bradley thought, this was simply the effect of liquor; journalists being journalists, they would have drunk well at the dinner. But when she spoke, there was strain in her voice as well.

'Where were you?'

'Walking around the lake,' he said.

'Around the lake? Were you alone?'

'No, I was with an official from the Chinese Foreign Ministry.'

'Really.' Her tone was dubious. Then she spoke more rapidly, in the low mutter which he was beginning to realise always accompanied strong feeling in her. 'I was worried,' she said. 'I went to your room and you weren't there.' She looked up into his face with an expression that had now become ambiguous, somehow combining accusation with entreaty; and he sensed that she was entering one of those modes where matter-of-fact calm might vanish.

'I didn't expect you to be back yet,' he said. 'Not until nine or later.'

'I came back a bit after eight. I took a taxi.'

'You can't have stayed long at the dinner.'

Her head ducked down as though he'd caught her out in a

misdemeanour. Then she said: 'No. I felt bad about letting you down. I couldn't eat, and I didn't want to be there. So I made excuses, and left. I shouldn't have gone.'

'Yes you should,' he said. 'It's part of your job, I realise that.'

'*No.* We'd made a date, and it was wrong of me to break it, no matter what the reason. I couldn't stop thinking about you. I only want to be with you.'

Now Bradley felt his doubts and reservations dissolving, and a wave of gladness went through him. And yet, at the same time, he had a sense of unnatural repetition, as though Erika and he inhabited a recurring dream together. The sequence being played out now had taken place before, when she came to his apartment from the Down Under Bar. But recalling this did nothing to check the surge of feeling that was pushing all his doubts aside. He was compelled by her, no matter what she did, and could not any longer contemplate her disappearing from his life. Even if she was luring him into some overwrought set of sequences whose compulsions and penalties were unpredictable, he was ready, now that she was in front of him again, to enter the dream willingly.

He reached for her, and she surged against him instantly, her hands moving over him, her lips wet on his, a fine dew of perspiration on her forehead, her breath faintly smelling of wine. It was as though her own repentance excited her, and her kisses had a frenzy that was new. But after a time, something seemed to change. Her body went lax in his arms, as though from a blow, and she drew back to look at him, frowning, her eyes scanning his, her expression suddenly suspicious. 'You haven't really forgiven me,' she said. 'Have you?'

'Of course I have.'

'So there *was* something to forgive.'

Bradley chose his words carefully. 'That's not what I meant. I missed you. I felt bad about not being with you. But if you thought the dinner was necessary for your story, I had no business objecting.'

'You're being a real diplomat, aren't you? But I think you're not sure now whether you want to go on with me.'

'There's nothing I want so much,' he said. 'But I'm not sure where we're going, to tell you the truth.'

For a moment she said nothing, her hands dropping to her sides. No longer touching him, she stood very straight, like a child awaiting punishment. 'What do you mean?' she said.

'Just what I say. I'm in love with you – and that means I don't want to lose you. But I'm not sure how you feel about that.'

A sort of alarm seemed to flicker in her face. Still speaking in a quick, child-like voice, she said: 'I suppose it scares me.'

Bradley closed his eyes for a moment, feeling something fall away inside him. He guessed that she had spoken without reflection, and that what she had uttered was the truth. 'Well, there you are,' he said. 'You're scared of permanence. So I have to be careful, don't I?'

'Do you? I think what you really want is to get out of this,' she said. 'You've decided I'm going to be too much trouble.'

'No.' He took her by the shoulders. 'That's nonsense. It's all in your head.'

Her reaction to these words startled him. She pushed away his hands and stepped back. 'In my *head*? Is that what you think? Well, you wouldn't want to be mixed up with a *head* case, would you, Mister Bradley? So you're free. Understand? You can go.'

With violent suddenness, she turned and ran across the room, disappearing through the doors on to the balcony.

He didn't immediately follow her. He stood still, telling himself that he was dealing with some sort of fear of abandonment, and with emotional responses that were grotesquely out of proportion to the things that seemed to trigger them. He should probably walk away, he thought, just as she'd challenged him to do; but it remained impossible to bring himself to do so. After a few moments, he crossed to the balcony doors, and stepped out.

Mild, warm air enveloped him: darkness like black fur. The small, pulsing lights on the lake appeared in front of him again, but at first it seemed that Erika had vanished. Then he discovered her, standing in a pool of shadow in the far corner of the balcony, leaning on the stuccoed parapet, her face buried in her folded arms. The sight of her drooping back pierced him, and he sensed that he was looking at a pain and desolation whose ultimate origins lay hidden, in another part of her life. He walked across to her and put an arm about her shoulders, and found that she was weeping. 'Come inside,' he said.

She turned, raising her head; the tears seemed to enlarge her eyes, and he was shocked at the despair in her face. When she spoke, her voice was tight. 'I'm sorry. Please don't leave me.'

'I won't leave you,' he said. 'Come inside.'

Once in the room she dropped limply on her bed, fully clothed, an arm across her eyes as though exhausted. He lay down beside her, a prisoner of the dream. Not touching, they lay silent for a time, faces upturned, the archaic mosquito net floating above them, giving off an odour of China in the 1930s.

He began to think that she'd gone to sleep; but when he put a hand on her shoulder, it seemed that he'd touched a spring. She twisted herself to face him, her arms going urgently about him; they tugged at each other's clothes, and he found that her body lay open and moist, as though grief had been an aphrodisiac.

Later in the night they lay talking, suspended in black air, high and calm and free above West Lake. Through the balcony's open doors, faint Chinese voices floated upwards. He could only just make out her face on the pillow beside him.

'You never talk about your childhood,' he said. 'Were you happy?'

'I was until my mother died. It devastated my father, losing her so young.'

'Were you fond of him?'

'Of course.' She spoke without expression, her voice flatter than usual, looking up at the mosquito net. 'My father was a very special man. He came through the War, and never talked about it. It wasn't easy for him, living in a country that saw Germans as the enemy. He had no time for the Nazis: he'd served his country because he had to, and he just wanted to forget it. When I was little, and he'd carry me on his shoulders – that was the happiest time in my life. But when my mother died, his life ended for him. If it hadn't been for me, I think he might have given up altogether. We were very close. But I don't want to talk about that.' Her arms went around him. 'I love to be with you, Brad. You make me feel peaceful.'

'I'm glad of that,' Bradley said.

She lay silent for a time; then she said: 'When I was a girl, after I lost my mother, Vincent helped me get through. He adopted me, in a way. He and I are like twins, he says, and it's true. We're both Geminis, in fact.' She laughed. 'Do you mind being involved with a twin?'

'Talking of Vincent – I think he may have a problem.'

He told her about his conversation with Lao. As he did so, the pale disc of her face turned towards him in the dark, and he sensed the fixity of her gaze. When he'd done, she raised herself on one elbow, looking down at him. 'Oh, fuck,' she said. 'He's an MSS man.'

'It seems pretty likely.'

'It's not just likely. That's what he bloody well *is*. And he's got you under surveillance as well as Vincent.'

'I don't think he's all that interested in me – he just wanted me to deliver his message to Vincent. Vincent's been a bit too daring in some of his cultural exchanges with the Peking intellectuals. We met an earnest young Marxist at Professor Liu's, and Vincent tipped a bucket on his orthodoxies. The bastard probably put in a report.'

'You don't sound worried.'

'Not really.'

'Then you don't know how bad this is. I've been here longer than you, Brad, and I do know.' Her voice had grown tense and hard; there was also an edge of fear in it. 'Where the Chinese system's concerned, you're an innocent,' she said.

'Maybe. But let's not get too paranoid about Mr Lao.'

'*Listen* to me!' She sat up straight, and pointed a finger at him. 'No Chinese official would make an approach like this to a member of a foreign mission, unless his bosses were seriously concerned. Did you say anything at all about Professor Liu? *Did* you? This could be crucial for Vincent.'

'No,' he said. 'Lao raised nothing specific. Take it easy. They just don't like the way Vincent talks, and they're issuing a warning. That's all.'

She lay back on the pillows beside him. 'I hope you're right,' she muttered. 'But I don't think so.'

Bradley put an arm around her. He'd not told her of Vincent's plan to help the Lius to defect, but he suspected she already knew: it seemed that Vincent told her everything. 'This country's like a very nasty boarding school,' he said. He spoke lightly, trying to banish her fear. 'Let's run away to Hong Kong.'

She huddled closer against him, and repeated what he'd said like a mantra. 'Let's. Let's run away.'

This was becoming their favourite fantasy. A fantasy was all it was, at present; but Bradley was beginning to suspect that like all fantasies, it held at its core a temptation towards reality.

2

A WEEK AFTER the Hangchow conference, Vincent invited Bradley to join him on a visit to the valley of the Ming Tombs. It was a place he found deeply impressive, he said, and he wanted Bradley to see it. Besides, it would do them both good to have a break from the Embassy: they could talk undisturbed. As always, Vincent had a purpose.

The tombs were some fifty kilometres from the capital, and Vincent had contrived to commandeer a car from the Embassy pool. They arrived at three in the afternoon, and left the car halfway along the Sacred Way that led to the tombs, telling the driver to wait. From here, they set off on foot down the long, stone-paved roadway.

It was almost empty. A few Chinese tourists drifted ahead of them, and a horse-drawn cart rumbled by, driven by two small boys. In front of them lay a vast, level valley, filled with groves of trees. Jagged blue mountains stood around its rim, and the only buildings to be seen, over miles of countryside, were the tombs of the Ming emperors: handsome, palatial residences of the dead whose orange-tiled roofs were scattered across the distance. The still, sunny air seemed to Bradley to carry a tang of the mausoleum, and the valley's venerable quiet was somehow both hostile and uncanny. In Ming times, Vincent had told him, for an ordinary citizen to set foot here meant death. Colossal stone statues towered among willows on each side of the road: frowning military generals; lions and elephants; mythical beasts. Fixed and unreal, these giant white figures from the ancient Ming past; fixed and unreal, this silent valley, with its willows and cypresses and warm red walls. Long after he'd been recalled from China, Bradley would see Vincent and himself as subjects of that unreality, walking down the Sacred Way: partly because of its atmosphere of warning, but principally because he would come to regard that afternoon as a fatal turning point: the point where Vincent began his progress towards downfall and disgrace.

'The only tomb that's been excavated is that of Wan Li,' Vincent was saying. 'The one who squandered the empire. After him, the eunuch Wei dragged the Ming down to its destruction. How great they were at their height, the Mings! Ruthless, though, I must admit. The founding emperor, Chu Yüan-chang, was a brutal genius, with the same sort of peasant cunning as Chairman Mao. Paranoid and merciless, like Mao – and carried out similar purges. Back in the 'sixties, a very brave scholar and Party official called Wu Han wrote essays and plays that used Ming history as a way of exposing the madness of Maoism. He paid dearly for it, poor soul. When the Cultural Revolution came, Wu's *Life of Chu Yüan-chang* was denounced by the Maoists as a criminal attack on Mao. He died in prison, under torture.'

Vincent shook his head, frowning; then his face brightened and he began to make his customary optimistic gestures, hands waving.

'Yet the achievement of the Mings remains almost unique in history. Think, Brad: nearly three hundred years of peace and order, with the arts and learning flourishing, a literate population, an enlightened scholar gentry caring for the people, and the Confucian virtues holding it all together! Nothing in Europe at the time could compare. I often discuss it with Liu Meng.'

Bradley was smiling indulgently, as he usually did when Vincent was buoyed up by one of his enthusiasms. 'How *is* Professor Liu, by the way?'

'Well. Speaking of which – in the utmost confidence, Brad – it may soon be time for me to make my move.'

Bradley glanced at him, frowning. '*How* soon?'

'Very soon,' Vincent said. 'I still have a little further to go in winning Meng's confidence. I dare not include Dorothy in the discussions, and the opportunities to talk to Meng alone are very limited.'

'For Christ's sake, Vin, think again,' Bradley said. For once, his calm deserted him, and he spoke with unusual vehemence. 'Look at the facts,' he said. 'A distinguished Chinese scholar, a member of the Party – and he suddenly asks for asylum in Australia, on an officially approved visit to an arts festival? The embarrassment to Canberra would be huge. They'll never bloody wear it, Vin. They want good relations these days – because what's at stake is trade. You *know* all that. And thanks to my mate Mr Lao, you know that the Ministry of State Security people are watching you. Not only that; they want you to *know* they're watching you. Give the idea away, mate, before you get in any deeper.'

'Certainly not,' Vincent said.

He had spoken sharply, and had come to a halt in the shadow of a giant Ming general, whose hand was on his sword-hilt and who looked down fiercely on the two of them. Vincent, whose head just reached the general's waist, laid a hand on the massive stone forearm, turning to face Bradley.

'Look here, Derek,' he said. 'You really must understand that I know what I'm doing. In my business, a great deal contributes to a decision like this: professionally, there's much more to it than you know. You see only the tip of the iceberg, and I simply can't give you any more detail. But be assured I'm a step ahead of the MSS people – and Professor Liu is totally onside. He's already passed me invaluable information – which hasn't been unappreciated in Canberra, I can tell you. And now that he wants to get out, I believe I have a duty to help him.'

'Has he said he wants to go?'

'Not in so many words. Obliquely. Our only conversations are in his apartment – and Dorothy's usually listening.'

'And Dorothy isn't receptive,' Bradley said. 'Is she? Dorothy's dead frightened of the authorities. If she knew what you were planning, she'd be scared out of her wits.'

'Very perceptive of you, Brad. Both of them live in fear: you've realised that. They fear that the humiliation and imprisonment they went through before could come back; they're never safe. And you've also understood what a brave and remarkable old man Liu Meng is.' He paused; when he went on, his rapid voice trembled with extraordinary emotion, and it seemed to Bradley that his face had become more pallid, making the blue of his beard more pronounced. 'Can you picture the hell he lives in – a man of his sensibilities, surrounded by stupid inquisitors? By spies for the Party like that odious Yang Wenfu? By materialistic deadheads to whom beauty is a closed book? All that Liu Meng cares about has been destroyed or devalued by Marxist tyranny – so why shouldn't he escape it? And why shouldn't I help him do so, and enable him to spend his final years in freedom? I regard it as one of the greatest opportunities of my life. And I need your help.'

'*My* help?' Bradley stared at him.

Fists clenched at his sides, feet apart, Vincent said nothing, his eyes narrowed behind their glasses; he stared back, and waited.

Bradley closed his eyes briefly, then sighed. 'Tell me what it is you want me to do,' he said.

Vincent smiled. 'Nothing very difficult, old chap. I want you to come with me on my next visit, and use your charm on Dorothy. That's all. Talk to her, so as to give me the opportunity to speak privately with Liu Meng.'

Bradley looked up at the fierce Ming general for a moment, while Vincent watched him. A process was beginning that would lead to nothing but trouble; he felt sure of that. Yet he could not deny Vincent what he asked for. 'All right,' he said. 'I'll make conversation with Dorothy. But that's as far as it goes, Vin. And I wish you'd think again.'

Vincent put a hand on his shoulder. 'I knew I could depend on you, Brad.'

As they spoke, the silence of the road was broken by the buzzing of a tractor, being driven towards them by a young Chinese farmer in sunglasses. A pretty Chinese girl in a wide straw hat rode beside him. Both smiled and waved as they went by, their faces innocent and open as those of children. They buzzed slowly out of sight, and the valley's ancient quiet descended again: dense and profound, like the weight of accumulated time.

THREE

1

UNTIL RECENTLY, FOREIGN Affairs had given Bradley the life he'd wanted. During his twenties, he'd enjoyed the forays into alien cultures that the Department had provided for him, and had found his official duties reasonably absorbing. He'd liked settling back in his seat on an international flight, savouring the thought of the unknown country waiting for him at the end of it, and knowing that when he arrived, to be enveloped by strangeness, he would join a group of fellow countrymen whose tastes and attitudes were similar to his own: all of them inside a cocoon of privilege which acted as a buffer against the difficulties and demands outside. And like many young men of his kind, he'd also secretly enjoyed those particular pleasures of the senses that were woven into such a life; moments so ephemeral as scarcely to be described in words, even to himself: shaving in his bathroom in an international hotel, prior to going out into the night of an unknown country, dabbing on aftershave whose scent became part of the night's excitement and threat; walking alone into a dark piano bar to be greeted by the chink of ice and the shallow yet inviting tinkling of jazz piano; peering through the dusk there, in which perfume and cigarette smoke mingled, to see a pretty woman smiling at him.

But his twenties were over. Next month, in July, Bradley would turn thirty-one. Not yet old, but no longer young, he saw the drab, well-marked road to middle age stretching in front of him, with its banal yet unavoidable questions. Was he still following a career that satisfied him? Would he still want it in five years? If not, should he change direction now? And was it time to be married? At thirty, the world said, it was time to be married; but where was the woman he truly wished to marry?

As though in response to this, the figure of Erika Lange had appeared at the entrance to the road, smiling at him quizzically. His addiction to Erika (which was how he continued to categorise his feeling for her) had shaken Bradley's usual equanimity. He was no longer floating though life; she'd created an intensity that resembled malaise. And Bradley would tell himself later that he'd not invited this condition. It had made its entrance with pleasant nonchalance; now, like a virus, it had taken possession of him. So should he ask Erika to marry him? Was this what she wanted? And was it what he wanted himself? He had a powerful impulse to ask her; and yet he continued to fear that final involvement would lead to regret. What the nature of this regret might prove to be was unclear. It was merely an amorphous shape – like so many other shapes to be seen on the drab road to maturity. Certainly the episode of hysteria in Hangchow had something to do with his unease; he was clear about that. But the episode remained unexplained, since Erika refused to talk about it. 'I was just upset,' was all she would say; then her lips would tighten, and she would say no more.

During that summer in Peking – in the months from July to October – he and she were together in whatever spare time they had. This should have meant that he came to know Erika better; and yet it seemed to Bradley that this was only partly the case. Certainly he learned more in the factual sense – facts that she chose to tell him – but whether this meant that he had truly begun to know her was another matter. Somehow, nothing seemed certain about her. Why this was, he still couldn't be sure – except that he sometimes suspected that what she told him about herself and her past was edited; perhaps even censored or distorted. His suspicion wasn't based on anything very tangible; it was merely something he sensed in her personality: a fleeting expression in her eyes at such times; a sudden, inexplicable with-drawal. Erika was not all of a piece, as other people were: this was the only way he could put it to himself. Her personality kept shifting, as her moods did, so that she seemed to present herself in fragments; and when he tried to bring her into focus, the fragments flew apart.

Even so, they were happy together, much of the time. When they were both light-hearted, Bradley would forget about his reservations, and find that he was blissfully happy – as Erika seemed to be. When they laughed together, they did so on a level where nothing could touch them; where the world lay below them, viewed from a height that only they inhabited. They laughed about trivial things, mostly to do with their colleagues at the Embassy, or diplomats from other embassies whose foibles amused them. The French ambassador – known as *le petit Louis* for his eighteenth-century arrogance – provided particularly rich material for comedy, since he barely condescended to acknowledge anyone below the level of ambassador, and refused to deal with journalists at all, whom he regarded as vermin. He had once cut Moira Paterson dead, when she attempted to interview him at a reception. Bradley was able to imitate him – he had a talent for imitations – with an accuracy that Erika never tired of. ('Do *le petit Louis*.') He could also reproduce Charles Morton's mooing tones, and on hearing this voice, Erika would immediately begin to laugh. And yet, at the same time, she was oddly respectful of the Ambassador, and deeply impressed that Morton had praised Bradley's report on the Hangchow conference, and had duly sent it on to Canberra. In fact, Bradley realised, Erika was very much a creature of the Department: in awe of its hierarchies, admiring of its high achievers. That Bradley was seen as a rising young diplomat, and that he carried out his work with effortless success, seemed to add to her regard for him. When he expressed his growing indifference to these things, she would sometimes look at him in puzzlement, he noticed: almost with doubt.

But all doubts, both hers and his, dissolved when they made

love. They were obsessed with each other to a degree where everything else in life had become two-dimensional: their work; the
repetitious round of diplomatic receptions; the ancient city itself.
All these things had lost their solidity, becoming a mere backdrop
to the adventure of their passion. Compelled to be apart for any
length of time, they made constant phone calls to each other;
reunited, they were flooded with delight. Her beauty was of a
kind that constantly presented new aspects of itself, so that
Bradley never tired of her, and could never take her for granted.
He was physically possessed by her, in a way that sometimes
disturbed him – since any addiction is disturbing. This possession
had partly been achieved through the manner in which she
continued to swing between opposite poles in their lovemaking.
In the dark, a frenzied and aggressive maenad would appear,
sinuous and surprisingly strong, pinning his shoulders with both
hands, her flesh unnaturally white, her narrowed, shining eyes
and thinly tightened lips expressing a passion closer to anger than
to love – only to be replaced by a humble, wan nymph who
abased herself in front of him, her hair hiding her face.

What did he know about her?

From sporadic conversations – mostly in bed, which was the
only place where she was inclined to dwell on her past, or on
intimate matters – he had pieced together the main phases in
Erika's career over the past decade: from her twentieth year, when
she had left Tasmania for London, until the August of last year,
when she was posted to Peking. She was evasive about much of
her life, and reluctant to dwell on detail – especially detail
concerning her emotional involvements – but Bradley discovered
that there had been three main phases in her progress since she
first went abroad, each of them set in a different country; and two
of these phases seemed to have ended with the break-up of a love
affair. It was as though Erika could only conclude a relationship
by fleeing the country where it was set.

The first phase was in London, where she'd gone in 1972 with fellow journalist Geoffrey Baxter. At first, in her references to this period, Erika had maintained that Baxter, who was twice her age, had simply been a friend and mentor, helping her to get established in London, and sharing a flat with her. She always spoke respectfully of him, and grew indignant when Bradley asked if they'd been emotionally involved, refusing to discuss it. Eventually however, she admitted that she and Baxter had in fact become lovers, living together for over two years. She confessed this to Bradley – as she did a number of things – on a night when she'd been drinking, and had ceased to be as guarded as usual.

She owed Baxter a lot, she said. When she'd arrived in Britain, she'd found a hack job on a little local paper in North London; six months later, thanks to Baxter's connections, she was working on the *Evening Standard*. But then, at the beginning of 1974, for reasons she didn't make clear, she had quit her job on the *Standard* and had successfully applied for a position with Australia's Department of Foreign Affairs, as a press officer with the Information Service. Her first posting was New York. She felt badly about leaving Baxter, she said; he had been very broken up. But she had to get away; to go in a new direction.

As Bradley knew, much of an Information officer's work was routine, from a professional journalist's point of view, belonging more to the area of public relations and official propaganda than to genuine reporting – but it carried many privileges. Erika now travelled on a diplomatic passport, holding the rank of First Secretary (Information). She had lived in a large and expensive apartment which the Government maintained on Columbus Avenue, with two Filipino maids to service it. Here, as part of her duties, she would occasionally entertain visiting officials and politicians. She had loved New York, where she had spent the next three years; she longed to go back there. Possibly because of her mixed German and Irish-Australian origins, Erika's looks were seen by many people as being those of a particular type of American woman – and since her accent was hard to place, she was sometimes mistaken for an American, by foreign speakers of English.

The New York period, in her sporadic references to it, was painted in bright, feverish colours, or else in the sinister black and silver of American night, with its swarming electric stars. The glamour of America – that glamour previously absorbed from films and magazines – had cast its glow over everything for her, and was accepted without question. There was fairy food there, and Erika had picked it up with both hands. Even an American breakfast in a drugstore in the morning, with eggs sunny side up and bacon and hash browns, was a small adventure to her, and remained so. She had found everything she wanted in America; had found, apparently, the country she had always waited for, and should have been born in, like those immigrants who immediately called it home.

She spoke of New York many times before the name Mike Devlin began to occur. When it did so, it seemed at first that Devlin was simply one of many contacts with whom she'd become friendly: a man she said at first was an official in the State Department, based in Washington, who came frequently to New York. Bradley got a blurred picture of a handsome Irish-American in his forties who was probably Erika's ideal of the perfect American male: one from the country's upper echelons, with a special understanding of the workings of American power. She would quote him as an authority on American foreign policy, and on Washington intrigues, with a deference that amounted to awe. And Bradley sensed a peculiar, almost nervous tension when she spoke of him – a tension which had not been there in her references to the deserted Baxter. Her voice would sink low, and her eyes would dart sideways in that particular way that both she and Vincent had when discussing matters that were secret. Finally, as though revealing dangerous information, she told Bradley that Devlin's position at the State Department had been a cover, and that he had actually been an operative in the CIA. It was not only the man she held in awe, Bradley sensed; it was what he was. She had an almost mystical reverence for espionage, which he suspected lay at the heart of her continuing respect for Vincent.

Bradley soon gathered that she and Devlin had been lovers — even though she had told him that Devlin was married and had children. This affair, it seemed, had been far more tormented than the last; her voice went very flat when she spoke of it, in a way that Bradley knew hid strong emotion. Devlin was a Catholic, she said, and was never going to leave his wife and children; but the feeling between them was so strong that neither of them could bear to end the affair. Finally something had happened that brought it to an end, she said, and in 1977 she was recalled to Australia. It was some time before she divulged the reason for this, and when she did so she was clearly distressed. It seemed she had become pregnant to Devlin, and he had arranged an abortion.

'Please don't discuss this with anyone,' she said. 'When I left the States, I had a sort of breakdown, and the Department gave me sick leave. I was shattered; I still think about the baby. They posted me to Jakarta when I was better. It took me a long while to heal — and Mike kept phoning me there. He even turned up on assignment, and stayed for weeks. You never know where Mike will turn up; he could turn up here. He was still in love with me; he still is, as a matter of fact.'

'And have you got over him?' Bradley asked.

'Need you ask? I'm in love with you, now. I'm so glad we met: you give me real peace, Brad. But Mike still hasn't got over me.' She smiled, gazing into space. 'If I picked up the phone and called him now, he wouldn't know what to do.'

'If I picked up the phone and called him now, he wouldn't know what to do.'

This statement kept coming back into Bradley's mind, possibly because the smile that had accompanied it had shocked him. It had been dreamy; complacent; almost proud. It told him that Erika took pleasure in her hold over Devlin, even though she had severed the cord. He tried to forget it, but it stayed in his mind like a warning. And Devlin himself, who had clearly been made of stronger stuff than her other lover, loomed like a shadow in their conversations. Somehow, Bradley sensed, it was her awe of Devlin's profession that kept the CIA man permanently alive in her mind. It was not simply that she found the profession of espionage glamorous; there was something more to it, he thought. He would not learn what it was from Erika herself; she was far too taciturn. All that Bradley could surmise was that her obsession with the world of secrecy lay hidden in her past, and in her imagination.

The imagination! It was from this old-fashioned territory – no longer given fashionable importance, and having about it a suggestion of childishness – that both her feeling and Bradley's drew its potency. She had not fallen in love with Bradley simply because of what he was; he represented something else to her. She had told him that he made her feel 'tranquil'. Was tranquillity what he represented – where Devlin had represented danger and high secrecy? Or was it significant that Bradley seemed to be the first man in her life who was the same age as herself?

Whatever the case, Bradley had to admit to himself that his love for her was also centred in the imagination. He was not merely in love with the Erika he knew in reality, but with an insubstantial counterpart: a woman he had seen in dreams. Her appearances dated back to his early youth, and she was nearly always seen on a long, straight highway at night: an empty road which ran through open grassland, in a country entirely foreign to him. There was always a wind there; she wore a light overcoat, well buttoned up, and the scarf that was knotted at her throat blew sideways, fluttering and dancing. Her eyes, in the dark, were pale and fixed and wide, and seemed to seek him out. They had held neither friendliness nor hostility, and their expression could not be read; but he had known that in some way she had recognised him, and that she waited in his future.

2

JUST WHEN HE thought he'd become acquainted with Erika's many faces, Bradley discovered another.

Late one evening, he knocked on the door of her apartment and heard her call to him to come in. He walked through the little hall into the sitting room: a room filled with ornaments, arranged on cupboards, the coffee table, and along the side-board – many of them wooden carvings and *wayang golek* puppets, acquired during her time in Indonesia. She was sitting at the dining table, hunched over a sheet of paper, and wearing reading glasses. He had never seen her in glasses before, and had not known that she wore them. He stopped in a sort of aston-ishment as she looked up at him, pen in hand, her eyes clouded, still lingering on something inward. And the woman he saw now seemed drastically different from the beautiful woman he was accustomed to. The glasses transformed her, making her face severe. She had tightened her mouth in concentration, making her lips thinner than usual, and this added to her look of severity.

Then she took the glasses off, pushed the hair back from her forehead and smiled, and was Erika again.

He walked over to the desk. 'I didn't know you wore glasses,' he said.

'Only for close work,' she said. 'I wear contact lenses most of the time. I'm half-blind, without them.'

Bradley hadn't known this either.

He stood looking down at the desk, and saw that a sheet of drawing paper lay in front of her, on which she'd drawn the figure of a young woman who resembled herself: a pretty blonde girl in a felt hat and raincoat, trudging through the rain. In the background was a skyline that looked like New York. Erika had used a fine-tipped black drawing-pen, and the drawing had a professional competence, its style resembling that of American comic strips. This skill, like her glasses, was something he'd not known about, and he stood looking down at the drawing with frank interest. But then, following his gaze, she snatched up the sheet and turned it on its face.

'I'm sorry,' he said. 'I didn't mean to pry. But you draw so well. Did you study it, at some stage?'

'No,' she said. 'But I've always liked to draw. Sometimes I wish I could hole up in a cottage in the woods somewhere, and just draw and paint – not to exhibit; just for myself.'

'I'd like to see some of your drawings,' Bradley said.

She looked at him; then got up and went across to a dark-stained cupboard set against a wall. She pulled out some loose sheets of drawing paper, carried them back to the desk, and set them down in a pile in front of Bradley. She stood beside him in silence, watching him as he looked down at the drawing on top of the pile. It was a full-length, black-and-white portrait of Vincent, standing behind a small table. Bradley was struck by its professionalism, and the quality of Erika's draughtsmanship. Her use of line was delicate and confident, the detail meticulous without being fussy. The likeness was also striking; but the way in which Vincent was dressed was very peculiar, causing Bradley to repress a laugh.

He seemed to be in medieval costume: a large, floppy felt hat, and a dark cloak worn over a white shirt and hose. He was not wearing his glasses. He held a wand in his raised left hand, as though about to perform a trick. On the table in front of him lay a sword, an earthenware goblet, what looked like a baton, and a coin. He was looking directly at the viewer from under his hat, and Erika had captured with great skill the gleam that his eyes took on when he wished to be compelling, and the slant of his long, beard-shadowed jaw. His expression was serious yet pleasant, and seemed to be asking the viewer to observe something: his trick, perhaps.

'It's a terrific likeness,' Bradley said. 'But why have you got him in that outfit?'

'He's the Magician,' Erika said.

Bradley looked puzzled.

'The Magician,' she repeated. 'From the Tarot. Don't you know the Tarot cards?'

'I've never even looked at a pack. Why the Tarot?'

Again the quick, sideways glance, as though wondering how much to tell him. 'Because the whole of life's in the Tarot,' she said. 'All the important secrets.'

She had spoken softly, with the conviction of a religious devotee, and Bradley looked at her in surprise. 'What secrets are those?'

Erika shook her head. 'That can't be told in two seconds.'

'I guess not. But tell me: do you and Vincent tell your fortunes with these cards?'

'Sometimes,' she said. 'But that's not what interests us most. It's the meanings in the cards themselves we care about.'

'So what does the Magician stand for?'

'He's the first card in the major arcana: the Greater Secrets. He controls the four elements. You can see them on the table in front of him: the sword for air, the cup for water, the baton for fire, and the coin for earth. The Magician can sometimes be a trickster – but he's really a teacher: a guide to the mysteries.'

'Sounds like a pretty suitable identity for a secret intelligence officer,' Bradley said. But Erika showed no sign of amusement at this. Expressionless, she turned over the sheet, revealing the next drawing.

Again, Bradley was startled. This sketch, also in black and white, showed a woman in a dance pose, naked except for a scarf which was tied on a slant about her hips. Her dark, heavy hair had been let loose, falling over her shoulders and greatly changing her appearance; but the likeness was unmistakable. It was Moira Paterson: he would have known her from the large, piscine eyes alone. She held her left foot raised, and stood poised on the toes of her right. Her arms were above her head, as though in exultation, and she held a pair of wands. Her gaze was trained somewhere to the left as she danced, her eyes half-closed, her lips parted in a smile. Had it been executed by a man, Bradley thought, this drawing would clearly have been a work of frank sexual homage: an image intended to arouse.

'That's the World,' Erika said. 'The last card in the major arcana: number twenty-one. Her dance is the dance of life. She represents cosmic energy – she's free from all earthly bonds.'

Bradley said nothing, staring at the drawing.

'Some experts on the Tarot say she's actually a hermaphrodite,' Erika said. 'That's why she wears the scarf. We can't be sure what's underneath it.'

Now Bradley turned and looked at her. She wore a smile that was humorously suggestive, her eyes meeting his with a teasing expression.

'It's Moira Paterson,' he said.

Erika's mouth bent wryly to one side, still with a hint of prurient amusement. 'Clever of you to see that,' she said. 'I must have done a better likeness than I realised. She was perfect for the World.' She scanned his face. 'You look shocked,' she said. 'Does a nude drawing shock you, Brad?'

'You and she are lovers,' he said. 'Aren't you?'

For a moment, they stood facing each other in silence. In the silence, Erika's face became transfigured by anger: an anger so intense that Bradley experienced a primitive thrill of fear. Her lips made a thin, downturned line, and her eyes seemed lit from within by fury, holding his as though to hypnotise him. Then, without warning, she slapped him across the face.

He stood for a moment longer, his sleepy eyes startled, his face slowly reddening, a blade of his plain brown hair fallen across his forehead. The echo of the slap seemed to fill the room. Neither of them spoke or moved, and Erika glared at him defiantly, as though daring him to return the blow.

Instead he turned away, and walked out of the apartment.

He thought of leaving the Embassy compound and going into the city: going anywhere to get away. But it was late, somewhere near eleven o'clock; the external world was out of focus, and there was a buzzing in his head. He went upstairs to his apartment, dropped on the bed fully clothed, and lay on his back in the dark, the fiery stinging in his cheek slowly subsiding. He had never before found himself involved with anyone like Erika Lange, and it seemed to the peace-loving Bradley now that he wanted nothing so much as to extricate himself. One hand over his eyes, breathing deeply, he strove to regain his accustomed equanimity.

Enough, he told himself. *It's enough.*

Saying this, he was encased by a numbness which he welcomed. Being in love with Erika had meant living with a deep, humming note of apprehension; now it might cease to sound. Dimly, he knew that regret probably lay waiting; but for the present, this didn't matter. All that mattered was to regain his balance, and to bring things to an end.

He switched on his reading lamp, and reached for a book on the bedside table: a study of Sir Francis Walsingham, and the political intrigues of the Elizabethan period. Like his numbness, its measured prose brought him a false peace; a feeling of sanity. He read for something like twenty minutes before the phone rang.

For some moments, he let it ring, knowing who it would be. No-one else would phone him in his apartment near midnight. His heart raced, and his mouth went dry. Apprehension was back, but with it came something else: an absurd relief. His peace had been false; his resolution empty. She was not prepared to let go, it seemed. He picked up the phone.

'It's me.'

This was no longer the voice of the fury who had slapped him; instead, it was the low, deep, penitent voice of her other self. He said nothing, trying to collect his thoughts, his study of Francis Walsingham lying open across his chest like a shield. The voice spoke again, even and soothing and placatory.

'I'm sorry. I'm really sorry. I shouldn't have done that. You shocked me.'

'I'm sorry I said what I did.'

'It's not true, what you said. It's true that Moira's got the hots for me; but I'm simply fond of her, and she makes a good model. I've never been to bed with her.'

Bradley was silent for a moment. He knew in the common-sense part of his mind that this was not the whole truth, and that he should make a final attempt to free himself. Erika would always bring him excitement, but would never bring him ease; she would very likely lead him into boundless grief, and he feared this.

'I've been thinking,' he said. 'I don't believe we'd make each other happy. I'm a bit too straight for you: that's what it comes down to. I think we should end it.'

There was silence on the other end: a silence filled with the vague, fluctuating humming that accompanied all phone calls in China. When she spoke, her voice was strained and tight.

'End it? I thought you loved me, Brad.'

'I do. That's the trouble.'

'And I adore you.' Her voice rose. As she spoke, it grew more and more rapid, and took on a note of desperation. *'You're the only man I've ever been at peace with, do you hear? So don't ruin it. Don't do this to me.'*

She paused, and for a moment Bradley was silent. Then he said: 'I think you and I are too different. I think we'll bring each other pain – so I'm trying to spare us both.'

He was convinced now that he was right in this: a notion that grew stronger as her agitation increased. And yet, in a treacherous corner of his mind, he knew that he would probably not succeed in breaking away from her, and was foolishly glad that he would not succeed.

Silence had followed his speech. Then she spoke again, with an almost threatening intensity.

'Come back down here, and I'll show you you're wrong.'

'I don't think that's a good idea,' Bradley said. 'Let's at least sleep on it, and talk about it tomorrow.'

This was a final ploy: a bid to create a distance between them where Erika might have second thoughts. Yet even as he spoke, he knew that it was fatuous: a gamble that part of him wished to see fail. He had found that when Erika sensed rejection, her response was one of extreme alarm; and this was what happened now. Her voice rose, taking on the note of hysteria he had heard in Hangchow.

'No! Come down here now! If you don't, I'll bloody well come up there, and beat on your door.'

Her squeezed voice held fury again: the mingled fury and pleading of a thwarted child. Before he could answer, she had hung up the phone.

Bradley knew that she expected him to call back; but he decided not to. He remained convinced that they both needed time to reconsider; and he only wanted to deal with Erika when she'd regained her equilibrium. He was not good at dealing with excess, he thought. Erika talked of peace, and he suspected it was the peace he brought her that she wanted, possibly more than love: yet when she had it, she shattered it. He lay quite still for some five minutes; then he picked up his book.

The phone rang again, making him start. The voice he heard when he picked it up this time had changed. It was slow and quiet and slurred.

'I have a good supply of sleeping pills here. I've taken some, and I think I just might take a few more. Good night, Derek.'

There was a click, and the connection was broken.

He stood up, drawing a deep breath. Then, in spite of himself, he laughed under his breath. He'd done his best by the sane part of his nature, he thought; he'd given sanity a chance. Now he moved towards the door, carried on a reckless wave of pity and desire.

It was a compound to which he'd become addicted.

A pattern had now been set: one which would not be broken. It was a pattern set by Erika, and in some ways it resembled her lovemaking: always wildly intense, and swinging between aggression and submission. Sometimes Bradley felt that they were figures in a theatre: a theatre whose script was in Erika's possession, and which he scarcely understood.

For weeks at a time they would be happy: exalted by the knowledge that they were lovers of a special kind. Erika had a way of looking at Bradley with deep tenderness in her eyes, and of lovingly touching his cheek, which made him briefly feel secure in her love after all. But then what he thought of as her other life would invade.

She would report to Bradley that Mike Devlin had phoned her from New York, and might come soon to Peking on Agency business. Even though it was over between them, she would probably have to meet Mike, she would say; he still loved her, and she felt for the way he suffered. Surely Brad could not object to that? Or Moira Paterson would demand to spend time with her, and Erika would go in to the city and have dinner with Moira in her apartment in the Qijiayuan diplomatic compound, staying there overnight, and rekindling Bradley's suspicions about the nature of their relationship. She seemed at such times to be possessed by another personality. Her voice would become flat and monotonous and defensive; she would insist on her right to continue to keep in touch with these admirers of hers, while demanding that Bradley should trust her; and if Bradley expressed any dubiousness, the raging child would appear. Finally, when she lay repentant in his arms, they would make love; and Bradley sometimes wondered whether the conflict had been fabricated in the first place in order to lead to this catharsis.

One thing, however, was slowly becoming clear to him. No matter how much Erika might seem to abase herself, or might plead with him not to leave her, this somehow never demeaned her or made her absurd, as it would have done most other women. In fact, even when her behaviour was at its most extreme, she never risked contempt or rejection; never lost control of the relationship. How this could be was baffling to Bradley at first; until finally he decided that her power lay largely in her beauty: a power she never had to doubt. As well, experience in the past would probably have shown her that the more tormenting she became, and the more she veered between unpredictable poles of tenderness and withdrawal, the more her lover would try to hold her. Should he become too secure, she would introduce new elements of doubt, to undermine his confidence in her devotion to him alone.

Bradley became very familiar with the concrete stairway in the residential block connecting his floor to Erika's: he seemed constantly to be running up and down it, often in a state of emotional turmoil. He was uneasily aware of the glances of his diplomatic colleagues when they passed him there, or in the corridors; they must surely know of the affair at this stage. Once Arthur Chadwick, who lived with his wife on the same floor as Erika, had nodded at Bradley with a knowing expression as he passed him in front of Erika's door, causing Bradley to suspect that the two of them were becoming the subjects of facetious speculation.

He now had a key to her apartment. One night, in the aftermath of a flare-up between them, he let himself in and found the sitting room empty. They'd been reconciled on the phone, but had not met since; Bradley had been compelled to attend a reception with the Ambassador, and had not been able to come to her until now. It was after eleven o'clock. Erika had said she would wait up for him, no matter how late he was, and had sounded unusually desolate. She hated being alone.

He called her name, but there was no answer. Puzzled and cast down, he assumed that she'd gone out, and began to look about him. A lamp was on at her little desk under the window; this was the only light in the room, which was thus half-dark. He walked over to the desk and found a number of sheets of notepaper lying there. On every one, over and over again, Erika had drawn the girl in the raincoat, trudging through rain-swept streets. She had told him the girl's name was Ella. He frowned, looking at these doodles. He guessed that Erika had drawn them in a state of distress, because of their rift; and the sheer obsessive number of them was disturbing. They suddenly seemed to him to be a proof of serious unbalance, and to hold some sort of meaning which would be a vital clue to her nature, if he could only decipher it. Who was 'Ella'? Was it Erika – or another? Erika refused to say.

He walked over and looked into the bedroom, expecting it to be empty.

But she was there, in the dimness, lying on the bed asleep, in a dark-blue frock she'd no doubt worn in the office, dully illumined by a light through the window. He tiptoed across to her, leaving the overhead light off. She lay on her face, absolutely motionless. A glass and a half-empty bottle of vodka stood on the bedside table. She'd been drinking, apparently, until she passed out.

He lay down beside her, and took her in his arms. She muttered in her sleep; then turned towards him, her arms going about him. There was no smell of liquor on her breath. But vodka leaves no odour, he thought; and he wondered how often she was drunk without his knowing it. She held her liquor well; like most journalists, she'd had a good deal of practice.

On a night soon after this, Erika spoke of the Tarot again.

'The people in the cards are always waiting for us,' she said. 'When I first saw them, I felt very strange: I already *knew* them. That's because they'd come into my dreams, ever since I was a child. I often study them; they help me to understand what's happening to me – or what might be in store. They act as guides. I saw *you* in the cards, before I ever met you.'

Bradley smiled indulgently. They were lying in her bed, in the half-dark; only a bedside lamp was on. 'Really? And which card am I?'

Erika smiled, and glanced at him. 'You're the Fool.'

He laughed. 'Thanks a lot.'

She put a hand quickly on his chest. 'No: I'm not mocking you. The Fool is the loose card in the Major Trumps. He's a jester, but he's also the Green Man. He's setting out into the world with everything still to learn. He's young and full of hope.'

'I'm glad to hear it. And which cards act as your guides?'

'Those to do with the Goddess. She's there in all her different aspects, in the Major Trumps. The Mother Goddess appears as the Empress. And the one called the Star is the Naked Goddess: mistress of earth and sea. She's called Astarte in the East; Artemis in the West.' Her expression had grown solemn. 'The Tarot's especially relevant at present,' she said. 'That's because the female principle's becoming dominant in the world again, now that patriarchy's over. People have to take her seriously.'

'And do you take her seriously?'

'Of course. I pray to her, when I'm in trouble. Once in New York, when I was in terrible despair over Mike, and on the edge of a crack-up, I felt her close to me. I actually felt her warmth, hovering over me. It saved me from doing something silly.'

Bradley, who took none of this seriously, began to feel uncomfortable. To change the subject, he said: 'You see the Magician as Vincent's card, and mine as the Fool. So which is your card?'

For answer, she threw off the sheet that covered them both. 'I'm the Star,' she said. Her gaze contained a mixture of flirtatiousness, pride and challenge, and a special little smile raised the corners of her lips: a smile he knew well, since it appeared when she wished to stimulate him, or to let him into a secret. She wore this smile when she flirted with men – even old and quite unattractive men – giving them sideways, half-childlike glances that invited confidences. It wasn't that she wished to get involved with them, Bradley had learned; it was because she seemed to need admiration, no matter from what quarter it came.

'How do you know you're the Star?' Bradley asked. He was postponing the moment when he would reach out and touch her.

'From my dreams. One dream keeps being repeated,' she said. 'I'm lying on a bed with nothing on, and a whole lot of people are looking down at me.'

'Who are these people?'

'I don't know,' she said, and her face grew serious; almost troubled. 'It's dark, and I can't see their faces. But they're all looking at me.'

They stood on the edge of the human torrents that flowed along Chang'an Avenue West. It was nine o'clock at night; they'd just emerged from Hongbin Lou, a Muslim restaurant where they'd eaten dinner.

October now, and an icy breeze was blowing up the avenue: a foretaste of North China's bitter winter. Erika was wrapped up in her long navy overcoat, while Bradley wore a ski jacket; but they both began to shiver, and to make small sounds of protest. They turned to each other, and laughed.

Neither spoke, and neither needed to: they had laughed out of a sense of pure wellbeing; out of pleasure in their love for each other; out of wry amusement at the autumn cold, which was serious but exhilarating. They had enjoyed their dinner of Mongolian hotpot, and had drunk a good deal of wine; they were happy, and looked at each other knowing they were happy. Erika's cheeks glowed pink with the cold, and her eyes shone; she wore a pale-blue knitted beret, pulled low on her head, and it made her look very youthful: closer to twenty than thirty. Bradley took her arm, and gripped it tightly.

'Marry me,' he said.

The words had come out without his thinking about them; without his even knowing that he would utter them. It was as though another voice had spoken from inside him, and he experienced a rush of alarm, mingled with reckless elation.

Her head came up very quickly, her smile fading; and her eyes, reflecting the streetlights, searched his with an expression that resembled dismay. When she spoke, he had the impression that her words, like his, had sprung from her without prior thought.

'I'm not ready,' she said.

'You're not ready?'

'No. I wasn't ready to hear you ask me that, Derek. I have to think.'

'All right,' he said. 'That's okay.'

She nodded. Then she turned and began to walk away, moving quite slowly; but she was quickly swallowed up by the remorse-lessly moving phalanx of Chinese, in their blue boilersuits and padded winter jackets.

Bradley stood looking after her. Did she expect him to follow? Or did she simply intend to disappear? Soon all that identified her was the pale-blue beret, bobbing among the multitude of black heads and fur-lined caps. But then she stopped on the kerb, turned, and looked back at him. Smiling, she raised her hand and beckoned.

He made his way though the crowd, dodging through what spaces he could find, conscious of the many almond eyes that followed his progress. When he came up to her she was smiling, and her expression was one of simple joy. She put her arms about his neck, leaning back as she did so to look into his face.

'Yes,' she said. 'The answer's yes, mister.'

'You know that nothing could make me happier,' Vincent said. 'I've always hoped that you'd marry her, Brad: I believe that you're the one to look after her.'

'You sound as though you planned it,' Bradley said. The words were intended to be light; but they came out almost like a challenge.

He and Vincent were walking in Beihai Park again, in mid-afternoon. It was still and cold and overcast, and both of them wore gloves, and ski jackets over their suits. The water of the lake was grey, and the bell-shaped tower of the White Dagoba looked forlorn, like something seen in memory. Vincent's gloved hands were clasped across his middle as he walked, as though to protect something valuable there.

'I didn't plan to entrap you,' he said, 'if that's what you mean.' His tone was guarded: the tone he usually used when discussing intelligence matters.

'Of course not,' Bradley said. 'But you make Erika sound as though she's emotionally fragile. Should I be concerned about that?'

Vincent came to a halt beside the white stone balustrade above the lake. He looked at Bradley sharply, as he used to do when they debated ideas. 'But you *know* that she's emotionally fragile,' he said. 'Don't you? And you must have taken that into account when you asked her to marry you. What more can I tell you?'

Bradley hesitated. There were many questions about Erika that he wanted to put to Vincent; questions he'd not asked before. Yet now he found himself uncertain about doing so. Partly it was because he dreaded to hear the answers; but also it was because he suspected that Vincent would evade being genuinely open with him. The silence extended, until Vincent finally broke it. This time his tone was conciliatory.

'Erika's not like other women,' he said. 'You've surely realised that, Derek. Secrecy is important to her – as it is to me. Don't try to pry into all her secrets, old chap, or you may end up losing her. And don't try to judge her in a conventional way. If you do that, you'll find yourself putting ugly labels on her – labels that are simply inadequate, where Erika is concerned.'

Bradley frowned. 'What sort of labels?'

'"Promiscuous",' Vincent said. '"Bisexual". Labels like that. To a limited mind, they'd fit, of course. But not where you're concerned, I hope. You must already know Erika better than that, and realise that although in a way those things are true, they're part of something larger: something extraordinary and wonderful. So don't try to cage the bird, or she'll fly away. Remember, it's you she loves. You offer stability, and she needs it badly.'

He smiled; then turned and began to walk on. Walking beside him, falling into silence again, Bradley was gripped by a chill that was not caused by the weather. Vincent had not dismissed his suspicions, he had confirmed them; and it seemed to Bradley now that he had known these things already, without any need for Vincent to spell them out; he had simply chosen not to believe them.

'There's a trauma in her past, of course,' Vincent said suddenly. 'That's at the root of it all.'

'What kind of trauma?'

'That I can't tell you,' Vincent said. 'You'll hit on it eventually, I feel sure.' He glanced at Bradley in a way that discouraged any further enquiry. Then, his face softening, he placed a hand on Bradley's shoulder, and his voice took on its most sentimental tone. 'She loves you, Derek, that's what matters. She's always gone with older men, and those affairs were bound to end badly. She's never loved a man of her own age: one who can bring her real harmony. Don't let her down, will you?'

'I'll try not to,' Bradley said. He could no longer look at Vincent. There was a taste in his mouth like metal.

3

WHEN ERIKA WAS absent, she became an idea: an entity whose form was always fluid. This morning, Bradley found that his notions about her had changed again.

It remained remarkably difficult to bring her into focus, and it would surely be unwise to take literally everything that Vincent had said about her yesterday, he thought. Even when she was present, Erika changed constantly; how then was he to reach any final conclusion about her? And why should he not believe that she wanted to begin a future with him where everything would be different?

The truth was that Bradley was now so deeply in love that he was prepared to deceive himself. The thought of losing Erika, despite the many tensions she created, was no longer tolerable to him; and it was too late now, he told himself, to try to step back again, or to reconsider his proposal of marriage.

When he went into his office, at nine o'clock, he found a note lying on his desk asking that he see the Ambassador as soon as possible. Walking along the corridor towards Charles Morton's office, he saw Erika coming the other way, in a crisp white blouse and skirt, accompanied by a female secretary from the Information section. This was the first time he'd seen her since yesterday's meeting with Vincent; he and she had not been together the previous evening, since she'd been visiting her friends at the British Embassy. Now, coming towards him, she raised her eyebrows and smiled, her face full of pleasure and the hopefulness of morning. As they passed each other, she murmured: 'See you tonight' – and in that moment, with its promise and its natural- ness, Bradley entirely rejected the picture that Vincent had drawn. This immaculate, confident, beautifully groomed young woman – a woman he knew to be fastidious to a degree, and almost old-fashioned in her concern for her reputation in the Department – could not be the figure that Vincent had hinted at. Both he and Vincent had drawn a profile from fictions and semi- fictions and dubious elements from her past: a profile that was surely distorted.

So Bradley reasoned, on the morning when the blow fell on Vincent and himself.

He sat on a straight-backed chair in front of the Ambassador's desk; Charles Morton sat behind it. The Ambassador was always extremely friendly to Bradley, adopting something of a fatherly tone with him, and he usually suggested that they sit in his green armchairs and have coffee. Today, however, he seemed to wish to be formal: there was no offer of coffee, and his manner was constrained. He fidgeted with his unlit pipe, which lay in a ceramic ashtray next to a framed photograph of his wife and grown-up daughters. Finally, he looked at Bradley directly, brushing back his ever-flopping, boyish grey forelock.

'I'm afraid I have something pretty serious to tell you,' he said. 'First, however, there are some things I want to make clear, Derek. In the short time you've been here, you've impressed me greatly with your performance. I like the way you go about things, and I know that you've been handling the Chinese officials with tact and skill. I believe you'll go far in the Department. For that reason, I was looking forward to working with you for the full length of your posting.'

Bradley's eyes narrowed at the use of the past tense. Seeing this, Morton held up his hand, and went on quickly.

'What I have to tell you isn't easy. The fact is, both you and Vincent Austin are being recalled. I'll explain why in a moment, but let me make one thing clear. Austin is being recalled because of a gross error of judgement. This is not so in your case: I believe you are entirely blameless. I'm very distressed that you have to go, and I hate to have to tell you this.' He looked down at his desk for a moment; then he looked up again, frowning. 'Firstly, I don't know whether you are aware of this, but your friend Austin is in fact an ASIS officer, working under cover.'

Bradley said nothing, leaving the Ambassador to conclude what he would from his silence.

'To tell you the truth,' Morton said, 'I never like having those people attached to an Embassy. I'm not awfully fond of spies: a necessary evil at the best of times. But one has no choice. I realise that Vincent is brilliant, and has apparently had a successful career in ASIS. I admired his obvious abilities – but I never felt easy about him. It seems I was right in that.' He picked up his empty pipe and examined it carefully; then he sighed, and looked up at Bradley again. 'I'll tell you exactly what has happened,' he said. 'Then you'll see my position, Derek – and Canberra's position as well. We're faced with the most enormous bloody embarrassment. It began with an assistant to the Divisional Chief in the Chinese Foreign Ministry contacting us here at the Embassy. I'm talking about the division that oversees relations with Australia and New Zealand, you understand. They asked to set up an appointment for me to personally call in at the Ministry to talk to the Divisional Chief. When they were asked the reason, the answer was that Mr Huang would make it clear when I came.' He cleared his throat. 'As you may know, Derek, that sort of low-key approach from the Chinese means it's something very serious. I knew straight away that we had trouble, and I was right.'

He drew out a leather tobacco pouch and began to fill his pipe, head bent, giving it his entire attention.

'When I got to the interview with Mr Huang, another man was present,' he said. 'He turned out to be a highly placed officer from their Ministry of State Security, and he was not a pleasant fellow. Looked like a thug, in fact. Lao Zheng, his name was.

What followed was quite the most distasteful interview of my career. Mr Lao more or less took over the meeting, and the accusation he made was that Vincent Austin has for some time been carrying on an underhand liaison with Professor Liu Meng, of Peking University. You know Professor Liu, I believe?' He looked up, putting his pipe in his mouth.

'Yes, I know him,' Bradley said. 'He and his wife are very good friends of Vincent's. Vincent and Professor Liu share interests in literature. I've become friendly with them too. I've visited their apartment a number of times, with Vincent. And I don't believe that you could call Vincent's relationship with Liu an underhand liaison.'

Once again, Morton held up his hand. 'You'd better hear the facts, before you comment,' he said. 'Professor Liu was giving Vincent occasional information on policy developments in the State Council. Vincent acquainted me with this, as he was bound to do, since he was reporting on it to his superiors in Canberra. What Austin did *not* tell me – or Canberra – was that he was planning to arrange for the Lius to defect.'

'I'm sure he would have done – once it became a possibility,' Bradley said.

'Please, Derek. I understand your loyalty to Austin,' the Ambassador said. 'But he should have mentioned this madcap scheme far sooner. Had he done so, I'm sure Canberra would have squashed it. Instead, what has happened is this. Dorothy Liu has gone voluntarily to the authorities to complain of him – probably without her husband's knowledge.'

'I see.'

Bradley sat very still, while Morton struck a match and began to light his pipe. It was a clean, well-maintained pipe, and the blue clouds he released were fragrant. Puffing, while Bradley watched him, he looked across at Wu Wei's scholar reading under the pine tree, and studied him with a mournful expression: perhaps he was thinking of Professor Liu. Finally he looked back at Bradley.

'The position is, I suspect, that Dorothy Liu was terrified. You know their history. She could see Liu losing his position, and the two of them spending their old age in another prison camp. So she told the authorities of Austin's suggestions, asking that he be stopped, and begging that she and Professor Liu should not be punished, since they had no intention of doing what Vincent suggested. The authorities have agreed to this, I'm told. I hope for the sake of those two old people that they keep their word.'

'So do I, Ambassador,' Bradley said softly. 'But that's a pious hope, isn't it?'

Morton shrugged. 'I suppose so.'

'I want you to know I greatly admire Professor Liu,' Bradley said. He was sitting with clenched fists, and trying to keep his voice even. 'He's a fine scholar, trapped among bullies and fanatics who can't even begin to know his worth. I can understand Vincent's wanting to get him and his wife out. I only wish it could have been done.'

'You knew about this plan?' The Ambassador looked at him sharply.

'Vincent mentioned the idea,' Bradley said. 'I told him that in my view, it could never work. The Lius were too old, too involved with their family here, and I could see that Dorothy would never agree. It's a tragedy.'

The Ambassador stared at Bradley, taking in his set jaw and clenched fists. What might have been a shadow of dubiousness had crept into his face, but his tone, when he spoke, was soothing. 'I'm glad you've been honest with me,' he said, 'and I understand your feelings. No doubt they do you credit, Derek, but it's not our job to get involved with such things, as you well know. I bitterly regret the way you've been drawn into it – but the fact is, you have been. This fellow Lao produced a set of photographs showing you and Vincent entering Professor Liu's apartment building. They were taken on different dates, apparently. The MSS people claim that you went there with Austin on three separate occasions. Would that be right?'

'Yes,' Bradley said. 'But why should I be expelled for that?'

'You shouldn't be, of course,' Morton said. 'But you know what their system is like. This situation is very serious – and you were indirectly involved, as the Chinese authorities see it. They are accusing Vincent Austin of conducting an intrigue with Liu: of "exchanging ideas hostile to the regime". That's how they put it.' He pointed his pipe stem at Bradley, and his face took on a degree of sternness. 'Austin could have been put in prison for that – but I'm relieved to tell you it won't happen. Instead, what the Chinese are saying is this: that it will be in the interests of both our countries if the two of you are quietly recalled – with an interval between your departures. If our Government cooperates, there will be no publicity. I've already talked to Canberra, and they've agreed. Their attitude is: Let's cut our losses – it could be so much worse. And you can see their point.'

'Oh yes,' Bradley said. 'I can see their point.' He sat back, feeling numb, and let his hands go limp. He didn't regret leaving China, but his immediate concern was that he would be separated from Erika.

'Please understand,' Morton said, 'there won't be a mark against you – as there will be with Austin, I'm afraid. ASIS will deal with him, of course: it's their problem. I can tell you, though, I don't think they'll look kindly on a cock-up like this. Your own case is quite different. You'll be given another posting very quickly, I'm sure. I want you to know that I'll be putting in my own report about you, and it will be absolutely positive. I'll show it to you before it goes off.'

'I appreciate that,' Bradley said.

Morton shook his head, and sighed. 'Foreign Affairs isn't an easy service,' he said. He nodded towards the photograph of his wife. 'I'm deeply interested in China, despite all its difficulties, but my wife has become quite unhappy here, and her health isn't good. My next posting will be my last, and she and I are both hoping I'll get Washington. But there are two more years to go, and one never knows.' He sighed. 'So you see, we all have our troubles, Derek.'

He stood up, and Bradley did the same. Morton came around the desk, and put a hand on his shoulder. 'Don't worry,' he said. 'I do assure you, I'll look after you.'

'Thank you, Ambassador. But who'll look after Vincent?'

The Ambassador pursed his lips. Then, without answering, he shook his head.

4

CHURNING AND RUMBLING, enveloped by the silver of a monsoon downpour, the ferry moved out fast from the Kowloon wharves, leaving behind it a complex village of junks. Bradley and Erika sat on a slatted bench on the covered top deck, holding hands in silence, staring into the high black night of Hong Kong's harbour, nursing an excitement which had no direct focus, which had been with them almost constantly over the past three days, and was expressed in the tightening of their hands.

The seats around them were packed with Chinese clad in every sort of dress but the blue cotton uniform of the austere Republic beyond Kowloon: young men in variegated sports shirts or light-weight business suits; girls in cotton dresses or the close-fitting, silk *cheongsam*; priestly old men with wispy beards, in the high-necked gowns of old China. Out in the raining dark, the shifting lights of freighters, passenger liners, junks, and the more dubious small craft of the South China Sea were blurred and enigmatic as stars. Ahead, on the other side of the channel, a grid of more stable yellow lights drew rapidly nearer: the skyscraper windows of Hong Kong, on its island.

Bradley was on his way home. He was booked on a flight to Sydney tomorrow morning, having spent three days here with Erika, staying in the Hong Kong Hilton. She had taken leave in order to be with him before he left, and they had spent this after-noon shopping and wandering in Kowloon, conscious that their time was running out. Now, as they sat in silence on the ferry, staring into the rain, he knew that their thoughts were running on similar tracks. They were trying to penetrate their future together: a future which – despite constant, serious and exultant talk about it, and despite a vision they had of it as large, thrilling, and beyond the ordinary – somehow remained unclear.

When he had told Erika that he and Vincent were to be recalled, she had stared at him in amazement for many moments. Then, with the impulsive quickness she often displayed, she murmured: 'I'll come with you.'

Bradley had asked her what she meant. Was she saying that she'd resign?

Yes, she said, she'd resign, and come back to Australia. But she'd have to give the Department at least a month's notice, which meant that she must serve out her time in Peking, and then follow him. Since Bradley would be based in Canberra, working on a desk in Foreign Affairs until he was given another overseas posting, she would join him there, she said, and look for work as a freelance journalist. When his future was clear they'd be married, and she'd go with him to wherever he was posted.

Bradley had been filled with elation at this. Except for his concern for Vincent, it seemed to him that his life was now moving towards fulfilment. But the next day, small shadows had appeared.

Erika's mood was no longer as joyful as his own, it seemed. A reaction had set in, mostly concerning Vincent's downfall. The day before – the day of the Ambassador's revelation – she had merely been shocked at what had happened. But then, having spent over two hours alone with Vincent in his apartment, she grew deeply despondent, almost as though his disgrace were her own. It seemed that they had jointly analysed what had happened, and the full extent of Vincent's disaster had sunk in. Erika's talk with Bradley revolved around this constantly. She had blamed Charles Morton and Vincent's superiors in ASIS for not standing up to the Chinese: almost irrationally, she saw them as betraying Vincent; and nothing that Bradley could say would persuade her otherwise.

Bradley had been allowed two more weeks in China before he left; but Vincent had been informed that he must leave on the day after the Ambassador had interviewed him. He had therefore spent a good deal of the day of the interview shut in his apartment, packing his effects and making arrangements for some of them – including his prized Cloud Pattern carpet – to be transported to Australia after he left.

Bradley had gone to see him directly after his own interview with Morton. He had found Vincent almost paralysed with shock, sitting in a chair and staring blankly in front of him, hands locked on his chest, his shoulders close to his ears. His voice had lost its usual resonance and vitality, and was low and almost expressionless.

'You were right, Derek, old chap. You were absolutely right,' he said. 'But I wouldn't listen – and I'm paying for it now.'

Bradley tried to reassure him, suggesting that when Vincent got back to Canberra, he'd find that ASIS had understood what he'd tried to bring off, and that he'd simply been unlucky. He was surely entitled to a failure now and then.

'No,' Vincent said. 'No. Failure's not tolerated in my game. I've already spoken on the phone to – certain people. My career's in ruins, Brad. Ruins.' He finally looked at Bradley. He had removed his glasses, and his eyes seemed more deeply sunken than usual. 'But it's not my failure that matters,' he said. 'It's what it may do to my poor Liu Meng. Dear God: all my fault.'

Abruptly, he put his face in his hands and kept it there. He was not weeping, but his attitude was that of one who weeps, and Bradley sat looking at his friend with mixed feelings. Although he pitied him, he also felt appalled at the possible disaster that Vincent had visited on the Lius; but he had put this from his mind now, and had begun to offer reassurance, reminding Vincent that the authorities had told Dorothy Liu that no blame would be attached to Liu Meng.

But Vincent had interrupted him, raising his face from his hands. 'No,' he said. 'Don't let's pretend. You know the Party's promises mean nothing.' His voice became small: almost pleading. 'Please, Derek – leave me. Come back later.'

When the ferry docked at the Wanchai pier, Bradley and Erika took a taxi back to the Hilton.

After they had washed and changed, they caught the lift down to the ground floor arcade to eat a light meal in the hotel's coffee shop. They had a craving for good coffee, and for the sort of Western snacks that had been unavailable in Peking; they'd eaten pancakes and toasted sandwiches here a number of times in the past three days. They had also developed a peculiar fondness for the coffee shop itself: a fondness that was quite irrational, since it was merely a variation on the sort of café that is found in international hotels everywhere. But their time together was running out, and, like other lovers in such circumstances, they were forming sentimental attachments to places and objects that were part of their fleeting happiness: landmarks that would soon disappear. The Cat Street Coffee Shop ranked high among these, and had almost become a refuge.

It was designed in chic imitation of a food stall for the Chinese poor. On one side of the long, dusky room, which had spotlights and fans in the ceiling, there was a shed-like bar with a sloping roof of galvanized iron, supported by crude wooden posts painted white, and with cheap matchstick blinds drawn halfway up. But there crudity ended. Low, elegant lamps hung in the area above the cash register, and pretty, painted birdcages, containing flowers instead of birds, were suspended above the bar. A row of Chinese counter-hands, in smart black suits and floral waistcoats, served snacks, coffee and drinks to the customers seated on stools there. Behind the bar, a long hatchway framed the kitchen, where cooks in tall white hats could be seen, stooping and nodding in a golden-yellow glow of culinary promise. All was rush and energy here: the money-charged energy of British Hong Kong. A team of

Chinese waitresses in tight red jackets and black trousers attended the small round tables set about the room, moving with electric speed, chattering incessantly to each other. The customers were a mixed crowd of Europeans and Chinese, all expensively dressed, some of the men in business suits, others in tuxedos, most of the women in cocktail frocks or evening gowns, ebbing and flowing and talking loudly, creating an atmosphere of expectancy, none of them here for long but clearly pausing on the way to more elegant and formal pleasures, in Hong Kong's bright-lit towers. Only Bradley and Erika lingered at their table, watching the shifting scene.

'This is our happy place,' Erika said. She reached across the table and took Bradley's hand.

'Right,' Bradley said, and laughed under his breath. 'The Cat Street Coffee Shop: our home from home.'

They went on holding hands, looking at each other, amused at their own silliness. Their table was by one of the shuttered windows looking onto the arcade; they had finished their toasted sandwiches, and were drinking their first cappuccinos. At the next table, a grey-faced European businessman in his fifties was sitting with his young Chinese mistress; his eyes lingered on Erika, as men's eyes so often did.

One of the Chinese waitresses alighted by their table like a bird. 'You want more coffee?'

'Why not?' Bradley said. 'We need to keep up our strength.'

Erika, still holding his hand, gave him her most knowing smile. 'You got that right, mister. This is our last night.'

'I don't need reminding,' he said.

'Soon you'll be in bloody boring Canberra. Where do you think they'll post you next?'

'No idea. I'd like a European city. There's a possibility of relieving in Vienna for a year.'

'That would be great. And we'll be married, and while you're working, I'll walk in the Vienna woods, or sit and sketch by the Danube. We'll go skiing.'

They had indulged in these fancies constantly, as they wandered through the teeming alleyways of Wanchai, or rode in the double-decker trams along Hennessy Road. They continued to look at each other; then both their smiles faded.

'I'll miss you,' she said. 'How will I manage without you?'

'We'll talk on the phone. It won't be long. Have they agreed to let you go in a month?'

She looked aside. 'I haven't told them yet.'

A faint chill ran through Bradley. 'Why not? I thought you'd do it straight away,' he said.

Erika didn't answer at first; she avoided his eyes, picking up the fresh cup of coffee the waitress had just put in front of her. She sipped; then she said: 'I talked to Moira, and she said it might put a black mark on me, going so quickly. She could be right: I need to think about it. Foreign Affairs has been good to me for a long time. It's been almost like a home: the only one I've had. They might need more time to replace me, and if they do, I think I should probably give it to them. I'll discuss it with Charles Morton, when I get back.'

'What the hell would Moira know? Just give them a month,' Bradley said. A sense that something was going wrong was stealing over him: a mounting, nebulous alarm which he tried to dismiss. 'They'll manage,' he said. 'We're starting a new life, aren't we? We're going to be married. What does it matter how much notice you give?'

She looked at him now as though he were speaking in a foreign language: one she could only just understand. 'Married,' she said, and looked down at the table, as though examining the concept. 'Yes. I suppose that does come first, doesn't it? It sometimes seems a bit unreal – being married.'

Bradley stared at her, saying nothing, and she closed her hand on his again, smiling into his face. 'Darling, don't be upset. I just want to do this the right way.' She now adopted what Bradley thought of as her professional voice: dry and rather boring, so that he had difficulty in attending to what she said. 'I'm not going to stop being a journalist, you have to understand that,' she said. 'My professional reputation matters to me, and it's important I don't leave Foreign Affairs in bad odour. I might want the Department's recommendation some time, and I don't want to mess up my CV. I also have certain standards of my own, Brad: I won't let my colleagues down.'

Bradley sat back in his chair. 'All right,' he said. 'How much more time did you think of giving them?'

'Three weeks more at the most,' she said. 'Is that so bad?'

'I guess not,' he said. 'Just don't let them extend it even further. Sorry: I was being a bit heavy. I just had a feeling.'

She stared at him, her eyes seeming to grow more pale than usual, perhaps through concentration. It was as though they were playing poker, he thought, and she had realised that he'd guessed what cards she held. The thought was absurd, and seemed to have no meaning; yet he could not dismiss it.

'*Stop* having feelings like that,' she said. 'I love you, and you'd better believe it.'

Going up in the lift to their room on the tenth floor, they stood in silence. There were no other passengers. The lift was driven by a Chinese dwarf dressed in the blue-and-gold silk robe of a nineteenth-century mandarin, wearing the traditional cup-shaped little hat. He smiled at them; he seemed to speak no English except to announce the floors, but they always greeted him. Like the Cat Street Coffee Shop, he was part of the transient world here that furnished their happiness: part of a dream from which they'd soon wake.

Inside their room, only the bedside lamps had been left on, and the curtains were open. The big plate-glass windows framed the darkness and the city's aerial lights and neons. Like the coffee shop, the room had a Chinese motif: bamboo furniture, and replicas of traditional silk paintings hanging on the walls. The covers were turned back on the bed, and a chocolate in gilt paper had been placed on each pillow.

Erika crossed the room and stood by the windows. Bradley

came and stood beside her, and they looked out in silence at Hong Kong's blazing tower blocks. Then she turned to him, with a sudden, almost savage movement he'd come to know well. Her face, tilted to look up into his, was livid in the half-light, her expression resembling anger, her lower lip creeping out. It was not anger, he knew, although it was almost as daunting. Her arms went around his neck.

'Now,' she said. 'Now.'

As they kissed, he pulled down the zip of her dress at the back.

His plane for Sydney left at ten. He had set the clock-radio by the bed for seven-thirty.

He woke to the muted voice of Rod Stewart singing 'I Don't Want to Talk About It'. Its volume increased; he opened his eyes, and reached out to touch Erika. But she was no longer next to him. He sat up abruptly, and punched the radio off. He looked about the room, which was still dim. It was empty, and there was no light on in the ensuite bathroom. Blinking away sleep, he began to comprehend that she was gone; there was no sign of the dark-green suitcase and matching cabin bag which she had packed last night and left by the dressing table. They were handsome bags: expensive-looking, like all her possessions.

He got out of bed and looked wildly about the room; then he checked the bathroom, which was also empty. Coming back towards the bed, he saw the sheet of hotel notepaper lying next to the radio. He picked it up and sat on the edge of the bed to read it, staring at the beautifully neat handwriting.

Dear Brad,

It's five o'clock, and I'm going. I'll have a coffee at dear old Cat Street, and then fill in time in the town until I catch my eleven o'clock flight for Peking.

I'm not leaving you, please understand that. I love you as much as ever.

So why am I going? Because there's something I have to tell you

*before you fly home, and I can't bear to tell you in person. I'd rather
set it out on paper.*

*I'm not sure that I want to be married. I've never been sure that I
want to be married, and don't want you to count on it. That's what
I had to say, and couldn't say to your face. I'm not saying I won't ever
marry you, please understand that – I'm saying I'm not sure. For now,
it might be better if we both stay free.*

*I'm going to think this over in Peking, and you should think it over
too. I'll talk to you on the phone. Please call me at the Embassy as soon
as you have an address in Canberra.*

I do love you. You're the nicest man I've ever known.

Erika

Half an hour later he sat in the hotel shuttle bus, staring out
blankly through the window as it pulled away from the steps of
the Hilton. The tall, handsome Sikh doorman in his red frock-
coat and white turban was opening the doors of arriving cars as
he always did, elevating an outsized umbrella over the heads of
the passengers to protect them from the latest monsoon shower.
Bradley found the sight of him unbearable: like the smiling dwarf
lift-driver, he had once been a figure in the special landscape
of happiness. Raindrops streamed down the window, obscuring
Bradley's view as the bus gathered speed.

It plunged down a decline now and entered a tunnel, whose
long, lamp-studded darkness closed around him like despair. He
leaned back in his seat, setting his jaw and closing his eyes. *Over*,
he said. *Over.*

Telling himself this, knowing it was finally true, he was
surprised to discover a sort of frigid and desolate relief creeping
over him. To be without Erika was to be free of unease, and the
constant gathering of anguish; and he knew that at some time in
the future he might welcome his release.

PART THREE

Master of the Registry

ONE

1

BRADLEY RAISES HIS head, and looks out the window of the sunroom.

The lights of six o'clock, faithful to their old magic, have begun to wink and dance down on Risdon Road, and in New Town's ultimate eastern distance. Colours, still perceptible in the landscape, are fading like dyes in aged fabric; watching them dissolve gives Bradley the sensation of slowly losing consciousness. The cypress by the gate has turned almost black, and the patchy gold of Lutana Rise has changed to the hue of sacking, dimly seen through the pale-blue smoke of dusk. Just beyond a swarm of new bungalows that will soon eat the Rise away, he can pick out the steep green roof of the house that he knows from the diaries to have once been Dietrich Lange's, on its ultimate curve of grass.

He's resolved to read the diaries strictly in order, not allowing himself to look ahead, and the one he picks up now begins in January 1983: the month when Vincent returned to take up duty at the ASIS Main Office in Canberra, following his expulsion from China.

In that year, Bradley had been out of the country. After a short spell on the Southeast Asia desk in December, following his own return from China to the national capital, he'd been posted to the Embassy in Vienna, relieving for a Second Secretary who was on a year's leave of absence. He'd seen nothing of Vincent before he left, since Vincent had taken a month's leave and had come down here to stay with Connie – presumably to seek peace and lick his wounds.

When Bradley had arrived back in Canberra a year later, in the January of 1984, he was offered a three-year posting in Singapore; but he decided not to accept it. He was finding diplomatic life increasingly unrewarding, and was tired of foreign travel; a desire for stability and a more contemplative existence had come uppermost, and he considered quitting the service altogether. Instead, he decided to apply for a position in the Office of National Assessments in Canberra. Its work was to sift and analyse all the intelligence information that was gathered by the various agencies and departments, as well as material gleaned from diplomatic reports, the media, and other outside sources. This now appealed to him far more than diplomacy, and he had put his case to the head of Personnel.

He had chosen a good moment, he was told; ONA had recently been asking whether some capable Foreign Affairs officers might be persuaded to come across to them. At the beginning of February, Bradley was informed that his secondment had been agreed to, and he found himself in an office at ONA, in the Defence complex at Russell. The transition had been a smooth one: Russell was just across Lake Burley Griffin from Parkes, where Foreign Affairs was located, and Bradley continued to stay in contact with former colleagues, who would sometimes appear at meetings. As he'd hoped, ONA suited him; he was soon wholeheartedly engrossed in the broad analysis of intelligence, and its national and international implications.

When he'd first arrived back from Vienna in January, Bradley had phoned Vincent. His reception had been disconcerting.

As soon as Bradley had announced himself, Vincent's voice had gone flat and toneless, like that of a man suffering from a serious illness.

'Ah yes,' he said. *'I heard you were here, Brad.'*

Bradley had suggested that they meet for a drink, and there was silence for a moment. Then Vincent said:

'Let's leave it for a bit. I see no immediate need to meet.'

'For heaven's sake, Vin. What does that mean?'

'I'm sorry, Derek. I don't wish to be rude. The fact is that the disaster in Peking has changed things. It's affected me rather badly. And I understand that you blame me in the matter of Professor Liu.'

'Blame you? That's not true, and you know it. Who said so?'

'Never mind. You were right, of course, but I found it disappointing that you judged me, as I'm told you did.'

Bradley began to protest, but Vincent cut in.

'It's simply not something I want to be reminded of, at present. I'll contact you when I feel better able to talk about it. Goodbye for now, Derek.'

The phone was hung up, leaving Bradley staring at the burring receiver.

He had resolved to contact Vincent again; but weeks went by, and he put off doing so. Nor did he see anything of him, although at that time they were both working in the Administrative Building in Parkes, which housed Foreign Affairs. Since ASIS had its own world on the fourth floor, separate from Foreign Affairs, Vincent's remaining invisible was not unusual. As well, Bradley learned, Vincent was working in the Registry, the cloistered section where ASIS kept its files, making him even more secluded from the rest of the building.

This had seemed a curious situation for an ASIS officer, since the Registry was staffed by clerical personnel; but he assumed that Vincent must be doing some sort of research, and put him from his mind. He suspected that Vincent was suffering from serious depression – and although Bradley knew that he should attempt to help him deal with it, he had resented Vincent's accusation, and continued to put off making another approach. Then he had moved across the lake to ONA, and the likelihood of encountering Vincent by chance diminished even further.

He opens the journal now, looking at the early entries for 1983. In many of them, he sees, Vincent addresses his old mentor, Professor Teodor Bobrowski, as though writing him an extended letter. This practice is maintained, somewhat oddly, throughout the diaries.

Bradley settles back to read. Within a few pages, he finds an account of Vincent's assignment to the Registry.

2

Vincent Austin's Diary

Monday, January 9th, 1983
MY DEAR TEODOR: as the new year opens, I find myself recording a fundamental change in my career – one which may lead to
unexpected fulfilment. I believe you will approve when I tell you
about it, and may well see it as something that has always been
part of my destiny. And it has come when I expected nothing but
disgrace!

Today, at nine o'clock, I had an interview with the Director
General: 'A', as he's known in the Service. My first day back on
duty since I went to Hobart on leave.

The debriefing I underwent on my return from Peking was so
unpleasant that I went home to Connie's to consider whether I
should resign – although this had not been suggested to me.
Brunton, the Head of Security, is a pompous idiot, and had made
the damage assessment as nasty as possible. He conceded that
since there had been no publicity over the Liu affair, I could still
eventually be posted to other countries – but he informed me that
for now I could expect to stay in Canberra, while my situation
settled down. As he so charmingly put it, there was a blotch on
my record which needed to fade away. I expected the interview
with the DG to be equally unpleasant.

Late last year, while I was in Peking, ASIS moved up here from
Melbourne – a fact which has significantly affected my future.
The interview took place in our new Main Office. ASIS is located

in the top two levels of the Administrative Building in Parkes, on King Edward Terrace. The building faces the National Gallery and Lake Burley Griffin; nearby are the National Rose Garden, and Parliament House. It consists of a rectangular central block with a number of projecting bays, faced with red granite and sandstone: a specimen of the pre-War Canberra style known as Stripped Classical, although its stark massiveness and giant entrance columns seem to me more Babylonian than Graeco-Roman, with perhaps a hint of 1930s Fascist. Staff enter at the back, on King George Terrace. I arrived there at eight-fifty and went through the heavy glass doors into the high grey foyer, showing my pass to the guards. I then took the lift to the fourth floor.

Here one enters a tight little vestibule, on the far side of which a security officer sits in an adjoining room behind a glass panel. Showed him my pass and he pressed a buzzer, allowing me through the door to our main offices. He directed me to walk down the corridor to a staircase that would take me up to A's office on the top floor. I walked along nut-brown carpet past a number of offices, including the one where Brunton had dealt with me in December. Down the Rabbit Hole. Except for a distant murmur of voices, it was all very quiet here, and no faces passed me in the passage that I recognised. Not surprising, since most of my old colleagues are posted in various countries abroad.

I was nervous. I had never met Richard Elliott, the new Director General, and knew only the bare facts about him. An ex-Naval officer, in his fifty-ninth year; served with distinction in World War Two; wounded and twice decorated. After that worked for many years in the Joint Intelligence Organization, and more recently was a strategic adviser in the Prime Minister's Department. I couldn't imagine how he'd handle my case. A reprimand in some form seemed likely.

His office, I discovered, was located in a structure that was also Babylonian in its block-like style, squatting on the roof of the building like a penthouse. His secretary showed me in immediately. She was a well-groomed, middle-aged woman who smiled at me pleasantly; this seemed a good sign, and I felt a little less downcast. The wood-panelled room was large, sparsely furnished, and full of light. The windows looked out to Lake Burley Griffin, blue in the morning sun, with the King's Avenue Bridge visible in the east, carrying traffic across to Russell, where I could pick out the pillar of the Australian–American War Memorial, topped by its eagle. The DG, who was sitting at his desk with the windows at his back, rose as I entered. A tall man, strongly built, with wrinkled black hair streaked with grey, and watchful brown eyes. A walking-stick leaned against the desk; he grasped it and came towards me, limping. It was his left leg that was affected: the war wound, no doubt. Leaning on the stick, he put out his hand.

'Vincent. I'm pleased to meet you,' he said.

His smile was warm – either naturally or by design – but his dark gaze had an opposite, veiled wariness, as it so often does in our profession. He gestured with his free hand at one of a set of well-upholstered beige chairs grouped around a coffee table.

'Come and sit down,' he said. 'Will you join me in a coffee? I'm in need of a heart-starter.'

I thanked him, and sat down. He placed himself in a chair where he was facing me directly, and leaned his stick against it. All the time he watched me openly and curiously, his friendly smile preventing this attention from being offensive.

'Well now, Vincent,' he said. 'It seems you've given us some anxious moments.'

'I'm afraid so, sir,' I said.

He put up his hand. 'Please call me Dick,' he said.

His secretary came in with a tray, and set out a silver coffee pot, milk, sugar, and two cups and saucers of delicate bone china. Elliott remained silent as she poured the coffee; when she'd gone, he leaned forward and pushed the milk jug towards me. As I added milk, he said: 'I've read the report on your debriefing, and I won't waste time discussing it, except to ask you this. Did you really think the Government would give its blessing to your plan for the Lius? That at this delicate point in our relations with China, they'd enable Professor Liu to defect?'

'I hoped so,' I said. 'But I'd like to point out that I intended to explore that though all proper channels before I made any move. The whole thing was blown prematurely because Dorothy Liu went to the authorities.'

He nodded, leaning back in his chair and watching me, his cup of coffee suspended. 'You liked Professor Liu, didn't you?'

I told him I held Liu Meng in the highest regard, and enlarged a little on this.

'You're a man of strong enthusiasms,' he said. 'Perhaps in this case, Vincent, you allowed your enthusiasm to override your judgement.'

'Perhaps I did,' I said. 'I feel very badly now about Liu Meng and his wife.'

'Not as much harm has been done as you may think,' he said. 'Our latest reports tell us that Liu was interrogated, but has been left in his position at the university.'

I was enormously relieved to hear this, and told him so.

He nodded, and said: 'Good. The question is, Vincent, what do you do now? You've clearly been an outstanding operative, and I don't intend to see you go to waste. As I see it, you were slack, but you didn't show yourself to be untrustworthy – so I'm going to take a chance on you. I've been looking at your record, and I'm particularly impressed with what you did in Singapore when you were based there. Building that set of Chinese agents was a real coup.'

He was referring to the affair through which I had made my mark in ASIS. The memory still gave me pleasure; but I was jolted back to reality now by a change in Dick Elliott's tone.

'However,' he said, 'this unfortunate episode of yours could have leaked to various foreign agents, as I'm sure you'll realise – so we'll have to take you out of circulation for a time. You'll need to stay here in Canberra – and I believe I've thought of a way to make use of that. I intend to put you to work in the Registry.'

I sat back. I probably looked sick. 'You mean you want me to work as a clerk,' I said.

His smile became amused and benevolent. He was enjoying this, I saw: he was perhaps one of those men who liked rearranging people's lives, divulging their plans to do so bit by bit. 'No, no,' he said. 'By no means. Allow me to explain, Vincent. Our move here from Melbourne hasn't been easy, as you'll know. We lost quite a few staff who refused to face the semi-rural joys of Canberra, and resigned. This means that a lot of our corporate memory has been gutted. I'm told that you have phenomenal powers of recollection – which means you carry a good deal of that corporate memory in your head. And this may make you ideal for the post I intend to create for you. Let's call it Operational Co-ordinator.'

I stared at him in bewilderment. 'I still don't understand,' I said.

He finished his coffee, put down his cup, and pointed at me. 'Attend, and you will,' he said. 'In about eighteen months, our files in the Registry will be computerised. But before that happens I want them analysed, from top to bottom. I don't want our most sensitive material pried into by computer freaks – so *you* will decide what gets pulled out and put in my safe up here, before that process starts. You'll have unrestricted access. The chief clerk in the Registry will work to your direction, and you'll report directly to me. You'll be the censor; and you might well become our internal historian, in the end – but that's by the way. Feel free to come to me at any time, if you hit on anything interesting. Liaise with me all the way. Does that appeal to you?'

'It does have an appeal,' I said. 'I'm an historian by nature.'

I had replied cautiously, keeping my face neutral, but my spirits had begun to lift. Someone else might have been downcast, seeing themselves being turned into a glorified clerk – but I could see real compensations. What Dick Elliott was doing was making me absolute master of the Service's innermost room, with access to the most secret files there: *the files that few people ever see*. In fact, dear Teodor, I was being offered entry to one of my earliest dreams: the door to the secret garden was opening, and what Elliott said next interested me even more.

'Good,' he said. 'And there's another aspect to this. You'll be in a unique position to analyse the qualities of our agents overseas, by studying the records. It's clear that you've been good at recruiting agents in the past; so that should be up your alley.'

'Yes,' I said, 'I see. And that will allow me to construct an overview of all the agents we have on the ground. That's never really been done before, has it?'

'No,' he said. 'I don't believe it has.'

He sat watching me, head on one side, seeming to wait for more. I had begun to think furiously; and now I began to put my thoughts into words. As I did so, I probably allowed my excitement to show – I believe I even began to wave my hands about – but I no longer cared.

'What this will mean,' I said, 'is that I'll be able to study *linkages* – to see where patches overlap that we could use to our advantage. Take the cases of Japan and Indonesia, Dick. Jakarta is a future competitor of ours for sales of coal and gas to Tokyo. We've got agents in both those countries – so we know of the more obvious dealings between the Suharto regime and the Japanese. But what if we were able to dig deeper?'

'Explain,' Elliott said.

'Suppose we were able to discover what sort of informal intelligence links there are between them,' I said. 'Links we don't know about, I mean. As you know, we always work with limited resources – we never have enough trained operatives. But with an overview of the agents we're running around the world, I might be able to suggest ways of pushing the boundaries, and setting things going without the need for more staff.'

Elliott continued to study me intently, one hand resting on his walking-stick. Then he said: 'I've had similar thoughts to those myself. When I took over here, I had notions of putting them into practice. I hoped when I was briefed by our senior officers that I'd get the sort of overview you're talking about – but I'm afraid it wasn't forthcoming.'

I said nothing, and waited.

'There's an old Russian saying,' he said: '"When trouble comes, make use of it." I can see you're the sort of bloke who may have the knack of putting that saying into practice. You could turn your present misfortune to good account – I hope so.'

I said I hoped so too, showing nothing of my inward pleasure.

But now Elliott frowned at me. 'Listen carefully,' he said. 'This is how it will be, Vincent. I'll give you access to the records of any agents you wish. I'll even give you access to my private files – those too sensitive to keep anywhere else but up here, in my personal safe. You'll make written reports to me, naming any agents you see fit. But you must understand that this is an academic exercise between the two of us. Don't go writing to our stations overseas – or to anyone else. No-one else must know of it – not even the Head of Security.'

I told him I fully understood this, and he heaved himself out of his chair. I stood up too, and he pointed his stick at me, swaying somewhat precariously. 'Don't let me down,' he said. 'I won't be able to save you. In fact, I'll have your balls.'

'I won't let you down,' I said.

'Fine,' he said. 'The Registry is our memory room – and you'll be the guardian of our memories. What could be more important, Vincent?'

TWO

1

'IN THE MIDST of life,' one of Bradley's ONA colleagues remarked, 'we are in Canberra.' The national capital had long been the subject of such jokes, and Bradley had by now heard most of them. A good sheep station spoiled. A set of suburbs in search of a city. This last was apt, since Canberra could scarcely be called a city at all, in the usual sense. Its official hub was a set of shops and offices called Civic Centre; but metropolis was not to be found there. There was little commerce and less industry in Canberra, and even the shabby underside and unappetising back-streets to be found in any true city were absent. Unnaturally flawless and orderly, Canberra seemed almost to be a full-scale model created by a town planner; and this, in a sense, was what it was.

Like Washington, Canberra had been created specifically to be the nation's capital: location of the Federal Parliament, Commonwealth Government departments, military establishment, foreign and intelligence services, and foreign embassies. But there the resemblance to Washington ended. Built to a design conceived by a Chicago architect on the eve of World War One, it had been erected among dry, remote sheep properties in the southern table-lands of New South Wales, seventy miles from the coast, like some extraordinary folly. Despite the fact that it functioned as a vortex of the nation's power, it lacked even the lineaments of a city. Instead – perhaps in reflection of the Australian dream of domestic fulfilment – it consisted of a set of model villages, each with its own shopping centre, occurring like islands among extensive bush reserves, and linked by curving, perfectly maintained highways. Cold in winter, when snow lay on the nearby Brindabella Ranges, and fiercely hot in the inland summer, it was a city of politicians, Byzantine hierarchies of public servants (themselves the subjects of jokes and folklore around the country), and foreign envoys. Most of its citizens came from somewhere else. Many found it boring – especially those whose jobs in Government had forced them to transfer here – and escaped when possible down to the coast, or to Melbourne or Sydney. The politicians camped here while Parliament was sitting, and then flew back to their various native cities around the continent.

When he had first come here ten years ago, to be trained at Foreign Affairs, Bradley too had found Canberra essentially tedious. Everything was recent; there was no presence of the nineteenth century; no patina of age. Its earliest buildings, both public and domestic, dated from the 1920s and '30s. Now, however, back here to stay – at least for the foreseeable future – Bradley began to see it differently.

Canberra might have a certain tediousness, but it was certainly not ordinary, he decided; when you came to look at it closely, it was extremely strange. Its vistas were those of a particular kind of dream: the sort where one is lost, and searches without hope for release, or perhaps for a reunion with people one cares about – only to find that one must move forever down endless, unfamiliar roads, or through coldly empty, blue-lit streets which are profoundly and subtly unnatural; which hide an unplumbable enigma, and might have been devised by one of the old surrealist painters: Max Ernst, perhaps, or Paul Delvaux. This was partly because of the capital's location, scattered as it was in a valley of the Molonglo River. The Chicagoan Walter Burley Griffin had seen this valley as an amphitheatre, and had linked its topography to his grand design for the capital. The surrounding mountains and bush-covered hills were its galleries, and Kurrajong Hill at its centre (the site of the projected

Parliament building which in four years' time would finally replace the provisional one below, on King George Terrace) was its dominant point, looking out over receding, circular terraces where the eye was led to monuments and key public buildings. An artificial lake, named after the architect, lay at the amphitheatre's centre, and many Northern Hemisphere trees had been planted, perhaps to harmonise with the embassies from the northern side of the globe: planes, elms, deodars and cypresses were all made to flourish through dedicated watering. If anything, the city faintly resembled Geneva: a Geneva set down in the parched yellow acres of the Australian Capital Territory. And the grand design worked: its vistas were impressive; even handsome. But they were also strange, Bradley thought, and somehow eternally subdued – partly because the ancient continent had thrown its blanket of primeval quiet over them, and partly because of the land which lay outside.

This was the Monaro, a few kilometres to the south. Mostly fenced off by graziers, the Monaro grasslands were naturally treeless plains, empty, beautiful and haunting, punctuated by flat-topped hills. They invited the spirit – but to what? Huge granite boulders rose in the grass there like monuments, in a region where the lost Aboriginal tribes had roamed over a century ago, leaving behind them a melancholy vacancy. The Monaro's spirit was perhaps the true spirit of the region, Bradley sometimes thought, brooding beyond the city limits.

March came, and still Bradley had heard nothing from Vincent. He had decided not to make any further effort at contact; instinct told him that it would not be well-received, and that he should wait for Vincent to make the first move – should Vincent ever wish to do so. That Vincent might have decided to end their friendship altogether seemed absurd and sad; yet Bradley guessed that it was possible. There was little doubt in his mind that the episode in Peking had changed his friend greatly; but it wasn't until the end of March that he discovered how drastic the change was. This came about through a chance conversation with one of Vincent's colleagues.

His name was Jim Dempsey. He was a senior ASIS officer, working on their Indonesia desk, with a long experience of that country. One afternoon, he came across the lake to Russell to brief a small group of ONA officers – Bradley among them – on the current situation in the Indonesian province of Irian Jaya. Such informal briefings by ASIS or Foreign Affairs officers were held on a regular basis, but Bradley hadn't encountered Dempsey before.

The small meeting room in the ONA building where the briefings took place was very plain, its only decoration a map of Southeast Asia. Despite the airconditioning, it had a soporific effect, especially on hot afternoons like this one. Seated with his ONA colleagues at the blond boardroom table, notebook in front of him, Bradley had sometimes found his thoughts wandering, and had tended to gaze out the window at the nearby lake, especially if the speaker failed to be compelling. But this was not the case with Jim Dempsey. He spoke forcefully, his resonant, booming voice filling the room. He was a tall, heavy man in his early sixties, running to flesh a little, with the build of a rugby footballer and a thatch of thick white hair combed into a high quiff in front, in the Elvis Presley style he had no doubt been faithful to since his youth. His pink face was genial, and his slightly bulging blue eyes shone with Irish-Australian good humour. He wore half-moon reading glasses to consult his notes, his massive head lowered; occasionally, looking up from under his eyebrows in a manner that suggested a bull about to charge, he would remove the glasses and gesture with them, to underline a point. He was essentially engaging and jocular, but there were moments when his eyes became entirely blank, and his face empty. It was an effect that was no doubt unconscious: a by-product, perhaps, of the years he had spent in his profession.

In mid-afternoon there was a short break, and the group drifted into an adjoining kitchen where an urn supplied hot water

for making tea and instant coffee. Returning to the meeting
room with his white, government-issue cup and saucer, Bradley
found Dempsey moving beside him, smiling expectantly as
though he hoped for conversation. Bradley decided to initiate it.

'I was interested in what you said about the Free Papua
Movement,' Bradley said. 'It seems to be a problem that's only
getting bigger.'

Dempsey halted, stirring his coffee, and studied Bradley pleasantly. 'OPM? Dead right, they're a problem,' he said. 'One the
Indons don't need, and that we don't need either, if the OPM
people get support from their brothers over the border.'

'I was talking to a Foreign Affairs officer who's just back from
Cairo,' Bradley said. 'He told me they suspect over there that
Colonel Gadaffi might be offering support to OPM. They iden-
tified some Papuan activists going through Cairo on a junket to
Libya.'

Dempsey raised his thick white eyebrows. 'Did they now?
That's interesting,' he said. 'It confirms a few titbits my lot have
picked up.' He sipped his coffee, and grimaced. 'This stuff is like
fucking detergent,' he said. 'However, one mustn't be churlish
about ONA's hospitality.' He put the cup and saucer down on the
boardroom table, and stood studying it with a severe expression;
then he turned back to Bradley. 'The Papuans have genuine grievances,' he said. 'We all know that. But purely from the point of
view of local stability, we must hope our Indonesian friends keep
the lid on the pot.'

'Can they do that, Jim?'

Dempsey smiled, and his booming voice became slightly softer.
'Our operatives in Indonesia are recruiting agents to inform us on
every aspect of the problem. One of these agents has access to a
top Indonesian Army general in Irian Jaya. The general seems
pretty confident. What he told our man was: "I have my eye on
everything that moves here. If a flea farts in Irian Jaya, I know
about it."'

They both laughed, and Bradley said: 'He sounds like Joseph

Fouché. "Where three are met together, I have always one listening."'

Dempsey stepped back a little, his mouth opening in a smile of surprised pleasure, and pointed at him. 'Fouché! Do you perchance have an interest in the French Revolution?'

'I do indeed,' Bradley said. 'Ever since university days. I read all I can find.'

'I too,' Dempsey said. 'It's my dearest hobby. We must have a yarn, Derek.' He looked quickly about the room, where the other half-dozen people here were all back in their chairs. 'I'd better sing for my supper again now,' he said. 'Or rather, for my lovely instant coffee. But when this is done, will you join me in a real coffee? Over at Civic, perhaps? I need to pick up some mail at the Post Office. We can talk French revolutionary politics. Much more entertaining than the current variety. What do you say?'

An hour later, at five o'clock, they sat under one of the white umbrellas of an outdoor coffee shop in Garema Place. The sun was still hot, and the jackets of their suits hung on the backs of their tubular steel chairs. The shadows of a line of plane trees were lengthening across the brick-paved plaza, which was crowded with shoppers from the nearby arcades and with placid-faced public servants in business suits, released from the Government office blocks here. On the other side of the plaza a carousel under a red-and-gold canopy revolved, emitting piped military band music which mingled with a Fleetwood Mac recording coming from a nearby music store. Yet despite these competing sounds, the square seemed essentially quiet, with none of the clamour of a city. It was as though all noise in Canberra came through a baffle.

Dempsey had nominated the coffee shop, which it seemed was a favourite of his, and they had driven here independently. Now he sipped his cappuccino, and exhaled with satisfaction. He had loosened his tie and unbuttoned the collar of his blue-striped business shirt, which was stretched to its fullest extent by the size of his shoulders and upper arms. Leaning forward, one large hand holding his cup, he made the round formica-topped table look toy-like. 'An extraordinary man, Fouché,' he said. 'That chilling bloody albino. A lot more formidable than Robespierre, in my view. If anyone founded the modern police state, Fouché did. His methods of surveillance are still what make totalitarian states work; and they're still of professional interest – wouldn't you agree?'

'True,' Bradley said. 'Lenin must have learned a lot from studying Fouché's police ministry.'

Dempsey nodded. 'Thorough,' he said. 'The bastard was very thorough. In the case of one plot that he nipped in the bud, every one of the plotters came to him and betrayed the others.' He chuckled. 'Fouché took a pride in that.'

'He must have been frightening to meet,' Bradley said. 'Even Napoleon was nervous of him, I believe. And he was never afraid of Napoleon. Once Napoleon said to him: "I ought to have you hanged." Do you remember that story? All that Fouché said was: "I am not of the same opinion, Your Majesty."'

Dempsey chuckled. 'Yes,' he said. 'A cool cat. He had a sense of humour, unlike most fanatics. The ultimate professional. But no pity. As pitiless as Stalin – or Mao. In the days of the Terror, he went through France like a bloody angel of death. He also organized public blasphemy. A donkey in a mitre, dragging the Gospels through the streets – that sort of thing. It used to upset me, thinking about that. But it's happened since, and will probably happen again. The enemy keeps popping up, wearing a different uniform, committing the same old crimes. The trick is to deal with him in cold blood.' With only a slight pause, but in a different tone, he said: 'That's something your friend Vin Austin hasn't learned, I'm afraid.'

Bradley leaned back in his chair, staring at Dempsey in silence. He made no attempt to conceal his surprise, and Dempsey looked back at him blandly, his eyes now entirely without expression. Then he said: 'I know what happened in Peking. A pity, that.'

Bradley had been wondering whether Dempsey's move to make his acquaintance was as unpremeditated as it had seemed. He had suspected from the beginning that Dempsey had something else in view besides discussing the French Revolutionary period, and he waited now to see what this was. But Dempsey allowed the silence to continue, and finally Bradley said: 'Yes, it was a pity. I'm sure you know how capable Vincent is. Now they seem to have buried him in the ASIS Registry.'

'You might say that,' Dempsey said. 'He's enmeshed in the files.' His fixed, unwavering gaze took on a glint of humour.

'What the hell have they done with him? Turned him into a filing clerk?'

'No, no. Nothing as demeaning as that,' Dempsey said. His tone was soothing. 'Hasn't he told you about it?'

'I've seen nothing of him since I got back. He seems to have become a recluse.'

Dempsey's eyes widened; he appeared to be storing this away for reference. 'So I gather,' he said. 'But I thought he'd make an exception in your case.'

'Why so?'

'You're very old friends, aren't you?'

A spy is never off duty, Bradley thought. Aloud, he said: 'You seem to know a lot about me.'

Dempsey held his gaze a moment longer, his face impassive; then he locked his hands and looked down at them, drawing a deep breath through his nose. 'That was a very messy fuck-up in Peking,' he said. 'And you were involved, after all.' Looking up again, he raised his large pink hand, palm outwards, to stave off protest. 'Indirectly, I know – and perfectly innocently. But involved, young Derek, nevertheless.'

He paused. At nearly thirty-three, Bradley found it odd to be addressed as 'young Derek'; but Dempsey's advanced age and jocular friendliness made it seem natural rather than patronising.

'We had to look at every aspect of it, and what led to it,' Dempsey said, 'and naturally you came into the net. But our main concern was Austin, and why he went off the rails like that. Yes, of course we know how competent he is. His service in Singapore at the end of the 'seventies, when he built up that list of Chinese agents, was bloody brilliant. You know about it? No, he wouldn't have told you.'

He smiled reminiscently, sipping his coffee.

'I called in at Singapore at the time,' he said, 'and Vin talked his scheme over with me. Like all great schemes, it was essentially simple; but no-one else had thought of it. A number of Southeast Asian Chinese were going into mainland China on business – often business coming off the back of Japanese investment. These people had high-level contacts in Peking, and Vincent asked the question: could they be recruited as agents? Soon he had a number of them on our payroll, and the links he set up were incredible – direct and indirect. One top Singapore business leader was close to a member of the Chinese State Council: a bloke who played a vital role in major resources decisions affecting Asia as a whole – and this country as well. Somehow Vin found out that these two characters came from the same village, and were blood-relatives, and that the Singaporean was heavily influencing the State Council guy's decisions. So Vin had one of his local agents get close to the business leader, and soon we had access to the direction of some key Chinese trade policies – long before anyone else.' He chuckled. 'I once watched Vin operating: it was a sight to see. There was a regional business conference held in Singapore with a big reception in a hotel foyer, hosted by the Japanese. Vincent took me up onto the mezzanine floor, and got out his special camera. He then proceeded to take mug shots of the business identities below. It gave him a record of which Southeast Asian businessmen were looking like buddies with which mainland Chinese officials. I can still see him, crouching around with his little camera, eyes gleaming. He's a character, no doubt about it.'

'He sounds like great value,' Bradley said. He looked away across the plaza, the image coming back to him of Vincent at night in New Town, carrying his big Speed Graphic: his course already set.

'He *is* great value,' Dempsey said. 'So why did he lose his judgement? That's what we had to ask ourselves, and that meant looking at his associations. This involved you, and of course that very fetching lady he's always been close to – Erika Lange.'

To hear Erika's name suddenly pronounced like this had the effect of a small electric shock on Bradley. Staring back at Dempsey, whose face remained impassive, but whose gaze was now subtly and politely curious, Bradley tried to conceal his reaction, as well as a quick stab of resentment. ASIS must know of his affair with Erika, if they had taken the kind of interest Dempsey was hinting at, and he wondered now how closely he and she had been watched.

'Vincent did what he did on his own initiative,' Bradley said. 'It had nothing to do with Erika – or with me.'

'No,' Dempsey said. 'No, of course not.' He had spoken on a mollifying note, and studied his folded hands again. 'We know that,' he said. 'The fact is that Vincent let his hatred of the Chinese regime and his feeling for Professor Liu overwhelm his judgement. He tried to do the bloody impossible, without thinking of all the negative factors involved. He forgot his training; he even forgot his basic duty to get things cleared at the top; he didn't keep Head of Security informed. So then things changed for him. In Intelligence terms, he went from green to amber. He could have gone to red, but it didn't end as badly as it might have. He wasn't declared persona non grata by the Chinese, and there was no protest and no publicity, as you know. But favours had to be done for the Chinese as a quid pro quo – and our masters weren't too happy about that.'

'So what happens to Vin now?' Bradley asked.

'It's already happened,' Dempsey said. 'For the time being, at any rate, he stays in the Registry.'

'But they can't do that, surely. He's not a bloody clerk.'

'He's not there as a clerk. As I understand it, Vincent's been asked to screen out what gets put away as highly sensitive, before it's all computerised. Quite a task. It should keep him busy for some time.'

He smiled; but Bradley looked dubious.

'I know, brother, I know what you're thinking,' Dempsey said. 'It's hardly like being out in the field, with the adrenaline running. But believe it or not, Vincent seems to like it. In fact, he's totally focussed on it, and in the year he's been there, he's become a bit of an institution. He's got a phenomenal memory – that's what impresses everyone. He seems already to have hundreds of files stored in his noggin: he's like a bloody human computer. It's the same talent he showed in Singapore. You can go to him and say: "Do you recall such and such an agent, or such and such a case?" – and he'll tell you. And it's not just a matter of simple facts. You can ask him: "What other cases could be precedents for this one?" – and he'll have an answer to that too. He's a bit of a treasure. But he's also an eccentric sort of bloke, if you don't mind my saying so. Asexual, as far as one can judge. There've never been any women – or men either. That's why being master of the Registry suits him, I imagine. We've even got a nickname for him: Vincent Regisaurus.' He chuckled.

Bradley laughed, and said: 'You're telling me he's become obsessive about it. I'm not surprised. That's what Vin's like.'

'He's become a little strange,' Dempsey said, 'to tell you the truth. He thinks he owns the files.' His voice dropped; he spoke softly and almost gently, as far as his big voice would allow. 'Paranoia's always a trap, in our game – we all have a goodly dose of it. I do myself. But Vincent possibly has a double dose. Do you mind my being frank about your old mate?'

'I guess not,' Bradley said, and found that he meant it. Suddenly, looking at the large pink face and the old-fashioned quiff of white hair, he thought he saw a sort of kindness in Dempsey – at the same time reminding himself that this could be a mask.

'In that case, I'll tell you what his real problem is,' Dempsey said. 'Vincent's an idealist. And that's not an indulgence an operative can afford.'

'Why so? I would have thought it's no bad thing.'

Dempsey slowly shook his head. 'Not how intelligence works,' he said. 'You should know that, even if you haven't been in the field. I was once in the Army, aeons ago – and our job's really no different from a soldier's. We carry out orders, which are sometimes nasty, we deal with the enemy by whatever means are thought suitable, and we don't intrude our own notions where particular situations are concerned. Not even when we know the enemy's house of cards could be knocked over, and we're asked to walk away. But Vin isn't built like that. Wouldn't that be your observation?'

'I really couldn't say. I didn't see him for many years – not until we were both in Peking. I'm not in a position to make a judgement.'

'Ah,' Dempsey said. 'I suppose not.'

They both fell silent, looking across Garema Place, whose crowds were powdered with the yellow inland sun of late summer: a sun that grew gentler now, with evening approaching. They had finished their second cups of coffee. The carousel was still revolving; from the music store, the Fleetwood Mac recording could still be heard. The ballad was 'Songbird'.

Dempsey suddenly roused himself, and looked at his watch. 'I must be off in a moment,' he said. 'My wife and I are having the grandchildren over to dinner. Little devils.' Then, as though struck by a sudden, final thought, he said: 'What I ask myself is: how much did Erika Lange have to do with Vincent's miscalculation – indirectly, I mean? They were friends from a very early age, weren't they?'

'Since schooldays.'

Bradley wondered if Dempsey heard the tightness in his voice. But Dempsey was looking down at his folded hands, carefully studying his steepled thumbs. 'That relationship has been unusual,' he said. He spoke in a musing tone. 'No romantic involvement, I believe – but over the years, she kept turning up on visits, wherever he was posted. And then they were both posted to Peking, where the drama took place.'

'I'm not sure what you're getting at.'

'I'm saying that Erika Lange is a strange one, and that she has a peculiar interest in Vincent's profession.'

He glanced suddenly over his shoulder. It was a glance Bradley was familiar with: a reflex action that he'd often observed Vincent perform, and which he thought of as the spy's glance. The only person at the table nearest theirs was a thin, middle-aged woman with short-cropped grey hair, in a black suit, who was eating a little cake and reading a document at the same time: no doubt a public servant who was taking work home with her. Reassured, Dempsey turned back again, and continued to study his locked hands. He had a massive immobility about him; he was not a man who fidgeted.

'I was under cover at the Indonesian Embassy in Jakarta, in the late 'seventies,' he said. 'I replaced Vincent there, who was moving on to Singapore. Erika had turned up there in 1977, just before he left. She'd had some kind of breakdown in New York – but Foreign Affairs, in their wisdom, had given her this new posting. The lady's an hysteric – as perhaps you know.'

Bradley said nothing. He was glad that Dempsey continued not to look at him.

'There was some quirky behaviour in the office,' Dempsey said. 'One or two unexplained outbursts. Well, that was no affair of mine. But then Canberra contacted me, and asked me to keep her under surveillance – the reason being that she was having an affair with one of my opposite numbers in the CIA. No need for you to know more than that, but there was enough to give us concern. The affair had begun in New York – but now this bloke kept turning up in Jakarta. Her meetings with him bothered us: we felt it to be a very unstable situation. On top of that, she seemed to know too much about our game. She wasn't just conscious of who was doing what, but over and above that, she was inquisitive. Always asking questions about intelligence matters – questions a press person had no business asking. All this was a bit of a worry, in an Australia-based officer.'

'I see. And you somehow connect this to Vincent's stuff-up in Peking. But I've told you: she had nothing directly to do with it.'

Bradley's tone was stiff, and now Dempsey raised his head and surveyed him. His kindly look had gone, and his prominent blue eyes were enquiring. 'You know that, do you?'

'I believe so.'

Dempsey laid a hand on Bradley's arm. He smiled, and the warmth came back into his face. 'Don't take offence, Derek. I'm not conducting an interrogation. I'm just an old spook who's been put out to grass, sitting on the Indonesia desk. Two years to go, and I'll retire. But I like Vincent Regisaurus, and I'd like to know what really went wrong, and see him back in the field.'

Bradley said nothing. The large, warm hand remained on his arm, and Dempsey leaned towards him. 'You're better off without her,' he said softly. 'Believe me. That lady is trouble.'

Bradley looked at him, struggling to control a surge of irritation. 'You seem to be very well-informed,' he said. 'I didn't know that ASIS took that sort of interest in my life.'

Dempsey removed his hand from Bradley's arm, still gazing at him benevolently. 'You're annoyed,' he said. 'Don't be, mate – there's no need. I told you: Lange was under surveillance. It had nothing directly to do with you; but then you came on the radar.'

'Sure. I understand,' Bradley said. He stood up, pulling on his jacket. 'I'm afraid I have to go,' he said. 'I have a dinner date. It was nice talking to you, Jim.'

Dempsey stood too, struggling ponderously into his jacket and picking up his battered briefcase. 'I too. My grandchildren await me,' he said. 'Pandemonium will rule, in the Dempsey household. I've enjoyed talking to you, Derek. Let's meet again – and we'll stick to history, next time.'

Bradley smiled briefly, and raised his hand. 'Sounds a sensible idea. Good night, Jim.'

He turned quickly, and walked away across Garema Place, sensing Dempsey's eyes on his back.

2

BRADLEY HAD ALWAYS been infatuated with the false god of permanence. He had never found it easy to see anything he cared for vanish into the past; he came close to being sentimental in this, so that phrases like 'gone forever' filled him with a yearning sadness.

Because of this, the loss of Erika had caused him grief: a grief which had persisted sporadically over the year following his departure from China. But underneath this grief, running in counterpoint, was a sense of deep relief. And relief, he knew, was the more truthful of the two emotions. He continued to regard happy tranquillity as his natural state and his natural destiny; his affair with Erika had been a shattering interruption, taking him into territories of storm and madness he had no wish to visit again. It had been intense and extraordinary, like nothing else in his life, and he recalled certain aspects of it with longing; but he had no wish to repeat it. He had known this within days of flying out of Hong Kong.

But severing himself had not proved to be as simple as he'd thought. For many months after their parting, she had kept him bound to her by telephone.

Most of her calls had been made from her apartment in the compound in Peking; others came from hotels in other Chinese cities, when her work took her there. The first call was made in December, three days after his return to the Department in Canberra. On his first morning in the Southeast Asia branch, the phone rang on his desk.

'Brad? It's me. I'm sorry.'

He stiffened, and sat up straight in his chair. The flat, oddly accented voice was chastened and humble; and yet it sent a thrill of alarm through him. It was a voice that promised calamities. One of his colleagues was seated at a desk close by, and could probably hear what he said. Bradley turned towards the window and spoke softly, without expression.

'Where are you calling from?'

'Peking. From my flat.'

'Why are you calling?'

There was silence for a moment; a silence in which the vast, hollow sighing of global distance could be heard. Then she said:

'Didn't you think I'd call? Didn't you want me to?'

'You wanted to be free. You're free.'

'I said I wanted to think it over. I've thought it over. I don't want to lose you.'

'What does that mean?'

'What it says. Jesus, Brad, why are you being so hard?'

'I can't talk here,' Bradley said. 'And anyway, there's nothing more to say, is there?'

'That's not true! We have to talk. I don't have a home number for you: give it to me, and we'll talk when you're there tonight.'

She rang him at nearly midnight, in the temporary flat he was renting. Without preamble, she began to speak in a rush, in the same chastened voice.

'I shouldn't have left you like that in Hong Kong, I know. But I was very confused and worried. I just wasn't sure about marriage. I'm still not sure; but I do know I love you: I can't bear to be without you.'

'Well, there it is,' Bradley said. 'You're confused. But I'm not.'

'What do you mean?'

Patiently, carefully, while sadness filled him like a rising grey water, he explained. He had reached an age where he knew what he wanted, he said, and he had wanted above all to marry her. But he knew that if she was not sure of marriage now, and had not been sure in Hong Kong, she never would be; and she would leave him in the end. It was better that they break off now, with no hard feelings. There were none on his part, he told her.

But she would not accept this. Her voice rose, filled with what sounded like panic. When he was posted to Vienna, she would find a way to come there, she said, even if it meant quitting Foreign Affairs. But he must understand how much her freedom meant to her; he ought to consider that they could live together in freedom, without constricting ties. She had to come and go as she pleased.

He understood how she felt, Bradley said, and he respected it. But marriage meant giving up some freedoms – a thing he had been willing to do, but which she was not. She would never give up being a loner. That was why they had to part.

She had protested, panic entering her voice again; but he had said goodbye for what he thought was the last time, and had put the phone down.

But it was not the last time. Calls now began which would disturb his nights for the next month, continuing until he left for Europe. They were always the same: always, monotonously, she would circle around the same points as those they had discussed in the first call. She insisted on her love for him, and he would almost begin to waver. But as soon as that happened, she would return to her original theme: that her need for absolute freedom could never change. She asked him to accept a contradiction, he found: that she loved him, but would never wholeheartedly cast in her lot with him. He must simply be there for her, while she came and went. Often she sounded like a despairing small girl, begging not to be abandoned. At other times she raged, and cursed him for his cruelty. Sometimes her voice was slurred, and he suspected that she was drunk. He wondered what would happen when the Embassy's accountants looked at her phone bill, which was surely becoming enormous. When his phone rang, he would experience a sort of dread; and yet, at the same time, his heart would race with a treacherous excitement, sapping his will to ignore the call.

Then the calls began to come as late as two and three in the morning, waking him from sleep. He began to hang up on her, brutally; but five minutes later, with impotent threat in her voice, she would ring him back. (*It's me. Don't you dare hang up, mister. I just want to say this.*) Sometimes this would happen half-a-dozen times in succession, until she desisted for the night. But although he wished fervently to be free of her, her voice had begun to rekindle his addiction, and he could not bring himself to leave the phone off the hook.

When he went to Vienna, there was only one more call, made to him at the Embassy. This time, when they came to the old impasse, Bradley had adopted a more uncompromising tone than usual, and it was she who hung up, weeping as she did so. He did not hear from her again.

He was finally free, it seemed; yet her hold was not quite broken. For some time, he was plagued by inconsequential memories. The sports bag containing her squash gear (she played on a court at the British Embassy), standing by the door of her Peking apartment. Her beautiful clothes, strewn on chairs and the floor (she was quite untidy, for so fastidious a woman). Her contact lens case, set on a bathroom shelf. The strange, accomplished drawings of her alter ego, endlessly repeated. The tough, downward line of her lips when she was unhappy. The humorous irony of her gaze, seeming always to contemplate some private joke. And he could not prevent her from entering his dreams: dreams of a life he feared to enter, but which filled him with a fruitless longing. She was a woman who had always seemed to belong to dream; now dream enclosed her completely, and it was difficult to distinguish the memory of the real Erika from the dream one. Sometimes she stood on the highway at night, with her scarf blowing sideways. In another recurring dream, he encountered her in a crowd.

The place was Marble Town: he knew that instantly. This was a town which was simply a name: a name that occurred in the chorus of an old American folk ballad called 'Every Night When the Sun Goes In'. Erika and he had heard it one night in Peking on the short-wave band of her radio, and had liked it. Whether a real Marble Town existed, he had no idea; but in his dreams its nature was both haunting and enigmatic, filling him with a sense of nearby menace; of wild risk; of some terrible and nameless fate. *I'm going away to Marble Town.* Surrounded by crowds, he was moving along its pavements now, past low buildings that were strange without his knowing what made them strange. And suddenly Erika appeared beside him, hurrying, not looking at him, trying to get past in the crowd: a small, slight young woman in a long gaberdine overcoat, open and loose like a cloak. Her fair hair hung across her forehead; she brushed it away with the back of her hand. Pale brilliance of her eyes: wide and glinting with the secret joke.

He knew she'd seen him, though she pretended not, and his old feeling for her overwhelmed him. He caught her eye and smiled, and she smiled back: a brief, cautious smile, her lower lip projecting. It was as though she smiled at a stranger, and this struck at his heart. Would she come back to him? He wanted her back, in the dream; but he feared that it had been too long. Her smile had seemed friendly; but the friendliness had been quite impersonal, and everything in him sank. She was on her way to somewhere else; always to somewhere else. A busy world waited to claim her; and he knew, standing there in Marble Town, old town of doom, that her life's chief excitement lay in journey. Farewells didn't really provoke sadness in her; she found them exciting, like arrivals. What she loved was transition. She loved being forever on the move: going through customs at an airport and boarding an international flight; getting into cars to go as fast and far as possible; phoning her lovers from distant places, where she could not be reached. The beloved must be stationary, while she must be moving – this was what excited her most. To love was to be constantly poised for departure, or else arrival.

Either would do.

*

He had leased a townhouse in the pleasant inner suburb of Red Hill, where he lived alone. The house was one of a pair, recently built: tile-roofed, faced with yellow stucco in the Spanish manner, with a courtyard at the back separated from its neighbour by a high brick wall. There were no front fences in Canberra – one of the many regulations imposed by the national capital to achieve aesthetic harmony – and Bradley's house and its neighbour stood exposed at the front. But there were few casual observers here: the houses were located in a cul-de-sac, in a domain of quiet where the only cars that passed were those of the residents, and where pedestrians from elsewhere seldom invaded, since going on foot was not made easy, in Canberra, and the car was dominant. As in most of the other districts of the capital, the bitumen roads and glaring white concrete kerbs were immaculate, only made untidy by the occasional yellow beard of wild grass, creeping in from the land close by.

Bradley's cul-de-sac was near Mugga Way – the highway that ran around the foot of the long, grassy ridge for which the suburb was named, and whose eastern and northern slopes skirted the expensive neighbouring suburbs of Forrest and Deakin. Sparsely grown with eucalypts and occasional casuarinas, Red Hill looked somewhat like an elongated loaf of bread – an effect that was heightened at present by the bleached, yellow-brown grass of Canberra's blazing summer, now coming to an end. The hill was set aside as a nature reserve; in other seasons, the calls of magpies, parrots and butcher birds filled the calm suburban air. But they were scarcely heard now, since these were the final weeks of the Red Eye cicada, whose road-drill droning is one of the loudest sounds in nature, driving all other creatures into silence. Denizens of the flaring inland heat, ancient heralds of mysterious rebirth, the cicadas had emerged from their underworld to dominate the day until now, only subsiding when the sun went, as though cicadas and the earth were linked on the same astral journey. Then, in the cool of the evening, on Red Hill's walking track, the local residents would exercise their dogs, and joggers would appear: perspiring bureaucrats and clerks who had exchanged their formal office-wear for fashionable tracksuits and sports shoes.

Bradley liked Red Hill; its quietness and semi-rural nature suited him, although he didn't spend a lot of time at home. He hadn't found his ideal house on the hillside, but this was something close to it. On most evenings, he ate out; his social life was sufficiently full to keep loneliness at bay, and the townhouse offered him a haven of peace when he wanted it. He had begun a relationship with an attractive young woman who worked in the National Library, who shared his interests in history and music, and with whom he went out to concerts and restaurants. They enjoyed being together, had a similar sense of humour, and laughed easily and often. It was an affair without tensions, with a mutual affection at its centre, and might grow serious; but Bradley wasn't hurrying it. Meanwhile, he was regaining his old contentment, and Erika had been fading from his mind. Now, however, Jim Dempsey had summoned her up again.

A week after their meeting, her call came. It was as though Dempsey had known she was coming back. Perhaps he had, Bradley thought.

It was a Friday night. At a little after eleven o'clock, Bradley locked his car in the garage, let himself into his house, and walked through the hall to the living room. He'd been out to dinner with a group of people from ONA, and had drunk a good deal of wine. He had heard the phone ringing as he came up the path, but now it had stopped. There was no red light showing in the answering machine, so the caller had left no message. He began to move towards the carpeted stairs to the bedroom.

As he did so, the ringing began again. The nocturnal silence of Red Hill was complete, without even the sound of a passing car, so that the sound of the phone was jarring. It stood on a table beside an armchair; he slumped into the chair and picked up the receiver.

'Derek? It's me.'

He sat quite still. Her voice was very distinct and close, and yet at the same time unlikely: a voice from a different dimension. Half-drunk, he was slow to answer; before he could do so, she spoke again.

'Are you there? Please don't hang up on me.'

'I won't hang up. Where are you?'

'I'm in Sydney.'

His mouth went dry; he took a long breath, and closed his eyes. 'So you're back.'

'Yes, I'm back. I've quit Foreign Affairs. Oh Brad, I do love your voice. It's a voice that makes me feel serene.'

'Thanks,' he said. 'Why are you calling?'

'Jesus. Always that same question.'

Her voice had dropped, suddenly full of despair. He said nothing, and waited.

'I really need to see you,' she said. *'Things are difficult for me at the moment. I want you to come to Sydney.'*

'How are they difficult?'

'I can't talk about it on the phone. Derek, I need you here with me. Please come.'

'When did you have in mind?'

'Tomorrow: Saturday. If you drive, you can be here by noon.'

'I'm not sure that I can do that. Why don't you tell me what this is about?'

There was a silence. Then she said:

'I could come to you, if you like. But perhaps you've got someone in your life. Is that the problem?'

'I'm sorry,' he said. 'I just don't think your coming here is a good idea.'

Another silence; then, when she spoke again, her voice had changed. Full of pain, it was the tight, dry voice of a much older woman.

'I see. You want me out of your nice tidy life, no matter what trouble I'm in. Well I just might come down there and make it untidy. How would you like that?'

Before he could answer, she had disconnected.

He sat by the phone, waiting for it to ring again, as it had always done in the past. But minutes ticked by, and the phone remained mute: a yellow plastic artefact that might never have carried her voice at all.

3

VINCENT'S HOUSE was in the suburb of O'Connor, on top of the hill of Wattle Street. This part of O'Connor was on a ridge, and looked out over a wide view.

When Bradley got out of his car and looked south between Wattle Street's lines of young oak trees, he could make out distant tower blocks beyond the suburb of Lyneham below, glowing in the sunset. The evening was pleasantly still and warm, and he loosened his tie; he'd come straight here from ONA. Birds twittered in the oaks, but there was no sound of cicadas; this was the last day of March, and their remorseless drilling had stopped some weeks ago, taking with it the worst heat of summer.

O'Connor was one of the newer Canberra suburbs, and most of the houses here dated from the 1960s. Vincent's proved to be one of these: a plain, two-storeyed brick house with a red-tiled roof, the upper storey rising box-like and domineering above the bungalows on either side. It was not a particularly attractive house, Bradley thought. Behind it, above its low brick garage, the slim, minaret-like telecommunications tower on Black Mountain could be seen, in the south-west. Bradley walked up the concrete path in front, through a minimalist garden of dwarf conifers, and climbed a set of pebble-cast concrete steps to the front door. He felt uneasy; it seemed to him likely that Vincent would be a good deal changed. But Bradley was here by invitation, and the invitation had been a warm one.

It had come in the form of a letter, addressed to him at home, and had begun affectionately: *Dear old chap.* It had gone on to apologise for neglecting him so long, and had asked him to call for a drink this evening – after which they might go out to dinner. There were many things Vincent would explain when Bradley got here, the letter had said. Bradley had phoned to accept, and their conversation had been brief; Vincent's tone had been brisk and neutral, neither friendly nor unfriendly.

Bradley rang the bell, and the door was opened almost immediately. Vincent stood smiling, holding the door wide, and it seemed to Bradley that he was thinner than before, and even paler, so that the blue of his beard was very marked. His white business shirt was creased, the collar open and the sleeves half-rolled up; a pair of black trousers gave him a more clerical look than usual.

'My dear fellow,' he said. 'It's so good to see you. Come in, come in.'

It was the old effusiveness; but Bradley seemed to detect a willed quality in it. He followed Vincent down the hall, and was led upstairs to a large room at the top of the house which had windows on three sides.

'My study,' Vincent said. He smiled with proprietary pleasure, and Bradley sensed from his tone that the room was important to him. 'We'll be comfortable here,' Vincent said. 'Sit down, do sit down, Brad.' He gestured at a straight-backed, Jacobean-style armchair which was placed in front of a big flat-topped desk on which a green-shaded banker's lamp provided the room's only illumination, except for the fading daylight through the windows. The desk was piled with papers and files, and a glass ashtray held a collection of cigarette butts. 'You'll have a Scotch? Yes? Water, no ice,' Vincent said. 'I remember.'

Bradley sat down and looked about him, while Vincent stood at a long cedar sideboard, pouring their whiskies. A dining table in the centre of the room was covered in books and papers. There was a leather armchair near the desk, and a set of bookshelves against the wall there reached to the ceiling. Four steel filing cabinets were set against the northern wall; above them was a large noticeboard, and a framed photograph of Connie Ross. All three windows had half-drawn, heavy brown curtains. The one on the eastern side looked down on to the street, the southern window surveyed the roofs and gardens that sloped towards Lyneham and the distant towers of Northbourne Avenue, while the window on the west framed the bush reserve that stretched from here to Black Mountain. Vincent had most of Canberra under his eye, and the room seemed like an all-purpose living area rather than a study; only a bed was missing. He clearly spent most of his time here, despite the size of the rest of the house.

Having handed Bradley his whisky, Vincent drew the curtains across all the windows except the one next to his desk, plunging the room into greater dimness. He then sat down behind the desk, giving Bradley an incongruous sensation of being interviewed, and raised his glass. The green glow from the banker's lamp illuminated his face from below, causing his deep-set eyes to look almost sunken, behind their spectacles. 'Cheers, old chap. It's been too long,' he said.

They drank, and Bradley exhaled in appreciation. Then he said: 'Yes, it has been too long. But that's not my fault, Vin.'

Vincent looked at him seriously, his glass arrested just below his lips. 'No,' he said. 'No. Not your fault at all, Brad. I want to apologise.'

'No need, mate. I understand.'

'No, Derek, you don't. When I came back here from Peking, I was in a bad way, and that continued for over a year. There were very few people I wanted to see. You would have been an exception, I assure you – but then, as I told you, I learned that you actually blamed me for what happened with the Lius. It hurt at the time – but that's all water under the bridge now. Besides, you were half-right.'

'Let's get this clear,' Bradley said. 'I believed what I said to you in Peking – that it wasn't a reasonable risk. But that's all: I never blamed you for what happened. Who on earth says that I did?'

Vincent looked into his whisky. 'Erika,' he said. 'She wrote to me.'

Bradley sat back. 'She was lying,' he said.

'Was she? That's possible,' Vincent said.

He was watching Bradley closely, and the melodramatic green glow and the shadows on his face made him resemble an interrogator in a period Hollywood film. Perhaps, Bradley thought, this was an effect Vincent wanted to create, absurd though that seemed.

'She was very bitter about you,' Vincent said. 'Emotionally shattered at the way you deserted her.'

'Deserted her?'

'That's right. You broke the engagement at the last minute, didn't you? I was very sorry to hear that.'

'Is that what she says? Jesus.' Bradley took a deep breath; then he shook his head. 'Well, it really doesn't matter now, Vin. Whoever broke it, we were both saved from a lot of aggravation. That's all I want to say to you about it.'

He drained his whisky and held his empty glass out at arm's length, in silence.

Vincent took the glass, watching Bradley's face. Then he said softly: 'I believe you, old chap. So let no more be said, except this: Erika has brought a lot of men pain, but where you two were concerned, I believed that things would be different. I thought that in you she'd found the man she truly needed. I had high hopes for you both. It seems I was wrong.'

Bradley shrugged, but said nothing, and Vincent got up and took their glasses over to the sideboard. Pouring fresh whiskies, he said: 'She's back in Australia. Did you know that?'

'Yes. She phoned me two nights ago from Sydney.'

'Really?' Returning with the glasses, Vincent looked at him sharply. 'And have you arranged to see her?'

'No.'

'And she hasn't tried to contact you again?'

'No. And I hope she won't.'

Vincent sipped his drink, back behind the lamp. 'And she didn't tell you what she wanted?'

'She said she was in some kind of trouble. Do you know what that might be?'

Vincent frowned at the desk in front of him. Without looking up, he said: 'She's been back for some months, living in Sydney. She left Foreign Affairs, as you probably know. She decided to go free-lance, and she hasn't found it easy. She's been trying to get into television journalism, interviewing for news and current affairs programmes – but I don't think any doors have opened for her. She's been having a tough time. In fact, I think she's getting a bit desperate. I've been helping her along financially, just between us.'

'I'm sorry to hear that,' Bradley said. His tone dismissed the subject, and he took a deep swallow of whisky. 'Tell me what you're doing in the Registry,' he said. 'Rearranging the files, I believe.'

Vincent narrowed his eyes. 'Who told you that?'

'I ran into one of your people. Jim Dempsey.'

Vincent snorted. 'Jim's too loquacious. A good old warhorse, but he really ought to guard his tongue.' He rummaged in a drawer of the desk, and pulled out a packet of cigarettes. Holding it up, he asked: 'You still don't?'

'No. And neither should you.'

'Yes, yes, I know. I'll give it up eventually, but I've been under a lot of strain.'

He flicked his lighter, lit up, inhaled with swift urgency, and then blew a long stream of smoke in front of him. The daylight through the window by the desk was gone, now; the room had become dark, and the banker's lamp was the only source of light, suffusing an area of the desk but striking neither of their faces directly. Vincent crouched close above the shade, his face tinted with its green more theatrically than before. The smoke from his cigarette eddied and drifted in the bright, downward light, composing a pale-blue screen there that grew more dense as they talked.

'"Rearranging the files" doesn't really describe what I'm doing,' he said. 'In fact, Brad, I've been entrusted with something remarkable. But I really must ask that you speak about it to no-one. Can you give me that assurance?

Bradley did so, and Vincent began to describe his new role, outlining the task he'd been given very much as Jim Dempsey had, but enlarging on it with a degree of detail that began to tax Bradley's concentration, as the effects of the second whisky took hold. There could be no doubting Vincent's passion for his new function. *Vincent Regisaurus*, Bradley thought, and smiled; but Vincent didn't notice the smile. As he spoke, he grew more and more animated, gesturing with his cigarette and waving his hands in the lamplight; at one stage, he got up and began to pace the room.

'The innermost secrets of the Service are all at my personal disposal,' he said, and his voice had taken on a throaty, gloating, almost caressing sound, as though he spoke of some private and perhaps shameful passion. 'The most secret of all files are in my care, Derek. Can you see what trust has been placed in me? And what it means?' He paused beside the desk, hovering over Bradley.

Conscious of Vincent's relatively recent disgrace, Bradley found a certain pathos in his pride in this new position as archivist of the firm's secrets; but he nodded solemnly, as though impressed. Not for the first time, he was puzzled by the almost mystical reverence that overcame Vincent when he referred to the hallowed zone of secrecy. It was as though the covert and the secret were not just that, but something more: sacred mysteries, perhaps. Despite Vincent's clerical air, Bradley had never thought of him as a religious man in the conventional sense – and certainly Vincent had shown no interest in religion, in its Presbyterian form or otherwise. But suddenly Bradley saw him as resembling a zealot: a follower of some transcendental system whose nature was arcane. His ecclesiastical-looking black-and-white dress this evening, together with the new, ascetic gauntness of his blue-chinned face, somehow suggested a priest of some kind, Bradley thought: one who was wrung by opposite visions of ecstasy and damnation. Aloud, he said:

'I'm not sure that I do see. What *does* it mean, in fact?'

Vincent looked at him quickly, his face stern. He then returned to his chair at the desk, folded his hands, and leaned towards Bradley. 'In telling you this, I'm trusting you absolutely,' he said. 'You do understand?'

'Yes, Vin, of course.'

Vincent paused, stubbing out his cigarette in the laden ashtray. When he spoke again, his voice was low and fervent.

'I believe I've seen an opportunity to turn my career around, and get back into the field,' he said. 'I'll do it by carrying out an analysis of the files – an area in which I happen to be rather capable. I'll be looking for links that my more limited colleagues have overlooked – and when I find them, I think I'll be able to expose some of the Soviet operatives and agents we have here in Australia: the ones who've never been entrapped, or even suspected. And I may also expose some moles in our own Service.'

Bradley stared at him. 'In ASIS? You think there are some?'

Vincent's stare became fixed. 'I'm certain of it.'

'But mate, is this really what you've been commissioned to do?'

Vincent's face closed. 'My commission is a very broad one,' he said. 'The DG made that plain. I'll work in my own way.' He frowned. 'I've probably told you too much, Derek.'

'If you don't know that you can trust me by now, maybe you should say no more,' Bradley said.

'You're right,' Vincent said quickly. 'We've been friends so long – there's no-one I trust more. It's so good to be able to talk to you again, Brad. There's no-one else I can be myself with, except you.' He leaned back in his chair, smiling, and studied Bradley with a new ease and openness. Then he said: 'You're getting to look more and more like your father.'

Bradley grinned, running his fingers through his faded brown hair. 'Part of getting older,' he said. 'We all end up looking like our fathers. Middle age awaits us, Vin. Maybe I'll take up golf, as well.' He stood up, looking across the room. 'What a lot of filing cabinets. Aren't you surrounded by enough of them at the office?'

Vincent had stood up too, and he surveyed the green cabinets with an odd expression: a mixture of proprietary pride and wiliness. 'Those are my insurance,' he said.

'I don't get it. Against what?'

Vincent hesitated. Then he said: 'I've trusted you with everything else – why not this? No-one else knows, and no-one else must ever know. This is my personal Registry.'

Bradley stared at him. 'You don't mean you're keeping duplicates?'

Vincent stared back, the light from the lamp reflected in his spectacles. 'The most important files, yes,' he said. 'Since I've come to believe that the Service has been penetrated, I thought it best.'

'But Vin, you know that's a crime, for God's sake. What if you're found copying them? How will you explain it?'

'I *won't* be found out,' Vincent said firmly. 'And no-one comes into this room. You're the first to do so – and the last.'

Bradley leaned back, digesting the seriousness of what he'd just learned. In bringing home duplicates, Vincent was carrying out an activity that was not only illegal, but one which seemed to indicate the growth of a disturbing and risky obsession. If it should somehow be discovered, his career would certainly be at an end, and serious charges would be made. Bradley wondered if he should try to persuade him to abandon the project; but he had begun to realise that Vincent had entered some rarefied, private level where he had abandoned all normal rules. Outside advice would be useless.

Over the next two weeks, Bradley heard no more from Erika, and assumed that she'd abandoned her threat to invade his life. But then two incidents occurred which destroyed his fragile peace.

The first took place at eleven o'clock at night, early in April. He was in his bedroom on the upper floor of the townhouse, preparing to go to bed. Outside, in Red Hill's silence, he heard the hum of a car approaching; headlights stroked the drawn holland blind on the window above the street, and were then switched off. At the same time, the engine of the car stopped, and he knew that it had parked directly outside. His neighbours never had visitors at this time, and Bradley assumed that somebody was calling on him, despite the lateness of the hour. He turned off the lamp beside his bed, crossed the room, and drew the blind aside a few inches.

The cul-de-sac was entirely empty except for a new-looking red Toyota sedan, parked across his driveway. The lights were out in its cabin. He waited for the driver to get out; but nothing happened. The car sat there, and its invisible driver didn't appear. Then, just as he was about to go downstairs and investigate, the engine came to life again, and the car moved slowly away.

The following night, at just after ten-thirty, exactly the same thing happened: the red Toyota pulled up across his drive and sat there in silence, without the driver appearing. This time, however, Bradley was in the living room downstairs. He moved quickly out the front door and hurried down the short concrete drive, walking in front of the car to peer through the windscreen at the driver, who was clearly illuminated by a nearby streetlight.

It was Erika, as he had half-known it would be, and she stared at him with an expression he remembered: one that mingled fierce accusation with alarm. Her face was blue-white in the artificial radiance, and her eyes were wide and staring. Bradley moved towards the driver's door, his heart thudding. But in that moment, Erika started the engine. The car lurched away from the kerb, barely missing him.

He stood in the middle of the cul-de-sac, in the cool April night of the suburb, watching its tail-lights disappear. Red Hill's silence was resumed, and it was as though she had never been here.

The night after that, the silent phone calls began.

The first was at midnight, waking Bradley from the edge of

sleep. Picking up the phone by the bed, he was greeted by silence on the other end; but he knew that she was there.

'Erika,' he said. 'Tell me what you want. I'm willing to listen.' There was still no answer, and he put the phone down.

Within a minute, it rang again. He picked it up and listened, saying nothing this time; the line was open, and he thought he heard her sigh. But still she didn't speak, and after a time he hung up.

An hour later, when he'd fallen asleep, the phone rang again. Cursing, he picked up the receiver, lying back on the pillow, listening to the hollow, live silence. This time, in order to sleep, he left the phone off the hook.

For the next two nights, the silent phone calls continued. He considered tracking her number and calling her back; but he always rejected it. If he did, the whole comedy of obsession, pain and abandonment would begin again, and Bradley remained determined to put that behind him. He would not keep an assignation again with the living woman; only with her shadow, in Marble Town.

4

WHEN BRADLEY RECALLED Vincent in that winter in Canberra, he would nearly always see him in the green-lit, smoke-wreathed lair of his study, on top of the house in O'Connor – always in the evening, since this was when Bradley would visit him. The curtains would be drawn back from the window beside the flat-topped desk, displaying the canopy of trees and suburban roofs that sloped down into Lyneham, and the distant lights glowing in the tower blocks on Northbourne Avenue. Vincent would sit behind the desk, a drink or a cup of coffee in his hand; and Bradley had come to realise that this was the only way Vincent felt comfortable about receiving him. The study had become a sort of hermit's cell; and Bradley sometimes wondered if Vincent had contact with any other human beings, other than his associates at ASIS.

It was now early June, and snow was on the Brindabella Ranges.

'I have news of Erika,' Vincent said. He drew on his cigarette, and tapped ash nervously into the ashtray. 'I really thought you should know. She called me from Sydney this evening, and she's very excited. She's finally broken into television journalism. She passed an audition with Channel Twelve in Sydney, and they've taken her on as an interviewer with *News Tonight*, their current affairs programme.' His eyes shone as he said this, like those of a proud father.

'I see. Well, wish her good luck,' Bradley said.

'Why don't you contact her yourself, Brad?'

'I don't think so, Vin. I'm sorry.'

Vincent sighed. 'She's going into a new phase of her life,' he said. 'She may actually learn to forget you, now. Is that really what you want?'

'Yes, mate. It really is. I'm involved with someone else, as I told you.'

'She's already done her first interview,' Vincent said. 'She spoke today in Sydney with Roy Cameron, the Western Australian mining magnate. They're screening it tomorrow night. I think you should watch, Brad.'

'Maybe I will,' Bradley said.

'Do,' Vincent said. 'Let me tell you, it's likely to create a bit of a stir.'

'How do you know that?'

'I was able give her some background on Cameron's interests overseas. Information he won't welcome.' Vincent pursed his lips. 'I don't wish to say more.'

The following evening, sitting in his living room in Red Hill, Bradley switched on the television set. It was six twenty-five: the programme would come on in a few minutes.

Twelve was a Sydney commercial channel, and *News Tonight* rated higher than any other current affairs programme, going to air nationally. The presenter, Bill Anderson, had been a popular figure for ten years or more, and its journalists were among the sharpest and hungriest in the country. Not for the first time, Bradley wondered how Erika had got herself in there, with no background at all in television journalism.

They led with the Prime Minister, whose towering, luxuriant white hair was impressive as always, recalling the wig of an eighteenth-century courtier. He submitted to an interrogation by Bill Anderson about the state of the economy, completing his response with a flight of oratory concerning the Government's fiscal achievements. Then he was gone, and Anderson began to speak about Roy Cameron. One of Australia's richest men, he had made his fortune with an iron ore mine in the Pilbara region, and copper mines in Queensland. Now Cameron was expanding overseas, Anderson said: he was one of the first Australian businessmen to go into a joint mining venture in China. Visiting Sydney today, he had spoken with Erika Lange.

Bradley found himself looking at a luxurious hotel room somewhere on Circular Quay, with a daylight view of the Harbour out the windows. Cameron and Erika sat facing each other in small brocade armchairs, on either side of a low coffee table. They were in medium shot, in profile. Cameron wore an open-necked shirt and tan trousers: he was a big, red-faced, fleshy man with a thatch of thick grey hair, and his belly bulged over his belt. He was smiling at Erika benevolently. She held a clipboard, and was as beautifully dressed as Bradley had expected, in a jade, high-necked blouse with full sleeves caught in at the wrists, and a long black skirt.

He had tried to prepare himself for the sight of her on-screen, but he had not anticipated the way in which the camera would deal with her. She was familiar (her hair worn as usual, falling towards one eye), and yet she was fundamentally different. He'd assumed that her looks would come across well, but not to the degree that they did. Her hair glinted gold in the lights like a helmet, and her skin had a pearl-like translucency; but most striking of all were her eyes, whose colour had intensified – perhaps because of her contact lenses, perhaps because of the lights – to an extraordinary, compelling azure. She proved to be one of those people whom the camera and make-up transform, as they do certain actors. The medium demanded good-looking women, and most of the interviewers on current affairs programmes were attractive; but Erika's beauty was startling. The camera had given her film-star looks – there was no other way to put it, Bradley thought.

She was putting her first question to Roy Cameron, but Bradley had not been listening; now, he tuned in, and found that she was speaking of Cameron's early days in the Pilbara, asking him to elaborate on the breaks that had propelled him to success. She spoke very clearly, seeming entirely relaxed and in control, her voice pitched low. Its flatness was still there; so was its almost masculine depth; but these too came across very differently from the way they did in life. Like her face, her voice was transformed, and took on an almost insidious seductiveness – all the more enticing since it seemed in no way contrived, and was apparently quite unconscious. Far from being flirtatious, she was very serious; this was her salient quality on-screen, and she only allowed herself a single, fleeting smile. The camera moved into close-up on the two of them, and her effect on Cameron (who was known to be something of a womanizer) became apparent. He was staring at her in open fascination, his lips parted in a half-smile, his eyes never leaving hers. As he went into his answer, the camera held him in close-up for a time, and then cut to a brief close-up of Erika, who was listening to him with total attention, leaning slightly forward. This was the first time the viewer had seen her at close quarters, receiving the full, mesmerising impact of the azure stare, which was directed off-camera to Cameron.

She prompted him now to further reminiscences of his early days, and he went into a degree of detail that was unusual for him; he was usually fairly close-mouthed. Questions about his copper mine in Queensland followed, and about further explorations he and his company were conducting in the region. Then Erika looked down briefly at the notes on her clipboard. Having done so, she raised her head to study Cameron in silence, as though uncertain about the way in which her next question should be put. He waited, smiling indulgently.

'I understand your company recently ventured into China,' she said. 'The first Australian mining concern to do so on a large scale. Can you tell us a little about that?'

Cameron rubbed his nose. 'Well, as you'll realise, China's new open-door policy has given us great opportunities,' he said.

'So we've gone into a cooperative venture with the Chinese Government: a big new copper mine in the north-east. It's doing very well indeed.'

'I'm sure it is,' Erika said. 'Near Harbin, isn't it?'

He raised his eyebrows. 'You're well-informed. Yes, somewhere near there.'

'Yes. And are you aware of the charge, Mr Cameron, that the mine employs slave labour?'

Cameron's face, in close-up, became a shade redder. He frowned, his eyes narrowing. 'No, I'm not. That's absolute rubbish, Erika. Where did you dig it up?'

The camera put Erika in close-up again, and her gaze now had a tragic quality, as though what she had to say gave her pain. She spoke softly. 'I served for some time in China as a Foreign Affairs officer,' she said. 'I heard this from a number of sources I trust. It may not be true, of course: I'm simply asking you to comment, Mr Cameron.'

Cameron glared at her. 'It's lying nonsense,' he said. 'That's my comment.'

Erika looked back at him without speaking for a moment, her head on one side. Her wide-set eyes had a wondering expression now, and her expression remained sympathetic, tenderly regretful, and at the same time genuinely puzzled. This clearly made what was happening exquisitely aggravating for Cameron. His mouth worked, and his jaw tightened, as though he were chewing on something.

'You see, Mr Cameron, your mine is close to one of China's secret gulags,' Erika said. 'Dong Yang is the main camp there, about eighty kilometres from the mine. Political prisoners are sent to that camp – and many of them are said to be forced to work in the copper mine. Have you heard that, Mr Cameron?'

Cameron's face had now become bloated and flushed with resentment. His mouth twisted to one side, and his eyes glinted. 'I've heard nothing of the kind,' he said, 'and I've made a number of personal visits there. This is the sort of fabrication cooked up by people hostile to the Chinese Government. And for you to air it on this programme is irresponsible.'

He stood, swaying heavily, pushing back the small brocade armchair.

'Your interview is over, young lady.'

The viewer was returned to the studio, where Bill Anderson sat at his desk, smiling at the camera. 'As you'll gather, Erika wasn't able to pursue that conversation any further. We've contacted Mr Cameron's company and told them that we're happy to give them every opportunity to refute the charge. So far, we've not had a reply. We have established, however, that the Dong Yang prison camp is located where Erika claimed it is, not far from the copper mine in which Mr Cameron's company is involved. We're also told by a number of China experts that stories about prison labour being employed there have circulated for some years. It goes without saying that *News Tonight* makes no charges in this regard. It merely asks questions – as our new reporter, Erika Lange, has so ably done. Welcome aboard, Erika. And now, a word from our sponsors.'

Bradley sat staring at an advertisement for insect-repellent. Then he got up and switched off the set.

That night he dreamed that he was on a bus, and suddenly found Erika sitting next to him.

In the dream, he was surprised and overjoyed to see her. Lips half-smiling, she looked into his face in the old way, her gaze warm and humorously questioning. She was stylishly dressed as always, in a navy-blue, lightweight car coat with a big collar, worn open over a pale-grey dress. She was friendly and relaxed, and they talked.

'You see?' she said, and treacherous hope woke in him.

But then her eyes flickered away, glancing about for something of greater interest. The bus was full of men and women laden with handbags, briefcases and magazines: the people she called her colleagues. They were all being carried to an important destination.

The bus stopped; everyone got out, and he saw with dread that this was Marble Town. He and Erika stood facing each other on the footpath, as the colleagues moved away towards a big glass building: a terminal of some kind. Out here on the pavement, a leather travelling bag slung over her shoulder, she looked slighter than she'd done on the bus; yet she gave the impression of being taller than she was. It had something to do with her fixed, confident, azure gaze, her erect carriage, and her determined lower lip.

'I have to go now,' she said. 'I'm on a flight to Zürich.'

He stared at her, stricken.

She raised her free hand, waggled her fingers, and silently mouthed: 'Goodbye.' She turned and disappeared, and grief flooded him.

Grief woke him, turning his body to stone; then it gave way to reluctant relief. He had lost her for the last time.

THREE

1

EARLY MORNING IN the sunroom. Sunlight seeps across Vincent's desk and floods the narrow space: the thin Tasmanian winter sun that becomes almost hot, when it strikes through glass. Outside though, Bradley knows, the air will be crisp and cold. Somewhere behind a curtain a lone blowfly is buzzing intermittently, and he wonders how it has survived, at this time of the year.

He picks up the binder in front of him, but pauses before opening it. This is the last diary: he's come to the final entries for 1984. He's kept to his resolution to read the diaries in chronological order, and has refrained from looking at these pages until now, despite a strong temptation to do so — these being the last months of Vincent's record.

Still he postpones beginning to read, staring at the view beyond the desk. The sun is flashing on the morning windows of quiet, empty Bay Road, signalling that promise of glory which is repeated by every fine dawn, despite all human pain and wretchedness. And looking across to the far green roof of the house on Lutana Rise, he allows himself to imagine for a moment that Erika is still there: Erika as she was in Vincent's photograph, in the casual cotton dress of childhood, head tilted back with a look of boy-like defiance. Then the sad fallacy of this is borne in on him. He is not viewing some magical stasis, but emptiness, illusion, and the immutable mystery of Time. Time! The house that Vincent used to watch with such devotion was long ago bought by some stranger, and the creeping tide of new bungalows has almost devoured the empty, tawny spaces of the Rise, turning it into just another suburb. Erika is gone. Vincent is gone, and only the shards of Vincent's fancies and ideas are left for Bradley to pore over.

Blackbirds are hopping on the little patch of dew-wet lawn below, as they did when he and Vincent were boys, and a small, serious girl in a felt hat and raincoat is passing the front gate on her way to school. The sky is clear; there are only a few pale smears of cloud above the low blue line of eastern hills, and the white, vertical smokes rising from the Zinc Works have a brilliant, festive look. It will be a fine day. He has left the door of the sunroom open, and can hear Connie coughing downstairs.

I'm the Star, he hears Erika say.

She had her wish, Bradley thinks. For a very short time, she did become a star, in the eyes of the world. During that incarnation, she ceased to be quite real: instead, she became an image.

2

Vincent Austin's Diary

Friday, July 20th, 1984

I'VE RECENTLY MET an interesting Soviet journalist, based here in
Canberra. His name is Peter Rykov, and he works for TASS news
agency. Fell into conversation with him at a British Embassy
reception. Spoke to him at first in my halting Russian (on which
he complimented me), and then in English. His English is excellent: he occasionally misplaces his definite articles, but nearly all
Russians do that. He's spent some years in the United States, and
is thoroughly Westernized, with a strong sense of humour. No
Soviet stuffiness or puritanism about him: what I imagine to be
the new breed of Russian. I've checked him out in the Registry,
and he doesn't show up in any of our files. To be sure of him, I'd
need to talk to ASIO; but I don't believe that he's KGB; here in
Canberra, their people are always under diplomatic cover at the
Embassy. He has no idea that I'm with ASIS, of course; I present
myself as a Foreign Affairs officer, based here between postings.

Tonight I met him again by chance in Bruno's Brasserie in
Manuka, where I often go for drinks and dinner at the end of
the week.

The place was crowded, as usual on a Friday. Located upstairs
off one of the arcades, Bruno's is popular with foreign embassy
staffers, Press Gallery journalists, and the various aides and func-
tionaries who circle anxiously around politicians. I like Bruno's.

The spicy, Central European cooking smells are appetising, and the murmuring voices of the diners have a promising quality. Lit by discreet fluorescent tubes in the ceiling and red candles on the dining tables, its main colours are black and silver: chrome bar stools and dining chairs with black vinyl backs; cloth-covered tables with chrome legs. I sat down on one of the stools at the bar, which is located on an inner side of the room under a canopy of stainless steel. I had just ordered a drink when I was tapped on the shoulder.

I turned to find Peter Rykov standing behind me, holding out his hand and smiling as though at a long-lost friend. It was a smile of unusual warmth, lighting up his face.

'Vincent!' he said. 'It's good to see you again.'

His grip was unnecessarily strong, but I managed not to wince. Tall and fit-looking, he gave me the impression of being an ex-military man – perhaps because he stood with a very straight back. There was nothing else that was military about him, except that he was dressed in a style of casual wear that has long gone out of fashion among Australian men of his age, being seen as too formal: navy blazer with brass buttons, collar and tie, khaki drill trousers with knife-edged creases. He did not immediately strike one as Russian; instead he had the sort of good looks that recalled leading British film actors of the 1940s and '50s: long face, narrow nose and finely cut features. He might in fact have been English or Danish, except for a sort of underlying toughness that I tended to see as Russian. His eyes were his only exotic feature, being of a striking cornflower-blue hardly ever encountered among people of Anglo-Saxon origin. I judged him to be in his mid to late thirties: his dark-blond hair was swept straight back, only the bays at his temples hinting at the imminence of early middle age, and his face was smooth and comparatively unwrinkled, except for deep lines running from the nose to the corners of the mouth. His full lower lip also had the set of maturity, and his long chin hinted at stubbornness.

'Are you alone? May I join you?' he asked.

I told him he was welcome, and he dragged up a stool. 'I've ordered a gin-and-tonic,' I said, and signalled to the barman. 'What will you have?'

'The same,' Rykov said. 'What could be better, at this time of day?'

He tilted his head back and narrowed his eyes, causing them to glint with a whimsical sharpness, while his smile became jocose and confiding. 'I've been at a press conference,' he said, 'held by your Prime Minister. I didn't learn much, but this man Hawke pulls the most amazing faces I've ever seen.'

To illustrate, he rolled his eyes upwards and contorted his face into a gargoyle-like expression that caused him to resemble Bob Hawke in aggressive debate. I had seen other journalists do this impression, but Rykov's was more accurate than most. I laughed aloud, and Rykov joined in. He had a big, deep laugh, and some journalists along the bar turned to locate it; seeing Rykov, they grinned involuntarily. It was the sort of laugh that drew people; it made you want to enter his orbit.

The barman brought two gin-and-tonics and I handed one to Rykov, who raised it in a silent toast, looking at me intently. It was difficult to look away: his eyes had a hypnotic quality. 'I think you told me at the reception that you served in China,' he said. 'How did you enjoy it there?'

'It had its moments. But it's pretty austere,' I said.

'I can imagine. No need to be polite to me about the People's Republic,' Rykov said. 'No-one in Soviet Union is impressed with the Chinese style of Marxism.'

I put out a feeler, at this. 'I believe things are changing considerably in the Soviet Union. I understand that people aren't required to be so orthodox about Marxism-Leninism as they were.'

Rykov swallowed a good half of his gin, and set it down with a rap on the polished wooden bar. 'I'll tell you the truth,' he said. 'Since the 'seventies, we have a generation in Russia who are bored shitless with Marxism-Leninism. Most of us only pay lip-

service to it – including those in Party and Politburo.' He looked
at me, and his smile became sardonic. 'Don't misunderstand me,'
he said, 'we're not on the verge of rebellion. But we've all had
ideology up to here.' He held his hand sideways against his
throat. 'We're interested in other things now,' he said. 'Even in
the 'sixties, when I was at university, we were more interested in
pop music from the West than in reading Marx. We were more
interested in Beatles than in Lenin. I tell you, Vincent, everything
Western used to fascinate me – and the new generation is the
same. They like little Elton John. He can't touch Beatles, in my
opinion, but there you are.'

'I hope they still listen to Russian music,' I said. 'You have such
great composers.'

Rykov looked at me quickly. 'You like Russian composers?'

I said that I did, and named some of my favourites. As I did so,
Rykov nodded vigorously, and his eyes became even brighter.
'And Shostakovich?'

'I haven't listened to much Shostakovich, I'm afraid.'

'You should. You should. Come to my flat one evening, and I'll
play you his great Seventh Symphony: the Leningrad. No Russian
hears it without weeping. I don't hear it without weeping. But I
have special reason. I come from there – from old St Petersburg.
This symphony was written in 1941, as a tribute to people of the
city, in the time when Nazis were bombing the shit out of
Leningrad, and its buildings were on fire. Shostakovich helped to
defend it. So did my father, actually, who was a general in Red
Army. I wasn't born then, but my father has told me something
about those days.' The glint of humour had gone from his eyes,
to be replaced by a different light: perhaps nostalgic; at the same
time bleak. He was no longer looking at me, but staring into the
mirror behind the bar, where bottles and rows of glasses winked
in a set of mirrors. 'They were the generation who had it hard,'
he said. He turned back to me and smiled, and his face was transformed again. It was as though he had removed a mask: one put
on without thought, and hastily got rid of. 'Well, Soviet Union is

changing,' he said. 'But we must wait for old men to shuffle off, before it can change much more.'

I began to be somewhat surprised by the general direction of Rykov's talk, coming as it did from a correspondent for the official Soviet news agency, and I wondered whether his sentiments were genuine, or a line put out with ulterior motives. One always had to consider that possibility, of course. There was a frankness and easiness about him, however, that made this difficult to believe, even though I knew from experience that his very easiness might well be part of his professional expertise.

'I'd like to see your native city,' I said. 'Alas, despite my knowledge of Russian, I've never been posted to the Soviet Union. When I picture Leningrad, it's the old St Petersburg of Dostoevsky's novels. I always see one of his characters mooching along beside the Neva, racked by some terrible conflict or other.'

Rykov screwed up his eyes in mingled amusement and surprise. Then he laughed appreciatively, clapping a hand on my shoulder. 'A lover of Dostoevsky! We have much in common, Vincent. You have read *The Possessed*? You remember Nikolai Stavrogin?'

I said I did.

'A wicked man, Stavrogin, but very interesting man,' Rykov said. 'The aristocratic revolutionary. Lost leader of Nihilists – charismatic leader who refuses to lead, and destroys himself. You remember this? Believe me, Vincent, this was a type that Russia would go on producing – and Dostoevsky knew it, even before the Revolution happened. A terrible reactionary, Dostoevsky – all that nonsense about Russia being saved by the Tsar and Orthodox Church. But he understood Russia like no-one else did, because he loved it.'

He finished his drink, and signalled to the barman. Then, in one of the sudden changes of direction that seemed habitual with him, he began to ask me about myself.

'You're married?'

'No,' I said. 'How about you?'

'Divorced,' he said. 'My fault. Women have always led me to

disaster. Can you introduce me to a nice Australian girl who won't do this?'

He let out his big laugh and changed direction again, asking me now who I thought would get the US Democratic nomination – Hart or Mondale.

'Perhaps Mondale,' I said. 'But it really doesn't matter. Reagan will beat whoever the Democrats put up, in November.'

'You think so? They say he is a rather stupid old man – how can the Americans vote for him? Because they like a film star?'

'He's no intellectual giant,' I said, 'but that doesn't mean he's stupid. He has a few clear values that he truly believes in, and that's what gets through to the people. It's probably what works best, in a leader. I'd suggest to you, Peter, that intellectuals make terrible leaders. They're too complicated and too self-willed, so they end up being given to excess: to tyranny. Look at Robespierre. Look at Lenin.'

Uttering this last name, I waited with interest for his response. He pushed out his full lower lip and looked sideways at me, seeming to consider.

'You may be right,' he said. 'But I have to tell you, Vincent, Star Wars is a worry. Our leaders truly believe that the Reagan is reckless, and is planning nuclear attack. They wet themselves about it. Andropov was convinced of it – and now that he's dead we have Chernenko as General Secretary: a member of the fucking old guard, who is backed by armed forces. So watch out – or we may all go boom.' Saying this, and arching his brows, he adopted an expression of comical apprehension, removing all tension from the discussion. 'It's the old men that worry me,' he added. 'The terrible old men with their rigid ideas, on both sides.'

As he spoke, live music began: a Hungarian gypsy air, cutting through the murmur of voices. Rykov turned, looking across to the dining area. In a far corner of the room, a plump, white-moustached old man in a frilled shirt and black waistcoat was playing a piano-accordion.

'Gypsy music is here,' Rykov said. 'This calls for goulash and red wine. Shall we eat, Vincent?'

We stood up from our stools. As we did so, Rykov put a hand on my shoulder again, his eyes shining. The music seemed to stimulate him. 'Gypsy music always reminds me of Dmitri Karamazov,' he said. 'You've read *Brothers Karamazov*? Of course. You remember how Dmitri makes off with the beautiful, crazy Grushenka, to an inn in the country? He organizes a wild party, a real orgy, and he asks the landlord for gypsies to provide the music – remember? "Get me gypsies!"' He laughed joyously at this, repeating: '"Get me gypsies!"' – and I began to laugh too. Then he went on: 'That's what I want from life, Vincent: a party with gypsies, and a crazy Grushenka beside me! What can the world give us to beat that?' He glanced slyly at me, head thrown back; and somehow it was as though he'd spoken in code: a code for something else that could not be spelled out.

I liked him, and his ebullience was infectious; but he was hard to read. He might well be what he seemed: a mercurial, easygoing journalist who was not over-respectful of the Soviet leadership, but who was not overtly rejecting it either. Or else he might be acting: but if his winning warmth and openness were feigned, he was a very good actor. Whichever the case, he exerted a charm whose nature was hard to analyse. It did not lie merely in the things he said, even though they compelled attention, and even though they were sometimes amusing. It could not be attributed to his good looks, since many dull people are good-looking. No; it somehow lay in a muted excitement he created: an excitement belonging to that mysterious zone beyond the ordinary which can never be netted in words, and is not even taken seriously by the worldly or the prosaic. It could only be seen in this case, I decided, as part of the mystery of personality; and its power was such that as we moved through the half-light of the dining room, with its flickering red candles and the murmur and laughter of its diners, Rykov seemed to be leading the way towards some illusory incident of great intensity, waiting at the centre of the evening.

Monday, August 6th, 1984

LAST FRIDAY, WHICH I took off from work, Peter Rykov drove me up to Sydney. My ageing Holden is in dock for repairs, and he offered me a lift. I was to stay with Erika for the weekend, in her flat in Neutral Bay. Peter told me he was staying with Russian friends, and would drive me back on Sunday night. He owns a very expensive sports sedan: a dark-blue BMW. His apartment in Kingston, not far from the Soviet Embassy, is also expensive. He invited me there one evening last week for a drink, and played me Shostakovich's Leningrad symphony, as he'd promised. The apartment was spacious, and its furnishings were of very high quality. An 'executive apartment'. TASS looks after him well, it seems.

We left Canberra at around nine in the morning. Fine weather for this time of the year, with winter sunlight. Out on the Federal Highway, I sank back in the BMW's leather seat with a pleasant sense of release. I believe the same mood was taking possession of Rykov: glancing at him, I saw that he was smiling, his eyes narrowed with a cat-like look of pleasure as the sun streamed through the windscreen. He's something of a dandy: he wore pigskin driving gloves, and a paisley scarf was knotted at his throat, tucked inside his blue linen shirt. He puts me in mind of a White Russian aristocrat. Maybe that's his actual ancestry, though it would never do to enquire: no doubt his family did all they could to obliterate it, after the Revolution. But his physiognomy gives him away: he's no *muzhik*.

As he drove, he began to talk to me about Erika. I'd suggested he watch one of her interviews on *News Tonight*, which he'd done; there have been more interviews since then, and I found now that he'd watched these as well, and had apparently been very impressed. This didn't surprise me, as Erika's ability in the medium has proved to be remarkable. Her success has been quite extraordinary: beyond anything one could have hoped for.

I can claim a modest part in this, since the fallout from the interview with Roy Cameron was considerable, setting her on her way as few other things could have done. Cameron has always been a figure of national interest, but until now no sort of significant scandal has been attached to him, except for rumours of his adultery with a striptease dancer, and a rather messy divorce. Now, here was real meat. Quite a few print journalists picked up on the story of the labour from Dong Yang prison camp, pursuing it relentlessly; they were able to confirm the camp's existence, and quoted a number of sources claiming that Cameron's mine did in fact employ slave labour – confirmation which gratified me considerably. Cameron's company has issued formal denials, of course, and so has the Embassy of the People's Republic – but Cameron himself has refused any further interviews, and clips from Erika's interview with him were run on a number of other television channels, including the national broadcasting network.

As a result of all this, and because of her striking appearance on camera, a number of small articles have been run on Erika herself: in a Sydney broadsheet, in the television section of a Melbourne Sunday paper, and in the big-circulation magazine, *Women's Life*. In that magazine, she was dubbed (ridiculously) 'the Deadly Blonde', because of what was seen as her entrapment of Cameron; and this label has since been applied in other papers. Such magazines are always looking for new stars, and they've gone a good way towards making Erika one, in a minor way. Since most of their stars are actresses from television soapies, or vacuous sports girls, Erika has novelty value, I suppose. She is seen to have 'refinement', and a certain degree of mystery, largely because her style is low-key and her accent difficult to place – and perhaps because she refuses to go into any personal detail about herself. The fact that she was in Foreign Affairs, serving in many countries abroad, impresses the magazine journalists; and although she has been careful to explain that she was a journalist herself, working in the Information Service, they have discovered that she held the rank of a diplomat, which has added to her unusual image. 'Glamorous ex-diplomat Erika Lange: *News Tonight*'s new star': this has been a typical headline. Beyond her professional background, the journalists have discovered very little, except for the fact that her father was a German immigrant married to an Australian – a discovery which prompted one media gossip columnist to compare her looks to Marlene Dietrich's.

Oh, my Erika! As well that they don't know you as I do!

All this publicity had of course interested Rykov, and he now questioned me closely about her. Then he said: 'So you're staying with her over the weekend?'

'Yes,' I said. 'She has a flat in Neutral Bay, with a spare bedroom.'

He glanced at me quickly, wrinkling up his eyes in that way he has, so that they glinted brilliantly in the sun through the windscreen, like chips of blue glass. His disbelieving smile was so light-hearted that I couldn't take offence. 'A spare bedroom! This sounds very proper,' he said.

'As I've told you,' I said, 'we have no romantic involvement. We're very old friends.'

'Yes, yes,' he said. 'Of course. You did tell me that. I'm sorry, Vincent. It's just that it's hard to believe you wouldn't be in love with a woman as pretty as that. Is she as pretty as she looks on television?'

'I believe you'd say so,' I said.

'And she's not involved with anybody?'

'Not at present,' I said, 'so far as I know.'

'Well, she's young,' Rykov said. 'Plenty of time to find the right man, I suppose. And perhaps her career is what she cares most about.'

'She's not so young as you might think,' I said. 'She's thirty-three.'

Again he turned to give me a swift glance, and this time his look was surprised. 'Really?' he said. 'She looks much younger. Wonderful what the camera can do.' He paused, his eyes on the road as we passed a truck. 'I found her interview with your Minister for Defence very interesting,' he said. 'I'd very much like to meet her. Purely on a professional basis, of course. Would that be possible, some time?'

'Certainly,' I said. There was silence for a moment; then I said: 'I'm meeting her for lunch in the city today. Why don't you join us?'

His smile broadened, expressing delight. 'Would that be possible? I wouldn't be intruding?'

'Of course not,' I said. 'I'm sure Erika would be interested to meet a TASS journalist.'

The car rounded a bend, and Lake George appeared on our right: waterless at the moment, but green with grass. Far out in the middle, white dots that were sheep showed bright in the morning sun; cattle grazed near a tawny stretch of sand. The lake extended to a long line of hills in the east, light-blue and mauve and very far off, looking like hills in a dream, or in some other country. Following my gaze, Rykov gestured as the car sped by.

'This is the place they call Lake George?'

I said it was.

'I thought so,' he said. 'And will you tell me, Vincent, why it's called a lake when it has no water in it?'

'It's a disappearing lake,' I said. 'Sometimes it's dry for years. Then it comes back, and it's filled with water for miles. No-one knows why.'

'Is that so?' He laughed, raising his eyebrows. 'I'm sorry, but this is very odd.' He glanced back, as it receded behind us. 'I like it though,' he said. 'I like the space.'

*

We got into Sydney just before noon. I'd arranged to meet Erika at twelve-thirty in the CBD, at one of the open-air restaurants on the terrace above Martin Place.

By the time that Rykov had put his BMW in a car park, and we had walked down George Street and up the hill of Martin Place, we were late. We climbed the pink granite steps to the crowded terrace in front of the MLC tower at twenty minutes to one, picking our way through office workers who perched on the steps like birds, eating their takeaway lunches. After Canberra's quiet, the noise of Sydney was distracting: piped music from loudspeakers; the chatter of hundreds of voices; the roar of traffic down in Pitt Street, magnified by the canyons of high-rise build-ings. But it was one of those fine winter days which suit Sydney best: bright, clear sun, without the heaviness and humidity that make the city so trying in summer.

I scanned the tables in front of the restaurant on the left of the steps, where Erika and I had arranged to meet. She was seated at a table under an umbrella, reading a newspaper. Since the restau-rants and coffee shops in the MLC Centre are favoured by stockbrokers, businessmen, banking executives and lawyers, business suits predominated here, on most of the women as well as the men. Erika was no exception: she wore a pale-blue linen trouser-suit, beautifully cut, but without the currently fashion-able power shoulders. They wouldn't have suited her slight figure, and she has always refused to follow fashions that don't suit her. A leather handbag of briefcase size leaned against her chair.

As we advanced on her table, a sixth sense told her of our presence. She looked up, putting down the newspaper and pushing back the hair from her forehead, surveying us both without expression, as is generally her way on first meeting. I apologised for the delay and introduced Rykov, informing Erika that he was the TASS correspondent here. They examined each other as I spoke, their eyes steady and enquiring, Rykov standing over the table with his usual military erectness. His face, as he looked at Erika, was alight with that humorous expectancy which I've come to see is typical of him, and he bowed slightly from the waist: a greeting from another century.

'I'm delighted to meet you,' he said. 'I'm a very big fan of your work, Erika.'

Erika raised her brows, and allowed him a faint smile in return. Meanwhile, a willowy adolescent waiter in black and white had arrived, hovering over us with folders containing the menu. He distributed these as Rykov and I sat down, and hurried off. I picked up the wine list, and scanned it for a moment. 'What do we say to a bottle of riesling?' I said. 'Shall I choose?'

Somewhat to my surprise, Erika and Rykov were still studying each other across the table; and I was struck by something odd. They somehow resembled each other, almost as though they were relatives. It was not just that they were both blond: it was something more specific, which I couldn't yet place.

Erika turned to me. 'Yes, Vin, riesling will be fine,' she said. 'You order. You always know the best wines. Unless Peter has some other preference.'

'I'm happy to leave it to Vincent,' Rykov said, and winked at me. 'He's the expert on Australian wine.'

Erika had opened her menu, and was studying it. Coming to a decision, she closed it again, and looked across at Rykov. 'So you're here for TASS,' she said. 'What sort of stories does your government want from you?'

'Anything of interest concerning your country,' Rykov said. 'Trade and defence matters, mostly. Political rows and scandals always of interest, of course. But there haven't been many lately.'

'And what do they think of the Hawke Government?'

Rykov grinned. 'They see it as very little different from the Fraser Government,' he said. 'Even though it's supposed to be Socialist, it's really quite conservative, isn't it? Labor backs the American alliance just like the Liberals. Nothing changes.'

Erika put her head on one side. 'Don't you think so? From a Soviet point of view, maybe that's so.'

'I was very interested in your interview with the Minister for Defence,' Rykov said. 'I learned a good deal about the Australian–American relationship from it.'

'I didn't get as much as I wanted,' Erika said. 'Scholes was pretty cagey.'

'He won't continue to resist you, I'm sure,' Rykov said.

There was another small pause; then Erika asked: 'And how long have you been in Australia?'

'About a year,' he said. 'Before this I was in New York for two years.'

'Really? I was in New York in the 'seventies. I loved it. What an energy there is in that town. Everywhere else seems slow, afterwards.'

'I know what you mean,' Rykov said. 'I liked it too. Every day is like an electric charge. No-one can accuse Americans of lacking vitality.'

'No. I suppose you find it a bit quieter in Canberra,' Erika said.

Rykov put his head on one side and pursed his lips judiciously. 'A little,' he said. 'What Canberra needs is a good slum.'

There was nothing very witty about this response, yet they both laughed as though there had been. It was the sort of behaviour which generally accompanies a mild flirtation, and which always looks slightly fatuous to the onlooker. The principals of course are oblivious, and such was the case now. Knowing my Erika as I do, I saw that she was interested in Rykov: to what degree, it was impossible to tell.

The waiter arrived with our bottle of riesling, and filled our glasses. When he had taken our orders for food, Erika raised her glass and said to Rykov: 'Anyway Peter, welcome to Sydney.'

'Thank you,' he said. 'Cheers.'

We drank; then Erika asked him: 'Do you miss the USSR?'

'Sometimes I do, of course,' Rykov said. 'But I'm not in a hurry to go back. The people are in many ways well-off now – but our society is bogged down.'

'What do you mean?' She had adopted her interviewer's voice.

'I mean that our country is in many ways frozen. The working class are secure, they can never lose their jobs, but they can't advance. They get complacent that way. Only at the top is there a lot of competition.'

'Really? You make it sound as if you have a class system. I thought Communism did away with that,' Erika said.

Rykov smiled with open amusement; he drank, then set down his glass. 'Of course we have a class system,' he said. 'I think you must know this, Erika.'

'And those at the top have all the privileges,' I put in. 'Isn't that so, Peter?'

He glanced at me quickly. 'More or less,' he said. 'Isn't that the way it always goes? Those who contribute most get the highest rewards. That was decided soon after the Revolution.'

'And what about you?' Erika asked. 'Where do you fit in on the social scale?'

'Me? I'm just a journalist.'

'Oh please,' Erika said. She was smiling, but her voice had gone flatter than usual. 'An overseas correspondent for TASS isn't just any old journalist, is he? You're nearer to the top of the heap than the bottom, I would have said.'

I thought Rykov might grow offended at this; instead he smiled broadly, and spread his hands. 'I've been lucky,' he said. 'My father was a major-general in Red Army, and I went to Leningrad State University; this put me in a strong position, naturally, and I got into journalism. I don't have much to complain of. But I'm critical of the way in which the country is going, and so are many of my comrades. We need better leadership than we have at present. The war in Afghanistan, for instance, has been a bloody big mistake. Andropov knew this at first – but then he got sucked in, and now he's gone, and his successors are floundering.'

'It does seem a mess,' Erika said. 'You agree that it's your Vietnam?'

Rykov put his head in his hands in mock despair. 'Please,' he said. 'Don't rub it in.'

'Did you report on the war?' I asked.

'Yes,' he said. 'I covered in 1980, for Radio Moscow. We had 80,000 troops there, just to hold the major towns, and to stop Afghan Army from being destroyed by rebels. We were getting nowhere, and nowhere was secure. I used to sleep with a pistol by my bed.' He had pushed back the sleeves of the blue linen shirt and had folded his hands on the table; he turned away now, and looked out at the crowds milling past our table, in their well-tailored suits and expensive casual wear. A pretty woman in sunglasses, wearing a low-cut white dress, passed close to us, and his eyes rested on her briefly. I noticed that his forearms were very muscular, and I found myself wondering whether Rykov was telling the truth about what he'd been doing in Afghanistan. I was more than ever convinced that he's a former military man – one who's kept himself at a peak of physical fitness – and I suspected that he'd been in the Red Army, serving in Afghanistan as an officer. I had no real justification for thinking this, of course; it was simply a hunch. A shaft of sun was striking under the umbrella to reach Rykov's face; in its strong light, which empha-sised the lines about his eyes, he suddenly looked less youthful than usual. I had discovered that he was thirty-eight, and he looked every year of it, just now.

He shook his head and smiled, and picked up his glass. 'But let's talk of more pleasant things,' he said.

Then Erika did an odd thing – although knowing Erika as I do, it should not have surprised me. She reached out and placed her hand on Rykov's bare forearm. He turned to her swiftly, his smile vanishing; then he looked down at her hand, which remained where it was. 'You have some bad memories, Peter,' she said. 'I can see that. Forget them. It's a lovely day in Sydney town.'

He looked into her face for a moment; then he laughed softly. 'So it is,' he said. 'And you make it lovelier, Erika.'

Nineteenth-century gallantry.

That night Erika gave me a simple dinner in the flat she's renting in Neutral Bay, on the North Shore. It's a unit on the seventh floor of a block in Rangers Road, and has a fine view of the Harbour from the balcony, looking over the tops of some giant camphor laurels. There's a small spare bedroom for me to sleep in.

Before dinner, we sat with our drinks on the balcony and talked. There's little restraint in our talk, but the days when we explored the arcane and the secret are gone – left behind with our youth. Gone, our dark and visionary adolescence, when I was the Magician, and she was white-browed Artemis. We're friends now, not conspirators, and in some ways Erika has become a stranger to me. But she's also a stranger to herself, and I believe I can still say that no-one has been closer to her than I am. Certainly not her lovers – not even Bradley – since they can't have known those secrets that she and I alone will always share. She's the only person outside the Service who knows what I'm doing in the Registry, and I was gratified by her pleasure and understanding when I first told her of my appointment. She came back to the subject now.

'You realise what the DG has done for you? He's made you master of the system,' she said. 'It's what we used to dream about, isn't it?'

'Yes. But I still need to make it work for me,' I said.

'You will, I know it. You'll pull off a coup, and be sent back into the field. I'm proud of you, Vin.'

As we spoke, the fast sub-tropical sunset was putting on its usual excessive display, beyond the balcony: sheets of pink and copper in the water, and the clouds in the west stained an ominous red. Over by Circular Quay, at the entrance to the city, the white-tiled sails of the Opera House were red-tinted too: the centrepiece of a stage-set. Flocks of flying foxes swooped and flapped in silhouette above the camphor laurels, like prehistoric birds of prey. Then the sunset was over, and darkness closed in. A huge container ship moved towards the Heads, black and hulking. A ferry hurried busily towards Mosman, spilling lights on the water as thick and yellow as syrup. Far across the Harbour, the windows of the eastern suburbs swarmed and danced.

We had fallen silent; now I turned back to Erika. 'How did you do it?' I asked.

She looked at me. 'How did I get in at Channel Twelve, you mean?'

'Yes. I've been wondering. It's all rather miraculous,' I said.

Her face had taken on that blank look I knew indicated caution with her. Oh, Erika, I know you so well!

'Luck,' she said. 'A colleague on the *Courier* introduced me to one of their network executives at a party. We got on well, and he agreed to get me an audition. They sent me out on a small, unimportant interview, and used it as a test. They liked it, and I was in.'

'Your executive must have been a nice fellow,' I said. Probing.

Her eyes narrowed. 'Actually, he's a pig,' she said. 'So is Craig Thompson, the network head. So are all the executives there. It's a male club, and they're the most sexist bastards I've ever met. They have absolute power, and what counts most with them, when they hire a female journalist, is sex appeal. One of the other women there told me she was sitting in when they were auditioning for a female anchor, and were running the tests on the screen. As each woman's test came up, Thompson would say: "*I'd* give her one – would *you* give her one?" If most of them said they would, the audition was successful.'

She was sitting with clenched fists, staring out over the balcony, her face entirely cold.

'I see,' I said. 'And have you been called on to do any of them favours?'

'No,' she said. She didn't look at me, but continued to stare into the dark. Then, in a very soft voice, she repeated: 'No. Except that I have to put up with being pawed now and then.'

I believe she was lying; I always know when she's lying. But I asked her no more questions, and the subject lapsed, as she clearly wanted it to.

We spoke about Bradley now, as we've done so many times before. On the occasions when she'd come and stayed with me in Canberra, Erika hadn't attempted to see Derek: I felt pretty certain of that. But I suspected that she'd phoned him. She's addicted to the telephone, which gives her intimate, drawn-out contact without physical presence. When she's with me, she will talk about Derek endlessly, agonising over the failure of their relationship, analysing the reasons for its ending, justifying her refusal to commit in the way that he wanted, and blaming him for what she calls his rigidity in rejecting her need for freedom. I listened once again as she went around in circles, with the deep monotony of neurosis: that neurosis which wants to resolve ir-reconcilable opposites; that deadly twist of the spirit which seeks to enjoy two opposed conditions at the same time, and can never understand why this isn't possible. Well, she is truly the Star now, and many men desire her, gazing at her image on the screen: why can she not simply glory in that?

'You say Derek tried to own you,' I said, 'and that this wasn't what you wanted. Very well: why don't you reconcile yourself to it? No-one can own you, we both know that. Freedom has a price, and the price is solitude. You're truly the Star now: and the Star shines alone.'

I had not directly referred to her secret persona for a very long time. We stared at each other, and both of us, I knew, were seeing the Naked Goddess, in those days when the Tarot and the world of secrets lay at the centre of our lives; those days when Erika was the embodiment of destiny and the divine. It was as though I had suddenly touched her on an intimate spot; a shadow passed over her face, and she looked down into her lap. 'I spread the Tarot recently,' she said, 'to see what hope it gave Brad and me. I just couldn't see him there. *You* were there, Vin: the Magician was in the middle of the circle, which was good. You predicted my success at Channel Twelve. But there were cards I didn't like. The Four of Cups reversed, meaning trouble and illness later in the year. And the ninth card was the Seven of Coins: a warning of loss. Bad cards, Vincent – and Derek wasn't there.'

'None of those bad things need happen,' I said. 'The cards simply give you warnings of what to avoid – you know that.'

She stayed silent for perhaps half a minute, looking out into the dark. When she looked back at me, her eyes had filled with tears. She pulled out a handkerchief from somewhere, sniffed, and wiped her cheeks. When she spoke, it was in a small, childish voice. 'I don't want to be alone. I wanted closeness as much as Brad did.'

'But only when it suited,' I said. 'At other times you wanted to disappear into the blue. I'm not being critical: I understand you, remember?'

'You understand too much,' she muttered. She looked out over the Harbour again, her eyes seeming to search for something among the lights. 'I really wanted to marry him,' she said. 'I wanted to have children with him.'

This surprised me, and I stared at her. She had never spoken of having children before.

Her eyes met mine defiantly. 'The clock's ticking,' she said. 'I'm in my thirties. I do want children, Vincent, before it's too late.'

'But you don't want permanence,' I said. 'And Bradley knew that. It's all over with him: you have to face that.'

She closed her eyes, as though in pain. 'I have,' she said.

I refilled our wine glasses, which stood on a little table between us; we drank, and said nothing for a time. We'd exhausted the subject, and I felt a sudden emptiness. There are times when she drains my spirit; and since our spirits are twins, I knew that hers was drained too. Finally, to change the subject, I asked her what she thought of Peter Rykov.

She looked at me quickly, eyes wide, adopting a careful expression. I know that expression: it means that she's been touched in some way. 'He's very charming,' she said. 'But something about him worries me. He's not what he seems.'

'You only think that because he's from the Soviet bloc,' I said. 'We always assume that about Soviet citizens, don't we? Usually with good reason. But in Peter's case, I think you'd be wrong. I believe he's just what he seems: a journalist, toeing the line for TASS, who now prefers the West, and hopes that things will change at home. He's no lover of the regime: you've heard the way he talks about it. He doesn't say very much – but when he does, he's critical. He has too much of a sense of humour to be a dedicated Communist. And being around Western journalists so long has probably had an effect on him. I intend to try to draw him out a little more, when I get to know him better. It's a case of softly, softly.'

'You're sure he's not KGB? He wouldn't be the first of them to use journalism as a cover.'

'I'm pretty sure he's not,' I said. 'KGB officers here are attached to the Embassy – they don't turn up as journalists. Besides, I went through the Registry. Rykov doesn't have a file. And if ASIO had anything on him, they'd have passed it on to us.'

'He's interesting,' she said. 'A man of the North: everything in him intense, like ice.' She smiled, and the smile was rather sly: an expression which might mean little, or something more.

On Sunday night, when Rykov drove me back to Canberra, an unusual exchange took place between us.

There's something about sharing a drive at night that creates an atmosphere of intimacy between two people. The situation invites confidences, even when the acquaintance has been a short one. Rykov's beautiful BMW, with its near-silent engine, was especially conducive to this: we seemed to be floating through the dark in a well-upholstered capsule, outside the barriers of mundane reality. In such a situation, even strangers will confide in one another. It was late; we'd eaten dinner in a restaurant in Paddington, and by the time we got onto the Hume Highway it was after ten o'clock. A heavy downpour had arrived, and the road ahead was hidden by sheets of silver. Rykov had drunk a good deal more wine than I had, and I wondered how steady his driving would be; but he seemed unaffected. He flashed around the big interstate trucks that crowd the Hume, steering through the spray from their wheels with a casual aggression which at first made me nervous. But I soon came to realise that he was a highly expert driver, drunk or sober.

We passed through the little town of Mittagong, with its gaudily painted Victorian buildings and fast food cafés for tourists, and were into the southern tablelands. The rain was left behind now. The sky was clear: a blue-black night, with sharp stars. I experienced the lightness I always do when I get up onto these tablelands; the humid heaviness of the urbanized coast was gone, and my spirits lifted. Even the dim, grassy spaces here, with their scattered, delicate eucalypts, had a quality that was different from the morose, olive-drab bush of the coastal flatland: there was a sense of freedom and release. Perhaps Rykov was affected by this as well, because now he began to talk, glancing at me occasionally in the dark of the car, his white, indistinct face reflecting the little lights on the dashboard. Coming through the last suburban scatterings of Sydney, we'd been mostly silent, and our talk over dinner had been on entirely trivial topics. It now became apparent that this conversation would be different.

'So what do you actually do, in Foreign Affairs? You've never told me,' he said.

Instantly, I became wary and alert, despite the fumes of the wine I'd drunk. I told him I was on the China desk at present: very routine work.

'You don't hope for another posting abroad?'

'Oh yes,' I said, 'but I'm in no hurry. I've been posted abroad a good deal, and I'm glad to be home for a while.'

He nodded, his eyes on the road ahead. 'I understand,' he said. 'We all want to be home, sooner or later. I too get homesick – but the trouble is, there's a part of me that doesn't want to go back at all.'

I had never made a direct critical comment to him about the nature of the Soviet system. Now I took the opportunity to do so.

'I think I can understand,' I said. 'Living in a one-party state must get a little restricted.'

I had dropped my bait, and waited. At first he said nothing, narrowing his eyes against the headlights of the cars in the opposite lanes. Then he said: 'It has its disadvantages. Although for someone like me, our system also has its advantages.'

I asked him what he meant by this.

'The system is clearly laid out,' he said. 'If you have the ability, and especially if you have a background the Party approves of, you can go far. You only have to keep your nose clean, and jump the correct hurdles.'

'And that was your case,' I said.

'That was my case – exactly. My father, who's retired now, was not only a high-ranking Red Army officer, but highly decorated: Order of the Red Star, and Order of the Patriotic War.' There was pride in his voice when he said this, and he paused for a moment. 'This helped, when I set my sights on university – and so did my background at school. I did all the right things. I was a Young Pioneer of the third class.' He grinned, glancing at me with a humorous glint in his eyes. 'Oh yes, I wore the red scarf,' he said. 'And I have to say I enjoyed it all: the camps, the sports, the marches; the bugles and the drums. It suited me.' He chuckled, and there was a kind of light self-mockery in his voice, now. I saw that the wine had affected him after all, making him loquacious, and perhaps a little nostalgic. 'I even liked the songs,' he said. '"The Anthem of the Young Pioneers". "The Little Joyful Drummer".' He began to hum the tune of one of these songs; then he sang a verse in Russian, breaking off to glance at me again, his expression now openly playful. 'We read books for boys by a writer called Arkady Gaidar,' he said. 'All about noble young Soviet heroes fighting enemies of the Motherland. I loved these books: I imagined I was a hero like that. But of course, this was all much more serious than your Boy Scouts. It was highly political. This was where they recruited us; when I was fifteen it led to my joining the Young Communist League: the *Komsomol*. I was well on the way to becoming a Party member. I was a believer, Vincent, and my life was clearly mapped out for me. After university, I knew that I wanted to be a journalist, and I was recommended to join the staff of Radio Moscow.'

'So life has been good to you,' I said.

Again the sideways glance, his intense blue eyes glinting in the stream of oncoming lights. 'Yes, it's been good,' he said. 'And if I ever had doubts about wisdom of our leaders, I kept them to myself. Everyone in USSR has those doubts – they wouldn't be human, otherwise, and they've had bloody good cause, in the past. As it happens, the year when Comrade Stalin was discarded as an icon was the same year in which I joined the *Komsomol*: 1961. That was when Khrushchev addressed the Twenty-second Congress, denouncing Stalinism, and asking that his body be removed from the mausoleum. Of course, this process had begun years before, when I was only ten: that was when Khrushchev revealed Stalin's crimes, at the Twentieth Congress. Shattering. I remember it, although I didn't really understand it then, because I saw how shocked my father was. He had revered Stalin without question; after all, Stalin had led us to victory over the Nazis in our Great Patriotic War – that was how my father saw it. Now he had to change his thinking. It wasn't easy for him.'

'I understand,' I said. 'Your father was clearly a loyal patriot – and Stalin had been the focus of his loyalty.'

'You could put it in this way,' Rykov said, and there was a note of appreciation in his voice. He clearly revered his father, and I had said the right thing. 'But like so many others,' he said, 'my father had been deceived by a man who had become a fucking monster.'

I now felt that I could take the opportunity to go further.

'I suppose that was inevitable,' I said. 'Stalin was a dictator, like Lenin before him – and dictators have a habit of becoming monsters, don't they? As Napoleon did. As Hitler did.'

Rykov's face became sober now, and he no longer looked at me. 'You're comparing Lenin to Stalin? And to Hitler?' His voice was soft, and had changed. It seemed to hold a faint note of threat, and it occurred to me that he would not be an easy man to cross.

'I'm afraid so,' I said. 'I hope you don't mind if I speak frankly.'

'Not at all, Vincent. This discussion is interesting,' he said, and now his tone was neutral. But he had given me a glimpse of his other side: one that it would not be pleasant to confront. 'Let's be open with each other,' he said. 'I don't often have a frank talk with someone on your side of the fence. Most Foreign Affairs officers are much more careful, and I grow tired of careful people. Let me say too that many people in Soviet Union would now agree with you that Marxism often got misused by our leaders.'

'But Peter, this is where I have to disagree,' I said. 'The germ of all that happened was in the theory itself. You must have studied the Marxist dialectic?'

Rykov sighed. 'I did, a long time ago. I found it very boring, to tell you the truth.'

'Well then,' I said. 'You'll know that Lenin was in fact utterly faithful to Marx. Marxism-Leninism followed Marx's prescription exactly. Lenin created the dictatorship of the proletariat, which was what Marx had asked for. But Marx actually despised the proletariat, didn't he? He said that the people themselves were not capable of creating revolution. It had to be done for them, by an elite of Communist intellectuals. Am I right?'

Rykov shrugged. 'This was reasonable, surely. People always need leaders.'

'Yes, but do they need autocracy? This was what Lenin and Trotsky created, wasn't it? It wasn't *really* a dictatorship of the proletariat – that was a fiction. Russia simply exchanged one sort of feudalism for another.' I paused, glancing at Rykov's face to see how he was responding. I had gone very far, in blaspheming the whole Soviet system; but I wanted to see if he was still a faithful son of that system. He drove in silence for a time; then he said:

'Remember, Vincent, when the Revolution came, in 1917, the people were half-starved and desperate, and sick of the war with Germany. After the Tsar abdicated, they were rising up every-where, calling for leadership that would rescue them from chaos. Russians always want that. They want the strong arm.'

'They certainly got it,' I said.

Rykov looked at me with raised brows, and laughed under his breath. Then he said: 'I think you feel strongly about all this, Vincent.'

'I feel strongly about tyranny everywhere,' I said.

'I too,' he said. 'But we are speaking of ancient history, and nothing can be done to change it now. Great upheavals always cause a lot of misery – all you can hope for is eventual improvement for ordinary people. Ours have suffered a good deal, while yours have been very fortunate. When I went to New York, it opened my eyes to just how lucky Americans are. But I also saw vice that has shocked me. In the USSR, we consider some aspects of the West to be not so attractive. Even Solzhenitsyn has this view. He published an article some years ago saying that the West was falling into decadence.'

'He may be right,' I said. 'We're losing our common values, with the decay of the churches.'

'You're a religious man, Vincent?'

'Not in a conventional way,' I said. 'But I don't think we can afford to deny the life of the spirit. If we do, we stunt ourselves. That's what Karl Marx did: he denied the spirit. He hated God; he was at war with God.'

'Come on now, Vincent,' Rykov said. 'How could Marx be at war with God? For him, God didn't exist. Marx was a materialist.'

'I always thought so too,' I said. 'But then I discovered that Marx *didn't* become an unbeliever. He'd been a believing Christian in his youth, and he didn't cease to believe – he simply began to hate God.'

Rykov gave me an incredulous glance. 'Excuse me, but what is your evidence for this?'

'The evidence is in a poem he wrote,' I said. 'Here's a quote from it: *I wish to avenge myself against the One who rules above.* You see? He wanted to make war on God – and he probably saw dialectical materialism as his weapon, drawing people away from their faith and even belief in the soul. And this gave us tyrants like Stalin and Mao, who had power without limits, who could order the deaths of millions, and who were treated like gods in earthly form. And that's what the fallen angels wanted, isn't it?'

At first, Rykov made no answer to this, but drove in silence. I'd chanced my arm in airing such views to a man who might well be a dedicated Marxist-Leninist, despite any discontents he might have with the current state of his country, and I waited for his response with a certain degree of nervousness. Finally, however, he slapped the steering wheel with his hand, and gave his big, full-throated laugh.

'Crazy!' he said. 'I think you are a crazy man, Vincent – and probably a religious nut. But I enjoy talking to you. In one thing you are right, though. The Soviets did all they could to free the people from the old religion: they saw it as superstition, cluttering up their minds. I have to tell you I know little about Christianity, in any depth: I was never taught about it, naturally. But my grandmother remained Russian Orthodox, and would go off to her church. I was fond of my old *babushka*, but her religion was just mumbo-jumbo to me. I'll tell you something: I believe only in what I can touch and feel – and what I can hit with this.'

He raised his clenched fist from the steering wheel, and gave me another smiling glance: one that seemed to hold an ambiguous hint of aggression. Or was it a trick of the dim light? He was certainly drunk, I decided: his eyelids were drooping a little now, and there was a very faint slur in his speech.

'When you've had to kill or be killed,' he said, 'you appreciate life at its simplest, most fundamental level – you don't need anything else. I have been in that situation, in Afghanistan.'

What a journalist had been doing taking up arms I didn't enquire; but I suspected again that he had actually been in Afghanistan with the Red Army, rather than as a correspondent. His eyes had gone back to the road, and we were quiet for a moment. To change the subject, I asked him whether he was hopeful about Russia's future. In answer, he returned to a theme he's touched on before, in Bruno's – but with some added remarks that surprised me.

'Yes, I'm hopeful,' he said. 'Even though Reagan and his Star Wars have brought us to the brink. We've been closer to nuclear war in the past two years than at any time since Cuban missile crisis – no doubt about that. But I have to tell you, Vincent, that much of this crisis is being kept alive now by paranoia among our leaders, as well as yours. Brezhnev began it when he'd already become gaga, preparing us for a nuclear first strike by United States – which I don't believe was really likely. Andropov whipped it up last year, with his Cold War speeches. But since Andropov's death in February, things have been getting calmer. Chernenko is old guard, but I'm told he doesn't think an American attack is all that likely now. And there is a younger member of Politburo called Mikhail Gorbachev who is urging his comrades to get back to negotiations. So I'm hopeful. And let me tell you something.'

He turned and looked directly at me for a moment, and his expression now had a remarkable seriousness and fervency.

'There is a new Russia coming,' he said. 'One that will have greater freedom, and that will get rid of dead wood. One that will be truly efficient and enlightened.'

'You think so?' I said. 'But who will be its leaders?'

His eyes narrowed as they returned to the road ahead, and his lower lip crept out. '*We* will,' he said.

'We?' I said. 'Who do you mean by "we"?'

He shook his head, not looking at me now, and laughed softly. 'Men like me,' he said. 'Men of my generation and background. That's all I mean.'

I suspect now that this was *not* all he meant; but the subject was clearly closed. We were passing the dark spaces of Lake George, and would soon be back in Canberra. We drove the rest of the way in comparative silence.

Rykov has certainly given me something to think about. He said little that was outrageously heretical, on our drive together, but his tone was scarcely that of a loyal Party member – and he seemed in the end to be hinting at dreams for a change of rule. I still consider it most likely that he's simply a journalist; but if he *is* actually a KGB officer, using TASS as a cover, it's another matter. In that case, he was being remarkably indiscreet – unless, of course, he wanted to create the false impression of being a dissident.

Perhaps it was simply the wine talking: he does seem to have a weakness for drink. There's something impulsive and reckless about him, just barely held in check.

Wednesday, August 8th, 1984

IN THE PAST two days, dear Teodor, I've continued to ponder my night-time conversation with Peter Rykov. I'm not speaking now of the question of his true allegiance – though this also continues to occupy me – but of the other themes that our talk stirred into life. When I spoke to him of Karl Marx's hatred of God, Rykov clearly thought me peculiar. I wasn't surprised; most people would think such a claim far-fetched. Until quite recently, I would have thought so myself.

Whatever Marx's final beliefs may have been, however – as distinct from his socio-economic theories – his influence on the twentieth century has been profound, and much of my life has been given to the shadowy struggle with those enemies that operate in his name. It therefore begins to seem to me that I should think more deeply about the nature of the doctrine of materialism which now holds whole societies prisoner.

We're accustomed to the notion of a world divided between those who believe in a non-material reality – the world of the spirit – and those who do not. *But what if this is not the full picture?* What if the materialist position is a mask – even when the wearer of the mask is sincerely unaware of it – concealing a wilful refusal to accept the existence of God? Such people may not, of course, have deliberately chosen evil – but they may nevertheless have placed themselves in a vacuum where evil can choose *them*. Since you are a Catholic, dear Teodor, I can use this word in the confidence that you'll accept it in its original sense. For most people now, of course, the very concept of evil is not merely seen as unfashionable but medieval – creating a little shudder of distaste, rather in the way that sexual terms did in Victorian times. But it has begun to dawn on me that evil may simply be a fearsome absence – and it was this that I had in mind when I said to Peter Rykov that we can't afford to deny the spirit. How I pity a man like Rykov, whose spirit can never rise to seek the invisible!

Writing this, I find myself thinking of my childhood walks with Kenneth Ross. His strange homily on Bald Hill, when he warned me to keep myself spiritually clean, had a powerful effect on me at the time – though whether it remained a formative influence on me over the years that followed, I can't be sure. Certainly orthodox Christianity had ceased to appeal to me by the time I entered university; I began then to drift away from it, like so many others in my generation. Where did I drift to? Not to materialism, certainly, but into a shadow world: one that often delighted me, but where I had no firm rock to take hold of. In this, I am a typical twentieth-century man. The decline of the main Christian churches (either clownish, apologetic parodies of their former selves, or mundane vehicles for social reform) has left us to wander aimlessly, shopping for beliefs. In my student days, Plato and his Forms inspired me, and I still consider them powerful as a poetic idea. Life has given me little time since to reflect on such things. I've adopted a sort of Hegelian outlook, I suppose, believing in a universal Mind or Spirit, manifest through the natural world, and through the human mind and spirit. This is delightfully vague, leaving me free to drift on.

In setting down these thoughts, I see I've not referred to the interest that Erika and I took in the Tarot. I suspect, dear Teodor, that you would not have approved of these activities; but I tell you, they were so seductive that even now I feel a stealthy pleasure when I summon them up. Is it perhaps true that there is something demonic in the Tarot? Could it have affected both Erika and me in a way that has prolonged itself? I've always dismissed such notions; but my thoughts keep returning to them, lately; and of one thing I'm sure. I need more rewarding mysteries now than those hidden in the Tarot; and I need more substantial secrets than those yielded up by espionage. I begin to understand that there is nothing that doesn't ultimately lead to the world of the spirit – either to darkness or to light.

When such notions come to me, I begin to suspect, dear Teodor, that I should perhaps give up the intelligence profession, and look for an entirely different vocation. At such times, I long for a life where I'd be able to give to others: a life that would reward my spirit. And when my thoughts turn down this path, I find myself thinking of my time in India, nearly a decade ago, on my first posting abroad.

One is very impressionable at twenty-five, and my encounter with India was one of the great experiences of my life. It continues to hover in my mind even now, sometimes colouring my dreams. During my two years at the Embassy in New Delhi, I grew deeply fond of the country, despite its many difficulties and frustrations, and despite the scenes of poverty that so shocked me when I arrived: scenes that I recorded in some detail in these diaries. I made many Indian friends, and I refused to insulate myself in the bubble of prosperous New Delhi, with its fashionable business class, well-off civil servants and expatriate Europeans – which was what so many of my colleagues did. On many an evening, I wandered alone through the crowded slums of Old Delhi, talking with the people in the lanes and shops: old and young men; eager children. I gave the children gifts, and distributed money to a chorus of beggars that followed me about; but I knew that this achieved little, and it troubled me. I still see the faces of the people I befriended – some of whom invited me into dark, crumbling little houses in back lanes, and served me with sweet tea or lurid soft drinks. They frequently come back to me in memory – the smiling, friendly young men; the eager children with their shining, intelligent dark eyes – as though they wait for me to return.

On my days off, I would take train journeys out to the villages of Uttar Pradesh – swaying through that enormous, level plain, its empty stretches of brown grass reaching to the horizon, its sadly few little trees a bright emerald-green. Scattered across those baking levels were scenes of poverty unchanged for a thousand years: men in loincloths working the fields with oxen and wooden ploughs; buffalo being driven along river banks by little girls in fluttering head-dresses; palm-thatched, primitive mud-brick houses whose walls were plastered with discs of cow-dung, to be used as fuel. And the brown plain, it seemed to me, gave off a low, monotonous droning: a droning that was malicious, undermining all human hope.

This hopelessness, I believed at first, was the changeless, insoluble condition of India's poor, as it was in the slums of Old Delhi. But I came to see that it was gradually being overcome. In the 1970s, a new prosperity was already appearing in the cities, while many organizations were working to alleviate rural poverty. But it was slow: painfully slow. So many small farmers and their families, out on those droning plains, and so many vital, intelligent children in the backstreets of the cities, were being wasted and destroyed! I wanted, in a vague and uninformed way, to help them; but then of course, as my work absorbed me, I put it from my mind – as so many others do.

Lately, however, these thoughts come back more frequently. I sometimes feel that in some way that I can't anticipate, India waits for me.

Sunday, September 2nd, 1984

ERIKA HAS MOVED to Canberra. Yesterday, Saturday, I called on her in her new house in Deakin.

She phoned me from Sydney three weeks ago to tell me of her decision. At first I was surprised, since most successful media people prefer to be based in Sydney. But Erika now specialises in interviews with federal politicians, and she'd decided, she said, that it would be convenient to live in the federal capital, rather than to be travelling down from Sydney all the time. Channel Twelve maintains a studio and a small camera crew in Canberra, so there are no practical difficulties. Even so, it emerged that her bosses had at first been reluctant – only giving in after she pleaded with them, promising to be in Sydney within hours whenever she was needed.

But convenience, I now find, was not her real motive. What that motive was I only learned yesterday.

I drove over to Deakin at eleven in the morning. Since her arrival, I'd met her a couple of times over lunch in Manuka, but had not yet seen her house; she'd been staying in a motel until last week. Now she wanted to show the place off. She seemed filled with excited pleasure, on the phone: she's leasing the house un-furnished, and has only just had her new furniture delivered.

'I've never had a proper house before,' she said. 'I'm afraid I've lashed out a bit, on the furniture.' This didn't surprise me; her extravagance has grown worse over the years, often getting her into credit card debt she can barely cope with.

As I drove around the long curve of Mugga Way, at the foot of Red Hill, I reflected that Channel Twelve must be paying Erika a very large salary: Deakin is one of Canberra's most expensive suburbs, and she'd told me that the house had three bedrooms and a swimming pool. What on earth could she want with such a large place, living alone?

A perfect day: deep-blue sky, a feathery breeze suggesting the nameless possibilities of spring, the sun warm but not yet hot. We sat on the lawn next to the swimming pool, having made a tour of the house.

It's an extensive, tile-roofed bungalow of salmon-coloured stucco, with a raised, stone-flagged terrace in front and a double garage underneath. It stands tucked away in Buxton Street: a crescent on the suburb's final edge, right beside Red Hill. The garden has a number of flowering trees, including two jacarandas. The swimming pool is a large one; camellia bushes grow in a rockery at one end, and some of the red flowers were floating in the water. Erika had set out coffee and Danish pastries on a big outdoor table of clear-stained jarrah, which had matching armchairs with yellow cushions; we were shaded by a giant white umbrella. She had bought this garden setting along with her indoor furniture, she told me. She'd clearly spared no expense: she'd even put in new curtains and planter shutters throughout the house.

We sipped our coffees in silence for a time, while the carolling of magpies came from Red Hill. The walking track that skirts the hill ran close to Erika's back fence, on top of a bank that was green with young grass. Most of the bank was screened from us by a line of grevilleas in the garden, but a section was visible through a gap. As I watched, a middle-aged couple wearing matching tracksuits passed, power-walking, like marionettes. Few other pedestrians had appeared; it was almost like being in a private parkland. The scattered, spindly eucalypts on the hill waved their glittering tops in the breeze, and the effect was joyous: a celebration of Erika's new life. She'd been for a swim before I came, and was clad in a cotton wrap: a multicoloured, sarong-like piece of cloth in purples, greens and blacks, tied in a knot under one arm, leaving her shoulders bare.

She had met me at the door in a black bikini. Her figure is still that of a girl of twenty-two: slim and unblemished. Her hair had been wet from her swim, and she was drying it with a beach towel. Before making coffee, she'd insisted on showing me through the house, excited as a child on her birthday.

The place was even more lavish than I'd expected. First, I was asked to admire the kitchen, with its long, gleaming counters, stainless steel oven, built-in, double-doored refrigerator, and new copper pots dangling in order of size from their hooks. I wondered how much use the pots would get, since Erika hardly ever cooks, preferring to eat out. Next, she showed me a main bathroom of five-star hotel standard, with a huge sunken bath, twin washbasins with chrome fittings, and a glass-doored shower recess. Then came a separate dining room, two spare bedrooms with generous ensuite bathrooms, and Erika's study, where she'd installed a white-painted desk, bookshelves, and a giant television set. Hurrying in front of me like a fay, her feet soundless on the deep, cream-coloured carpet which was everywhere in the house, she led me after that to a sitting room as large as a foyer, with two three-seater sofas covered in expensive floral linen, a chair with a pattern to match, and a large, glass-topped coffee table strewn with glossy fashion magazines. I expressed admiration, and she kissed me on the cheek. Then she spun around and led me on again, to the main bedroom.

Its king-sized bed had a fitted, cream brocade cover scattered with bright cushions. There were two antique bedside tables, and a chaise longue whose fabric matched the bed cover. Like many of the rooms, this one featured the wooden planter shutters that Erika had installed. They were closed, so that only a little sun was filtered through the slats, and the room was dim. There was a smell of her perfume in the air.

She looked at me cheekily, smiling. 'So. You like, mister?'

'I'm overwhelmed,' I said. 'But can you *afford* all this?'

She nodded, her hands on her hips, her eyes teasing and evasive, like those of a child telling fibs. 'I'm running a line of credit,' she said.

It was a phrase she'd used in the past, and we both knew what it meant: she was getting in deep financially, and didn't care.

I laughed, and said: 'I won't be able to bail you out this time. It's all on too big a scale.'

'You won't have to, sweetie,' she said. 'They've already told me they'll renew my contract at Twelve, and increase my salary when they do. They say they have evidence that their ratings have gone up because of me. You do realise what that means, Vincent?'

'It means you're truly the Star,' I said.

Our eyes held, and her face became solemn; I had spoken in our old code, summoning up that past we seldom mentioned, now. A curious feeling entered the bedroom, and I sensed an invisible flutter in the dim, perfumed air. We were back in our Secret Room, just for a moment.

'Right,' she said softly. 'And I think I deserve all this. Clothes, as well. You want to see them?'

She crossed to the sliding mirrored doors of the wardrobe, and drew two of them back with athletic vigour, using both hands. Reflected in the mirror as she did so, she glanced shrewdly, briefly, at her own semi-nude image. She can never resist it. 'I've been shopping,' she said, and gestured at the wardrobe's interior. Her manner now was jaunty, with an undertone of defiance, as though she anticipated criticism. 'These are my summer outfits.'

The amount of clothing hanging from the rail was more than I could have imagined that one woman could possibly wear: suit after suit and dress after dress in light materials, in the muted, soft colours she favours. Underneath were racks of shoes: numberless, disappearing into the dark recesses of the wardrobe. Most of the dresses were of Irish linen, she told me. The shoes were mostly Italian.

336 The Memory Room

I laughed. 'You've gone mad,' I said.

'No I haven't,' she said. 'I've bloody well earned all this, Vin.' Smiling triumphantly, she shook her locked hands above her head, like a boxer celebrating victory. As she twisted her torso, I was touched by the sight of her navel: that innocent navel of the girl-child I'd once loved. I wanted to go down on my knees and kiss it; I wanted her to be Princess Aura again. Then we would both be safe from Time and despair, in the storeroom in Connie's house in New Town.

But that could never come back. The flow of Time would not be stopped; Erika was a woman of thirty-three, not the lost orphan I'd loved, and neither of us, I suspected, would ever find the sort of harbour that other people did: home, partner, children. We had been chosen for some other fate: but what it was, I no longer knew. Incongruous pity filled me: pity for her, in this moment of her triumph. Here she was, in her huge, unnecessary house, with these beautiful, unnecessary clothes which I guessed she had bought on an impulse that was essentially a child's: to 'make up' for something. But what that something was had never been clear to me; I only knew that she'd never found enough rewards to heal her hurt. Was it the loss of her mother? Or love and fear of Dietrich Lange, her frightening, handsome father, and her memories of that time in the steep-gabled house on Lutana, when she lay in bed in the dark, waiting for his footsteps to pause outside her door, and the handle to softly turn? Another love might have healed her of that, I thought; but it seemed that such a love had not been possible. Not yet, at any rate; and perhaps not ever.

Meanwhile, here was my Erika: blessed with a success that still seemed unreal, all alone in a house from a home-decorating magazine, sleeping alone (so far as I knew) in her beautiful king-sized bed, making snacks in that vast kitchen where the oven would stand unused, and probably drinking too much vodka at night. For how long would it last, this new phase? It was only another of her temporary halts; nothing was more certain than that. Success had come very quickly; and in the television world, it could be snatched away just as fast. Yes, she was happy at this moment – euphoric, even – but underneath was that deep unease, that enormous, engulfing sadness I had sensed when she stood under the bridge with me in Risdon Road, the rain dripping from her schoolgirl's hat. That kind of sadness can never be banished; run from it though we may, it will always catch up with us, we who are born to serve it.

Erika had dropped her hands now; they hung at her sides, and she stood with her weight on one foot, her gaze meeting mine with a look of enquiry. She had understood, and her smile faded; we can still tune in to each other's thoughts. But she made no comment; instead she turned, reaching into the wardrobe to draw out her cotton wrap. Throwing the purple and green cloth about herself, knotting it beside her left breast, she stood with her back to me, looking at me over her shoulder. 'I'll make us coffee,' she said. 'Come out to the pool. I've got something important to tell you.'

It was nearly one o'clock, and the sun had grown much warmer. I was glad of the shadow of the umbrella, and shaded my eyes against the flashing light from the pool. Soon we'd go into the kitchen for lunch: Erika had promised me an omelette. During the time we'd been sitting here, a cordless phone she'd put down on the table beside her had rung three times, and she had carried on long, urgent conversations, punctuated by excited bursts of laughter. All of the calls had been from people at Channel Twelve: contact with Sydney was essential at all times, it seemed.

In between calls, she'd been talking to me about her work: of interview techniques and difficult interviewees, and of the importance of maintaining a good relationship with her producer, and the Head of Current Affairs. She also spoke of the resistance that the network executives had shown concerning her move to Canberra, and of her efforts to persuade them; but the important topic she'd promised me hadn't yet materialised. I sensed that it would, but she seemed to be approaching it with reluctance.

'Why did you actually want to come to Canberra?' I asked. 'Not just to be near Parliament House, surely? Sydney's got a lot more attractions, God knows.'

She didn't immediately answer; she seemed to be gathering her thoughts. Finally she said: 'It's nice to be near *you*, for one thing, Vin.'

'Thank you,' I said. 'But what's the real reason? Do you want to tell me?'

She looked past me towards Red Hill, and her expression made me stop smiling. It was grave, and had a fixed intensity, as though she'd sighted something extraordinary in the middle distance. It was a look I'd seen in the past, and didn't welcome; I found it more ominous than promising.

'Because now I've met the man I've always looked for,' she said.

I stared at her, and waited. Her voice had been quite toneless.

'You mean you don't know?' she said. 'You don't know who it is?' She seemed genuinely surprised now, looking at me. 'Don't you read the papers?'

I laughed; I found the question ludicrous, since I wasn't really used to Erika's growing fame. It's a specialised fame, of course: the sort that's achieved by broadcasting personalities. Scarcely to be compared with that of film stars or political leaders, it's restricted to a particular orbit: women's magazines, gossip columns, and those sections of the newspapers that deal with the media. These are not areas I tend to take an interest in – though I'd searched the media sections of the newspapers in the past two months for any pieces that might deal with Erika. Sometimes I'd been rewarded, and had clipped the stories for my files – but I'd come across nothing about a romantic association.

'I'm sorry,' I said. 'Have I missed something?'

Instead of answering, she got up from her chair and walked to the end of the table, where a small pile of magazines was lying, held down by an empty flower pot. She pulled out one of these, came back to her chair, and began to flick through the pages. It was *Who's In*, a mass-circulation weekly devoted to articles on media personalities, film and television reviews, and general show-business gossip. She folded it open at the page she wanted, and pushed it across to me.

I found myself looking at a page of coloured photographs, all of which seemed to be of prominent media people, together with marriage partners, de factos or hangers-on. It was headed 'Out and About', and the pictures were accompanied by the sort of vapid comment typical of such features. The largest picture, on the top right, was of Erika and Peter Rykov.

They seemed to be in a crowded foyer, and were looking at the camera with questioning expressions, brows raised. He was in a dark suit and tie; she wore a black halter-neck dress. They made a handsome couple; but this was not what struck me most. What tugged at my attention once again was the curious likeness between them: that likeness which had puzzled me when they first met. This time, I thought I'd identified its source. They had similar, prominent lower lips, which they tended at times to push out in the same way, giving them a faintly pugnacious air. They were doing so in the picture, probably because the sudden appearance of a photographer had disconcerted them. This, and their blondness, made them seem almost like brother and sister.

I looked up: Erika was smiling at me expectantly. Then I looked down at the picture again, shaking my head. The caption underneath it read:

Erika Lange, knife-wielding interviewer from Channel Twelve's News Tonight, *seen at the opening of the new Jonathan Montgomery play at Sydney's Waterfront Theatre. Erika's escort is handsome TASS journalist Peter Rykov. Is this a romance across the Iron Curtain? Erika denies it, but the glamorous couple are seen about everywhere.*

'Oh dear,' I said. 'Oh dear, oh dear.'

She frowned. 'Is *that* all you've got to say?'

I sighed. 'It started soon after I introduced you,' I said. 'Didn't it?'

She looked away, her eyes roving over the pool and the swaying eucalypts of Red Hill. 'Fairly soon,' she said. 'He phoned and asked me to dinner.'

'He moved quickly,' I said.

'It was all quite formal for a while,' she said. 'But it's not formal any more. Peter's not like anyone else, Vin. I've never loved a man in this way. Not Derek, not anyone. I want you to understand.' She looked at my face, and saw nothing there to encourage her. 'Oh fuck,' she said softly. 'How can I *make* you understand?'

'I'm trying,' I said. I paused, giving myself time to think. 'When people say they're in love,' I said, 'all one can do is take it on trust. One can't enter into it, any more than one can enter into someone else's grief. The words always come out the same, don't they? The same old platitudes, for a feeling that's supposed to be unique each time. I'm prepared to believe this is special, if you say so – but let me remind you, dear, it was special with Brad. It was special with Mike Devlin.'

'No!'

She had almost shouted, and I turned and looked at her. We were sitting side by side at the head of the table, half-turned to each other. She had brought her fists down on the arms of her jarrah chair, and leaned forward now to glare at me. 'You don't see because you don't *want* to see,' she said. 'You don't understand because it's a feeling you've never had, and *can't* have!'

I sat still and silent: this was cruel of her. Instantly, she saw it, and leaned forward to put a hand over mine. 'I'm sorry,' she said. 'I didn't mean that. But if you don't understand, Vin, no-one will. I've been looking for Peter all my life, and now I've found him.'

The magazine was lying on the table between us. As we spoke, I'd been glancing at the photograph: looking at Peter Rykov. And now I saw it. I understood now: understood more than she thought, more than she understood herself. I was remembering Dietrich Lange, in that ancient time in boyhood when she had taken me into his study. His weary face and long German head came vividly back to me, with the light-blue eyes and full lower lip that Erika had inherited; and now I knew who it was that Rykov most truly resembled. Erika had found her father.

I took out my cigarettes and lit one. I've been trying to quit again, lately, but in moments of tension or anxiety, I find it impossible not to light up. I pulled the saucer from under my coffee cup to use as an ashtray, while Erika watched me, waiting for my response, her expression somehow mingling exultation with unease. The effect was whimsical: it made me want to hug her. Instead I blew out smoke, and said:

'You've found him only to lose him. You do realise that?'

'But I don't intend to lose him,' she said. 'We must never be separated.'

'You're talking nonsense,' I said. 'There's only one end to this story: he'll be recalled to the Soviet Union. He's got no control over that, and no way of getting out of it. You must know that.'

She looked down at the magazine and frowned. 'Of course I know,' she said. 'But it could be a long time off.'

'But eventually it *will* happen,' I said. 'So this is a temporary affair. Is that what you're telling me?'

'I'm saying no such thing,' she said. 'What I'm saying is that this is the man I want to be with all my life.'

She was sounding quite irrational, causing me to grow exasperated. 'Please,' I said, 'explain what you mean. How are you going to achieve this? Do you imagine you can go back to the Soviet Union with him? Highly unlikely. And certainly Rykov could never stay here.'

'He might,' she said. But her tone was suddenly lifeless, telling me that she knew this was nonsense. Knowing her sudden mood-swings as I do, I began to feel unkind for pressing her; but I made myself do so.

'No,' I said. 'That's impossible. So you just haven't faced that part of it, have you?'

'Maybe not,' she said. She stared into the broken, leaping light on the swimming pool and fell silent, as though mesmerised.

I reached out and took her hand. 'Peter must know that any permanence for you two is out of the question,' I said. 'Doesn't he?'

'He says he'll think of something when the time comes,' she said. 'And I have to believe he will.' She looked at me. 'We sometimes talk about it half the night,' she said. 'We make all sorts of mad plans. We're driving each other crazy. Sometimes I don't even want to go in to the studio. Interviewing some stupid politician suddenly seems pointless.'

'Don't think that way,' I said. 'You could lose everything you've just achieved.'

'That's what Peter says.'

She contemplated the pool again, her eyes wide and rueful, and I watched her in growing concern. I looked down at the couple in the magazine: the beautiful, confident-looking woman; the handsome, hard-looking man. These were the sort of people who were the stuff of suburban fantasies: dream people, riding high above the ordinary world; impervious to the demands and ennui of ordinary life, existing on a plane where only achievement and excitement mattered. But oh, my Erika, I know better than anyone what a precarious line you tread, and how easily you could come to grief, as you've done in the past! I know only too well that you could plunge from your mythical height – and in fact, I begin to see signs that you may topple at any moment.

What should I do? Should I talk to Rykov?

Thursday, November 8th, 1984

I SEE I'VE made no entries of any consequence here for two months. A good deal has happened which I should now account for. I'm referring to the situation between Erika and Peter Rykov.

One thing that is clear to me is that the affair is actually different from her others, just as she claimed. Why, I'm not finally able to know. Erika gives me clues, of course, in her monologues on the phone and when we meet; but despite her extravagant statements about the depth of feeling between them, there's a dimension that she and Rykov inhabit of which I can know nothing. It's not only their sexual passion that's a closed book to me; it's that other, shared passion which is located in the imagination. This is truly a region of mystery (as she and I have always understood), and only the two protagonists in a love affair can know its special nature, since it's unique in each case. Clearly, this has a strong hold on them both – as well as that predictable animal lust which I don't wish to know about.

Peter and I are so alike, Erika has said to me. *It's extraordinary. It's as if we came from the same mould.*

Hearing such a declaration from my twin of former years gave me pain, but I concealed it. She had not made such a declaration about any of her former lovers – not even about Bradley – and I knew that something different had occurred in this relationship with Rykov. She might almost have been speaking of herself and me, in our youth; and in doing so, she was cutting the last thread that linked us to that past, and giving herself to Peter Rykov heart and soul. That she and Rykov *are* truly alike is something I'm bound to admit – and it's not just a matter of their looks. They are clearly alike in temperament; and this is where both their joy and their anguish probably lie. Rykov (unlike Bradley, for instance) is as temperamentally volatile and unpredictable as Erika – and this has proved to be an explosive combination. The affair, though apparently full of intense happiness, is also unpredictable and tormented to an extreme degree – and I am often involved in this. I'm involved (God help me!) because I've become a confessor to them both.

Until yesterday, I was confessor only to Erika. The phone is her confessional: when it rings, these days, I know that I must prepare myself to listen to a long recital about Rykov. That flat, seemingly reasonable voice of hers will sometimes hold me for half an hour at a time, and all that's required of me is to listen: just as I so recently did to her monologues concerning Derek. But the conflict which is her central theme now is of a fundamentally different kind. Where Bradley wanted a kind of commitment that Erika wouldn't give, it's she who now wants a promise of permanence from Rykov: this man who is a citizen of an entirely closed society, and who must inevitably be forced to go back there! Perversely, she seems to have found the one man she wishes to be bound to, but who cannot be bound because of what he is.

I'm the recipient of frenzied reports of breakdown; even of pointless, tearful appeals for help – which of course I can't give. She and Rykov are more or less living together – sometimes in his apartment in Kingston, sometimes in her house at Deakin – and at the climax of one of their quarrels, Erika is given to rushing out to her car and simply driving away, without telling Rykov where she's going, and without knowing herself. On these occasions, she will often phone me from a call box out in the countryside, or from the bar of a hotel in some little bush town, and pour out her grievances and fears. These speeches are usually so rambling that I'm seldom able to understand what the quarrel has been about –

or else I find it's been triggered by something so trivial that I can barely refrain from laughing. The only clue she has given me to an actual, serious problem is to claim that Rykov is 'possessive', and hostile to the men who sometimes approach her in public, having recognised her from her television appearances. He also resents the claims that are being made on her by the channel, which take her away to Sydney.

But whatever the causes of these tensions, I know why my Erika behaves as she does – know it, I suspect, better than Rykov does. When she flees in her red Toyota, it's not only to escape from her own hysteria, and from a problem at the heart of the relationship which she probably refuses to face; it's because flight itself secretly stimulates her, whatever the degree of her distress. Perhaps (I'm guessing here) the whipping-up of distress is actually an excuse for the flight, and a part of the excitement it creates. I doubt that she's actually conscious of this, but there's one thing I know: to be speeding in her car to no destination, leaving behind a man in turmoil, a man who adores her, and who is anxious about her whereabouts – this is what she secretly savours. For a time, racing towards the horizon, she goes back to her special nowhere: to a place far off, where nobody knows who she is – and these southern tablelands, with their wide grasslands, their distant hills and mountains, their big skies and scattered little towns, provide the perfect landscapes for her flights. She can stop in one of the townships and have a coffee or a drink; she might even have a little adventure, flirting with a man in a bar or a café, or simply talking to a woman serving behind a counter. She has then become *someone else*; she has escaped into her other life. Once, she went as far as Jindabyne, in the Snowy Mountains.

But there can only be one end to it, every time: she will go back, somewhere before nightfall; or at the worst, before midnight. She will stop at another call box somewhere (how she loves call boxes! For Erika, coming across a public phone is like the sight of a bar for an alcoholic), and telephone Rykov: contrite, loving and anxious. *'I'm sorry.'* I can hear her voice.

She can't bear to be away from him for long; that much is clear. And she's probably addicted to their wild reconciliations.

Yesterday evening, I became Rykov's confessor as well.

This has made things really complicated: a distraction in my life that I'm beginning to find quite difficult. Between the two of them, he and Erika are leaving me little mental peace; yet I feel a compulsion to remain involved.

Rykov approached me in Bruno's. I was sitting at the bar there at around seven-thirty; I'd been working late at the Registry, and had just come in. I was tired, and planned to have dinner alone and then go home.

His voice spoke in my ear, from behind.

'Vincent. I'm glad I find you here. We have to talk.'

I swung around on my stool, and immediately noticed that Rykov seemed paler than usual, in the soft, indirect lighting, and that his lips were tight. My heart sank; I guessed immediately that his approach concerned Erika in some way.

'Hello, Peter,' I said. 'I was just about to eat. Will you join me? We can talk over dinner.'

A stool next to mine was vacant, but he didn't sit down; he continued to stand over me. When he answered, his deep voice was so low that his words were almost drowned by the loud talk and laughter rising along the bar. 'Thank you, no,' he said. 'I have no appetite, at present. I'm asking a favour of you, Vincent: I need your help. Postpone your meal and come with me – my car's outside. We can't talk about this here. I only ask for half an hour of your time. I'd be grateful.'

I stared at him; he had an air of authority which seemed to convey that I had no choice. It was a kind of polite bullying, made effective by his strong physical presence, and I half-resented it. Besides, I was hungry, and wanted my dinner. But my curiosity was aroused. As he stood there, tension seemed to radiate from him in waves, and I noticed that he was clenching and unclenching his hands. He was dressed with an informality that was unusual in him: jeans and an open-necked shirt. It was as though he had simply rushed out of the house without any thought for what he had on. I guessed that he'd been drinking, though I could smell no liquor on him.

A few moments later, we were speeding around Arthur Circle in his BMW, headed west through the blue-lit evening in the general direction of Deakin. Because of this, I assumed that we were going to Erika's place; but he had told me nothing. Since getting into the car he hadn't spoken; he simply drove, his lips compressed, his eyes wide and staring. It was as though he was seeing some deeply troubling vision up ahead.

If this was the famous Russian temperament, I'd had enough of it, I decided. I asked him if he would mind telling me where he was taking us, and my tone must have warned him that I was growing irritated. He glanced at me quickly, and said:

'I'm sorry, Vincent. I should have told you. I thought we would go up to the Red Hill lookout. It's quiet, and we can talk. Afterwards, let me buy you dinner in the restaurant.'

He took the car at alarmingly high speed up the narrow drive that winds on to the top of Red Hill, swinging recklessly around the bends. Fortunately, we passed only one other car coming down. He jerked to a halt near the restaurant that sits beside the lookout area, and I opened my door with relief.

As soon as I stepped out, my edginess dissolved. Here on this dark, quiet height, whatever troubles Rykov had to relate would surely fall into perspective. It was a calm, windless night with a clear sky, and the air up here was delicious: the weather I like best, before the heat of Canberra's summer sets in. An orange glow came through the glass walls of the small, circular restaurant, illuminating the car park. Figures could be seen inside, but out here the asphalt expanse was deserted: an expanse that was unnaturally neat and clean, like everything else in Canberra. It's a tourist spot, mainly frequented by day.

Still without speaking, Rykov and I walked across to the neat concrete kerb on the eastern side, with its border of native flowers and grevilleas, and stood looking out over the city's lights. The moon was up, almost at the full, and it was bright enough for the colours of the flowers to show clearly. Next to us was a giant aloe, its green and yellow spikes as high as our heads. In the smokeless air, the lights of the districts to the north and east winked and danced with intense brilliance. Beyond, I could make out Lake Burley Griffin, shining in the moon, and the dark, distant cone of Mount Ainslie.

'I like it here,' Rykov said. He was looking out at the lights. 'I like to look down on Canberra.' He pointed, and grinned. 'Think of all that wrestling for power going on down there: your politicians worrying about their popularity, the parasites worrying about the politicians, and the journalists digging dirt on them all. Eh? It all seems so silly, up here. Don't you agree?'

'I suppose so,' I said. 'Until you go back down. Then it's all real again.'

'I guess you're right,' he said. 'But it's mostly for very small stakes, in Australia. I wonder why they bother. Your journalists ought to try digging for dirt in Moscow: the sort that can get you killed.'

I said nothing, and he turned and looked at me. The moon and the lamps in the car park made his hard face look paler than ever, and suddenly older. 'Erika's gone,' he said abruptly. 'She's disappeared.'

This was the first time that one of her flights had been reported to me by Rykov; until now, I'd learned about them only from Erika herself.

'She does that,' I said. 'I wouldn't worry.'

'Yes,' he said, and his tone was remarkably bitter. 'She does that.' He paused, looking down at the lights again. Then he said: 'But this is different. We quarrelled, and she drove off to Sydney. She did a show last night and should have been back today. Instead, she phoned me and told me she was staying in Sydney with a girlfriend – but she gave me no phone number, and hung up. Since then, I've had no contact. I've tried the television studio, but they have no number for her – or say they haven't. This gives me concern, Vincent.'

'She has a number of female friends who are journalists,' I said. 'I wouldn't worry: she's no doubt staying with one of them.'

He narrowed his eyes. 'Perhaps,' he said. 'Or perhaps with a man.'

I thought it better to say nothing to this, and waited. He swayed; he ran his fingers through his dark-blond hair and some strands fell over his forehead, making him look in disarray: he was usually so well-groomed. He'd certainly been drinking, I thought, or he wouldn't have spoken to me like this. As though reading my mind, he laughed softly. 'I make myself foolish – that's what you're thinking, my friend. Am I right?'

'No,' I said. 'But she's not with a man, I feel sure. Erika's seriously in love with you – you must know that, Peter. So I wonder what you've actually brought me up here to ask me?'

His smile faded; he studied me, and I wondered if he'd grow suddenly angry, as drinkers are inclined to do. Instead, he said:

'I'm worried about her safety. She has never before failed to contact me. She may be in some sort of trouble: this is my concern. I thought it might be your concern too, Vincent. You and she are very old friends, after all.'

'I don't imagine she's in trouble,' I said. 'Erika knows how to handle herself.'

He drew a deep breath, studying my face as though for clues. 'You know her well,' he said, 'and you're right when you say that this is something that she does, this running away. We quarrel; she runs out of the apartment and gets in her car and drives off. I stand at the window, watching, knowing that she'll be back. Sure enough, usually within five minutes, back comes the little red car – like something on a rubber band.' He laughed under his breath, his mouth down-turned and unamused. 'At other times,' he said, 'it may take hours. But this time is different, Vincent.' He shook his head. 'To people who don't know her well, Erika seems very cool, very organized and calm. No doubt this is how they see her at her studio – and this is how the television audience sees her. That's how she seemed to me, at first. But in certain circumstances, she has no control, this woman: I learn that more and more. Sometimes, she will scream like an infant. No words – just a scream.'

'Yes,' I said. 'That's when she can no longer bear what's happening.'

Rykov raised his brows at this, and looked at me in silence. Then he said: 'So you know. And you know that she's capable of anything – and therefore, that anything might happen to her. She behaves more like a Russian than a woman of German extraction.'

'She's Irish on her mother's side,' I said. 'Celts are also unpredictable.'

'What a combination,' he said, and stared gloomily at the ground. Then, suddenly, he put his hand on my shoulder, gripping it tightly. I don't like to be touched in this way, and it made me uncomfortable.

'I think you can tell me a lot that I don't know,' he said. 'That's the real reason I'm talking to you, Vincent. You and Erika have been friends since you were children. You're very close – I know this. But you've never been lovers – this is what Erika tells me. Is that really true?'

'I'm not bound to answer that,' I said. 'But for what it's worth, yes. It's true.'

His hand remained on my shoulder, his face quite close to mine. 'I believe you,' he said. 'And I apologise for such intimate questions. But please bear with me, Vincent, because this woman is a mystery to me, she is not very balanced, she's in some ways like a child, and I think you are the only person who might help me to understand her – to help her. Erika and I have so much in common, and both of us say we have never loved anyone else like this – yet still I don't know her. How does one explain that?'

'One doesn't try,' I said; but I don't think he heard me. He was staring down at the lights again, and his hand dropped at last from my shoulder.

'I need to know more,' he said. 'You understand? I wouldn't talk like this to you otherwise; there is nowhere else I can turn. Erika is a danger to herself – you must know this, Vincent. Don't you?'

'I'm not sure what you mean,' I said.

'She has twice threatened suicide since I've been with her,' Rykov said flatly. He waited as though I might explain this, tilting his head back in that way he has so that he seemed to look down on me from a height, narrowing his eyes so that their bright blue gleamed with extra vividness. I think he knows how effective this is, just as he knows how engaging his looks are.

'She's given to depression,' I said. 'Those are false alarms, I'm sure. You'll have to be understanding.' Suddenly, I felt sorry for him. Clearly he saw me as the doorkeeper who could unlock Erika's secrets for him, but who was stubbornly refusing to do so; and I decided to try to help him. 'There are some women who are special,' I said. 'It's a quality that's instantly recognisable: people sense it. It might be described as a touch of divinity. Actresses sometimes have it. And such women can never completely belong to anyone. They know it themselves.'

Rykov looked at me blankly; he began to laugh, but then stopped. 'And you're telling me that Erika is like this? Divine? This is what the problem is?'

I nodded. 'And yet she loves you,' I said. 'Both things are true.'

He went on staring at me, and I could see that he'd decided I was not to be taken seriously. 'I have to hope you're wrong,' he said. 'You have a strange way of looking at things – as I already know. I'm sorry I troubled you, Vincent.' He gestured towards the glow of the restaurant. 'Shall we eat?'

'That seems a good idea,' I said.

During the meal, he said no more about Erika; but I knew he was exerting iron self-control.

Friday, November 9th, 1984

ERIKA CAME TO me this evening, without warning. From my
window, I watched the red Toyota pulling up in front of my
house at about eight o'clock. I went down and greeted her, and
led her upstairs.

'I think you must live in this study of yours,' she said. 'That is,
when you're not in the Registry. Don't you ever use the *sitting*
room, Vin?'

'Hardly ever,' I said. 'I prefer being up here.'

'Yes,' she said. 'Among your files. In your eagle's nest.'

She looked about her, surveying my filing cabinets and books.
She was sitting sideways in the leather armchair, her legs dangling
over one of its arms, casually dressed in a fawn rollneck sweater
and jeans. I had mixed gin-and-tonics for us both, and sat with
mine behind my desk, studying her. She seemed happy tonight –
even elevated – her face softly lit by my desk lamp. I had no other
light on in the study, and we were surrounded by shadow which
enclosed us like a tent, the way I like it. The curtains weren't yet
drawn, and the lights winked down on Northbourne Avenue. I
savour these times, when she comes to me here at night: it's almost
as though we're back in the Secret Room. That's when I feel that
though others may love her, she'll always belong to me.

'I got your messages on my answering machine,' she said. 'So
I thought I'd better come over. You sounded so *anxious*, Vin.'

It was true. What Rykov had told me last night had worried

me, and I'd made a number of phone calls to her home during the day. All I'd got had been her answering machine.

'Yes, I was worried,' I said. 'So was Peter Rykov.'

She frowned. 'He spoke to you, did he?'

'That's right,' I said. 'You just disappeared, as I understand it.'

'I didn't disappear. I was in Sydney,' she said, 'staying with Moira Paterson, who's just back from the Middle East. I cut off contact with Peter because we'd had a terrible row. I wanted time to collect myself.' She paused. 'I was very upset,' she said. 'It had all become too much. I talked the affair over with Moira, and she advised me to break off with him. It seemed the only way to end the pain.' She glanced at me quickly, almost furtively, before taking a swallow of the gin, and I gave her an ironical smile. That advice was predictable: there was little that I didn't know about Moira, and the relationship between them.

'But you didn't break it off,' I said.

'No,' she said. She was looking into her drink now, and her face had become unusually serene. 'I couldn't,' she said. 'I love him too much.'

'I hope you've been to see him,' I said.

'Of course,' she said. 'We've been together all afternoon, at his apartment. He had to file a story this evening, so I came over here. Everything's made up between us.'

'For now,' I said, and let the statement hang in the air.

She looked at me calmly. 'I mustn't lose him,' she said, 'and he mustn't lose me: that's what we both know now. I want him to stay in Australia – or at least, to stay outside the Soviet Union. I'd go with him anywhere: to any other country. I'd even go back there with him, except that they'd never allow it. He says that he'll hang on here, and work on getting a posting to another Western country when this one ends. I have to accept that, for the present. He'll find a way – I know he will.'

'He's a Soviet citizen,' I said. 'And no matter what he may say, he's a patriot. I think he loves Russia. Most Russians do. You shouldn't underestimate that.'

She swung her legs to the floor and sat forward, her elbows on her knees. 'A patriot. You may be right,' she said, and her voice had gone soft and fond, while her expression remained serene. 'There are things I still don't understand about Peter. And yet he's the man I've waited for, without even knowing it. Do you know, Vin, when I was a girl, I made drawings of him? It's true; I can prove it: I've still got some of those sketches.' She looked at me with hopeful eagerness: the face of the young girl in New Town. 'If I showed them to you, I think you'd be surprised,' she said. 'It's Peter Rykov's face. Can you believe that?'

'Oh yes,' I said. 'I can believe it.'

A sad wave went over me. She had found her father, I thought; and now she would have to lose him again.

She finished her drink, leaned over to put it on the desk, and sat back in the armchair. She began to talk now about her latest interviews on Channel Twelve, discussing them at some length. Content to be with her, but finding her journalistic projects less than interesting, I let my attention wander a little, sipping my gin. When she discusses practical matters, her flat voice becomes even flatter, and it's easy to drift. But then I heard her say something about Pine Gap.

'Pine Gap?' I said. I sat forward, closer to the lamp. 'You did a story on the American communications base?'

'Didn't you see it? It caused a lot of interest,' she said.

'I don't always see your show,' I said. 'Tell me about it.'

'Peter suggested it, and he was right,' she said. 'There's such an interest in Star Wars at present, and Pine Gap's hooked in to Star Wars in a big way – we all know that. So I interviewed Scholes, the Minister for Defence. He was very evasive.'

'He would have been,' I said. 'You wouldn't have got much.'

'No,' she said. 'But I was able to ask a lot of questions he didn't like.'

'I'm sure he didn't,' I said. 'But tell me, dear: was it really a good idea to be questioning the most sensitive and secret aspect of our defence alliance with the United States?'

She looked across at me quickly, with that air of low-key, mischievous excitement that intelligence matters have always stirred in her. It was as though we were discussing the plot of *Ella* again, or the latest spy thriller. 'Don't be so pompous and official, Vin. I'm not actually criticising the alliance,' she said. 'But the public have a right to know about these things, and I have a right to put the questions. It's my job.'

I sighed, and said: 'I'm sure you believe that. But I look at it from a rather different perspective.'

'I actually had some pretty good background,' she said. 'Aren't you going to ask me where I got it?'

'I'm sure you'll tell me,' I said.

She leaned further forward and lowered her voice. 'I went to a party over in Griffith last week,' she said, 'at the home of some fellow who was Personal Private Secretary to a federal minister. It was one of those parties where journos and public servants and political staffers mingle. I got talking in a corner to a public servant called Harold Ward, who said he was a very big fan of mine.' She smiled in a way I knew well: a smile which acknowledged the chronic susceptibility of men. 'What that meant was that he wanted to get into my pants,' she said. 'He was desperate to impress me. A boring, pudgy guy with big thick spectacles: hopelessly unattractive. But he was hugely pleased with himself, and he did turn out to be quite a big wheel: a First Assistant Secretary from the Department of Defence. We got talking about Star Wars, and that led to Pine Gap.'

'I see,' I said. 'And he was so anxious to impress you that he broke confidentiality.'

She nodded, ignoring my tone. 'What he told me was that one of the agencies in Defence had been asked to prepare a top-secret briefing paper for the Minister: for Gordon Scholes. I think some of the military brass were behind it. It wouldn't even be seen by members of Cabinet – but Ward had been asked to check it through when it was done, and report on it to Scholes. And he gave me some titbits about the topics it dealt with. He said that because of Star Wars, the Americans are more dependent on Pine Gap than ever before.'

'Obviously,' I said. 'What else did he tell you?'

'He filled me in on the questions that the Minister had been given to raise in Cabinet – swearing me to secrecy, of course. Even most members of Federal Parliament don't know what goes on at Pine Gap, Vin – you know that. So what the paper did was to set out questions that the Government might want answers to, before it signs a new lease for the facilities. Where does America's control over Pine Gap stop, and Australia's control begin? Can Australia have more access to the information collected there? And are there secrets at the station that even our Government doesn't know about? That sort of thing.'

'I see,' I said. 'Well, you certainly rattled a few cages.'

'When I told Peter about Harold Ward, he was very interested,' she said. 'He's usually madly jealous of men who come on to me like that, but he saw Ward as useful. Ward had asked me if we could have a drink some time – I'd brushed him off, but Peter suggested I take him up on it. Peter told me I could get an even bigger story for *News Tonight* if I could manage to pump Ward about the US Naval Communications Station at North West Cape, in Western Australia.'

'Really?' I said. 'Why was that?'

'He told me that from a Soviet point of view, North West Cape is even more important than Pine Gap,' she said. 'He said it's not just an intelligence base, but a command and control centre. It communicates with Australian and US Navy ships in the Indian Ocean and the western Pacific – did you know that?'

'Yes,' I said. 'I know that.' By now, my face must have shown my disquiet; but she seemed not to notice. Serene and unheeding, she continued to talk.

'It can issue instructions to American nuclear submarines to launch their missiles,' she said. 'It also intercepts Soviet communications. Peter says the Kremlin see it as a major threat. He says they see a nuclear war launched from subs as something that could happen at any time – so if war broke out, North West Cape would be a number-one target.' She looked at me with an awed expression, head on one side. 'I never even heard of the place before,' she said. 'So I thought I'd ask you about it, and see what you think, Vin.'

This is what has come of our games, I thought. Aloud, I said: 'Rykov does seem to know a lot. And what sort of questions did he suggest you ask your randy First Assistant Secretary?'

She squinted past me, apparently trying to remember. 'Just general things,' she said. 'Nothing top-secret, Vin: relax. What the base's capabilities are. Whether they plan to upgrade it, at any time. That sort of thing. Peter would like to get a story for TASS as well.'

'I'm sure he would,' I said. I drained the last of my gin and sat looking at her. We can still pick up each other's thoughts, and she quickly picked up mine.

'No,' she said. She shook her head and smiled reassuringly. 'Don't be silly, Vin. Peter's not working for Soviet intelligence – you checked that out long ago, remember? He's just a correspondent. Besides, KGB people don't use journalism as a cover in Australia. *You* told me that, Vin.'

'But they do use TASS as a cover in other countries,' I said. 'They might have decided to do it here as well.'

'Listen to me,' she said. 'Peter hates their system, and he loves the West. When he lived in New York, it changed his whole way of thinking: he realised he'd been fed nothing but lies about the West, and that Soviet society was a tyranny. I *know* him, Vin. He means what he says.'

'He believes in a new Russia,' I said. 'That doesn't suggest that he's cut his ties to his country, does it? He's still deeply involved with it.'

'Yes,' she said. 'And doesn't that go to prove what I'm saying? That he has no time for the present system?'

'Perhaps,' I said.

'You think he's using me?' Her eyes had widened with mild

indignation, reflecting the lamp. 'Don't be bloody silly, Vin. I've told you – he's not asking me to get vital intelligence information: just stuff of public interest. A good story.'

'It's a little more than a good story,' I said. 'It would greatly interest his compatriots at the Soviet Embassy, whatever you may think. But leaving that aside: suppose Rykov did turn out to be KGB. Just suppose it. What then?'

She looked at me for a moment without speaking – and now she wore that peculiar expression I'd first seen when she was twelve: a mixture of guilt and stubbornness, when she was set on a course that was forbidden. She looked down into her lap, fingers locked, clicking her thumbnails together. The clicking was the only sound in a silence that prolonged itself for perhaps half a minute. Finally she looked up, brushed her hair back from her eyes, and spoke in a low, sulky voice.

'I'd still love him.'

I stared at her in deep concern, and a sort of amazement. Now I saw that for all her adult skills, Erika had not essentially changed since our days in the Secret Room. Espionage, which had long ceased to be glamorous to me, was still an area of dark romance to her; and if Rykov was a spy for that system, with its long history of genocide and misery, it did nothing to lessen his appeal. In fact, I thought, it probably added to it, giving him a forbidding charm. Oh, my Erika! You are not immoral, I see, but amoral: a child, titillated by that which is both seductive and menacing. (*The footsteps in the corridor. The handle softly turned on your bedroom door. The bedclothes thrown back by a big hand.*) Evil has a glamour all its own, and you are one of those who are entranced by it.

I came from behind the desk and stood over her, putting a hand on her shoulder.

'Do you remember our games? Do you remember *Ella*?' I said. She nodded, saying nothing.

'It's not a game now,' I said. 'You could cause serious trouble, if this goes the wrong way. So will you do something for me? Will you just hold off on the North West Cape story, and hold off on talking to your Mr Ward, until I do some checking?'

She nodded again. 'Check all you like,' she said. 'You'll find nothing's wrong with Peter.'

She looked up, and her smile had returned: still serene, yet somehow wily. Perhaps I imagined this. I hope so.

Sunday, November 11th, 1984

NO WONDER THAT Erika's story on Channel Twelve created a stir. Pine Gap, out in the desert near Alice Springs, is run by our colleagues in the CIA, and is one of the largest and most secret defence satellite communications systems in the world. It's the ground control and processing station for satellites engaged in signals intelligence collection: a vital link in the American Star Wars system. Most of it is under ground, and sealed off entirely from public or any other scrutiny; consequently, it's the subject of much bizarre conjecture.

However, although the story will have embarrassed the Government, I doubt that the loose-tongued Mr Ward from Defence was able to tell Erika much that was of vital intelligence interest to the Soviets. My understanding is that the Russians already know most of what there is to know about the station, in the broad sense. What they'd be vitally interested in – and quite unable to find out – would be the precise nature of the signals that come in there. They would want to crack the codes. I hardly think that Ward is in possession of information like that; nor can I believe that Erika would be foolish enough to publicise it if he did. And yet I grow more and more worried.

What worries me most is the fact that Peter Rykov was so interested in the story. Is it possible that he'll urge Erika on to find out more specific information – of a kind that would be of interest to the Soviet Embassy? His asking Erika to pursue Ward to get information about the US Naval Communications Station at North West Cape is particularly disturbing. The more I turn this over in my mind, dear Teodor, the more I'm forced to entertain the possibility that I've so far rejected: that Rykov is in fact a KGB operative. If he's not, he's certainly behaving like one, and it's clear that I must do something.

I've culled through the Registry again, and have still found nothing on him. But of course, he'd be more likely to have a record with our internal intelligence people than with us. I should have checked this before with our Counter Intelligence section. I'll do so first thing in the morning.

Thursday, November 15th, 1984

AT LAST: INFORMATION on Rykov. But like so much intelligence, it's inconclusive.

Three days ago, I walked down the corridor to the Counter Intelligence section and spoke with Bill Turner, the officer in charge. Bill, whom I've known for some years, was immediately cooperative. He has an opposite number in the Australian Security and Intelligence Organisation, and was able to get him on the phone immediately. This officer ran a check on Rykov there and then, while I sat in front of Bill's desk.

'ASIO doesn't have anything specific,' Bill told me, when he put down the phone. 'But it seems that Comrade Rykov's on their watch list. After all, he was given a visa, so it can't be anything conclusive, right? But they ask would you like them to check again with the FBI? It should only take a few days.'

I said I'd be grateful; and this morning Bill phoned me, and asked me to come down to his office.

I entered the glass cubicle with a surprising feeling of nervousness, and sat down in front of Bill's desk again. He leaned back in his chair and grinned faintly at me, a look of conjecture in his eyes. Bill is a tall, amiable, broad-shouldered man who's shiny bald: he looks more like a banker than an intelligence officer, and if I had to get troubling news, I was glad it would be coming from him.

'According to the FBI report there's a question mark on your mate Rykov,' he said. 'The FBI believed he was KGB but couldn't prove it – so he somehow slipped through the cracks when he came out here. It seems he took an undue interest in defence matters over there – more than a TASS journalist should have done – and he was suspected of having contacts in the military and the State Department who were feeding him information. They also think that he may have served as a KGB officer in Afghanistan – but again, their information isn't clear-cut. By the way, he's got something of a history as a wild boy: drinking and womanizing. But that's no crime: it makes him more likely to be a journalist, right? Maybe that's all he is: we should keep an open mind, Vin.'

'We should indeed,' I said.

But I came away more troubled than ever.

Friday, November 16th, 1984

AT SIX O'CLOCK this evening I left my house and walked out of O'Connor down the long hill of Wattle Street, bound for Diamond Kate Carney's bistro in Lyneham, at the foot of the hill. I'd arranged to meet Erika there for a drink. Erika's fond of Kate's, which is reputed to be a lesbian meeting-place – though this is never very obvious, and the bistro attracts a variety of customers from all over the city.

My reason for arranging our meeting wasn't a pleasant one. Last night, on her programme, Erika had carried out an interview with a recently retired Australian Navy commander, and the subject had been the North West Cape Communications Station. He had been based there, and was presented as something of an expert on the facility. Like many another retired military man, he was clearly enjoying his moment in the limelight, and probably knew less than he affected to do. But he had announced that the Americans were about to put in a whole new generation of equipment there – and this revelation, which was thoroughly irresponsible, gave me some concern. Erika had launched the interview without warning me, despite my request that she postpone it, and I lurched down the hill nursing something very like anger. The oak trees were out in pale-green leaf, casting traceries of shadow on the road, and I was soothed for a time by the charm of this, and by the bright, still twilight; but the drilling of cicadas had begun, announcing the onset of summer, and it seemed to increase in intensity as I approached the Lyneham shopping centre. Brutally loud and challenging, like the roar of a crowd at a football game, the din of these uncanny insects caused a sinking in my belly, resembling the expectation of some shattering, unwelcome event.

Lyneham, like most districts in Canberra, is miniature, and so is its shopping centre. A small supermarket; an antique bookshop; a newsagent. There's very little else; one is through it almost as soon as one arrives. Diamond Kate Carney's is next to the newsagent. As I passed the newsagent's doorway, my attention was caught by a banner featuring the cover of a national women's magazine, propped on a stand on the footpath. The headline announcing its cover story read: *ERIKAMANIA*. At first, the meaning of the word didn't sink in; but then, coming to a halt, I saw that it was splashed across a photograph of Erika, which filled the entire cover. Below it was a sub-heading: *Channel Twelve's star interviewer becomes a sex symbol.* Bemused, I studied this phenomenon for some moments before going on into Kate Carney's, making my way past the tables under umbrellas out in front, where the first wave of customers had begun on their Friday night drinks.

I stopped just inside the doorway. Kate's is half-dark inside, and has a vaguely secretive atmosphere. I saw why the place appealed to Erika. Odd and interesting encounters seem possible here, and no doubt are. The semi-darkness was just as well, I thought, since Erika would probably attract more public attention than usual, with that banner standing in the street. I couldn't yet see her, and stood peering about. The bistro is named after a famous Sydney vice queen of the 1920s, who controlled most of the brothels in Darlinghurst. A blow-up photo of her hung above the bar, in cloche hat and fox-fur stole, a diamond gleaming in each of her smiling Irish teeth: an icon, no doubt, for the Sapphic element among the clientele. The place was spacious and yet somehow intimate, with a slight, agreeable shabbiness – its décor authentically 1920s. Pop music of that era, at a discreet volume, was coming over the amplification system. Dark-red ceilings and red carpet. Spotlights and fans in the ceiling. At the far end was a raised stage for musicians (none here at the moment), with a baby grand piano, and footlights permanently on. There were booths around the walls with worn leather cushions on the seats, while dark-stained wooden tables and chairs filled the centre of the room. Most of these were occupied, and I scanned them for Erika, but without result. I turned to the bar, which had a brass foot-rail and a wall of mirrors behind, reflecting the fugitive lights in the room. Three pretty girls in frilly white blouses and black waistcoats were serving there, and I ordered a whisky. Then, my eyes adjusting to the dimness, I turned and surveyed the room again.

This time I saw her, seated in one of the booths on the far side. On the other side of the table between them, engaging her in conversation, was a tall, thin, bearded man in a pale-blue lightweight suit, whom I didn't recognise. I walked across, carrying my whisky, and it wasn't until I'd almost reached them that Erika looked up and saw me. She smiled instantly – that joyful, fond smile that will never allow me to be hostile for long – and called my name. The man looked up as she did so, and stood up from the bench, facing me and bending slightly, as tall men are inclined to do.

'Vincent, this is Doctor Blaumanis,' Erika said. 'Doctor, my friend Vincent Austin.'

Doctor Blaumanis shook my hand, his grip somewhat loose and fleeting. In his other hand he held a glass containing a Bloody Mary; Erika was drinking the same, I noticed. 'I must apologise,' he said. 'I am intruding. I took the opportunity of introducing myself to Miss Lange because I so much admire her work. She is a remarkable interviewer. So penetrating.'

He was well-spoken, with a pronounced accent; I had thought he might be Polish, but his name seemed to come from one of the Baltic countries. He was exceptionally spruce, in his summer suit, crisp white collar and dark tie; his beard was trimmed in the

Vandyke style, his pale cheeks clean-shaven, and his moustache also neatly trimmed. He had a high forehead, and his lank, back-swept hair receded at the temples. Like his beard, it was brown with some grey in it, and I judged him to be about fifty. His grey-green eyes were fixed and hard-looking, studying me from under low-set brows. His effect on me, though he smiled agreeably, was somehow not pleasant. But I put this down to my mood, and his intrusion.

I agreed that Erika was a fine interviewer, and added that she seemed to have become a sex symbol as well.

Erika made a face. 'So you've seen that bloody magazine,' she said. 'It's so embarrassing. Come and sit *down*, Vin. Doctor Blaumanis, won't you come and finish your drink?'

But Blaumanis held up his hand, to my relief, and shook his head. 'No, no,' he said. 'I must not take up more of your time. It was very good of you to speak with me – and now I must be off to my club.' He downed what remained of his Bloody Mary in a single gulp, set the glass carefully on the table, and turned to me. 'Good to have met you,' he said. He bowed again, and seemed almost to click his heels. Then he was gone, moving swiftly across the room.

I slid into the bench opposite Erika. 'I assume he was trying to pick you up,' I said.

She shook her head. 'People talk to me all the time,' she said. 'I don't think I like being famous. Just because they see you on the box, they think they *own* you in some way. I have the most awful people bail me up in shopping centres: chattering women; sleazy men. "Erikamania". For fuck's sake.'

'What sort of doctor is this Blaumanis?' I asked. 'An academic?'

'No,' she said. 'He's a medical doctor. It wasn't clear whether he's still practising. He's a Latvian. He's off to the Baltic Club, down the road.'

She looked away, seeming not to want to discuss him. This, of course, aroused my curiosity, and I asked her what he had wanted to talk about.

'My interviews, of course.' She drank the last of her Bloody Mary, and frowned. 'He was obviously intelligent, and not on the make,' she said. 'That's why I let him sit down. He'd seen my Pine Gap interview – and the one last night on North West Cape.' She avoided my gaze, saying this. 'He's obviously obsessed with the Cold War, and he wanted to talk about the current build-up of tension between the US and the Soviet Union. His obsession's natural, I suppose, since the Russians grabbed Latvia. You know what these Baltic refugees are like: they do *dwell* on it, don't they? But I didn't really take to him. He made me nervous, actually; and he began to say things that were odd.'

'What sort of things?'

She shook her head again, apparently wanting to dismiss the subject. 'He seemed to want to *warn* me about things: I wasn't very clear what. Told me I was very brave and outspoken, but that interviews like the Pine Gap one could attract a lot of attention, and get me into hot water. He told me I should be careful. He said he could get me useful contacts, if I wanted. People who'd come here from the Iron Curtain countries.'

'Did he indeed?' I said. 'Did he have any other helpful advice?'

She leaned back, and sighed. 'He's just a Latvian doctor with a bee in his bonnet. Don't start to put your periscope up, Vin. Let's talk about something else.'

'Yes, let's,' I said. 'Let's talk about North West Cape.'

She glanced down at the table, where her narrow hands rested side by side, looking somehow defenceless. For a moment she said nothing, and I waited. As I did so, my eyes strayed to the bar, where three young women in light summer blouses and tailored jeans had half-turned towards us. They were looking across the room with eager expressions; one of them pointed, and they began to laugh excitedly, their heads close together. Erika was wearing a stylish, sleeveless dress of expensive-looking pale-green linen, the neckline of which was cut low, showing a hint of cleavage. I saw her now as her various admirers must see her: she looked like a fashion model, and I began to realise that conducting a conversation with her in public would be rather like being on a stage. It was the first time that her growing fame had directly affected me, and it gave me an uncomfortable feeling; it was as though she and I had entered a different reality from the one we'd always known.

'I *thought* you'd bring that up,' she said. 'I didn't tell you because the opportunity arrived suddenly, and there wasn't time. The Defence Minister had refused to give me another interview: he was pissed off about the Pine Gap piece. Then suddenly I was put on to this Navy commander who'd actually been attached to the North West Cape base. It was a golden opportunity.'

'The man was a fool,' I said. 'He knew bugger-all – but what he did let out was damaging to American security, and damaging to ours. It's amazing how some of these military characters lose their loyalty to the country when they're put out to graze.'

Her eyes avoided mine, wandering off to the trio of women at the bar. They were still looking across at her, and one of them smiled. Erika smiled back, and it was the same warm, promising little smile that she gave to men who interested her. The young woman looked startled, then delighted. One of her friends nudged her, and they went into private laughter again, heads close together. Then Erika turned back to me, the smile fading, her eyes growing cold.

'Look, Vin, I don't have to get your permission to do an interview,' she said. 'I'm doing my job in the best way I can – and I have to be the judge of what issues I take up.'

In all the years we had known each other, we had hardly ever quarrelled, and I had seldom grown angry with her; but I was truly angry now. She saw it, and once again her eyes flew away, going to her admirers at the bar, and then to a mixed group of young men and women who were staring at her from a nearby table, their smiles resembling those of long-lost friends.

'This wasn't an ordinary issue,' I said. 'It could damage our national security in ways you don't seem to grasp – as well as our defence alliance with the United States. It has to be off bounds, even for journalists. Your Latvian friend is right: you could get into trouble, blundering into top-secret territory like that. If you could just get your mind off your devoted fans for a moment, I might be able to make you understand why.'

She looked back at me swiftly, at this, and I saw that she had suddenly been transformed. Her eyes had taken on a bleak, hostile shine, and her face had frozen into an expression I knew all too well, though I'd seen it only a few times since our childhood. She had been seized by one of those rages of hers which I knew might cause her to do something unpredictable. But she spoke in a clear, clipped voice.

'Don't you bloody *dare* talk to me like that, Vincent.'

She appeared to struggle with herself for a moment, her mouth working. When she spoke again, it was in a low, furious mutter.

'I'm out of here.'

She snatched up the big leather handbag from the bench beside her, slid out of the booth, and then made one of those exits of hers which generally draw a good deal of attention, and which in this case drew most other eyes in the room that had not already been watching her – half-running between the tables, past her wondering admirers at the bar, and so out the door.

I followed slowly, self-conscious and avoiding all eyes; but when I emerged into the lingering daylight, it was in time to see the red Toyota speeding away down Wattle Street.

I'm concluding this entry at three o'clock in the morning. I was woken from sleep – as I half-suspected I would be – by a call from Erika at two. Now I have too much on my mind to go to sleep again.

The phone beside my bed must have rung for some time before I became conscious and answered it, clawing it from its cradle and falling back on the pillow.

'I've rung to apologise,' she said.

This voice was entirely different from the one that had last spoken to me. It was the voice of Erika at twelve: the voice of my orphan, wanting only to be cared for and forgiven, making my heart tremble. Oh, Teodor, if that Erika came back and stood before me, and we could both be children again, I would have all I could ever want in life! But it can never happen, I know; I must cease to think in this way.

I'd let silence hang between us, and now she spoke again.

'*I shouldn't have run out on you – but I was very upset. You're still the best friend I have, Vincent, and when you speak to me like that, it really cuts me up.*'

'I'm afraid I did speak harshly,' I said. 'I'm sorry for that, dear. Am I forgiven?'

'*Of course,*' she said. '*I know you're concerned for me; that's why you're so important to me, Vin.*'

'In that case I hope you'll listen to what I'm saying,' I said. 'Trying to break open our most crucial defence secrets for the titillation of a mass audience – how can I put it? It does the country no good, and it can do *you* no good. It's not like exposing political corruption, is it? If you were doing that, I wouldn't have a word to say. But this is in a very different area. An area it does you no good to enter.'

'*I understand what you're saying,*' she said. '*But because I'm a journalist, it's hard for me to think the way you do, Vin. You must see that.*' She had spoken very low, without expression, and paused for a moment. Then she said: '*This is a terrible time to be phoning you – but I'm alone here in bed, and I feel very sad. Sad and spooked.*'

'That's okay. I'm always here for you,' I said. 'But what's happened to Peter?'

'*He's in Sydney,*' she said. '*He had to go up there to cover some international conference on trade with Japan. I miss him.*' She paused again; I knew she wanted to stay on the phone, and I waited. '*It's funny,*' she said. '*That Latvian seemed to be saying almost the same thing as you.*'

'Really? I can't quite see why he took it on himself to do that,' I said. 'I'd be wary of Doctor Blaumanis, if he turns up again.'

'I hope he doesn't,' she said. *'I've been thinking about some of the things he said. He gives me a bad feeling, now that I think about him.'*

I'd begun to have a vague sense of disquiet about the Latvian myself, and I asked her to tell me exactly what things she was referring to.

'He talked a lot about the Pine Gap interview,' she said. *'He seemed impressed with the background I had. Then he got onto his Cold War hobby horse: Ronnie Reagan's hard line with the Soviets, and the standoff between them. The whole world's divided into two camps, where a guy like Blaumanis is concerned. He even said Canberra was split down the middle. He said he assumed I must talk to people from both sides of the fence – that's the way he put it. Then he asked me point-blank whether I'd spoken to anyone useful on the Soviet side. You can imagine what that made me think.'*

'That he was talking about Peter Rykov? A bit unlikely,' I said.

'Do you think so? I wish I did,' she said. *'Naturally I told him a journalist never discloses sources.'*

I asked her what more Blaumanis had said.

'He said something to the effect that after the interviews on Pine Gap and North West Cape, I'd have disturbed people in my own camp, but that I'd also be of interest to people in the other camp.'

She paused, and I prompted her to go on.

'He went on about the position of a journalist cultivating sources from the Soviet side. Called it a tricky business. One thing he said sticks in my head: "If you do have a source from that side, their people will guess who it is: you can be sure of that. And then you'll both be closely watched." I felt he was actually issuing me with some sort of warning. I asked him why he was pushing this line with me, and he got all sympathetic and soothing. He just wanted to be helpful, he said. He'd lost own his country to the Soviet Union, and he knew how tough the Russians could be, and what they could do. In a small national capital like Canberra, he said, they'd soon realise if I had a close relationship with a Soviet source: that was all he was saying.'

'It might mean nothing more than it seems to do,' I said.

'*You're wrong,*' she said. '*He was warning me to stay away from Peter – I'm starting to feel sure of it.*'

'That sounds a bit paranoid,' I said. 'Put the idea out of your mind, dear, and go back to sleep.'

I didn't feel as sanguine as I sounded; nor did I inwardly dismiss the possibility that she was right in her suspicions. But I didn't want her to be any more anxious than she already was, tonight. There was silence for a moment. Then she said:

'*I wanted to talk to you about Peter.*' Her tone had changed: it was quick and urgent. '*We didn't get a chance in Kate Carney's,*' she said. '*I was going to talk to you there. Peter wants to stay with me.*'

'To stay with you? I don't understand,' I said.

'*I told him I couldn't go on with him as we were,*' she said. '*That I'd break it off. And then he said that he'd think about staying in Australia, rather than lose me. That he might ask for asylum.*'

For a moment I said nothing. My heart had begun to race, and I chose my words carefully.

'Might?' I said. 'That doesn't sound very definite.'

'*It's not. Peter mustn't know that I've told you this – and nobody else must know about it, or it could get back to his people. Promise me that, Vincent. Swear.*'

I said I promised; then I asked her when Rykov might make up his mind.

'*I don't know,*' she said. '*How can I know? He's not even sure himself. He's very tormented about it.*'

'We'd better not discuss this any further on the phone,' I said. 'I'll call you tomorrow night and we'll arrange to meet. Then we'll talk. Now I must get some sleep. Good night, dear.'

She said good night, in a flat, sober voice, and I put down the phone.

Monday, November 19th, 1984

THIS MORNING, I had a meeting with Jim Dempsey. I'd thought of going to the Director about what Erika told me last night, and perhaps I should have. But I found I couldn't do it – not yet.

I needed first to seek the advice of a fellow professional: one who was shrewd as well as tough. Dempsey immediately came to mind. He's often crude, and can at times be irritating – sometimes making me feel that I give him cause for some secret amusement. But his larrikin manner hides a sharp mind, and he has a sympathetic side; even, perhaps, a sentimental one. And above all he's an old hand, who knows everything there is to know about the game: an old-fashioned patriot, and a man I can probably trust. So I phoned Dempsey on the internal system as soon as I got into the office, telling him I needed to consult him about something important, but not saying what it was. He told me to come along at eleven, his big voice genial as always, booming out of the phone.

His glass office was like all the others on the fourth floor, but was made more pleasant than some by having a window looking out over the trees towards Parliament House. Sun was streaming in at present, making the place cheerful, despite its impersonality. But Dempsey would have made it cheerful anyway, with his humorous bonhomie; he greeted me and shook my hand with an air of delight, as though my company gave him special pleasure. I knew it was just his customary manner, but it helped me to face what I feared would be a difficult interview. I sat down in front of his desk, where a framed photograph of his grandchildren sat among files and newspapers, and went through my account. It was one I'd rehearsed very carefully.

I told him that Erika was having an affair with Peter Rykov and wanted to marry him. I went on to say that Rykov had urged her to cultivate the loose-tongued Mr Ward at Defence, in order to get whatever information she could on the US intelligence bases – though I stressed that Rykov may simply have done so in his capacity as a TASS journalist. I told Dempsey about the ASIO report on Rykov, saying that it was inconclusive, and I also mentioned Doctor Blaumanis's odd conversation with Erika. I concluded with my vital news, telling Dempsey that Rykov had spoken of seeking asylum, in order to stay here with Erika. I emphasised that he hadn't made up his mind, and that there was nothing we could do until he did. Then, without making any comment of my own, I sat back.

Dempsey sat quite motionless, massive behind his desk, looking at me in silence. His white eyebrows had shot up, and his large, somewhat protuberant blue eyes seemed to grow even larger. All humour had now left his face. He slowly loosened his tie and unbuttoned the collar of his shirt, freeing his pink jowl of constriction, and picked up a ballpoint pen from his desk. Still looking at me, he held the pen horizontally between his fingers and thumbs as though it were a spirit level, or some delicate device whose purpose was obscure. He looked down and studied it, and looked back at me again. Then, in a much quieter voice than usual, he said:

'And you've spoken to no-one else.'

'As I told you,' I said. 'I wanted another opinion before I spoke to Dick Elliott – and I trust yours absolutely. The thing is, there's no proof that Rykov's KGB. Ostensibly, he's a TASS correspondent who's fallen in love, who prefers the West, and wants to jump ship and stay here.'

'You think so.' It sounded like a statement, not a question.

'I'm simply not sure,' I said.

Dempsey threw down the pen and sat forward, his gaze fixed on my face. 'I saw those interviews the beautiful Erika did,' he said. 'What did you think of them, from an intelligence point of view?'

'Unfortunate,' I said. 'But no great damage done.'

'I'm surprised you think so,' Dempsey said. 'There were no vital secrets aired – naturally. But indirectly, the discussions would have been of great interest to our Soviet friends here – in particular, the North West Cape interview. Erika got that dickhead from the Navy to tell her that the Americans are putting in a whole new generation of equipment there. For fuck's sake, Vincent, don't you know what that means? Where's your training gone? You've been too long among your files, my boy. It alerts the Soviets to the fact that all they know about the base is about to be wiped out, and that they'll have to start collecting their intelligence all over again. That's pretty bloody important, wouldn't you say?'

Somewhat embarrassed, I agreed that it was, and Dempsey leaned further across the desk.

'I accept that Erika is an old and close friend of yours,' he said. 'I always found her charming myself – if a little erratic. She was fascinated by our game, I remember, in a romantic sort of way. Now look what it's led to. I can't pretend to approve of her capers, even if she has become a television star. She was a Foreign Affairs officer once, and really ought to know better. However, there's nothing to be done about that. Rykov's another matter.' He paused, and suddenly smiled. It was a predatory smile, surprising in such a genial man. 'In my opinion, he's KGB; but we need to prove it,' he said. 'If he is, and if he *did* decide to defect, what we'd have on our hands would be rather big – the biggest thing since the Petrov affair.'

'I realise that,' I said. 'On the other hand, Jim, I have to say again that he may be just what he seems: a TASS correspondent who's thinking of seeking asylum, and making a life here with a woman he's in love with.'

But Dempsey continued to smile, slowly shaking his head. 'He's got to be KGB,' he said. 'And if he is, mate, and if he did defect, the KGB chief of station at the Embassy here would go ballistic.' He got up suddenly to close his office door, glancing along the corridor before he did so; then he threw himself into his chair again, so that it creaked in protest. 'And what we also have to consider,' he said, 'is that the *rezidentura* at the Embassy may already know about Rykov's intentions.'

'I've thought about that,' I said. 'But it seems unlikely; he's sworn Erika to secrecy, and he doesn't know yet whether he'll jump or not. They may be keeping a watch on his affair with Erika, though. As you'll know, the people at the Soviet Embassy routinely spy on one another – and presumably on their correspondents here as well.'

'True, brother,' Dempsey said. 'So it's likely they've bugged his apartment. If so, they'll have heard the love-talk that goes on, and they may already know that he's flirting with the idea of asylum. Unless, of course, he has no such plan, and is simply telling the lady a lot of lies.'

'In which event, he's certainly KGB,' I said.

'Exactly. But suppose again that although he's KGB, he genuinely *wants* to defect.' Dempsey leaned back, his eyes gleaming with the excitement of the hunter. 'Think what it would mean if our people could debrief him, brother! He could well give us the names of all the important local informants – all the traitors inside the system. The KGB have very highly placed people here feeding them information on stuff like Pine Gap and North West Cape – and the last thing they'd want is a scandal frightening those agents. Their whole Australian network could come unravelled: the bastards would be frantic. I'd greatly enjoy retiring with that under my belt.'

He was going too fast, I thought; and I reminded him that the FBI hadn't been able to prove that Rykov was a spy.

'Okay,' Dempsey said. 'Then it's up to us to prove he is. Or rather, it's up to ASIO. I've got some mates there; I'll ask them to stake him out. Tap his phone. Watch his comings and goings. You know the drill.'

At this, I felt a pang of something like shame. Since Rykov spent a good deal of time at Erika's house, this meant that she would very likely be placed under surveillance as well. But there was no turning back now; all this was the routine stuff of our profession, and I'd had many strategic conversations over the years like the one I was having with Dempsey. What made it different now was that one of the subjects under surveillance was very dear to me. And it suddenly occurred to me that the Russians might well have begun to watch Erika as well. They might have bugged her phone, or even the house itself, if they'd found a way of getting inside.

'As to this Doctor Blaumanis,' Dempsey said. He paused, running his fingers through his thick thatch of hair, and looked out the window at the distant white Parliament House building. 'He may be just a nosy Balt who wants your friend's attention,' he said. 'He probably read tittle-tattle about her and Rykov in the gossip magazines, and used it as an excuse to issue his little warnings. But we shouldn't dismiss him. Most Eastern Europeans who came here as refugees after the War are fanatical anti-Communists – and that's probably what Blaumanis is. But there are others who've come since who are different: the Soviets have allowed them to emigrate as sleepers. When the time's ripe, they're activated as agents. We should check Blaumanis out with ASIO, and find out what kind of Balt he is.'

He stood up, and I did the same. He came around the desk, smiling now with glad anticipation, and clapped a heavy hand on my shoulder.

'I'm glad you came to me, Vincent,' he said. 'I realise you can't feel easy about Erika's involvement. Neither do I. But let's wait and see how the dice fall. If Comrade Rykov finally decides he wants asylum, she'll have her happy ending – if not, she'll be saved from being used. Right, brother?'

I knew that this was true. Why then was I gripped by a sort of guilt?

Sunday, November 25th, 1984

FOR SO MANY years, the Game has come first with me. I've given my life to it. The Great Game! I'm suddenly remembering the heroes of my dreaming adolescence: those agents of the British Raj in the deserts and snowbound passes of Central Asia, pitting their wits against their opposite numbers, the secret agents of the Czar. Even after I'd begun to experience the long hours of tedium and the endless exploration of detail which is the mundane reality of the Game as it's played today, my devotion to it didn't fade; and the brief moments of excitement, when they came, made the routine worth it. Ah, my dear Teodor, I was born for the world of secrets, whatever form it might take! You knew that.

But lately, a change has overtaken me. The world of secrets doesn't come first with me any more. What I seek now – and can't find – is the zone of the innermost spirit. It too is an area of secrecy; and at present it eludes me. This change has come over me slowly and insidiously: a feature, perhaps, of early middle age. Is this why I feel a certain shame about today's conversation with Erika? Shame that I'm now playing the game of subterfuge even where she's involved?

This is not to say that I've lied to her directly. The deceit lies in what I've kept back.

The day after my discussion with Dempsey, I phoned Erika and made an appointment to visit her at home in five days' time.

I had something important to talk about, I said. I have to assume now that her phone may be tapped, so I refused to be more specific than that, and told her not ask me for details. I also insisted that we meet alone; I didn't want Rykov present.

Today was the appointed day, and I drove over to Deakin in the late afternoon.

We sat on stools at the counter in her big, pristine kitchen, with its hanging, unused pots and pans, drinking iced apple juice. It was very hot: we are almost into December, when the summer's furnace door will open fully, and there will be no relief. Outside, in the tawny spaces of Red Hill, the droning of cicadas was at full volume, like the sound of the dry white heat itself. Rykov was away in Melbourne, Erika said, and she had no news to give me: he had still not made up his mind to begin the course of action that would break his life in half. For someone from the Soviet Union, she said, the decision was a terrible one. He could never go back: it would cut him off forever from family and friends, and he worried in particular about his father, of whom he was deeply fond. He dwelt on the fear that his defection would bring his father into permanent disgrace; this was the way their system worked, and the idea was hard for him to bear, she said. In fact, he was in a state of anguish. They both were.

'I understand that,' I said. 'But in the end it's a decision only he can make.'

I then began to discuss what would happen once Rykov made up his mind to stay here. I felt confident, I said, that my people would allow me to be the one who conducted the first interview with him; after that, he would be dealt with by officers from ASIO, since internal matters were their affair. I said nothing of my discussion with Dempsey; nor did I tell Erika that Dempsey's colleagues in ASIO had now put Rykov under surveillance. I was absolutely correct in not doing so, of course; and whichever way things went, it would be in her best interest. But I didn't feel proud of my silence.

Erika listened to me without comment, nodding and frowning

in a distracted manner, sipping her iced drink. She seemed nervous, I thought, as though her mind were on something else. The Federal Election campaign is in full swing, and Channel Twelve's demands on her for political interviews have intensified, so that she is constantly in a state of high tension. But I knew that her mind was mainly on Rykov: Rykov, who was almost certainly deceiving her, just as I was.

Long ago, I thought, she'd fallen in love with the world of deceit: now its sad mists were gathering about her.

Thursday, November 29th, 1984

DEMPSEY CAME ALONG to the Registry this morning, and sat down in my office. ASIO's first report on Rykov had reached him, and he handed me a copy.

Although what the report told us didn't prove beyond doubt that Rykov was KGB, it came pretty close to doing so. ASIO had acted quickly, and he had now been under surveillance for a week. During that time, he had made two visits to the Soviet Embassy, and the tap on his phone had recorded a number of brief calls to the librarian in their archives. These calls had been translated, and had proved to be mundane messages setting up appointments to pick up books. However, Jim's friends in ASIO knew the librarian to be a link to the KGB chief of station, and believed that Rykov was setting up meetings with the *rezident*.

Dempsey sat back, pushing the notes aside on my desk. He was looking at me benevolently, but I could sense his anticipation: his readiness to spring. 'I think it's time for you to get him on the hook,' he said softly.

'I can't guarantee that,' I said. 'He won't make up his mind.'

'Then you and the beautiful Erika must help him to,' Dempsey said. 'The ball's in your court, brother.' He still appeared bland, but his tone had an insistence that left me in no doubt that decisive action was expected of me.

Last week, Jim and I went together to the Director General, to acquaint him with the situation. Once he had taken it in, Dick

Elliott showed a powerful degree of enthusiasm. He lost no time in contacting his opposite number at ASIO, and gaining agreement that our two organizations would work on the Rykov case together. This was unusual, since the ASIO people would normally have resented ASIS invading their territory – but because of my friendly relationship with Rykov, and my long acquaintance with Erika, it was agreed that I should make the initial moves. And Elliott made it plain to me that if Rykov does come over, and does prove to be a KGB officer, it will be a real coup, and a boost to my career. In other words, I'll have redeemed myself – which means that I'll be sent back into the field again.

I wish that I could feel more gratification. In other circumstances, I might have been exultant. Instead, because Erika stands at the centre of this, I feel little else but shame and dread.

Monday, December 3rd, 1984
TONIGHT I MET Erika in Kate Carney's.

Eight o'clock. We sat in one of the booths on the worn leather cushions, facing each other. Although this was a Monday night, the place was crowded; laughter came from the bar, and from the tables in the centre of the room, competing with the usual piped music from the 1920s. Erika was dressed very casually, for her: in fact, she was almost drab, in a tan blouse and khaki lounge pants; she wore little make-up, and sat huddled forward, her hair half over her face, as though to avoid being noticed. She succeeded; no-one seemed to be looking at her. She was drinking brandy-and-dry; she'd finished the first one very quickly, and I'd just bought her another.

'You know what I'm waiting to hear,' I said. 'That Peter's come to a decision.'

She shook her head. 'No. But he soon will, I hope. I'll be away in Sydney from tomorrow until next Saturday: the channel's going to be running post-mortems about the Government's re-election, and why Peacock lost, and I may get an interview with Peacock. I've told Peter that when I get back, I hope he'll have decided.'

No smile. She hadn't smiled when we met, either. Drawn and tense, she wore the particular little frown that I know is a sign of anxiety in her. The light-blue of her eyes seemed lighter, diluted, the pupils small as though from the effect of a drug. She takes too many sleeping pills; this may have been part of the reason. As I looked at her, I became conscious of the sound of a live piano, rising above the voices. Up on the stage at the far end of the room, with its hectic footlights, a small, middle-aged man in a yellow shirt and black waistcoat was seated at the baby grand. He had lank hair falling over one eye and heavy-framed glasses, and looked like a pre-War Cockney comedian. Smiling at the audience, he leaned forward to an overhead mike as he played, and began to sing: as always in Kate's, a song from the 1920s.

Pack up all my cares and woe,
Here I go,
Singing low,
Bye bye blackbird . . .

As I listened, I gazed in silence at Erika's face. As though to memorise her, I studied her myopic, wide-set eyes, pouting lower lip, sideways-falling hair. *Bye bye blackbird.* I was in an anxious state myself, and my thoughts weren't coherent: I had the sudden, irrational notion that my orphan and I might not see each other again for a long time.

'Look,' I said, 'I want to talk to Peter. I think if I do I might be able to draw him out. If he can actually tell me that he wants to come over, I can handle it for him. I promise you.'

She stared at me, and her frown deepened. 'You wouldn't let him know I'd told you anything,' she said. 'Would you, Vin?'

'No,' I said. 'But please do what I ask. Tell him that if he'll talk to me, I can help him. He needn't know that you and I discussed it. Tell him to phone me at home, in the next few days. If he doesn't, no harm's done. It's up to him. Will you do that?'

Her eyes remained fixed on mine. She had the appearance now of somebody affected by shock. She spoke, but I couldn't hear her above the laughter and the music. I asked her to repeat.

'Yes,' she said. 'I'll do it.' Then, almost without a pause, she spoke again, in a low mutter. 'Vin: I'm frightened.'

'There's no need to be,' I said. 'This can all be handled without any problems.'

'That's not what I'm talking about,' she said. 'I'm talking about that bloody Latvian doctor.'

'Blaumanis? I said. 'Has he surfaced again?'

'I got here early,' she said, 'I was having a drink at the bar, and he came up and cornered me again. He started out with smarmy compliments, and then he began to get offensive. He talked about a picture he'd seen in some paper showing me with Peter Rykov. He told me that a TASS man was just as much a Soviet official as any of their other people out here, and he began to warn me off seeing him. He was pretending to be concerned – but that's not how it came out. He told me that becoming involved with Peter would disturb *them* – always *them*. He knew what the Soviets were capable of, and innocent little Australians didn't. The same line as before, but he seemed to be getting almost threatening. He ended up saying the most ugly things about Peter, calling him a womanizer and a drunkard. At that stage I told him to mind his own bloody business, and walked away. I wish I'd slapped him.'

'He's a nuisance,' I said. 'I'll have him checked out. But you know how these Balts are; they hate the Russians. He's just got a bee in his bonnet.'

But she shook her head, her mouth tightening, looking across at the bar. She drew a deep breath. 'That bastard frightens me,' she said. 'I don't know what he wants. And all of it's coming at once: that's what spooks me. I'm not sleeping well, and Peter and I have these long conversations through the night – '

She broke off, looking down at the table. I put my hand over hers, and spoke gently.

'It will all work out,' I said. 'Just ask Peter to phone me.'

Friday, December 7th, 1984
EIGHT O'CLOCK AT night. I sit here in my study as usual: but nothing is as usual. I'm waiting on a call from Erika; meanwhile, I intend to record what took place yesterday. Although my mind is in turmoil, I must do this clearly and dispassionately, as though I were writing up a Contact Note. I need a clear head, and a calm spirit.

On the evening of Wednesday – the day after Erika left for Sydney – Rykov suddenly phoned me here at home: a thing he'd never done before. The sound of dropping coins told me he was in a call box.

'*Vincent? You know who this is?*'

'Yes,' I said. I'd immediately recognised his deep voice with its faint accent, but refrained from addressing him by name.

'*I have a favour to ask,*' he said. '*It's vital that I speak with you tomorrow evening. I hope you'll cancel whatever other engagements you have. It's very important, Vincent. Can you do that?*'

My heart began to race. I wanted to ask him what this was about, but forced myself to refrain; I could tell that he wanted to keep it brief.

'I believe so,' I said. 'Where can we meet?'

'*It involves a short drive out of town: thirty or forty minutes,*' he said. '*I hope you don't mind that.*'

'Tell me where to go,' I said.

The location he'd chosen was surprising. I was to drive to the satellite town of Queanbeyan, and then go a little way south into the country, taking the road that runs to the old mining town of Captain's Flat. About halfway to Captain's Flat, I would come to a junction where another road led off to Bungendore. I should continue along the Captain's Flat road for about a kilometre, until I came to a point where a sign read: O'Hagan's Flat. There was no settlement there, he said: just grazing country. He would be there at seven-thirty. If I was late, he would wait for me. He asked if I had this clear; when I said I had, he immediately hung up.

I know the area quite well, having visited it on my drives about the region. The section he'd chosen for our meeting was empty grazing land akin to the Monaro, rolling south towards the hills around Captain's Flat, beyond which lie the plains of the Monaro proper. He clearly wanted to ensure that our meeting had no witnesses – and this elaborate degree of caution could only mean one thing: he'd discovered that he was under surveillance.

Yesterday, Thursday, I set off in the Holden at ten to seven, giving myself forty minutes to get to the meeting point. It had been a hot day, but was now beginning to cool off. Daylight saving has begun, and it was still an afternoon of thick, golden sunlight and long shadows when I turned onto the road to Captain's Flat. Passing through a tract of scrubby hill country, I came out into a plain in the valley of the Queanbeyan River, and soon passed the junction of the road to Bungendore.

Very few cars were on the road here. I drove slowly now, looking for the signpost that Rykov had mentioned. I was passing through open grazing country, guarded by barbed-wire fences on either side of the road and stretching away to a rim of low hills, pale and uncertain as smoke. Far out on these green and tawny flats, black dots of cattle were visible, and a distant house and some sheds, beside a line of gums. The sign, when I came to it, was very prominent, with nothing to be seen behind or in front of it but grass. *O'Hagan's Flat.* No such place was marked on my road map, but here stood the sign, supported on two posts in the bleached white grass at the road verge. It was now five past seven. As I drew up, I sighted Rykov's blue BMW, parked beside the road perhaps a hundred yards further on.

I decided to leave my car here, and walk down to him.

Out on the road, I was surrounded by the level, extending spaces of this Monaro-like country under its big expanse of sky, in which small white clouds floated high up. Silence here, except for the rushing of a light, steady breeze, carrying the scent of dry grass. Rykov's car, glinting in the sun and reduced to a toy by the space between us, was the only sign of life. A truck roared by, and then the place was empty again. The bitumen road, with its winding white line, ran off into the south-east, bounded by the hills that cluster along the Great Dividing Range, blue-grey and olive in the first haze of sunset: a haze that was honey-coloured now, glowing on the paddocks of the graziers. And scattered through the grasslands, I saw, were those curious rock formations peculiar to the region: clusters of grey granite boulders, some of them round, some of them peaked like steeples, suggesting the remains of buildings erected here by some vanished culture: one perhaps pre-dating the Aboriginal nomads.

I was now extremely tense, and it was symptomatic of my tension that this naïve notion revolved in my head as I walked, and that the landscape began to take on an unnatural hue, deeper than that caused by the sunset. Nearing the BMW, I took off my sunglasses and squinted, trying to see if Peter was sitting inside. But the haze, and a gleam on the rear window, made it impossible to tell. I came quite close before the driver's door opened and he stepped out; he must have been watching me in the rear-vision mirror. He stood leaning against the car, casually dressed in a dark-blue shirt and khaki slacks, his hair fluttering in the breeze; he too was wearing sunglasses, but I assumed that his eyes were on me. He looked even bigger and more powerfully built than usual, his long shadow stretching across the bitumen beside him. When I came up to him, he took the glasses off, thrust them into the pocket of his shirt, and held out his hand.

'Vincent,' he said. '*Preevyet.*'

'*Preevyet,*' I said.

As we shook hands, he tilted his head back and screwed up his eyes in that way of his, looking down on me in silence; and a hint of his whimsical smile appeared, as though we shared an old joke. But it was fleeting, and his face became sober to the point of sadness. In that moment, I had a sudden surge of sympathy for him; I had always liked him, and in other circumstances, I thought, we might have been friends. We stood facing each other beside the car, and he waved his hand at the grasslands.

'As you can see,' he said, 'no danger of our being seen together.'

I affected surprise. 'I don't know why that should concern you,' I said. 'No doubt you'll explain, Peter. We might have found somewhere nearer town, mightn't we?'

'Of course,' he said. 'But the choice is sentimental. I often come out to this country to get away from things. So I thought it would be a nice place for you and I to have our last talk.'

'You're going away?' I asked.

He didn't answer immediately. Running his eyes over me, he pushed out his lower lip in that manner which reminds me of Erika, and pointed at my chest. 'I assume you're not wired up,' he said.

I pretended to show amazement. 'Wired up?' I said. 'What on earth do you mean?'

'Vincent, Vincent, let's cut out the games,' he said. 'You're not a Foreign Affairs officer: you have senior rank in your country's overseas intelligence service. And I'm an officer of KGB, with the rank of major.'

I stared at him for a moment. Then I said: 'And why are you telling me this, Peter?'

'I'm telling you because it's all over,' he said. 'I'm being recalled to Moscow. So first, let me assure you that I carry no recording device – and I'll accept that you don't, if you tell me so.'

'Yes,' I said. 'You have that assurance. Now tell me what this is about.'

Instead of answering, he took my arm, and drew me off down the road. 'Let's walk,' he said.

We walked in silence, until we reached the white-painted railings of a little bridge. A creek flowed under the road through a culvert here, and we stopped and leaned on the top rail of the bridge, watching the bright, clear water flow off through the grasslands to the west. Nearby, some black cattle grazed on a low rise, among the monumental boulders. For some moments, Rykov said nothing. When he finally spoke, his voice was low and sardonic.

'You know, Vincent, your ASIO people are pretty fucking clumsy,' he said. 'Do they really think, when they sit outside my apartment in their cars and all the rest of that nonsense, that I don't see it, with my training? They tried to tail me this evening, of course, but I've thrown them off. And do they really think that the *rezidentura* at the Embassy will fail to put two and two together and to run a check on *you*? You have an interesting record, by the way, Vincent – and I wonder why an ASIS officer is wasting his time in Canberra. I also wonder whether it was you who blew my cover, and alerted our clumsy friends in ASIO. But you won't tell me that, and it all doesn't matter now, anyway. I fly out tomorrow, returning to Moscow.'

I strove to control my expression. 'Tomorrow? But why so soon?' I asked. 'You've done nothing that would give us grounds to expel you, surely.'

He turned from the railing and frowned at me. For a moment he seemed to struggle for words. 'Before I tell you,' he said, 'let me say something else. I like you, Vincent. You're a strange fellow, with your funny theories: in many ways you are not really the usual intelligence operative, if you'll pardon my saying so. Perhaps this is why I like you. So I'm not speaking to you now in my official capacity, but as *myself*, Peter Rykov – and all that I'm going to say to you is personal. Just as it was that night on Red Hill. Do you understand? It can have no importance to your people, since it has no relevance to intelligence. What it concerns is my relationship with Erika.'

'I see,' I said.

'I'm forgetting the rules, to talk like this,' he said. 'Should this conversation somehow reach my people, it would do me harm. But that's a chance I choose to take. I'm choosing to trust you, Vincent.'

As he spoke, the breeze flung some of his words about, and left others very clear; sometimes a passing car half-obscured them. It was like listening to a radio broadcast through interference.

'I won't report it,' I said. 'You have my word.'

He surveyed me as though measuring my sincerity. His right hand was clenched into a fist, at the level of his belt. The wind lifted his hair like a sheaf of dark straw, and he brushed it from his eyes. 'Okay,' he said, and looked away for a moment. He spoke softly now, as though to himself. 'Okay. I have to trust you, anyway.'

I had taken out my cigarettes, and bent sideways to light one against the breeze; I noticed that my fingers were shaking, and saw that he noticed this too. I was thinking hard, my training causing me to search for hints of a ploy. But I was inclined to conclude there wasn't one: this really was about Erika.

'Give me one of those,' he said.

I passed him a cigarette; he leaned forward with it in his mouth, and I held a lighted match between his cupped hands. It went out in the breeze, but the second match was successful. He drew deeply and then straightened up, exhaling a long stream of smoke that was whipped away on the wind. 'I'm here because I want you to speak to Erika for me,' he said. 'I want you to do it on Sunday, when she gets back from Sydney.'

'She believes you're asking for asylum,' I said.

'So she told you that,' he said. 'Now I understand. This would have been a very big thing for your people, wouldn't it?'

I didn't respond to this; instead, I asked: 'Does she know that you've decided not to do it?'

He shook his head. 'No,' he said.

'And you want me to be the one to tell her,' I said.

'Yes,' he said. 'If you'll do me this favour – and I beg that you will, Vincent. I'm asking it because of the very old friendship between the two of you: this strange friendship that I've never understood. You are like brother and sister, I know that. So I'm asking you to speak to her after I'm gone, and to pass on what I have to say now.'

I looked at him, and he read my expression.

'You think I'm a shit,' he said, and I noticed that his accent, usually only just discernible, seemed to be more pronounced. 'Don't bother to deny it,' he said. 'I don't blame you. But please listen, Vincent, to what I have to say. It will be the truth, I promise you.'

He paused, and looked across to the cattle grazing on the rise. Deep shadows had gathered among the boulders there; the sunset was now well advanced, and a broad band of pink, stretching across the sky above the grasslands in the west, was reflected in the water of the creek. Rykov reached into his back pocket, and drew out a silver hip-flask. He unscrewed the top and handed it to me.

'Time for an evening snort,' he said. 'Join me in a vodka, Vincent: a farewell drink.'

I thanked him, and took a couple of swigs. The vodka was cold and hard as it hit the back of my throat, and when I lowered the flask, the sunset colours in the landscape flared around me with a new vividness. I handed the flask back to Rykov, who wiped the top on his sleeve, threw back his head, and took four or five long gulps. He must have almost emptied it. He exhaled, looking at me with a fleeting smile, screwed the top back on the flask, and thrust it into his hip pocket. Then he began to speak.

He spoke with a display of feeling which surprised me more and more as he went on. It could not have been feigned. He had half-turned from the railing of the bridge, and his gaze held mine so that we faced each other in the attitude of opponents. God knows what we looked like to the occasional passing motorist. As he spoke, and the light slowly failed, he fluctuated constantly between measured coldness and an unchecked warmth that I thought of as peculiarly Russian – though my experience of Russians has been limited. He spoke fast, and the flood of words was so considerable that I have little hope of recalling them all: but I intend to record what I can. Some were wrenched away by the remorseless breeze.

'I saw Erika at first as a useful source of information,' he said. 'Journalists usually are. Of course I was attracted to her; but the fact that she was a source came first. And when she did that Pine Gap interview, and told me she'd obtained leaked information for it – this was a real windfall. You're a professional; you'll understand me when I say that it was my duty to follow up in every way I could. But I got no truly top-secret information from her: understand that too, Vincent. Erika didn't set out to betray your country's interests. She saw me purely as a journalist, and gave me the sort of information that excites a fellow journalist. She has no idea what is merely spicy information in such a case, and what is vital intelligence – and her admirer in Defence passed on very little that was crucial. That sort of bloody fool is not in possession of what is crucial: CIA sees to that. But she did deliver juicy titbits about the US–Australian defence relationship. That made my *rezident* at the Embassy very happy, and brought me some compliments from Moscow Centre.'

He drew deeply on the cigarette, looking down now into the creek below, and then threw it into the water. I'd not seen him smoke before; he was obviously an abstainer who was lapsing.

'Then it all changed,' he said, and turned back to me. 'You know why.' I had the impression now that he was exerting all his discipline to contain his emotion; and the way in which he spoke next reinforced this impression. No doubt the vodka did something to fuel it; but I began to suspect that he was on the edge of some sort of crack-up.

'Listen to me, Vincent. I'm confiding in you now as a man, not as an operative,' he said. 'Why? Because I want you to tell this to Erika: all of it, whatever the consequences are.' He stared at me, the blue of his eyes hypnotically vivid; then he gestured towards the grasslands and the dimming sky. 'I'm speaking in this way because here I'm free to do so,' he said, 'and soon, back in Moscow, this sort of freedom will be gone. So let me tell you, Vincent, if you don't already know: there's something that can happen between a man and a woman which the word "love" is inadequate to describe. I didn't know this before. I was married once to a very correct woman whom I didn't really love, and I've had many women since – with various degrees of satisfaction. But Erika for me isn't like other women. Erika is different. Well, you told me that. You warned me, one might say.'

He paused, as though I might comment; but I said nothing. He drew slightly closer, peering into my face as though to read my expression. He needed to do so: the sun had now set, darkness was flowing through the paddocks like dull water, objects were obscure, and all the colours in the landscape were seeping away.

'I think I fell in love with her because she's a little bit mad,' he said. 'Perhaps *more* than a little bit mad. But you know all about her madness: right, Vincent?' Without waiting for an answer, he suddenly put another question to me. 'Tell me this: do you believe in reincarnation?'

'I haven't thought about it very much,' I said. 'I don't rule it out.'

'I hadn't either,' he said, 'but now I think it may be true. This is because Erika and I seem to have met before – in an earlier life. We both know it: we both *remember* each other! You understand what I'm saying? It's as though we've been waiting for each other. We knew each other's faces; we know that we've been in love before. We almost remember what happened to us.'

I studied him now with a little rush of sympathy – this big, hardened man who had told me he was a pure materialist, believing only in what he could touch and feel. Now he was talking of belief in the transmigration of souls. *The spirit will not be denied*, I thought. Aloud, I said:

'And now you're going to leave her. Do you realise what this will do to her?'

I had put in the knife deliberately, and his mouth went thin as he stared at me; then he closed his eyes. When he opened them again, a car passed with its headlights on, lighting up his face. It was very pale: a white, suffering mask. 'I realise very well,' he said.

'Look, Peter,' I said. 'You can still defect. I'll do everything I can to pave the way.'

He shook his head. 'What I'm going to tell you now will perhaps make you despise me,' he said. 'But listen carefully, Vincent. When I first told Erika I was thinking of asking for asylum, I did so with the knowledge of my chief of station. A strategy, to make it easier to continue with the affair: not to lose my hold on her. She wants very much to marry me, and we both said we'd like children; we talked about it a lot. Then it became real: I realised that I could not bear to leave her. I decided that this was what I actually wanted to do: to stay here, and never to lose her. And I began to move towards it.'

'So for God's sake – why have you turned back?' I asked.

He let out a long breath, shaking his head. 'There are many reasons,' he said. 'One of the big reasons is my father. I know what the bastards would do to him if I defected. My disgrace would be visited on *him*. My mother is dead; he has only my sister and me. He's old: a true patriot, and a decorated hero who's proud of his country, in spite of its faults. I've told you this, I think. He's proud of me too; and I tell you, my disgrace would kill him.' He paused; then he said: 'It may very well be possible that I'm in trouble anyway. When my chief of station told me I was recalled, he said it was because ASIO had identified me, and so I would no longer be able to operate here usefully. But he also said that I was becoming too involved here. I knew what that meant: too involved with Erika. The *rezident* doesn't like me: he's an old Stalinist type who sees me as a womanizer, with bourgeois tendencies. They all watch each other, at the Embassy: no doubt they've been watching me. I'll find out when I get back to Moscow. And then – '

He broke off, and I waited for him to continue. But he abandoned whatever he'd been going to say.

'But still you'll go back,' I said.

'There's another reason,' he said. 'Patriotism.' He drew in breath, and sighed. 'Patriotism is out of fashion in the West, right? But not with us. It's hard for a Russian to betray his country. I'm no exception. I guess I'm like my father.' He suddenly raised his open hands, as though in a gesture of surrender; then he let them drop, and his voice grew hoarse and strained. 'You are looking at a man who is torn in two,' he said.

'I'm sorry,' I said. I was deeply uncomfortable, and could think of nothing else to say. Despite the extravagant way he'd been speaking, the pain in his voice had affected me, and his face, in the dark, was drained in a way that affected me too.

He gestured towards the veiled grasslands. 'I like your country,' he said. 'It has its own beauty, and I like the sense of space. I also like the people. But I thought very hard about being here, living as an exile and a traitor, and I knew I couldn't do it – not even for her. I would be empty – a shell. And you won't be offended, Vincent, when I say that we are standing at the bottom of the world here, from my point of view. Some day this may be an important nation – but not yet. Only these American bases make it a serious player in the game that you and I are involved in. Nothing else.'

'If the game's still important to you, I suppose that matters,' I said. 'Are there any other reasons for your leaving?'

He nodded. 'We've had some discussions about the Soviet system, you and I. I was careful then, but I'm not being careful now. I'll tell you directly: I no longer believe in a one-party state, or in Marxism; and I want to be one of those who turn it around when the time comes. The system will fall, Vincent – perhaps sooner than you think. Then I hope that my friends and I will build a new Russia.'

'You've never said who you mean by that,' I said.

He looked at me in surprise. 'We in the KGB,' he said.

'Naturally. The best go into our service: the very best. Where else is there to go, for a gifted young Soviet man or woman? We haven't got the outlets you people have. And when the time comes, we'll be the only ones capable of running the country. Meanwhile – '

He broke off and drew a deep breath again. His face had been briefly filled with ardour; now it seemed to shrivel. 'Time to go,' he said, and looked out into the dark as though searching for something. A half-moon had risen above the grasslands.

'Tell me what you want me to say to Erika,' I said.

'Tell her what I've said to you,' he said. 'That's all. Then she can judge me – and I think I know how she'll judge me.' He closed his eyes. 'Tell her I'll see her wherever I go. Just tell her that. And now I'll say goodbye.'

'*Da sveedanya*,' I said.

'*Da sveedanya*.' He held out his hand, and I took it. He gripped my hand hard; a car passed, and lit up his face, and its sadness is in front of me now, as I write. 'We give up a lot for our country, in our line of work,' he said.

'Some of us do,' I said. 'Good luck, Peter.'

'You're not walking to your car?'

'No,' I said. 'I'll wait here for a bit.'

He nodded once, turned away, and marched off up the road, carrying himself with his usual military erectness.

I stood where I was, by the railings of the bridge, watching him go. I had forgotten how dark it gets in the countryside; soon his straw-coloured head and dark-blue shirt could only just be made out, in the black. A truck suddenly appeared in front of him, its headlights powering out of the darkness and lighting him up like a figure in a film. Then the dark closed around him again, and I turned away and looked out over the paddocks.

The moon had become brighter, and I could just make out the water of the creek and the nearby rise, with its boulders. The cattle had disappeared. I was filled with a helpless sadness, and had no desire to go back to town; I wanted to climb through the barbed-wire fence and lie down in the grass out there: in the pale, dry, comforting grass, among the strange rocks of the grasslands.

Today, Friday, I woke late, at about seven-thirty. This morning Rykov would be going – flying out of Canberra to Sydney, and then boarding a flight to Europe, later in the day. I wondered what he'd done with his beautiful BMW, and whether it was even his car.

Although I'd be late at the office, I continued to lie in bed, thinking. Erika wasn't due back in Canberra until tomorrow – which gave me a little time, I thought, to prepare myself to break the news to her. I decided not to phone her in Sydney today; her response would be extreme, and would almost certainly wreck whatever work she was carrying out. Better to spare her that, I decided, and to deliver my message face to face.

But of course, this wasn't to be. A short time after I'd eaten breakfast and was sitting in the kitchen over coffee, the phone on the wall beside the counter began to ring. My belly hollowed out as I stared at the shrilling instrument, and the bright morning sun ceased to look cheerful, taking on an ominous glare. This would almost certainly be Erika calling; she'd have failed to get through to Rykov yesterday and this morning, and her sixth sense would have told her that something was wrong. I hurt inside for her, and at the same time resented the role that Rykov had forced on me. For a moment, I considered not answering; but then I decided not to postpone a conversation I'd otherwise spend the day dreading.

As soon as I said hello she began to speak, without announcing herself and without preamble.

'I need your help. Peter's disappeared. He wasn't answering the phone at his apartment yesterday, or the day before. Not this morning, either. I've phoned a journalist I know in the Press Gallery, and he hasn't seen him there in days. I know he wasn't going inter-state on business this week – so where can he be?'

I began to prepare an answer; but before I could speak, she rushed on.

'He'd always call me: it doesn't make sense. He's got my number here at the motel. We always talk to each other every day, when we're away from each other. Something's happened: I know it. I've got a recorded interview with Andrew Peacock this evening. How can I get through that when I'm this anxious? Please, Vin: will you try to find him?'

'I'm sorry,' I said. 'I really am, dear. But I can't help you.'

She heard the sorrow in my voice, and possibly the apprehension as well. Instantly, her own voice rose, and its tone of anxiety became even sharper.

'What do you mean, you can't help? You can find anyone if you want to, Vin. Do you mean you won't?'

'I mean I can't,' I said. 'Peter's on his way back to Moscow. He flies out first thing this morning.'

There was an empty pause. *'No,'* she said.

It was not loud; it was a simple murmur of pain and denial.

'Listen to me,' I said. 'Please listen carefully, Erika.'

Then I began to explain, telling her everything, choosing every word with care, and feeling the receiver grow slick with perspiration in my hand. I offered no comments or speculation, but simply transmitted to her, so far as I was able, every word that Rykov had said. I believe I spoke gently, and yet with a certain detachment – doing so in the hope that this would help her to face what she had to face. But I also dwelt on Rykov's love for her, and of the anguish I'd witnessed.

While I spoke, she made no further response; no sound. If the line had not been open – and its hollow sound told me that it was – I would have begun to suspect that we'd been cut off. When I'd concluded, the faint, almost subliminal sighing of the open line was all that I heard for many moments more. Finally she spoke, in a lower voice than before, repeating the same monosyllable: the same incredulous, outraged denial, like the moan of a wounded animal.

'No.'

'Erika,' I said. 'Listen to me.'

But she was no longer listening to anything. The monosyllable was repeated three times, but this time very low, as though from far away.

'No. No. No.'

Then she hung up. I sat on the kitchen stool by the phone, staring at the burring receiver. She hadn't given me the name or phone number of her motel, so I couldn't call her back. It was time to leave for work; but I felt pretty sure that she'd call me there, during the day.

This didn't happen, however; and when I got home here this evening, there was no message on my machine.

It's nearly midnight, and still she hasn't called. I'm very tired, and will go to bed now. I hope that she managed to carry out her interview with the Opposition Leader successfully; it would have been hard for her. I also have the shameful hope that she won't call me during the night, which she's capable of doing. Better to talk to her in person, when she arrives back in Canberra tomorrow. I'll need then to summon up every reserve of concern and love. Yes, love. For who else will love my orphan now?

Monday, December 10th, 1984

THIS ENTRY WILL be very difficult to write. I was mentally quite
unable to do so yesterday. My thoughts fly about, and tears keep
overwhelming me. I'm also subject to fits of trembling, which
won't seem to stop. Soon I intend to abandon this diary altogether – but before I do so, dear Teodor, the record must be
completed.

Then you'll read it all, I hope – since I've decided that my
journals will shortly be placed in your care.

In my last entry, I see that I expressed the hope that Erika
wouldn't call me during the night. But this, of course, was what
she did, as she's done so often before.

Ascending very slowly from deep sleep, I lay listening as the
ringing of the phone grew louder in my brain, like mechanical
cries of distress. The illuminated dial on my bedside clock read
five past two. I was filled with a profound tiredness – a tiredness
that had been with me since my meeting with Rykov – and I was
still half-asleep when I reached out and picked up the receiver.

'It's me,' she said. 'Did I wake you?'

'Yes,' I said. 'What is it? Are you all right?'

A pause followed; I was too tired to prompt her, and waited.
She sounded tired herself; her voice was flat and low, and without
expression.

'I know this is a lot to ask, but I want you to come to me,' she said.

'Erika, how can I do that? You're in Sydney,' I said.

'No,' she said. *'I'm here in Canberra, at home.'*

I propped myself on one elbow, fully awake now, and switched on the table lamp beside me.

'But what about your interview with Peacock? You were recording it this evening, weren't you?'

'Yes,' she said. *'But I walked out and drove back here.'*

'You walked out? On the Leader of the Opposition? Oh, Lord,' I said.

'I couldn't go through with it,' she said.

'I know how you must be feeling,' I said. 'But how will Channel Twelve respond to this?'

'I'll be finished, I should imagine. I don't give a stuff,' she said. *'Now that Peter's gone, I don't care.'*

I closed my eyes, filled with despair for her. I searched for words that would help, and instead found myself uttering platitudes.

'You may think that now,' I said. 'But however badly you feel, it will pass. Please don't act in haste; please don't wreck your career.'

'It's already wrecked,' she said. *'But I don't want to talk about that; it's not why I called. I just want you to come to me.'*

'I'll come first thing in the morning,' I said. 'I'm dreadfully tired tonight, and you must be too. You've driven all the way from Sydney. Get some sleep, dear.'

'I can't sleep,' she said. *'I'm afraid.'*

'Afraid? What are you afraid of?'

'I don't know. I'm just afraid.'

Her voice remained flat and deeply weary; drained of life. But it held no serious note of fear, so far as I could tell. Or at least, I wanted to believe so. The fact was that I had such a reluctance to go to her at that hour, that I would only have done so had she been in serious danger. She had asked me to come to her before, late in the night, and I'd gone – only to find when I got there that she simply wanted to talk: a thing she could have done on the phone. It would be the same this time, I thought. I understood her grief, but her talk of fear made no sense. She would weather this storm, as she'd done the others. Yet part of me knew that her love for Rykov was different from her other involvements – even the one with Bradley. Knew it, and pushed it away.

'Go to sleep, dearest,' I said. 'Sleep will do you far more good than a visit from me. I'll be there first thing in the morning, I promise you. Call me again if you need to.'

'*So you won't come,*' she said. It was a flat statement, made without hope.

'Not unless it's absolutely urgent,' I said. 'Is it?'

'*I suppose not.*' Her voice sounded very small and distant now; there was a pause, and when she went on she seemed to be talking to herself. '*He was everything to me. When he held me, I felt safe, for the first time. I've never felt like that before.*'

'We'll talk in the morning,' I said.

'*You promise you'll come then, Vincent?*'

'I promise,' I said. 'At eight o'clock. Good night, dear.'

She didn't reply; instead I heard her sigh, and then she hung up. I lay back on my pillow, and turned off the lamp. Did I feel guilt? Not then; not then, God forgive me.

At just after eight, I drove over to Deakin. Having slept, I was thinking more clearly, and now felt less sure that I'd been wise in refusing to go to Erika last night. It wouldn't be true to say that I had any sort of premonition: I merely nursed apprehension about the state in which I'd find her. Otherwise, my principal thoughts were practical: I was considering what strategy I'd suggest she might adopt to try to retrieve her career at Channel Twelve.

The day was already hot, and the capital was still half-asleep, this being Saturday. The traffic was sparse on Mugga Way, and the ambassadorial residences and their high-walled gardens looked empty, like abandoned film sets. Buxton Street, when I got to it, was equally deserted: rolled newspapers lay uncollected in the driveways and on the neat green lawns, and the curtains and blinds of the bungalows were still drawn. No-one was about.

I parked my car across Erika's driveway and got out, squinting at the hot blue sky. Sunlight gleamed on the tiled roofs and windows in the crescent, and the drilling of cicadas had already begun on Red Hill, more unnaturally loud than usual in the Saturday quiet. I walked up the short driveway, which was strewn with the fallen purple flowers of the big jacaranda on the lawn, and climbed the front steps of Erika's salmon-coloured bungalow. Standing on the stone-flagged terrace, I pressed the button of the electric doorbell. Somewhere nearby, a dog barked twice, and a man in a white bathrobe emerged from the house on the other side of the road, picked up his newspaper and went in again. Erika didn't appear, and there was no sound from inside; I assumed she might still be asleep, and rang again. After waiting for something like a minute after the chimes had ceased, I went down the steps and walked around to the back.

The sun flashed with empty brilliance on the water of the swimming pool, and a used green coffee mug stood on the big outdoor table. I wondered how long ago Erika had left it there, having sat here alone with her coffee in her beautiful back garden. There was a pathos about it, that mug. Across the back fence, on Red Hill, the drilling of the cicadas rose even louder, and the leaves of the swaying eucalypts glinted like metal. A lone jogger in singlet and shorts pounded by on the walking track: the only human figure to be seen on those droning yellow slopes, in this bright, silent morning that I'd begun to find ominous.

I knocked on the back door. I knew now that I should have come last night; knew already, in a corner of my mind, that something was wrong. I waited only a short time before trying the door. It was unlocked.

The kitchen – immaculate as ever, with its gleaming counters and its beautiful copper pots dangling in correct order from their hooks – was empty. I called her name. There was no answer.

I went through the door that took me into the carpeted hallway, calling again, quite loudly. A vase of wilting roses stood on a hall table. The house was silent, its only odours those of furniture polish and a faint, stale perfume. Calling, I looked into her study, and then into the big sitting room. No sign of her. Surely, if she was asleep, she would have woken by now, I thought. I moved across to the bedroom, the door of which was ajar. I called again, waited briefly, pushed the door wider and then went in, my feet making no sound on the deep cream carpet. I found that my heart was beating hard, and my mouth was dry. The room was very dim: the planter shutters were closed on all the windows, and it took a number of seconds for my eyes to adjust. The air was stuffy; there was a faint medicinal smell in here, and a stronger odour of perfume. Through the shutters, the drilling on the hill outside could still be heard: muted, frenetic and intolerable.

Erika was lying on her back on the big double bed that stood on the far side of the room. She was covered from the waist down by a single sheet; above it she was naked, and her whiteness shone dully in the dimness, like phosphorescence. There was a stillness about her which caused my throat to tighten so that I could scarcely breathe. This was accompanied by a sudden sinking inside me, shocking and profound. Everything waved in front of my eyes; but I made myself continue to look at her. She was lying with her right arm outstretched towards the antique bedside table that stood next to her. She seemed to be reaching for the telephone. Had she been trying to call me? Her head, supported by two pillows, was turned slightly towards the phone. Her hair was spread across the pillows, and the lock that so often fell across her left eye was doing so now, making her look slightly raffish. Her stillness had an aura that was different from that of sleep. There is only one stillness like it. And yet I tried to tell myself that sleep was what this was, in those last seconds before I moved towards the bed. She had taken a sleeping pill last night, I told myself, or had been drinking, and this had made her sleep very heavily. A brandy bottle stood on the bedside table, which helped me with this notion.

Then I reached the bed and stood beside her, and knew that I could deceive myself no longer. Her eyes were closed, and her face seemed peaceful, at first; but now I saw the downward curve of her lips. They were grim, as though she had come to some final and terrible realisation. They transformed her, making her face appear like a Gothic carving. At the same time, her body looked very young: innocent and defenceless, like that of a young girl.

Scarcely knowing what I was doing, I drew the sheet up and covered her to the shoulders. My head was swimming, there was a swelling in my throat, and a strange singing in my ears; but I forced myself to concentrate. On the table, beside the phone and the bottle of brandy, was an empty water glass with a trace of the brandy in it, and a small bottle. I picked it up, and read the label: *Nembutal.* Yes, these were the sleeping pills she took so often; and the bottle was almost empty.

Erika, I said, and I reached out and placed my hand on one round shoulder.

The flesh I touched had the final coldness of stone. I quickly took my hand away, and closed my eyes. The swimming in my head and the ringing in my ears threatened to engulf me now, and I went and sat down on the chaise longue, against the wall opposite the bed.

I sat for a length of time that had no dimension for me, until finally the swimming and the ringing stopped. I could no longer look at the white, motionless figure on the bed, with its outstretched arm; instead, I found myself staring across the room at the sliding mirrored doors of the wardrobe – that wardrobe which held the wonderful array of clothes she'd shown me when I first came to the house, when her success had just begun – and I saw myself reflected in the glass: a crouched figure whose face, it seemed, was as white as Erika's own. And suddenly, like a phantom, she appeared to me over there, just as she'd been on that day: alive and exultant in her black bikini, pulling back the door with that elastic athleticism she'd had since her schooldays.

'So. You like, mister?'

The swelling in my throat grew bigger and bigger: intolerable. I found that I was weeping now, making ugly noises in the silent, scented room. As I wept, the drilling of the cicadas from outside seemed to bore into my brain.

O Erika, my orphan, my lost twin! I had not wept like that since my other twin died.

But all weeping stops in the end, leaving us merely empty. We're not able to bear those emotions that match the size of our great calamities; were they to grow to their true size, they would consume us. Instead, we take refuge in blankness: the same weary blankness that children know when they cease to cry. And in fact we return to childishness, after such weeping, and look about us for comfort, or at least an escape. But unlike children, we find no comfort: only the refuge of numbness.

Numb, I sat there, on Erika's elegant chaise longue. Finally, my mind still empty, I stood up, and walked out into the hall. At first, I didn't know what my intentions were; but then I found that my mind was working again. There had been no note beside the bed; before I telephoned the police, I wanted to see if she had left one anywhere else.

I went into her study. There was a scattered pile of notepaper on the white-painted desk, with a ballpoint pen lying beside it. Next to it was a chaotic heap of papers and cardboard folders. She had never been a tidy woman. There was no sign of a note; the notepaper had merely been used for doodling. I picked it up, and shuffled through it. There must have been a score of sheets, and on every sheet, over and over again, a drawing of Ella appeared: Ella of the Secret Service, in her hat and raincoat, sometimes walking with her head down, at others directly facing the viewer. In some of the drawings her face was smiling; in others it expressed utter sorrow. When had Erika made these obsessive, repeated doodles? Last night, I decided, just before she died. She had drawn her childish self – that second self known only to her and to me – as though by doing so she would finally be free, walking backwards into Ella's

hermetic paper world: that world of jejune adventure we had both
believed in, where no sorrow lasted long, and despair had no
dominion, whatever discouragements Ella might face.

Erika, I said. *Erika.*

I was shaking steadily, and realised that this had been going on
for some time. I drew out another sheet of paper, buried at the
bottom of the pile. This proved to be a sketch of Peter Rykov,
beautifully executed in pencil. It was a good likeness, but made
him a little more handsome than he was; she had idealised him.
At the same time the likeness to her father – whether rendered by
intention or unconsciously – was striking. I set the sheet aside,
together with the drawings of Ella, to take away with me. Then I
began to look through the pile of papers and folders.

Most of them were related to her television work, and there
seemed to be nothing of interest; but then my eye was caught by
a document that proved to be Erika's will, drawn up by a firm of
solicitors in Civic Centre. Attached to it with a paper clip was a
single sheet headed: *To Whom it May Concern.* My own name
jumped out at me, and I began to read. The statement was typewritten, signed by hand, and was brief. It named me as the
executor of Erika's will, and said that in the event of her death I
was to wind up her affairs and arrange her burial. She had only
one living relative in Australia, it said – a sister of her mother's in
Victoria, with whom she had little contact – her father's family all
being in Germany. She therefore wished me, Vincent Austin, as
her closest friend, to be in charge of any final arrangements. Her
solicitors held the original of the will, and a copy of the statement
I was reading.

I put the sheet down. How long ago had she drawn up these
documents with the solicitors? Certainly not in the past few days;
yet she'd never mentioned it to me, and had never asked me to act
as her executor. I didn't look through the will; I couldn't face it.

There was a phone on the desk, and I began to dial the emer-
gency number. I found that I was shaking so much that it was
difficult to punch in the triple-zero.

*

I was with the police at the house for what seemed a good deal of the morning, but was probably much less. There were two of them, both young men with heavy faces. I sent them into the bedroom alone; I was glad I had covered her with the sheet. When they discovered who Erika was, I seemed to detect a veiled prurience in their expressions; but perhaps I imagined it. They also seemed suspicious of me, at first; but showing them my Foreign Affairs pass helped, and I got them to phone Jim Dempsey at home to confirm my identity. I then showed them the copy of Erika's will, and the statement concerning me. From that point on, I was treated as though I were her nearest relative – especially after I said that I would be responsible for arranging her funeral, and would meet all costs. They talked to me in respectfully hushed voices, tactfully ignoring the fact that I continued to have fits of trembling. They seemed to assume that this was a straightforward case of suicide, and that there were no suspicious circumstances. So did I, at that stage. This was a Coroner's case, they told me: there would have to be an autopsy. Tomorrow being Sunday, it would very likely be carried out on Monday.

We were talking in the study, and the phone there rang a number of times. I didn't pick it up; I let the answering machine record the messages. Someone from Channel Twelve in Sydney came on twice, asking Erika to call him urgently. The studio would soon have to be told what had happened, and I suggested to the police that they call Erika's solicitors first thing on Monday, and inform them of her death. The solicitors could be the ones to release the news to the studio, and to the press. I would speak to the solicitors later that day. All this I managed to convey to the police with difficulty, since my trembling continued, and a space was opening up in my brain: a space that would stay there for the rest of the day, making rational thought impossible.

One of the police called the Coroner's Office after that, and a panel van arrived a short time later. I didn't watch when Erika was carried out to it; soon afterwards, I was free to go.

The rest of the day is not entirely clear in my mind. I recall driving away from the house, but after that memory shows me nothing but a blur of streets and roads until I'm outside the city. I had no idea where I was going; I only knew that I couldn't bear to go home. All I wanted was to keep on driving towards nowhere, as Erika used to do. Steering the car was difficult, since tears would suddenly blind me, and the space in my brain made it difficult to concentrate, and my fits of trembling continued. I had no thoughts: it was hearing Erika's voice in my head that brought on tears.

My next memory is of finding myself on the Monaro Highway, headed south. I drove fast through the noonday heat, taking no notice of the empty plains that extended beyond the road. Mirages shimmered above the bitumen, and once I nearly collided with a truck, which made me grin like an idiot. Finally I reached Cooma, capital of the Monaro, where I parked the car and walked the streets for what must have been many hours, breathing the cool air of the high country and staring blindly at the people and the shops. The faces here (country people; tourists) looked innocent and happy, and I envied them: they moved through a different reality from mine, on the other side of a transparent screen. Stray pictures of that quiet little town float back to me, but nothing is clear; the space in my brain persisted, and I moved in a daze. Occasionally I would make idiotically banal observations to myself (*There it is, then. So it's all over.*) – but mostly I didn't think at all. I had no appetite, and ate nothing all day. I recall going into a bar and drinking beer; and later I seem to have sat in a café over a pot of tea, staying there for hours. A young waitress with an open country face smiled at me, I remember; but then, seeing my expression, her smile faded into uncertainty.

Memory now shows me the Monaro Highway unravelling in front of me again, at sunset. I was headed back to Canberra; but somewhere near seven o'clock, a short time after leaving Cooma, I pulled the car into a lay-by and got out. I did so without thought; without seeming to know why I did it.

I stepped to the edge of the road. In front of me stretched the plains of the Monaro, receding into distances which I found my spirit had been hungering for. And I realised now that I'd stopped here to do what I'd thought of doing when I said goodbye to Rykov: I would walk out on to those grasslands and stay there, in absolute solitude. I'd no doubt be trespassing on the domain of some grazier, but there was no sign of life here at all, except for a group of sheep in the middle distance, and I climbed through the wire fence and set out over the pale-green levels, with their clumps of bleached white tussock-grass and their scattered structures of granite.

One of these groups of grey boulders attracted my attention, and I walked towards it. From a distance, the cluster seemed small; up close, however, they proved to be quite massive, resembling a group of megaliths. I sat down in the grass, and leaned my back against the sun-warmed stone. I had heard that deadly snakes were common on the Monaro, but I was indifferent to that. Empty, in this empty and beautiful place, I breathed the pure air, hearing my own breathing, registering the sudden calls of birds and the faint whirr of cars on the highway.

Time passed, and I was barely aware of it passing. Darkness came, and I was looking up at the constellations, brilliant in this untainted air. There was the Southern Cross and its pointers, low in the south-east; and there was brilliant Sirius, just rising. In the north, I could just make out the Seven Sisters. How little I knew of the stars, I thought; how little I knew of many things. But this would change, because my old life was over – I knew that now. I didn't yet consider precisely how it would change, but of this one fact I was certain: that it would do so completely, and at once.

At around ten o'clock I became aware that I was cold, and decided to go. Before I went, I said a prayer for Erika, not knowing for certain to whom I was praying. Not to Uncle Kenneth's Presbyterian God, certainly, but to an overarching presence which seemed very close, here on these plains, among these enigmatic rocks, under these wheeling constellations.

Praying for her, my orphan, I began to weep again, knowing that I would be guilty all my life of failing to go to her when she'd called me; knowing that had I gone, I might have saved her. When I'd ceased to weep, I paused before setting out for the road, leaning against the boulder; and my old habits of thought reasserted themselves. I began to analyse Erika's death.

I had not doubted that it was suicide; but was this really the case? When she'd begged me to come to her, she'd said that she was afraid. What had she been afraid of? What had she told me recently that she feared?

Then I remembered, and clenched my hands.

Blaumanis, I said. *The bloody Latvian.*

Sunday, December 16th, 1984

ERIKA'S MEMORIAL SERVICE was held yesterday at St John's Anglican Church: quite a pretty little building in Reid, over a hundred years old, dating back to when this region was simply a farming community. I organized the service, but kept myself anonymous. A few members of the press were there, some Foreign Affairs people, and a number of vulgar onlookers. The eulogy was delivered by an odiously smug executive from Channel Twelve. I stood at the back.

The Director General has refused to take any action on Doctor Blaumanis. Nor will he allow me to do so. This despite the fact that enquiries I've made with ASIO have revealed that the Latvian is clearly a Soviet agent.

ASIO have nothing specific on him in regard to covert activity, but they say that his posturing as an anti-Russian patriot is clearly false. Over the years he's been identified by ASIO operatives attending meetings held by a number of Communist Party front organizations, including the New South Wales Peace Council and the Russian Social Club in Sydney. Of course he doesn't do this openly, or his cover in the Latvian community would be blown. Instead, he attends under a false name. He's a Soviet sleeper, and I have little doubt that they directed him to assassinate Erika.

I spoke a number of times to Dick Elliott and Jim Dempsey about this, and said that we should press for an inquest. But both of them rejected the proposition as fantastic.

Dear God, why are they being so blinkered and obtuse? Why

can't they see that there was enough at stake for the Soviet *rezidentura* to have wanted Erika removed? Had Peter Rykov defected, as Dempsey himself has pointed out, his debriefing could have delivered us their entire Australian network of informers; and his infatuation with Erika would have been seen by the Soviet Embassy as the sole cause of the disaster. True, he'd been recalled, and defection was no longer a threat; but how could they be sure he hadn't given Erika information about the network? As a prominent journalist, she was a walking time bomb: they'd have reason to fear that her bitterness over Rykov's desertion might cause her to make the list public. It's my belief that Blaumanis went into the house as she slept, and gave her a lethal injection. His medical knowledge would have made him the ideal agent to carry this out.

I've spelled this out to Elliott and Dempsey in every way possible; but it's useless. I'm shouting in the dark. They accept the likelihood that Blaumanis was an agent, but their opinion is that he was told by the Russians to speak with Erika about her association with Rykov in an attempt to frighten her off. Nothing more: they won't accept the notion that he murdered her. This is the 1980s, they say; the Russians don't do this sort of thing now. And when I suggested that I liaise with the people in ASIO to investigate Blaumanis further, the DG grew quite agitated, and flatly forbade it.

This means that I'm helpless: without the cooperation of the Service I can't pursue him, and he'll get away scot-free. I grew very angry; I spoke to the DG in a way I have never spoken to my superiors before. I even shouted. Finally, Elliott told me outright that the notion of Blaumanis's having murdered Erika was absurd, and sprang from my being 'overwrought'. Not to put too fine a point on it, he was saying that I've had a nervous collapse – and he advised that I see the Senior Defence Psychiatrist for counselling. I was deeply insulted at this, and walked out of his office.

Monday, December 17th, 1984
MY SUSPICIONS WERE wrong. It was suicide, after all.

I am empty, as I write this. Today Dick Elliott called me into his office to tell me that although the Coroner's finding won't be announced for some weeks, he had used his powers to obtain a copy of the pathologist's report. He read it to me aloud, and I'm ashamed to record that when he had finished, I wept. It states that Erika died of the effects of a massive overdose of Nembutal, combined with a quantity of brandy. No foul play is suspected, and there will be no inquest.

Dick Elliott was very kind to me, as I sat there in distress. When I tendered my resignation – which I'd decided to do even before we had our discussions about Blaumanis – he told me not to act in haste, but instead to take two years' leave of absence. He valued me too much to see me leave the Service, he said; he understood my strain and grief, and wished to see me take time to recuperate. He was willing to let me go almost immediately, since he understood my desire to get away; and he offered me help with a plan I've conceived for a new life abroad.

Although I have no intention of ultimately returning to the Service, I agreed to take unpaid leave. I also accepted Dick's offer of help. But what I really intend to do, once I'm overseas, is to disappear for ever. You see, dear Teodor, what I long for (as many a burnt-out spy has done before me) is *a one-dimensional life* – and to achieve it, my old self must be discarded. As you know, the life we have in espionage is one of constant duality, and I'm desperately tired of duality. To serve people – to help people in need, which is what I intend to do – will be the opposite of this. A life of giving: this will truly be one-dimensional! Do you see?

For a long time, I've felt lost. Now, everything is opening up. The future may be largely unknown, but I'm no longer lost.

I will fly out immediately after Christmas, on the 27th. Apart from Elliott and Dempsey, only three people will know after I leave that I still exist: Aunt Connie, my friend Derek Bradley, and you, dear Teodor. These diaries – records of the life of a former secret intelligence operative – will be placed in your keeping, to be kept or destroyed as you see fit. They may have a certain psychological interest for you – as well as providing you with a full explanation of what has become of me, and why. As an expert on what thriller-writers call 'the secret world', you may possibly be interested to see how one recruit to that world – the recruit you made! – was led there initially by his hunger for another: an arcane zone without the hard, practical purposes of the spy world. Those purposes are essentially mundane, as you know – however vital they may seem in those rare, crucial moments of intrigue that cause history to swerve: those moments that so excite us, we who lurk unseen in history's anterooms. Ephemeral and beguiling as news, the secrets of the spy world can only exert their power in the present; after which they dissolve, to be replaced by new secrets, in history's pitiless flow. But in that *other* secret world – a world whose features are as faint as distant music, as hazy as the Kingdom of Faery – the arcane and the secret have purposes that are in no way practical. In fact, their purposes can't be stated, since they evade being dealt with in words. Thrilling and indefinable as certain scents, troubling and enticing as those long, long dreams that revisit us from childhood, they belong in the end to myth, and so can never die.

This, dear Teodor, was the secret world that recruited me first – just as it did my Erika. But both of us made the mistake, once we left childhood behind, of seeing espionage as its worldly face.

That mistake has now destroyed Erika, and came close to destroying me. In a sense, it *has* destroyed me, since my old self and my old life are gone.

I was a romantic of the suburbs: a stepchild of the old Cold War. It has scarcely touched my native hemisphere, that contest of giant shadows – yet it loomed above my life nevertheless, and drew me into its ranks. Then, in its dying days, it plunged me into its darkness.

I intend to survive, nevertheless; and the only way I can do so is to create a new self.

I fought the enemy as best I could. New enemies will emerge, no doubt; they always do. But they will be for others to fight.

Goodbye: and I like to think that you will wish me well.

FOUR

1

BRADLEY LOCKED THE door of his car and paused for a moment, looking at Vincent's house. Flocks of small birds were in frantic final chorus in the oak trees that ran down Wattle Street, and the upper storey of the house rose box-like and severe against the evening sky. The windows all had their curtains drawn, and the place already looked untenanted; but then Bradley recalled that it had always looked like that. He went up the drive and mounted the pebbled steps to the front door, opening it with the key that had been delivered to him this morning.

The study upstairs was dim as always, the heavy brown curtains drawn over the windows.

Filing cabinets; bookshelves; dining table and sideboard; big, flat-topped desk: all in place. Only the picture of Connie Ross seemed to be missing. The atmosphere here, now that the room was empty, suggested even more strongly than before that its function was that of a sanctuary: a place of secrecy, subject to a single owner. Vincent's presence was strong, and Bradley heard his voice: its measured, mock-clerical tones; its archaic slang. *Old chap. Old bean.* He drew back the curtains on most of the windows, letting the late sun seep in. It was stuffy here, with a lingering smell of Vincent's cigarette smoke, and he took off the jacket of his suit and threw it on the armchair beside the desk. He opened a window on the western side, and stood looking out to Black Mountain, where the distant telecommunications tower glinted in the sun. The house had the hollow sense of waiting of all houses that are empty, and an odour that was not yet musty but might become so, adding itself to the smell of Vincent's ghostly cigarettes. He turned, and surveyed the study again.

The desk was neater than usual, with nothing on it except a blank notepad, a bottle of fountain-pen ink, an ashtray, and a clipping from a Sydney newspaper. Bradley sat down in Vincent's swivel chair, and picked up the clipping.

It was the front page of the paper, and was dated December 11th: over two weeks old. Bradley found himself looking at a photograph of Erika Lange. It was a head and shoulders shot, no doubt taken for publicity, and she looked at him directly, as she often used to look, smiling with closed lips, eyebrows raised as though querying something: the vagaries of men and the world, perhaps. He'd seen this picture a number of times in the past fortnight, in various papers and magazines that had run stories on her death. He closed his eyes for a moment, frowning; then he sat staring at the headline.

POSSIBLE SUICIDE OF TOP TV JOURNALIST
Death of Channel Twelve's Erika Lange

He didn't read the story; he'd already read it too often, in other papers. He wondered why Vincent had left the clipping here; had he forgotten to take it, when he was packing?

He leaned over to his jacket on the chair, reaching into the inside pocket and pulling out the foolscap envelope containing Vincent's letter. It had been brought to his house at eight o'clock this morning by the chief clerk of the ASIS Registry, and it had also contained the key to the house. Now he spread the letter on the desk in front of him: three handwritten sheets. Vincent had neat, spiky handwriting which was easy to read; he was one of those increasingly rare people who still used a fountain pen.

Wednesday, December 26th, 1984

Dear Derek,

By the time Hilda Maxwell brings you this on Friday, I'll be overseas. I leave first thing tomorrow. I'm sorry, but I can't tell you at present where I'll be. The reasons are dealt with fully in my diary, which I trust you'll read.

Let me just say that Erika's death has led me to this decision. I didn't see you at her memorial service at St John's. I can understand your reasons. Of that, I'll say no more.

I'm saying goodbye to no-one: I'm simply disappearing, to start life anew. Regard me as a missing person. Whether I'll make contact again after this – with you, or with anyone else – is something I've yet to decide.

Before I go, I have some favours to ask. You have always been my best friend, Derek – though lately, we've drifted apart – and I'm confident you won't let me down.

I've told Hilda to ask you to go to my house on Friday – as soon as possible after she brings you this letter. The key of the front door is enclosed here. Please go up to my study and look in the drawers of my desk. You'll find there a number of ring-binders – five altogether. These contain my diaries for the past two years. I want you to take them away with you. I'm letting the house, and the agents will be arranging for the uplift and storage of everything else at the beginning of next week.

What I'm asking of you as well is this: that you take the diaries down to Hobart when next you have time to make the trip. They're to be delivered by you in person to Teodor Bobrowski. I've written to tell him to expect you, and I'm sure he'll be pleased to see you. You do understand: deliver the diaries by hand. On no account are they to go through the post.

My second request is that you visit Aunt Connie, who will also know that you're coming. She too will be pleased to see you; she was always fond of you, as you know. My reason for this request is that the balance of my diaries – and there are many, going back to my early youth – are all at Connie's. They are in a room that you know of, at the end of the sunroom. It's locked, but Connie has the key. Those diaries too are to be delivered to Ted Bobrowski, completing the set. He will expect them – I've told him in my letter that as I go into my new life, these records of my old one are all bequeathed to him.

There are other papers and materials in that room. These I'm bequeathing to you, Derek. They may be of interest; keep them or destroy them, as you see fit. I only ask that you show them to no-one else.

I've kept a very full record of my life – why, I'm not quite sure. They say that spies are often frustrated novelists, but I doubt that this is so in my case: I've never had ambitions in that direction. I think the reason for my compulsive record-keeping may be connected with my fatal attraction to secrecy. I've always felt that my life had meanings that were elusive, and difficult to grasp; meanings merely hinted at, lying at the edges of things: perhaps in some odd corner of a landscape, or on the outskirts of a town, or in connection with particular people: people who seemed to hold the keys to a mystery I had only half-grasped. And by writing things down – by simply recording them – I thought that their hidden meanings might somehow emerge, as more mundane clues emerge in those records to do with espionage which I've analysed through-out my career.

Alas, ultimate meanings seldom did emerge for me. Who knows though, Brad: you may see them in these archives of my life's progress, even though I can't. Which brings me to my final request.

I hope that you'll stay in Hobart for some days – Connie will be delighted to put you up – and read through all the diaries before you deliver them to Ted.

Why do I ask this? Because now that I'm going, I want you to know all there is to know about my story – which is also Erika's. You and I set out on the same path together, sharing that unique friendship of very young men which can never be repeated, and I feel you are somehow owed an insight into how our paths were always destined to diverge. You will also learn the true nature of my relationship with Erika, and more about Erika than you now perhaps know. I can only hope that it will help you to come to terms with the sadness you must surely feel about her. If it doesn't, please forgive me.

In many ways, Brad, you and I saw life for a time through the same eyes. Young provincials in our sheltered southern island, remote from the centres of power, we were possibly more aware of the marvels and menaces of the world than those who live in their shadows, since they lit up our imaginations with a glow created by distance, like far lights at night. Except for Erika, no-one was as close to me as you; and you gave me a kind of fellow-feeling which she couldn't do: that of an honest, uncomplicated man. Does that sound patronising? Far from it: honest, uncomplicated men are not so common any more, and you are the sort of man that I could never be, but greatly wished to be. More, you gave me a family life: the only true family life I ever had. I remember your parents with deep affection, and those evenings of warmth and easy closeness in the little house in Pirie Street. You'll find a record of those evenings in my early diaries – but you'll also find much else that you won't have imagined. I want you to know all! And what I hope is this: that if you begin my story there, in our happy days in New Town, and read it to the end, then the meaning may emerge for you which still eludes me.

Meanwhile, goodbye, dear Brad. Had I told you to your face that I loved you, I would have seen you respond with simple embarrassment. And so I put it on paper instead, speaking as men did to each other in the eighteenth century – with unashamed affection.

Your
Vincent

Carefully, Bradley re-folded the letter, and returned it to its envelope. Then, pushing back the swivel chair, he began to open the set of drawers on one side of the desk. The first drawer was empty; the second two, which were deep, contained the five ring-binders Vincent had referred to. Bradley piled them on top of the desk, opened one of them, and began to look through it.

Something like five minutes went by; then he heard a noise downstairs. He sat back, and listened.

There was the distinct sound now of the front door closing, followed by feet coming up the stairs: a heavy tread, with no attempt at stealth. Bradley stood up behind the desk. He was still standing there when Jim Dempsey came through the door and halted. He was carrying the jacket of his lightweight khaki suit over his shoulder, hooked on his index finger; like Bradley he'd clearly come here from the office, and had loosened his tie. He raised his heavy white eyebrows, but otherwise betrayed no surprise.

'Young Bradley,' he said. 'What brings you here?'

'I had a key,' Bradley said. 'Did Vincent leave one for you as well?'

'I cannot tell a lie,' Dempsey said. 'No he didn't. But we old cracksmen have our methods of gaining entry.' He smiled waggishly, crossing to the leather armchair where Bradley's jacket lay, and threw his own on top of it. 'Warm in here,' he said, looking up at the ceiling. 'Not even a fan.' He moved across to the Jacobean-style armchair in front of the desk: the one in which Bradley had so often sat in the past, talking to Vincent. While Bradley stood staring at him with an expression of blank enquiry, he lowered himself into the chair, holding both the arms. 'I think we need to talk,' he said.

Bradley sat down again. 'I think we do,' he said. 'Would you like to tell me first why you've broken in?'

Dempsey smiled, his bulging blue eyes shining with their usual good humour. 'Why not?' he said. 'After all, you arrived before me, entering in a legitimate manner.' Then he ceased to smile, and his face became neutral: neither friendly nor unfriendly. 'Firstly, however, we need to have something clear,' he said. 'You're in ONA now, and you're bound by the same code of discretion as I am. So I assume I can rely on that?'

'Naturally,' Bradley said.

'All right,' Dempsey said. He paused. 'How much do you know about Vincent's departure?'

'Not a lot,' Bradley said. 'We didn't see much of each other over the past few months. He's asked me to take charge of these.' He gestured at the diaries, in their red ring-binders.

Dempsey's eyes narrowed as he looked at them. 'And what exactly are they?'

'Personal diaries,' Bradley said.

'Purely personal?'

'Purely personal,' Bradley said. 'And I'm asking you again, Jim: why are you here?'

Dempsey half-turned in his chair and gestured at the four steel filing cabinets on the far side of the room. 'To go through those,' he said.

'And what right have you got to do that?' Bradley said.

Dempsey heaved a sigh, and rubbed the side of his chin. 'Considering your friendship with Vincent, I can understand your getting pissed off,' he said. 'But just bear with me, brother, and I'll hope to make you understand. First, though, let me get this over with.'

He got to his feet and crossed heavily to the filing cabinets, pulling at the top drawer of the one nearest the door. It came open. 'At least I don't have to pick their locks,' Dempsey said. He peered into the drawer. 'Empty,' he said. In silence, he pulled open the drawers of all the cabinets, one by one. Slamming the last one shut, he straightened up and grunted. Then he crossed the room and threw himself into the chair again.

'All empty,' he said. 'I'm not sure whether that's good or bad.'

They stared at one another for a moment. Remembering the files from the Registry that Vincent used to copy and bring home to be stored in these cabinets, Bradley had become increasingly tense; now, he felt relief. He wondered what Vincent had done with them. Destroyed them, perhaps; he hoped so. Dempsey had folded his hands in his lap; he looked down at them as though meditating, his brows raised. Then he looked up at Bradley again, as though coming to a decision.

'I'm here because our Director General has a concern about Vincent,' he said. 'And I've got to say to you, Derek, that it's a concern I share. Don't get me wrong: you and I have discussed Vin before, and you know the high opinion I have of him. A very talented operative, with an unusual mind. But he seemed all the time to be running to some agenda of his own. I never found out what it was.'

'I guess he's not your conventional spy,' Bradley said.

Dempsey smiled faintly. 'Who is? But our concern at the moment is this. Vincent has been known to take top-secret files home with him: an absolute no-no, as you'll realise. It would normally mean dismissal – or worse. He did it once when he and I were in Jakarta together, and got a dressing-down from the Head of Security. He survived it – he had a knack of surviving, and you'd never suspect him of anything subversive. He just seemed to think he was a law unto himself, and the files obsessed him. He got over-involved; he wanted to build up his own private system. That's why that work in the Registry suited him so well. When that laser beam was focussed, it made incredible breakthroughs. It was all in the way he analysed the material. We'd be puzzling over something for months, and then he'd hit the nail on the head. It was all about linkages – Vincent saw them where no-one else did. He scored some real hits, and Dick Elliott was delighted.'

'But you think he may have brought some files here,' Bradley said.

'It did occur to us,' Dempsey said. 'We had to know. But it seems whatever was in there has all been cleaned out.'

'I'm sure it would all have been his own personal stuff,' Bradley said.

'Yes. We have to hope so, Derek.' Dempsey appeared to consider pursuing the subject further. But then he straightened himself in his chair, cleared his throat, and changed the subject. 'It was because Dick Elliott really valued Vin that he decided to look after him,' he said. 'He's put him on two years' leave of absence, instead of accepting his resignation. You know this?'

'No. I know almost nothing,' Bradley said. 'All Vin says in his letter to me is that he's going abroad to start a new life.'

'That's it,' Dempsey said. 'That's his idea: a new life. But what the DG proposed was that Vin keep his options open. Then, in two years, he can come back to us if he wants to.'

'I doubt that he will,' Bradley said.

'So do I,' Dempsey said. 'He's had a kind of nervous break-down: it's happened to many a good operative before him.'

'How bad is it?'

'He's not ga-ga, if that's what you mean,' Dempsey said. 'It's what you might call an emotional collapse – largely to do with Erika Lange's death.'

Bradley said nothing, his face composed and still, and Dempsey paused. Then he sighed, looking away out the window and appearing to study the telecommunications tower on Black Mountain.

'What a bloody waste,' he said, and his voice had sunk to a throaty murmur. 'Such a lovely, talented woman. But it was always likely to happen, from my observation of her. She was the suicidal type. What the shrinks would call a borderline personality.'

Bradley closed his eyes for a moment; then he looked at Dempsey again. 'The shrinks have categories for everything,' he said. 'But do you really think that a woman like Erika can be tidied away with some bloody clinical label?

'Maybe not,' Dempsey said. 'Maybe not, brother.' He looked back at Bradley, his head cocked on one side. 'I'm sorry. I guess it's not easy for you to talk about this.'

'It's all right, Jim,' Bradley said. 'I've long ago moved on. But it's very sad.' He squinted, and pinched the bridge of his nose; then he sat back, seeming consciously to relax. 'You're sure it was suicide? She was addicted to sleeping pills. She might have miscalculated.'

'No doubt at all,' Dempsey said. 'We have the report. She took a hell of an overdose of Nembutal. That's lethal stuff. So you're right, Derek: we're looking at a very sad story here. According to Vincent, she was depressed about losing Peter Rykov, the TASS correspondent who was pulled back to Moscow. A very volatile affair, as perhaps you've heard. A case of two pretty turbulent people in a state of co-dependency.' He grinned faintly. 'Sorry, I'm using psychiatric jargon again. It's a bad habit.'

Bradley said nothing, watching him.

'As I told you, Erika's death hit Vincent very hard,' Dempsey said. 'He even began to be irrational. That's why the DG set out to do all he could for him. He's got a good heart, Dick Elliott, but he's also shrewd. It made sense to help Vincent with his plans, and get him abroad as soon as possible – away from the Service.'

'Plans?' Bradley said. 'What plans does Vin actually have? I don't even know where he's gone.'

Dempsey leaned back, hands folded on his stomach. 'No harm in telling you, I suppose. He's gone to New Delhi,' he said. 'He's attracted to northern India, apparently – seems to have wanted to get back there ever since he was posted to Delhi in the 'seventies. He told Dick and me that he planned to try to work with some sort of voluntary organization to alleviate poverty.' He smiled. 'He sounded a bit like a missionary, which didn't entirely surprise me – he's always reminded me of an unfrocked clergyman.' When Bradley didn't return the smile, he said quickly: 'Vin wasn't inter- ested in religious organizations though; he made a point of that. And Dick Elliott was able to help him. Dick's got contacts in an outfit called Volunteer India. It asks for people who can bring specialised skills to various areas: agriculture; education; social welfare – that sort of thing. He's given Vincent an introduction.'

'I see.' Bradley sat in silence for a moment. Then he said: 'I hope he'll be happy. It ought to be an improvement on spying.'

Dempsey looked at him quickly, catching the sardonic note in his voice. 'Don't despise the trade too much,' he said. 'The country needs old whores like me, when the nasty buggers appear. And they always do, brother – they always do.'

'No offence intended,' Bradley said. 'I was thinking of Vincent.'

Dempsey stood up, looming beside the desk. He picked up his jacket from the armchair and began to haul it on, struggling to get one of his beefy arms through a sleeve. 'I know you were,' he said. 'The thing is, my boy, people like Vincent are attracted to the Service for all sorts of odd reasons. They often have too much imagination – and that can cause a crack-up.' He sighed, then brightened, beginning to smile at Bradley. 'Whereas I, for example, have no imagination, and here I am on the verge of retirement with all my marbles intact.'

Bradley stood up too, running his fingers through his hair, and came from behind Vincent's desk. 'Come on, Jim – I'll buy you a pre-New Year drink,' he said.

'What a bloody marvellous idea, mate.'

Bradley followed Dempsey out the door. When he closed it behind him, sealing off the room and its presence, it seemed to him that he was taking his leave of Vincent forever.

2

AN AFTERNOON IN March, the air cooling, the sun coming and going at the whim of slow-sailing clouds. The colouring of the day is changing from moment to moment, as it so often does in the island: colour giving way to monochrome; monochrome flooded by colour again. Birds like frowns on the glassy autumn air. Intensities of a cold climate.

Walking up the little hill of Pirie Street, a large overnight bag slung from his shoulder, Bradley is re-entering the past, watched by those rows of houses that once saw him walk to school. Tall Edwardian chimneys; leadlight glass and little front porches from the 1920s and '30s, all seemingly suspended in the eras of their birth, as though in an airless room: an impression reinforced by autumn's ancient quiet. It's a quiet broken only by sparrows, which flutter in bursts from front gardens, and wheel and chitter above the power lines. Five o'clock. Only one car goes by; nobody else on the footpath. On Bradley's right, the houses and their gardens are perched on a ridge which is buttressed by a high brick wall; he runs his hand along the bricks as he passes, as he used to do at five years old.

He's not been home for over three years, and his stays have always been brief: dutiful, hurried trips to see his parents. He will not visit them this time: the house further down Pirie Street has been sold, and his parents have retired to the island's east coast. A taxi brought him here from the airport, dropping him off in the New Town Road; on an impulse, Bradley decided to cover the remaining distance to Connie Ross's house on foot.

He's come to the top of the hill. He drops his bag and pauses on the corner of Bay Road, surveying the scene that has opened to the north down Pirie Street: that view which lies at the heart of memory.

The sun has come out from behind a bank of cloud, sending down long, dazzling rays. A golden-brown glow touches roofs and garden trees, and the narrow ribbon of Pirie Street is brilliantly lit up, running downhill into the valley where it meets Risdon Road and the mock-Tudor gables of the old Maypole Inn – passing, halfway down, the familiar red roof of the Californian bungalow where Bradley's earliest dreams took shape, which Vincent saw as his only real home, and which now is inhabited by strangers. Past Risdon Road, Pirie Street appears to continue up the rise on the other side of the junction; but it's no longer Pirie Street there, having melted into Main Road – the old main highway that takes traffic out to the north, and the island's heart. On top of the rise, Main Road meets the blue screen of the ranges, with the peak called Collins Bonnet looming in the west, and the square stone tower of the Congregational church, with its grey hipped roof, standing among pines to the east: an after-image from the 1840s. Beyond, in Glenorchy, are those outskirts of the town where Bradley and Vincent wandered at night in their student days, filled with the excitement of the world.

Bradley continues to linger, his gaze led on by the triple-crosses of telephone poles. In the glow that is briefly transfiguring all New Town's hills and valleys, the poles recede up Main Road until they become minute, seeming to lead to a region of illusion, as they used to do in his youth: a land outside reality. For fleeting seconds, the scene awakens in him that surge of joy he used to know then: an expectancy that he and Vincent shared. And perhaps, he thinks, both of them in their different ways were formed by these ephemeral revelations. Cut off in their native island from the larger world, they made do with mirages: states of delight more seductive than anything the real world had to offer.

A cloud bank swallows the sun, and Pirie Street and Main Road and the hills beyond the town become themselves again: a modest, circumscribed landscape he long ago left behind. Yet delight lingers, and Bradley is glad of it. Somehow, in a way that he may never understand, the hidden region exists, in a dimension of its own.

He stoops, picks up his bag, and sets off down Bay Road to Connie Ross's house.

AUTHOR'S NOTE

This is a work of fiction, and its characters and events are entirely invented. It should therefore be understood that the officers of the Australian Secret Intelligence Service portrayed here, from the Director General downwards, are all fictitious, and not based on any actual counterparts. The same applies to the Foreign Affairs officers at the Australian Embassy in Peking, from the Ambassador downwards: they are in no way based on any of the staff who were serving there at the time.

The sequences that take place in China in 1982 belong to an era when the Chinese Government had recently replaced Wade-Giles with Pinyin for the transcription of Chinese names. However, I have mostly stayed with Wade-Giles, both because the old names were still hanging on among English speakers in that year, and because I find the traditional names so much more attractive, rich as they are with historical and literary associations.

Backgrounds are as accurate as I can make them, but I have taken a few small liberties. For example, I have kept trams running in Hobart long after the folly of their removal.

A number of officers in Australia's overseas service, some retired, some still serving, have given me generous help and advice with this novel. I offer them my grateful thanks.

The first third of the book was written with the support of the Literature Board of the Australia Council, and I wish to record my appreciation.